PHARMACOLOGY III

B. Pharm. Semester VI

Dr. SACHIN V TEMBHURNE

Assistant Professor,
Department of Pharmacology,
AISSMS College of Pharmacy,
Pune.

NIRALI
PRAKASHAN
ADVANCEMENT OF KNOWLEDGE

N1710

Pharmacology III   **ISBN 978-93-5164-655-6**

First Edition : **January 2016**

©   : **Author**

Published By :   Polyplate

NIRALI PRAKASHAN

Abhyudaya Pragati, 1312, Shivaji Nagar,
Off J.M. Road, PUNE – 411005
Tel - (020) 25512336/37/39, Fax - (020) 25511379
Email : niralipune@pragationline.com

☞ DISTRIBUTION CENTRES

PUNE

Nirali Prakashan : 119, Budhwar Peth, Jogeshwari Mandir Lane, Pune 411002, Maharashtra
Tel : (020) 2445 2044, 66022708, Fax : (020) 2445 1538
Email : bookorder@pragationline.com, niralilocal@pragationline.com

Nirali Prakashan : S. No. 28/27, Dhyari, Near Pari Company, Pune 411041
Tel : (020) 24690204 Fax : (020) 24690316
Email : dhyari@pragationline.com, bookorder@pragationline.com

MUMBAI

Nirali Prakashan : 385, S.V.P. Road, Rasdhara Co-op. Hsg. Society Ltd.,
Girgaum, Mumbai 400004, Maharashtra
Tel : (022) 2385 6339 / 2386 9976, Fax : (022) 2386 9976
Email : niralimumbai@pragationline.com

☞ DISTRIBUTION BRANCHES

JALGAON

Nirali Prakashan : 34, V. V. Golani Market, Navi Peth, Jalgaon 425001,
Maharashtra, Tel : (0257) 222 0395, Mob : 94234 91860

KOLHAPUR

Nirali Prakashan : New Mahadvar Road, Kedar Plaza, 1st Floor Opp. IDBI Bank
Kolhapur 416 012, Maharashtra. Mob : 9850046155

NAGPUR

Pratibha Book Distributors : Above Maratha Mandir, Shop No. 3, First Floor,
Rani Jhanshi Square, Sitabuldi, Nagpur 440012, Maharashtra
Tel : (0712) 254 7129

DELHI

Nirali Prakashan : 4593/21, Basement, Aggarwal Lane 15, Ansari Road, Daryaganj
Near Times of India Building, New Delhi 110002
Mob : 08505972553

BENGALURU

Pragati Book House : House No. 1, Sanjeevappa Lane, Avenue Road Cross,
Opp. Rice Church, Bengaluru – 560002.
Tel : (080) 64513344, 64513355,Mob : 9880582331, 9845021552
Email:bharatsavla@yahoo.com

CHENNAI

Pragati Books : 9/1, Montieth Road, Behind Taas Mahal, Egmore,
Chennai 600008 Tamil Nadu, Tel : (044) 6518 3535,
Mob : 94440 01782 / 98450 21552 / 98805 82331,
Email : bharatsavla@yahoo.com

niralipune@pragationline.com | www.pragationline.com
Also find us on 🇫 www.facebook.com/niralibooks

Foreword ...

The study of Pharmacology is an essential and important part of pharmaceutical and health care education. Pharmacology involves the study and description of drugs and their effects on the whole body. The classification of drugs, pharmacological actions, adverse effects, drug interactions and information regarding their doses are the topics discussed in this book

There is need to understand body physiology and pathophysiology before study of pharmacology. The systematic compilation of all information such as physiology, pathophysiology and pharmacology in a single book is a difficult task. Dr. S.V. Tembhurne, by his experience has achieved this for the better understanding of the subject by the students.

The book is written in a concise manner with probable questions at the end of each chapter which will help the students in revising the chapter thoroughly.

I congratulate Dr. S. V. Tembhurne for his excellent work and I sincerely hope you will gain as much insight as I did from these chapters.

Dr. Ashwini R. Madgulkar
Principal
All India Shri. Shivaji Memorial Society
College of Pharmacy, Kennedy road, Pune.

Acknowledgement ...

I would like to express my sincere thanks to my wife Dr. Babita and my family.

I am deeply indebted to Dr. Dinesh M. Sakarkar, Principal, SNIOP Pusad; Dr. M. N. Saraf, Principal Bombay college of Pharmacy; Dr. A. G. Jagtap, Bombay college of Pharmacy; Dr. Sohan Chitlange, D. Y. Patil college of Pharmacy, Pimpri, Pune; Dr. S. N. Sakharwade, Department of Cosmetic L.A.D. College Nagpur, for their guidance, suggestions and cooperation that has gone a long way in helping me to write this book..

Thanks are also due to Dr. Mangesh Bhalekar, Dr. Santosh Gandhi, Dr. Shashikant Bhandari, Dr. Mrunali Damle, Mrs. Swati Kolhe, Prof. Rahul Padalkar, and other staff members of AISSMS, COP, Pune for their kind co-operation.

I would like to acknowledge the excellent efforts of Mr. Jignesh Furia and his staff of Nirali Prakashan, Pune for bringing out this book in the least possible time.

Dr. Sachin V. Tembhurne

Preface ...

Pharmacology involves the study of the drug action on the body. It includes finding out how a particular drug produces beneficial and adverse effects on the body. Pharmacologists aim to develop a better understanding of drugs and their actions on biological systems for the improvement of human health.

An undergraduate student of pharmacy always faces problem in understanding the subject because of unproven disease mechanism and lengthy language. In an attempt to remedy this, texts of this book are given in point wise and in precise manner along with illustrations whenever is necessary which will help the student in understanding and remembering the text.

The book covers the brief pathophysiology, updated classification of drug, pharmacokinetic profile, pharmacological actions, adverse effects, contraindications, drug interaction and uses in detail for each drug. The text cover the disease mechanism whenever is necessary which will help to understand treatment module. For exam point of view a book also covers the important questions at the beginning and at the end of each chapter. I have hoped that this book of pharmacology will simplify the subject for the students of pharmacology.

Pune

Dr. S. V. Tembhurne
stembhurne@gmail.com

Syllabus ...

Topic No.	Name of the Topic and Contents	Hours
	Pharmacology of drug shall includes : classification, mechanism of action, pharmacological actions, pharmacokinectics, therapeutic uses, adverse effects, drug interactions, contraindications, dosages, treatment of poisoning (if any) Pharmacotherapy shall include: Pharmacology of drug/s used for clinical management of diseases/ disorders	
	SECTION I	
1.	**General Anesthesia:** Stages and Principles of Anesthesia, Pharmacology of Intravenous and Inhalational Anesthetics.	02
2.	**Local Anesthetics:** Pharmacology of injectable and surface anesthetics, Clinical Uses and techniques of administration of local anesthetics	02
3.	**Alcohols and Alcoholism:** Pharmacology of Alcohol, and management of chronic alcoholism. Treatment for alcoholic liver diseases	03
4.	**Psychopharmacological Drugs:** Antipsychotic, anti-anxiety, Sedative, Hypnotics, Antidepressant, Antimanic drugs	08
5.	**Antiepileptic Drugs:** Classification of epileptic Seizure, Pharmacology of one prototype drug from each class of antiepileptic drugs used in Grand Mal, Petit Mal epilepsies.	04
6.	**Pharmacotherapy of Parkinson's Disease and Alzheimer's Disease**	04
	SECTION II	
7.	**Opioid Analgesics and Antagonist:** Classification and Pharmacology of opioid Analgesics (Morphine), opioid Antagonists.	04
8.	**Pharmacology of Non-steroidal Anti-inflammatory Drugs**	03
9.	**Pharmacotherapy of Rheumatoid Arthritis, Osteoartritis and Gout**	03
10.	**Drugs used in Respiratory Tract Disorders:** Pharmacology of drugs used in Bronchial asthma, COPD and Cough.	04
11.	**Drugs used in Gastrointestinal Tract Disorders: (i)** Pharmacotherapy of Peptic Ulcers-Pharmacology of Proton Pump Inhibitors, H2-Receptor Antagonists, Mucosal Defense Enhancers, Antacids and cytoprotectants, **(ii) Pharmacology of** Emetics and Anti-Emetics, **iii)** Pharmacotherapy of Constipation, **(iv)** Pharmacotherapy of diarrhea.	08

***

Contents ...

***

Chapter 1

GENERAL ANAESTHETICS

Objectives

After reading this chapter, the student will be able to:

➢ Understand the goals of general anaesthesia

➢ Justify the use of preoperative medications in general anaesthesia

➢ Enlist the different stages of anaesthesia

➢ Explain dissociative anaesthesia

The goal of general anaesthesia is to produce analgesia, unconsciousness and amnesia. These terms are as follows:

- **Analgesia**
  o Loss of pain perception.
- **Unconsciousness**
  o Loss of awareness of one's surroundings.
- **Amnesia**
  o Inability to recall what took place.

History of Anaesthesia

- Ether was synthesised in 1540 by Cordus.
- Ether was used as anaesthetic in 1842 by Dr. Crawford W. Long.
- Ether was publicised as anaesthetic in 1846 by Dr. William Morton.
- Chloroform was first used as anaesthetic in 1853 by Dr. John Snow.
- Local anaesthesia with cocaine was discovered in 1885.
- Thiopental was first used in 1934.

- Curare which was first used in 1942, opened the "Age of Anaesthesia".

Basic Principles of Anaesthesia

- Anaesthesia is defined as the abolition of sensation.
- Analgesia can also be defined as the abolition of pain.
- "Triad of General Anaesthesia".
  o Need for unconsciousness
  o Need for analgesia
  o Need for muscle relaxation.

General anaesthetics (GA) are potent CNS depressants

It is the most severe state which involves intentional use of a drug to induce CNS suppression. Combination of opioids, narcotic and volatile anaesthetic result in no pain and a state of unconsciousness. The suppression of all CNS functions result into sedation, sleep, depressed reflexes, amnesia and unconsciousness.

Risk Factors Associated with GAs

- CNS factors
- Cardiovascular factors
- Respiratory factors
- Renal and hepatic function

Mechanism of Action of GAs

- The general anaesthetics act on ligand gated ion channels but not voltage sensitive ion channels. The GABA-A receptor gated chloride channel is the most important of these (Figure 1.1). Many inhalation anaesthetics, barbiturates, benzodiazepines and propofol potentiate the action of inhibitory transmitter GABA to open chloride channels.

- Action of glycine (activate chloride channels) in the spinal cord and medulla are augmented by barbiturates, propofol and many inhalation anaesthetics. This action results in blocking the responsiveness of painful stimuli mediated by fluorinated anaesthetics and barbiturates. In addition to this glycine also inhibits neuronal cation channel gated by nicotinic cholinergic receptor.

- Nitrous oxide and ketamine do not affect GABA or glycine gated chloride channels rather they selectively act on NMDA type of glutamate receptor. This receptor gated mainly calcium selective cation channel in the neurons and their inhibition appears to be the primary mechanism of anaesthetic action of ketamine as well as nitrous oxide. The volatile anaesthetics have little action on this receptor.

- Neuronal hyper polarisation caused by general anaesthetics has been ascribed to activation of a specific type of potassium channels, while inhibition of transmitter

release from presynaptic neurons has been related to interaction with certain critical synaptic protein.

- Local anaesthetics act primarily through blocking axonal conduction while the general anaesthetics appear to act by depressing synaptic transmission.

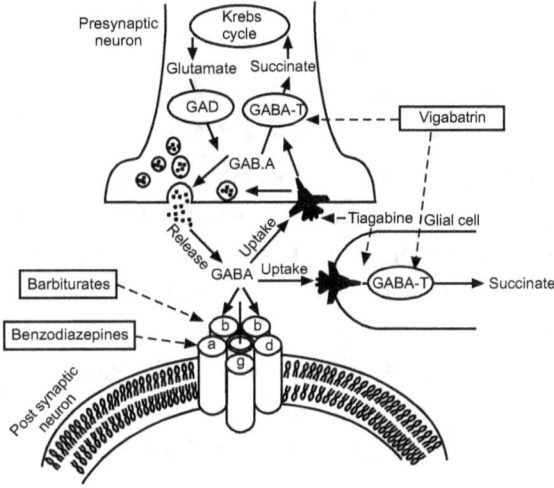

Fig. 1.1: GABA receptor

Stages of Anaesthesia

There are four stages of anaesthesia. They are explained below.

Stage 1: The analgesia stage

Stage 2: The excitement stage

Stage 3: Surgical anaesthesia

Stage 4: Medullary paralysis.

Stage 1: The analgesia stage

The analgesic stage begins with the inhalation of anaesthetic and lasts up to the loss of consciousness. Pain is progressively abolished during this stage. Patient remains conscious, can hear and see, and feels a dream like state. Reflexes and respiration remain normal. Though some minor and even major operations can be carried out during this stage, it is rather difficult to maintain this state. It is therefore limited to short procedures.

Stage 2: The Excitement Stage/Stage of Delirium

It starts from loss of consciousness to beginning of regular respiration. Excitement is seen and the patient may shout, struggle and hold his breath; muscle tone increases, jaw are tightly closed, breathing is jerky; vomiting, involuntary micturition or defecation may occur. Heart rate and BP may rise and pupils dilate due to sympathetic stimulation.

No stimulus should be applied or operative procedure carried out during this stage.

Stage 3: Surgical Anaesthesia

It extends from onset of regular respiration to cessation of spontaneous breathing. This has been divided into four planes which may be distinguished as

- Phase1: Roving eyeballs. This plane ends when eyes become fixed.
- Phase 2: Loss of corneal and laryngeal reflexes.
- Plane 3: Pupil starts dilating and light reflex is lost.
- Plane 4: Intercostals paralysis, shallow abdominal respiration, dilated pupil.

Stage 4: Medullary Paralysis

In this stage, there is cessation of breathing to failure of circulation and death. Pupil is widely dilated, muscles are totally flabby, pulse is thready or imperceptible and BP is very low.

Pharmacokinetics of Inhalation Anaesthetics

- Inhalation anaesthetics are gases or vapours that diffuse rapidly across pulmonary alveoli and tissue barriers. The depth of anaesthesia depends on the agent (MAC is an index of potency) and its partial pressure (PP) in the brain, while the induction and recovery depend on the rate of change of PP in the brain.

- Transfer of anaesthetics between lung and brain depends on a series of tension gradient which may be as

$$\boxed{\text{Alveoli} \rightarrow \text{Blood} \rightarrow \text{Brain}}$$

Elimination

- When anaesthetic administration is discontinued, gradients are reversed and the channel of absorption (pulmonary epithelium) becomes the channel of elimination.

- Most of general anaesthetics are eliminated unchanged. Metabolism is significant only for halothane. Other are practically not metabolised.

Classification of General Anaesthetics

(A) Inhalation anaesthetics

(a) Gas

(i) Nitrous oxide (blue cylinder): Prototype anaesthetic gas

(ii) Cyclopropane (orange cylinder): Have a rapid onset of action and a rapid recovery

(iii) Ethylene (red cylinder): Less toxic than most of the other gas anaesthetics

(b) Liquids

Ether, Halothane, Enflurane, Isoflurane, Sevoflurane, Desflurane and Methoxyflurane.

(B) Intravenous anaesthetics

(a) Inducing agent: Thiopentone sodium, Methohexitone sodium, Propofol and Etomidate

(b) Slowly acting drugs

(i) Benzodiazepines: Diazepam, Lorazepam, midazolam

(ii) Dissociative anaesthesia: Ketamine

(iii) Opioid analgesia: Fentanyl

Inhalational GAs

- Inhalational anaesthesia refers to the delivery of gases or vapours to the respiratory system to produce anaesthesia.

- **Pharmacokinetics:** Inhalation anaesthetics get uptake, distributed and eliminated from the body.

- **Pharmacodynamic:** The Pharmacodynamic effects of these agents depend upon the MAC value. The dose of inhaled anaesthesia represented by percent in inspired mixture.

Nitrous Oxide

- It was prepared by Priestly in 1776 and its anaesthetic properties were described by Davy in 1799. It is characterised by inert nature with minimal metabolism. It is colourless, odourless, tasteless, and does not burn. It is a simple linear compound. It is not metabolised in the body.

- The major difference of nitrous oxide for its low potency and its MAC value which is 104. It is a weak anaesthetic and powerful analgesic. It is therefore recommended to use other agents for surgical anaesthesia. It has low blood solubility (quick recovery).

- Minimal effects of nitrous oxide are observed on heart rate and blood pressure. It may cause myocardial depression in sick patients and has little effect on respiration.

- Toxicity of nitrous oxide is mainly due to manufacturing impurities. The effects which occur due to presence of large concentration of gas in alveoli called second gas effect or concentration effect and this is observed at the beginning while at the end diffusion hypoxia occurs.

- It inhibits methionine synthatase (precursor to DNA synthesis) and also inhibits vitamin B-12 metabolism.

Ether

- It is a highly volatile liquid, produces irritating vapours which are inflammable and explosive.

- Ether is a potent anaesthetic, produces good analgesia and marked muscle relaxation by reducing Ach output from motor nerve ending.

- It is highly soluble in blood, induction is prolonged and unpleasant with struggling, breath holding, salivation and marked respiratory secretions (atropine must be given as premedication to prevent the patient from drowning in his own secretion).

- Post anaesthetics nausea, vomiting and retching are marked.

- It does not sensitise the heart to adrenaline and is not hepatotoxic.

Halothane

- Halothane was synthesised in 1956 by Suckling. It is a halogen substituted ethane.

- It is a volatile liquid, easily vaporised, stable, and nonflammable.

- It is the most potent inhalational anaesthetic and the MAC value is found to be 0.75%.

- Efficacious in depressing consciousness. It is very soluble in blood and adipose tissue.

- Halothane inhibits sympathetic response to painful stimuli and driven baroreflex response (hypovolemia).

- It sensitizes myocardium to effects of exogenous catecholamines which results in ventricular arrhythmias.

- It decreases respiratory drive represented by shallow respiration and depresses protective airway refluxes which are mediated by central and peripheral response to CO_2 and O_2 respectively

- It also depresses the myocardium by reducing intracellular calcium concentration.

This lowers BP and slows conduction. Halothane also produces mild peripheral vasodilation.

- The side effects to halothane are rare. It may result in Hepatitis (1/10,000 cases) which is characterised by fever, jaundice, hepatic necrosis and death. Metabolic breakdown products of halothane are hapten-protein conjugates which produce immunologically mediated assault. The immunological reaction is exposure dependent.

- Halothane also produces malignant hyperthermia which is due to intracellular release of calcium from sarcoplasmic reticulum causing persistent muscle contraction and heat production. The incidence of malignant hypothermia was observed in 1 of 60,000 cases when given along with succinylcholine while in absence of succinylcholine the risk of incidence was reduced to 1 in 260,000 cases.

- There is rapid rise in body temperature, muscle rigidity, tachycardia, rhabdomyolysis, acidosis and hyperkalemia to halothane.

Following measures are considered as treatments for Halothane toxicity

- Early detection, hyperventilation, bicarbonate administration, IV dantrolene (2.5 mg/kg), ice packs/cooling blankets, use of lasix/mannitol/fluids, ICU monitoring. In susceptible patients pre-operates with IV dantrolene, keep away inhalational agents and succinylcholine.

Enflurane

- Enflurane was developed in 1963 by Terrell and was released for use in 1972. It is a stable, nonflammable liquid and pungent in odour. The MAC value is 1.68%.

- Enflurane a is potent inotropic and chronotropic depressant and decreases systemic vascular resistance which results in drastically low blood pressure and conduction.

- It inhibits sympathetic baroreflex response and sensitises myocardium to effects of exogenous catecholamines which results into arrhythmias.

- It stimulates salivary and respiratory secretion. Respiratory drive is greatly depressed; produces the central and peripheral responses such as increased dead space, widens A-a gradient and produces hypercarbia in spontaneously breathing patient.

- Metabolism of Enflurane takes place one-tenth that of halothane and it does not release quantity of hepatotoxic metabolites. Metabolism releases fluoride ion which cause renal toxicity.

- There is alteration in the epileptiform EEG patterns of the patient.

Isoflurane

- Isoflurane was synthesised in 1965 by Terrell and introduced into practice in 1984.

- It is an isomer of Enflurane and does not have carcinogenic effect. It is nonflammable and pungent in odour.

- Pharmacokinetically it is less soluble than halothane or Enflurane and the MAC value is 1.30%.

- Compared to Enflurane, systemically isoflurane depresses respiratory drive and ventilatory responses, it also depresses the myocardial activity and inhibits sympathetic baroreflex response. These effects are comparatively less than enflurane.

- It also sensitises myocardium to catecholamines which is less than halothane or Enflurane.

- Isoflurane produces most significant reduction in systemic vascular resistance and results into coronary steal syndrome and increased intra coronary pressure. It has excellent muscle relaxant property which potentiates effects of neuromuscular blockers.

- Side effects of isoflurane are less due to its metabolism which produces low potential of organotoxic metabolites. It does not have any activity on EEG activity like Enflurane, though it produces broncho irritating and laryngospasm.

Sevoflurane and Desflurane

- Sevoflurane and desflurane has low blood solubility and produces rapid induction and emergence. They have minimal systemic effects and produce mild respiratory and cardiac suppression. Compared to others they have few side effects but are expensive.

- Desflurane has distinct property in their high volatility, lower oil: gas partition coefficient and very low solubility in blood and tissue because of which induction and recovery are very fast. Patient can be discharged few hours after surgery.

- Sevoflurane is polyfluronated anaesthetic which is intermediate between isoflurane and desflurane, thus there are no problem in induction.

- Sevoflurane does not cause sympathetic stimulation and airway irritation even during rapid induction.

Intravenous Anaesthetic Agents

The first attempt to use of intravenous anaesthesia was by Wren in 1656. In this he use the opium as intravenous anaesthesia for his dog. The same was as anaesthesia in 1934 with thiopental. In many ways these agents meet the other requirements by producing the muscle relaxants activity. They produce appealing and pleasant experience.

(A) Inducing Agents

Thiopental

- Thiopental is a barbiturate. It is water soluble and alkaline in nature. It produces dose-dependent suppression of CNS activity and results in decreased cerebral metabolic rate (EEG flat).

- Systemically thiopental produce rapid onset of action and ultrashort recovery period. It has varied effects on cardiovascular system. it produces mild direct cardiac depression resulting into lowered blood pressure and compensatory tachycardia (baroreflex).

- It also produces dose-dependent depression of respiration through medullary and pontine respiratory centers.

- By intravenous route the onset of action begins in 1 minute and duration is around 20–30 min. $T^{1/2}$: 3–8 hours; metabolised in the liver, excreted in the urine.

- The side effects of thiopental are noncompatibility, tissue necrosis (gangrene), tissue stores. Laryngospasm occur generally when respiratory secretion or other irritant are present, it can be prevented by atropine premedication and administration of succinylcholine immediately after thiopentone. Succinylcholine and Thiopentone react chemically thus they should not be mixed in the same syringe.

- Occasionally it is used for rapid control of convulsion. Intravenous infusion of subanasthetic doses can be used to facilate psychiatric verbal communication with psychiatric patients.

Methohexital

- It is similar to thiopentone and three times more potent.
- It has a quicker and briefer (5-8 min) action.
- Vascular complications are rare.
- It is more rapidly metabolised than Thiopentone.

Etomidate

- Structurally etomidate is similar to ketoconazole.
- It has direct CNS depressant (thiopental) and GABA agonist activity.
- Systemically it produces little change in cardiac function in healthy and cardiac patients. At mild dose there is dose related respiratory depression.
- It also decreases the cerebral metabolism and suppresses the production of steroid from adrenal and is not suited for continuous IV use. It is poor analgesic.
- The side effects of etomidate are pain on injection because of presence of propylene glycol. It also produces myoclonic activity, nausea, vomiting and cortisol suppression.

Propofol

- Propofol produce rapid onset and short duration of action.
- Myocardial depression and peripheral vasodilation may occur. It is not water soluble so result in pain. It also produces minimal nausea and vomiting

(B) Slower Acting Drugs

Benzodiazepine (BZD)

- Benzodiazepine produce sedation and amnesia by potentiating GABA receptors.
- It produces slower onset and emergence. BZDs are poor analgesic: an opioid or nitric oxide is usually added if the procedure is painful.
- BZDs decrease muscle tone by central action, but require neuromuscular blocking drugs for muscle relaxation.
- They do not provoke postoperative nausea or vomiting. Involuntary movements are not stimulated. The anaesthetic action of BZDs can be reversed by flumazenil

Diazepam

- It is often used as premedication for seizure activity and rarely for induction.

- It has minimal systemic effects in which respiration is decreased with narcotic usage.
- It is water insoluble thus produce venous irritation.
- It is metabolised by liver and is not redistributed.

Lorazepam

- It has slower onset of action (10-20 minutes) and generally not used for induction
- It is used as adjunct for anxiolytics and sedative properties. The amnesic effects are more profound.
- It is similar to diazepam. It is water insoluble and produce venous irritation

Midazolam

- It is more potent than diazepam and lorazepam.
- Induction is slow thus the recovery is prolonged.
- It may depress respirations when used with narcotics. It has minimal cardiac effects. Due to its water solubility it is non-irritating.

Dissociative Anaesthesia

Ketamine

- Pharmacologically ketamine is related to the hallucinogen phencyclidine.
- It interrupts cerebral association pathways thus is called Dissociative anaesthesia.
- It stimulates central sympathetic pathways. The primary site of action is the cortex and subcortical area; not in reticular activating system.
- Ketamine has been recommended for operation on the head and neck, in patient who has bled, and asthamatic patients (relieves bronchospasm).
- It is good for repeated use; particularly suitable for burn dressing. It may be dangerous for hypertensive and in ischemic heart but is good for hypovolemic patient.
- The main characteristic of ketamine is stimulation of sympathetic nervous system which results into increased heart rate, blood pressure and cardiac output.

- It maintains laryngeal reflexes and skeletal muscle tone and in emergence can produce hallucinations and unpleasant dreams.

Clonidine

- It is selective α_2 adrenergic agonist and used as an antihypertensive agent.

- Sedation and analgesia are produced due to the stimulation of central α_2 adrenoceptors.

- It is administered before surgery; clonidine reduces the dose of anaesthetic/ analgesic drug, resulting in less overall depression of cardiovascular function for the same level of anaesthesia.

Narcotic agonists (Opioids)

- Narcotics have been used for years. It was used during the civil war for wounded soldiers due to their analgesic action.

- Predominant effects of narcotics are analgesia, depression of sensorium and respirations.

- Mechanism of action of narcotics is receptor mediated which are given in Table 1.1.

Table 1.1: Receptor-mediated effects of narcotics

Receptor	Effects
μ (mu)	Analgesia, respiratory depression, euphoria, physical dependence
κ (kappa)	Analgesia, respiratory depression, sedation, miosis
σ (Sigma)	Dysphoria, hallucination, tachypnea, tachycardia

- Narcotics agonist produce minimal effect on cardiac at usual doses but there are no myocardial depression observed. Bradycardia is observed when large doses are administered.

- Narcotics produce peripheral vasodilation and histamine release which results into hypotension.

- Side effects are nausea, chest wall rigidity, seizures, constipation, urinary retention.

- Meperidine, morphine, alfentanil, fentanyl, sufentanil are commonly used narcotics.

- Naloxone is pure antagonist that reverses analgesia and respiratory depression nonselectively and effects may recur when metabolised.

Other Agents

Muscle Relaxants

- Current use of inhalational and intravenous agents does not fully provide control of muscle tone. Muscle relaxants were first used in 1942 and since then many new agents have been developed to reduce the side effects and lengthen the duration of action.

- Mechanism of action occurs at the neuromuscular junction (Figure 1.2.)

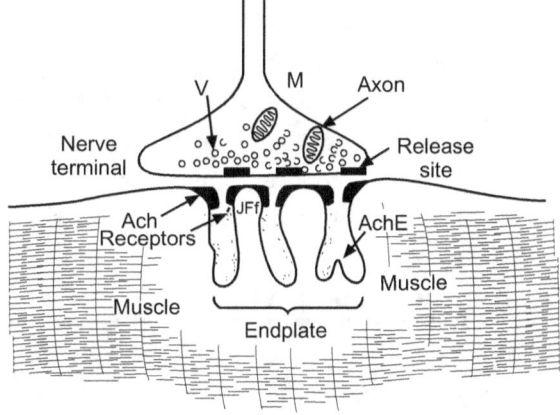

Fig. 1.2: Neuromuscular Junction

1. **Non-depolarising Muscle Relaxants**

- These agents competitively inhibit end plate nicotinic cholinergic receptor.

- The intermediate acting agents produce the action for 15-60 minutes e.g. atracurium, vecuronium and mivacurium.

- The long acting agents produce the action for over 60 minutes e.g. pancuronium, tubocurarine and metocurine.

- The major differences in both long acting and intermediate acting agents are the effects on the renal function.

- Tubocurarine suppresses sympathetics and produce mast cell degranulation while the pancuronium blocks muscarinics receptor.

- The action of non depolaring agents are reversal by anticholinesterase which inhibit acetylcholinesterase e.g. neostigmine, pyridostigmine, edrophonium. Muscarinics stimulation is the major side effects of such inhibition.

2. **Depolarizing Muscle Relaxants**

- These agents depolarise the end-plate nicotinic receptor.

- Succinylcholine is used clinically.

   o It has short duration of action due to plasma cholinesterase.

   o Side effects are fasciculations, myocyte rupture, potassium extravasation, myalgias and malignant hyperthermia.

   o It also produces sinus bradycardia because of activation of muscarinic receptor.

Drug Interactions with GAs

- Use of antihypertensive with general anaesthetics results in marked fall in blood pressure.

- Use of neuroleptics, opiods, clonidine and monoamine oxidase inhibitor potentiate the anaesthetics effects.

- Use of halothane with adrenaline sensitises the heart.

- Corticosteroid and general anaesthetics can precipitate adrenal insufficiency and cardiovascular collapse.

Agents Involved in Balanced Anaesthesia

Preoperative medications

o Sedative–hypnotics

o Opioids

o Antiemetic

o Anticholinergics

o Antihistamines

o Neuroleptics

o Narcotics

The use of preoperative medication is important due to the following reasons.

- For relief of anxiety and facilitated smooth induction.

- Amnesia for pre- and postoperative events.

- Supplement analgesic action of anaesthetics and potentiate them so that less anaesthetics is needed.

- Decrease the secretion and vagal stimulation caused by anaesthetics.

- Antiemetics effect extend to the postoperative period.

- Decrease acidity and volume of gastric juice so that it is less damaging if aspired.

Sedative-antianxiety drugs: BZDs have become popular drug for preanaesthetics because they produce tranquility and smoothen induction; there is loss of recall of preoperative events. They counteract CNS toxicity of anaesthetics.

Promethazine: It is an antihistaminic with sedative, antiemetic and Anticholinergics properties. It is particularly used in children.

Anticholinergics: Atropine or hyoscine has been used, primarily to reduce salivary and bronchial secretions. The main aim of their use now is to prevent vagal bradycardia and hypotension, and prophylaxis of laryngospasm which is precipitated by respiratory secretion. They dilate pupils; abolish the pupilary sign and increase signs and chances of gastric reflex by decreasing tone of lower esophageal sphincter.

Glycopyrrolate: Is a longer acting quaternary atropine substitute. It is a potent antisecretory and antibradycardiac drug; acts rapidly and less likely to produce central effect.

Neuroleptics: Chlorpromazine, trifluoperazine or haloperidols are frequently used in premedication. They relieve anxiety, smoothen induction and have antiemetic action. However they potentiate respiratory depression and hypotension caused by the anaesthetics and delay recovery.

Involuntary movement and muscle dystonias can occur, especially in children.

Antihistamines: These are H_2 blockers. generally used for patients undergoing prolonged operations and obese patients who are at increased risk of gastric regurgitation and aspiration pneumonia.

Ranitidine or Famotidine given night before and in the morning benefit by raising pH of gastric juice; may also reduce its volume and thus chances of regurgitation. Prevention of stress ulcer is another advantage.

Antiemetic: Metaclopramide preoperatively is effective in reducing post operative vomiting. By enhancing gastric emptying and tone of LES, it reduces the chance of reflux and its aspiration. Extrapyramidal effect and motor restlessness can occur.

Domperidol is nearly as effective and does not produce extrapyramidal side effect.

Opioids: Morphine or pethidine relieve anxiety and apprehension of the operation. It produces pre- and post operative analgesia, smoothen induction, reduce the dose of anaesthesia required and supplement poor analgesic (thiopentone, halothane) or weak nitrous oxide anaesthetics.

Use of opioids are now mostly restricted to those having preoperative pain. When indicated fentanyl is mostly injected just before induction.

Questions on this Chapter

1. Discuss in detail the different stages of anaesthesia.
2. What are the balanced anaesthesia explain in details.
3. Write a short note on dissociative anaesthesia.
4. Write a short note on Inhalational Anaesthetics.
5. Discuss the mechanism of general anaesthetics.

Chapter 2

LOCAL ANAESTHETICS

Objectives

After reading this chapter, the student will be able to-

➢ Distinguish between the effects of local and general anaesthetics

➢ Understand the characteristics of local anaesthetics

➢ Understand the mechanism of local anaesthetics

➢ Distinguish between the features of amide vs. ester linked LA

➢ Enlist the toxicity profile of LA

CATEGORIES OF ANAESTHETICS

- **Local anaesthetics:** Local anaesthetics (LA) are the agents used to cause absence of pain sensation and feeling in a designated area of the body. They not produce the systemic effects associated with severe CNS depression.

- **General anaesthetics**: The agents from this category produce depression of Central Nervous System (CNS) and are used to produce loss of pain sensation and consciousness.

The other important differences between general and local anaesthetics are given in Table 2.1.

Table 2.1: Characteristics of Local and General Anaesthetics

Target	General Anaesthetics	Local Anaesthetics
Site of action	CNS	Peripheral nerve
Area of body Involved	Whole body	Restricted area
Consciousness	Lost	Unaltered
Care of vital Functions	Essential	Usually not needed
Physiological trespass	High	Low
Poor health of patient	Risky	Safer
Use in non-cooperative patient	Possible	Not possible
Major surgery	Preferred	Cannot be used
Minor surgery	Not preferred	Preferred

Preanaesthetic Medications

Following are the agents given prior to induce anaesthesia to prevent or minimize the adverse effects of anaesthesia. (For detail refer page no. 1.9, General Anaesthesia).

- Sedative hypnotics
- Antiemetics
- Antihistamines
- Narcotics.

LOCAL ANAESTHETICS (LAs)

Introduction

- Followed general anaesthesia by 40 years. Koller used cocaine for the eye in 1884. Halsted used cocaine as a nerve block.
- First synthetic local anaesthetic was procaine in 1905. Lidocaine was synthesized in 1943. The action of local anaesthetic can be produced by sensation of cooling effect. Clinically used LAs have no/minimal local irritant action and block sensory nerve endings, nerve trunks, neuromuscular junction, ganglionic synapse and receptor (non-selective) i.e. structures which function through increased sodium permeability.
- They also reduced the release of acetylcholine from motor nerve endings. Injected around a mixed nerve they cause anaesthesia of skin and paralysis of voluntary muscle supplied by that nerve.

Classification of LAs agents

Injectables

(1) Low potency, short duration:-Procaine, Chloroprocaine.

(2) Intermediate potency and duration: - Lignocaine, Prilocaine.

(3) High potency, long duration: - Tetracaine (Amethocaine), Bupivacaine, Ropivacaine, Dibucaine (Cinchocaine).

Surface anaesthetics

(A) Soluble

- Cocaine
- Lignocaine
- Tetracaine
- Benoxinate

(B) Insoluble

- Benzocaine
- Butylaminobenzoate (Butamben)
- Oxethazaine.

Occasionally used local anaesthetics in other countries: Mepivacaine, Etidocaine, Cyclomethycaine, Dyclonine, Proparacaine.

Anaesthetics which are local irritants and other prominent systemic activity Propranolol, Chlorpromazine, H_1 antihistamine, Quinine.

Estered linked local anaesthetics: Cocaine, Procaine, Chloroprocaine, Tetracaine and Benzocaine.

Amide linked Local anaesthetics: Lignocaine, Bupivacaine, Dibucaine, Prilocaine, and Ropivacaine.

Mechanism of action of LAs

Mechanism of action of local anaesthetics is by reversibly blocking of sodium channels to prevent depolarisation. Anaesthetic enters on axioplasmic side and attaches to receptor in the middle of the channel see figure 2.1.

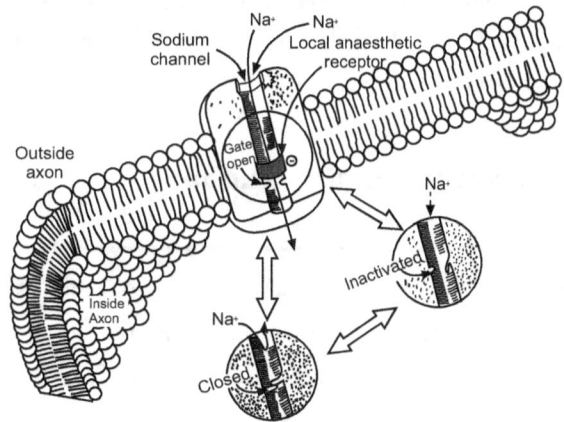

Fig. 2.1: Sodium channel

Characteristics of LAs

(1) **Linear molecules** that have a lipophilic and hydrophilic end (ionizable).

   (a) Low pH resulted to drug present more in ionized state and unable to cross membrane.

(b) Adding sodium bicarbonate converted the drug into more in non-ionized state and is able to cross the membrane.

(2) Two groups: Esters and Amides.

(a) Esters metabolised by plasma cholinesterase.

(b) Amides metabolised by Liver microsomes by dealkylation and hydrolysis.

Features of Amide LAs (compared to ester LAs)

- Produced more intense and longer lasting anaesthesia.

- Bind to α_1 acid glycoprotein in plasma.

- Not hydrolyzed by plasma esterase.

- Rarely cause hypersensitivity reaction; no cross sensitivity with ester LAs.

- Because of their short duration, less intense analgesia and higher risk of hypersensitivity, the ester linked LAs are rarely used for infiltration or nerve block, but are still used on mucous membrane.

Pharmacokinetic of Local Anaesthetics

- Soluble surface anaesthetics are rapidly absorbed from mucous membranes and abraded areas; but absorption from intact skin is poor. Procaine is negligible bound to plasma protein, but amide LAs are bound to plasma protein.

- After oral ingestion both procaine and lignocaine have high first pass metabolism in the liver. Thus, they are not effective orally for antiarrhythmic purpose.

Toxicity Profile of LAs

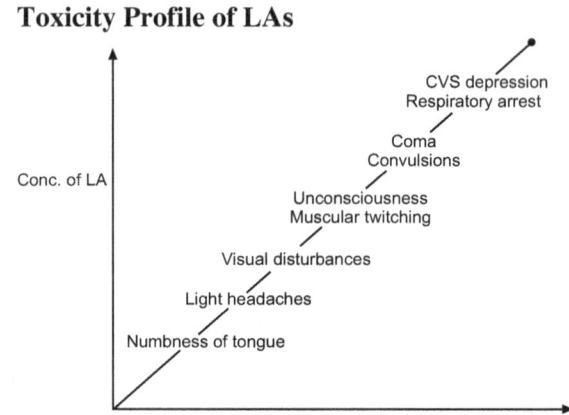

Fig. 2.2: Toxicity profile of LAs: at increasing the concentration of local anaesthetics in plasma resulted into dose dependant toxicity the first toxicity sign is numbness of tongue and as the plasma concentration of LA increase result into above toxicity.

LOCAL ANAESTHETIC ACTION/ TOXICITY

- **Central nervous system**
  - Initially, LAs produces lightheadedness, circumoral numbness, dizziness, tinnitus, visual change.
  - Later, drowsiness, disorientation, slurred speech, loss of consciousness, convulsions observed in patients.
  - Finally, there is respiratory depression.

  E.g. Cocaine having more potent action on CNS.

- **Blood vessels**
  - Fall in blood pressure due to sympathetic blockage, relaxation of arteriolar smooth muscle.
  - Toxic doses of LAs produce cardiovascular collapse.

- **Cardiovascular**
  - LAs produce myocardial depression and vasodilation results into hypotension and circulatory collapse. They also have quinidine like antiarrhythmic action.
  - Procaine cannot use as antiarrhythmic agent because of short duration of action

and propensity to cause CNS effect, but its amide derivative procainamide is a classical anti-arrhythmic action.

o	At high dose they induce arrhythmias.

o	Bupivacaine is more cardiotoxic.

o	Lignocaine is used as an antiarrhythmic.

- **Allergic reactions (less than 1%)**

	o	The allergic reactions may be due to the use of preservatives in LAs or metabolites of esters.

	o	Rash, bronchospasm.

Prevention and Treatment of Toxicity

- Toxicity to use of LAs primarily from intravascular injection or excessive dose. For prevention of the following aspect should be considered:

	o	Aspirate often with slow injection.

	o	Ask about CNS toxicity.

	o	Patients have continuously on monitor.

	o	Prepare with resuscitative equipment, CNS-depressant drugs and cardiovascular drugs.

Individual compounds

Cocaine (Obtained from *Erythroxylem coca*)

o	South American Indians used to induce euphoria, reduce hunger, and increase work tolerance in sixth century.

o	Many uses in head and neck-strong vasoconstrictor, no need for epinephrine.

o	Mechanism is similar i.e. blocks sodium channel, also prevents uptake of epinephrine and norepinephrine.

o	It may lead to increased levels of circulating catecholamine thereby results in tachycardia, peripheral vasoconstriction.

o	Safe limits (200-400 mg) - use with epinephrine clinically.

Procaine

o	It is the first synthetic local anaesthetics introduced in 1905.

o	It is not surface anaesthetics.

o	PABA is released on hydrolysis of procaine which can antagonise the antibacterial action of sulfonamide given to treat the infection.

o	Procaine penicillin injected i.m. acts for 24 hours.

Lignocaine

o	It is introduced in 1948.

o	Lignocaine hydrochloride is used both topically and by injection.

o	It blocks the nerve conduction within 3 min. whereas procaine may take15 min.

o	Cross sensitivity with ester LAs is not seen with lignocaine.

o	Central effects of lignocaine are drowsiness, mental clouding, altered taste and tinnitus.

o	Overdose may cause muscle twitching, convulsion, cardiac arrhythmias, fall in BP, coma and respiratory arrest.

o	It is rapidly metabolised in liver by dealkylation to form monoethyl-glycinexylidide and glycine xylidide.

o	Lignocaine is a popular antiarrhythmic.

Prilocaine

o	It is similar to lignocaine but does not cause vasodilation at the site of infiltration and has lower CNS toxicity due to larger volume of distribution.

o	It is readily metabolised in liver and kidneys. The principal metabolite excreted in the urine is o-toluidine. This is believed to cause methaemoglobinaemia.

Eutectic Lignocaine/Prilocaine

o	It can anesthetise the intact skin after surface application.

Tetracaine (Amethocaine)

o	Tetracaine is a ester of Para Amino Benzoic Acid (PABA), it is more potent and more toxic due to slow metabolism.

o	It is used for surface anaesthesia and spinal anaesthesia.

Bupivacaine

o It is a potent and long acting (180-360 min.) amide linked LAs, used chiefly for infiltration and regional nerve block, epidural and spinal anaesthesia.

o It has high lipid solubility; distributed in tissue organ than in blood after spinal and epidural injection.

o It is more prone to prolong QT interval and also cause cardiac depression.

o It should not used for intravenous regional analgesia.

Ropivacaine

o It is a congener of Bupivacaine, equally long acting but less cardiotoxic.

o It blocks the fiber involved in pain transmission.

o It is used for postoperative and labour pain; it can also be employ for nerve block.

Dibucaine (Cinchocaine)

o It is a most potent, most toxic and **longest acting LA (180-600 min.).**

o It is used as surface anaesthetics on less delicate mucous membrane (anal canal) and occasionally for spinal anaesthesia of long duration.

Benoxinate

o It is a good surface anaesthetic for the eye; has little irritancy.

o 0.4% solution rapidly produces corneal anaesthetics.

Benzocaine and Butylaminobenzoate (Butamben)

o Both are PABA derivative that can antagonise sulphonamide locally.

o It is hydrolyzed by esterase in the plasma to 4-aminobenzoic acid.

o It has very low aqueous solubility; these are not significantly absorbed from mucous membrane or abraded skin.

o Produce long lasting effect without systemic toxicity.

o It is often used in combination with other drugs for temporary local relief of pain associated with dental procedures, sore throat, hemorrhoids and pruritis.

Oxethazaine

• Topical anasthetics, unique in ionising to a very small extent even at low pH values.

• Effective in anaesthetising gastric mucosa despite acidity of the medium. It is generally administered along with antacid because it afford symptomatic relief in gastric, drug induced gastric irritation, gastroesophegeal reflex and heartburn of pregnancy.

METHODS OF ADMINISTERING LOCAL ANAESTHETICS

Following are discussing the methods of administration of local anaesthetics

• Topical/Surface anaesthesia.

• Infiltration anaesthesia (infiltered under the skin in the area of operation).

• Conduction block (injected around nerve trunk).

    o Field block

    o Nerve block

• **Spinal anaesthesia** (injected in sub-arachnoid space).

• **Drug used in spinal anaesthesia:** Lignocaine, Tetracaine, Bupivacaine, Dibucaine.

Complications of spinal anaesthesia:

o Respiratory paralysis - Pulmonary complication

o Hypotension due to sympathetic blocker

o Headache

o Neurological complication

o Septic meningitis

o Nausea and vomiting.

• **Intravenous regional anaesthesia:** These are mainly used for upper limb and orthopedic procedure.

- **Epidural anaesthesia:** Lignocaine and Bupivacaine are most popular epidural anastasia. It divided into three categories depending on the site of injection.
  - **Thoracic:** Used generally for pain relief from thoracic /upper abdominal surgery.
  - **Lumber:** Produce anaesthesia of lower abdomen, pelvis and hind limb.
  - **Caudal:** Given in sacral can produce anaesthesia of pelvic and peripheral region, used mostly for vaginal delivery, anorectal and genitourinary operation.

Duration of action of both anaesthesias is prolonging by adrenaline. Cardiovascular complications are similar to spinal anaesthesia but neurological and headaches are less.

Questions on this Chapter

1. Write the classification and pharmacological actions of local anaesthetics.
2. Write short note on surface anaesthetics.
3. What are the Injectables local anaesthetics?
4. Discuss different methods for administration of local anaesthetics.

Chapter 3

ALCOHOLS AND ALCOHOLISM

Objectives

After reading this chapter, the student will be able to:

➢ Distinguish between methyl alcohol and ethyl alcohol

➢ Explain the characteristics of Alcoholic Liver Disease

➢ Explain the manufacturing process of alcohol

➢ Justify the usefulness of disulfiram and naltrexone in alcoholism

METHYL ALCOHOL
(METHANOL, WOOD ALCOHOL)

• It is known as wood alcohol since it is prepared by destructive distillation of wood.

• It is poisonous and so it is not suitable for human consumption.

• Formaldehyde, a metabolic product of methyl alcohol damages optic nerve leading to blindness.

• Ethyl alcohol may be give in case of poisoning with methyl alcohol.

• Ethyl alcohol is metabolised preferentially over methyl alcohol, so methyl alcohol is excreted unchanged.

Ethyl Alcohol - (Ethanol)

• Alcohols are hydroxyl derivatives of aliphatic hydrocarbons. Study of pharmacology of alcohol is important due to its presence in beverages and due to alcohol intoxication rather than as a drug.

Alcohol is manufactured by fermentation of sugar and the process of fermentation is continued till the content reaches approximately to 15%. This reaction is inhibited by alcohol itself.

$$C_6H_{12}O_6 \xrightarrow[\text{In yeast}]{\text{Zymase}} 2CO_2 + 2C_2H_5OH$$

Pharmacokinetics of Ethanol

Absorption, fate and excretion: Alcohol is absorbed in the stomach (25%) and small intestine (75%). It is metabolised in the liver as follows and elimination takes place via urine.

1. Ethyl alcohol $\xrightarrow{\text{Alcohol dehydrogenase}}$ Acetaldehyde

2. Acetaldehyde $\xrightarrow[\text{Aldehyde dehydrogenase}]{}$ Acetyl CoA

Acetyl CoA is further metabolised to carbon dioxide and water.

Pharmacological Effects of Alcohol

1. **External**: Externally alcohol acts as a-

   (i) Astringent as it precipitates proteins.

   (ii) Refrigerant as it produces the cooling effect on the surface of the skin.

   (iii) Rubifacient as it dilates the cutaneous blood vessels.

   (iv) Detergent as it dissolves the sebaceous secretions.

(v) Antiseptic as it destroys micro-organisms.

2. **Gastrointestinal tract:** Alcohol increases the gastric acid secretion and thereby produces a carminative effect.

3. **Liver:** Long term consumption of alcohol causes fatty liver.

4. **CNS:** Initially excitation occurs because of depression of higher inhibitory centers. This is followed by progressive depression, drowsiness, sleep and unconsciousness as the dose increased.

5. **CVS:** There is cutaneous vasodilation at moderate dose of alcohol. This produces a feeling of flushing and warmth. There is slight rise in blood pressure and increase in heart rate when a concentrated form of alcohol given which this is due to reflex action.

6. **Respiration:** There is slight increase in the rate of respiration at moderate dose of alcohol while larger doses produce respiratory depression which may be fatal.

7. **Kidney:** There is decreased secretion of anti-diuretic hormone resulting in increased output of urine (diuresis).

8. **Sexual function:** Alcohol produces erection of sexual organ due to loss of inhibitory control.

9. **Food value:** There is rapid utilisation of alcohol which gives rise to energy but it is not a true food because the energy produces is not sufficient even for basal metabolism.

Interactions

• Synergistic effects are observed with antidepressant, antihistaminic, opioids and anxiolytics. There is marked CNS depression and motor impairment may occur.

• Acute alcohol ingestion with tolbutamide results in inhibition of tolbutamide metabolism while chronic alcohol results in increased in metabolism.

• There is increase in hypoglycemic activity of insulin and sulfonylureas after ingestion of alcohol.

• Administration of aspirin and other NSAIDs in alcoholism cause more gastric bleeding.

Contraindications

Alcohol is contraindicated in peptic ulcer, hyperacidity and gastroesophageal reflux patients. There is precipitation of seizures when used in epileptic patients.

Toxicity

• There is nausea, vomiting, hangover, flushing. Accidents may occur if vehicles are driven or machinery operated after moderate to heavy drinking.

• Hypotension, hypoglycemia, respiratory depression and gastritis occur after acute alcohol intoxication.

• Chronic alcoholism causes atrophic changes in GIT, degenerative changes in liver and nerves.

ALCOHOLISM

Alcoholism is a major social problem and is also known as alcohol dependence. In alcoholism there is psychological and physiological dependence on alcohol. Alcoholism is a social evil as it disrupts interpersonal, family and work relationships.

At early stages some sign and symptoms that indicate alcoholism are need for alcohol at the beginning of day or at the time of stress, hiding alcohol from family, irritability when the alcohol is not available,, insomnia, nightmares, anxiety etc.. At a later stage of alcoholism symptoms such as memory loss, tremors, hallucination, confusion, rapid heartbeat, sweating are observed. Decline in sexual interest and potency, shortness of breath, accumulation of fluid in body part, liver cirrhosis and neurological impairment is also observed.

There are many factors that contribute to alcoholism but exact cause is not fully understood. These factors include depression, dependence, anger, divorce. Hereditary factor may also contribute to alcoholism.

Clinical Manifestations and Complications of Alcoholism

Liver cirrhosis is a major health complication caused due to chronic use of alcohol. It is the major cause of death in alcoholism. Some possible complications of alcoholism are as follows-

1. **General**

1. General appearance of an alcoholic person changes at the time of alcohol withdrawal or at the time when the alcohol is not present in the blood. Some of these are as follows:

    *   Hand tremors
    *   Excitability, irritability and nervousness
    *   Disturbance of sleep pattern (REM sleep pattern)

2. Yellow colour of skin in alcoholism indicates liver damage.

3. Alcoholics suffer from vitamin B deficiency that results in dry, red, itchy skin called seborrheic dermatitis.

4. There is blockage of salivary duct due increase in stickiness of saliva and swelling of parotid gland.

5. There is swelling of tips of fingers causing puffiness. There is also increase in the size of lower part of nose due to increased in nasal sweat gland .

6. Drinking of alcohol during pregnancy results in risk of premature birth, low birth weight and fetal alcohol syndrome

2. **Gastrointestinal Tract**

*   Dyspepsia occurs in which there is feeling of discomfort after eating.

*   There is sign of gastritis due to inflammation of stomach and GI tract.

*   Recurrent diarrhea occurs due to changes in the motility of gastrointestinal tract. There is malabsorption of food due to increased in propulsive activity of the small intestine.

*   There is inflammation of stomach and colon that causes recurrent abdominal pain.

*   Alcohol consumption also causes pancreatitis. Alcohol has direct toxic effect on the pancreas which causes change in secretion due to pancreatic irritation and damage. There is increase in protein concentration in the pancreatic juice. The most common symptoms of pancreatitis are constant and severe epigastric pain, nausea

and vomiting within one or two days after heavy alcohol consumption.

*   Alcohol causes change in blood sugar level due to release of insulin from pancreas resultingin hypoglycemia. This decrease in blood glucose level causes the liver to produce glycogen to replace lost glucose which results in increase in blood glucose level in turn causing hyperglycemia.

*   Alcohol causes increased acid production resulting in destruction of stomach lining This leads to formation of ulcers and causes gastrointestinal bleeding.

*   The major toxic effect of alcohol is enlargement of liver due to accumulation of free fatty acids in liver called alcoholic fatty liver. Over a period of time there is necrosis of liver resulting in jaundice, hepatomegaly, liver pain, fever and ascites formation.

*   Liver cirrhosis results due to advanced necrosis and scarring of liver.

3. **Cardiovascular related**

*   Alcohol consumption causes irregular heartbeat.

*   There is shortness of breath and signs of congestive cardiac failure.

*   Alcohol decreases the oxygen carrying capacity of blood. Nutritional deficiency specially of vitamin B 12 due to alcohol consumption lead to formation of immature RBCs and WBCs. Defects in RBCs maturation leads to enlargement of RBC and causes anemia.

*   Alcohol also cause dilation of peripheral blood vessels leading to loss of body heat. Thus, regulation of body temperature is impaired.

4. **Respiratory System**

*   Alcohol has toxic effects on lung tissue and alveoli resulting in loss of elasticity and air capacity of lung This condition is known as chronic obstructive pulmonary disease (COPD).

*   Due to irritation and inflammation of lung tissue and bronchi recurrent chest infection and pneumonia occur. Alcohol also suppresses the immune system

compromising the body's ability to fight infections.

5. Musculoskeletal

- There is improper nourishment of muscle tissue resulting muscle wasting. This is characterized by acute pain in the upper arms, shoulders and pelvic area.

- Chronic use of alcohol increases the level of enzyme serum creatinine and phosphokinase resulting in muscle cramps and weakness.

6. Renal System

- Chronic use of alcohol decreases the efficiency of kidney function. There is leaking of blood cells and albumin which may impart red colour to the urine.

- Alcohol suppresses the release of anti-diuretic hormone (ADH) from the pituitary gland resulting in polyuria or diuresis. The extent of diuresis depends on alcohol concentration in the blood.

- Alcohol also disrupts electrolyte balance. There is decrease in the excretion of sodium and chloride. Loss of magnesium causes slowdown of mental process.

7. Reproductive System

- Calcium is very essential for ovaries to work efficiently. Alcohol interferes with the absorption of calcium resulting in decreased in efficiency. It also disrupts the regular menstrual cycles.

- In males, alcohol increases estrogen and decreases the testosterone level resulting in development of feminine features such as breast enlargement, loss of facial hair etc. Alcohol has a direct toxic effect on testes causing them to atrophy, decrease in plasma testosterone concentration and decrease in fertility.

8. Laboratory Values

- Alcohol increases the various diagnostic parameters of various systems such as increase in the uric acid level, increase in triglycerides level, increase in mean corpuscular volume and increase in alkaline phosphatase.

9. Central Nervous System

- Alcohol impairs the brain functioning and causes loss of memory particularly of recent events. Impairment of memory occurs due to brain cell damage.

- Cessation of alcohol results in seizures. Threshold of seizures depends upon the level of alcoholism.

- Peripheral neuropathy occurs due vitamin B deficiency because of alcohol use. Vitamin B deficiency leads to deficiency in the production of enzymes which are needed to maintain the covering of nerve cells. Deficiency of these enzymes causes destruction of nerve cells due to which tingling, numbness, as well as muscle weakness, loss of balance (ataxia) are experienced.

- Large amount of alcohol affects the REM sleep resulting in insomnia and nightmares.

- Alcohol withdrawal results in hallucination, delirium, tremors, insomnia, depression, irritability and increase in blood pressure,

MEASURES AND TREATMENTS

Preventive measures

Following are some measures to prevent development of complications and further health hazards of alcoholism.

- Moderate use of alcohol.
- Set the limit of alcohol
- Don't drink without dilution and don't drink alone.
- Take vitamins supplements.
- Don't drink and drive.

General measures

- Stop drinking
- Get the medical help when physical withdrawal symptoms occur.
- Keep appointments with doctors and counselors
- Change lifestyle and friends circles or any other factor that encourages drinking.

Medical Treatment

- Some drugs namely disulfiram, naltrexone, topiramate, produce some beneficial effects in alcoholics. Disulfiram causes unpleasant physical symptoms when it is given along with alcohol. So patient refuses to drink because of fearing an antabuse reaction..

- Disulfiram, by instilling patients with a fear of an "Antabuse" reaction should they drink, may make for enough sober time for patients to benefit from a psychosocial approach. Given the risks associated with disulfiram, cases must be highly selective and disulfiram should generally not be prescribed to patients who are not committed to sobriety, as they generally end up drinking while taking it. This includes patients who want disulfiram so that they can "dry out" for a few weeks.

- Naltrexone, in a dose of 50 mg daily, may be use to reduce the craving and damping the reinforcing euphoria of a drink. Thus there is reduction in the number of drinking days and increase in the chances of abstinence.

- Topiramate, in a dose of from 100 to 200 mg is demonstrated to reduce the drinking days as well. It also reduces the amount of alcohol consumed on and increases the number of abstinent days.

- Drugs used for withdrawal symptoms include benzodiazepines, tranquilizers, antipsychotics and anticonvulsants (if seizures occur).

- Relapses are common; most occur in the first 6 months. Only about 50% of alcoholics achieve a year of continuous abstinence. The physician therefore must guard against becoming frustrated and must likewise help the patient to keep up his morale.

GUIDELINES FOR SAFE DRINKING

- On an average 1-2 drinks per day is usually considered safe.
- Not more than 3 drinks on any one occasion should be consumed.
- Consumption of >3 drinks per day is associated with documented adverse health effects.
- Do not drive or engage in hazardous activities after drinking.
- Do not drink if an interacting drug is being taken.
- Subjects with any contraindication should not drink.

ALCOHOLIC LIVER DISEASES

Alcoholic liver disease (ALD) is a major health issue worldwide. It ranges from simple steatosis to development of liver cirrhosis and hepatocellular carcinoma (HCC). There are no FDA-approved treatments available for ALD. At present, abstinence remains the cornerstone for successful treatment of ALD.

A number of risk factors have been identified which influence the development and progression of liver disease. They are-

- The most important risk factor is the quantity of alcohol ingestion. As per the reported data the risk of cirrhosis increases with the ingestion of >60 – 80 g / day of alcohol for 10 years in men, and >20 g / day in women.

- Drinking of beer or spirits likely to be associated with more risk of liver disease than drinking of wine.

- Women are more sensitive to alcohol mediated hepatotoxicity and may develop more severe ALD at lower doses and at shorter duration of alcohol consumption.

- There is also involvement of individual's racial and ethnic heritage in liver injury. There is higher ratio of alcoholic cirrhosis in Hispanic and African-American males as compared to Caucasian males.

- Protein calorie malnutrition is an important risk factor in the development and outcome in a patient with alcoholic liver disease. Mortality is higher in malnourished persons.

- Deficiency of vitamin A and E also increase the risk in development of liver disease.

- There is also some impact of diet on the alcoholic liver disease. Diet rich with polyunsaturated fatty acid potentiate the development of alcoholic liver disease while saturated fatty acid has protective role.

- Obesity and excess body weight have been associated with an increased risk of ALD.
- There is significantly higher rate of alcohol dependency in those children who are adopted in alcoholic family as compared to non-alcoholic family.
- There is higher prevalence of alcoholic cirrhosis in a monozygotic twin compared to a dizygotic twin.

Therapy

There are numerous therapies investigated and suggested in an attempt to reverse the stages of liver disease. The therapy depends on the stage of the disease and specific aim of therapy. The patients of alcoholic cirrhosis show several complications including the evidence hepatic failure and portal hypertension; thus these patients are treated as same as non-alcoholic. Additional attention has be paid to other organ dysfunctions associated especially with alcohol. Following are a few suggestive therapies in alcoholic liver disease.

Abstinence

Continuous use of alcohol is associated with progression of liver disease thus abstinence from alcohol is a cornerstone therapy in order to prevent further liver injury, scarring, and possibly liver carcinoma. Abstinence is beneficial as it reverses fatty liver. Abstinence also improves the outcome of histological features of hepatic injury.

Nutritional support

In alcoholic liver disease significant protein calorie malnutrition is a common finding. There is deficiency of vitamins and trace elements such as vitamin A, D, thiamine, folic acid, pyridoxine and zinc. Thus all the patients of alcoholic liver disease should be treated aggressively with vitamin therapy. Nutritional supplementation in mild to moderate alcoholic hepatitis during the first week of hospitalization has been reported to decline the in the serum bilirubin level.

Corticosteroids (Prednisolone)

The characteristic inflammatory response occurs in alcoholic liver disease. Corticosteroids have well known effects on immune response. The corticosteroids provide beneficial effects in alcoholic liver disease by reducing the cytokine production and suppressing the production of acetaldehyde adduct as well as decrease in the production of collagen.

Oxpentifylline (Pentoxifylline)

Pentoxyfylline is a phosphodiesterase inhibitor used in the treatment of intermittent claudication which is a symptom that describes muscle pain caused by too little blood flow. It improves the response of red blood cells to deforming stress. It also modulates the transcription of TNF-α gene by inhibiting the outcome of TNF-α

Antioxidants

There is evidence of increased oxidative stress in alcoholic liver disease. Use of antioxidant such as silymarin (milk thistle), S-adenosyl methionine in alcoholic liver disease have been reported to be beneficial.

Phosphatidylcholine

Phosphatidylcholine is a super nutrient and and has been proved to be extremely beneficial in the treatment of alcoholic liver disease. It has protective and beneficial effects against ethanol induced fibrosis by decreasing the activation of stellate cells to transitional cells. It also stimulates the collagenase activity. There is also indicated to decrease in the activities of cytochrome P450 2E1 (an oxidative enzyme concerned in alcohol metabolism) and modulating TNF-α.

Questions on this Chapter

1. Write a short note on alcoholism.
2. Write the clinical manifestation and complications of alcoholism.
3. Write the pharmacological actions of ethanol.
4. Write the preventive measures and treatments of alcoholism.
5. Write short note on alcoholic liver disease.
6. Write the treatments for alcoholic liver disease.

✳✳✳

Chapter 4

ANTIPSYCHOTICS

Objectives

After reading this chapter, the student will be able to:

➢ Describe the term psychosis and mania

➢ Understand the characteristics of psychosis

➢ Describe the various pathways involved in Schizophrenia

➢ Write the classification of Psychotropic drugs

➢ Write the neurological side effects of antipsychotics

INTRODUCTION

- Psychotropic agents are those which have primary effect on mental processes.

- Based on the manifestation, psychiatric disorder can be categorized as **psychoses, mania, depression (affective disorder) or neuroses**.

- **Psychoses:** These are severe psychiatric illnesses with serious distortion of thought, behaviour, capacity to recognise reality and of perception. In this case, the patient is unable to meet the ordinary demands of life. It consists of the following characteristics.

- Acute and chronic brain syndrome (cognitive disorder).

- Functional disorder: Serious alteration in emotions, thought and behaviour e.g. schizophrenia (split mind)-splitting of perception and interpretation of reality-hallucination, inability to think coherently.

- **Mania:** Hyperactivity, uncontrollable thought and speech associated with violent behaviour.

- **Depression:** sadness, guilt, physical and mental slowing, self destructive ideation.

- **Neuroses:** These are less serious illnesses in which the patient is able to understand the reality. Depending on the severity of its features, it can be categorized as-.

  Anxiety, obsessive compulsive disorder, reactive depression, stress, hysterical

SCHIZOPHRENIA

- Schizophrenia is a group of heterogeneous, chronic psychotic disorders.

- The major symptoms include hallucinations, delusions, and abnormal experiences, such as the perception of loss of control of one's thoughts. Patients lose empathy with others, become withdrawn, and demonstrate inappropriate or blunted mood.

- The disorder has a strong genetic component, as demonstrated by a concordance of 40 to 50% between monozygotic twins, but no objective physiological or biochemical diagnostic tests exist.

- Schizophrenic symptoms have been divided into two major categories. Positive symptoms and negative symptoms.
- Positive symptoms are those that regarded as an abnormality or exaggeration of normal function (e.g., incoherent speech, agitation). Antipsychotic drugs are generally more effective in controlling these signs.
- Negative symptoms are those that indicate a loss or decrease in function, such as poverty of speech content or blunted affect.
- Both types of features are observable in most patients. Negative signs are considered to be more chronic and persistent and less responsive to some antipsychotic agents. Although any of these symptoms may undergo partial remission, persistent dysfunction and exacerbations are typical. See table 4.1.

Table 4.1: Psychotic symptoms

Positive Symptoms	Negative Symptoms	Cognitive Symptoms
• Delusion • Hallucination • Disorganized speech • Disorganized behavior • Agitation	• Passivity • Apathetic Social withdrawal • Stereotyped thinking • Anhedonia • Attentional impairment • Emotional withdrawal	• Impaired verbal fluency • Problems with serial learning • Problems with focusing attention • Concentration

PATHOPHYSIOLOGY

Key Dopamine Pathways in schizophrenia and mania

(a) **Mesolimbic pathway:** Hyperactivity on this pathway is associated with positive symptoms of schizophrenia.

(b) **Mesocortical pathway:** Deficit in dopamine in this pathway is associated with negative and cognitive symptoms of schizophrenia.

(c) **Nigrostriatal pathway**

- It is a part of extrapyramidal system and controls motor movement.
- Blockade of D2 receptors causes:
- o Deficiency in dopamine in this pathway and thus movement disorder such as Parkinson's disease.
- o Hyperkinetic movement such as tardive dyskinesia.

Dopamine pathway involve in schizophrenia and Mania

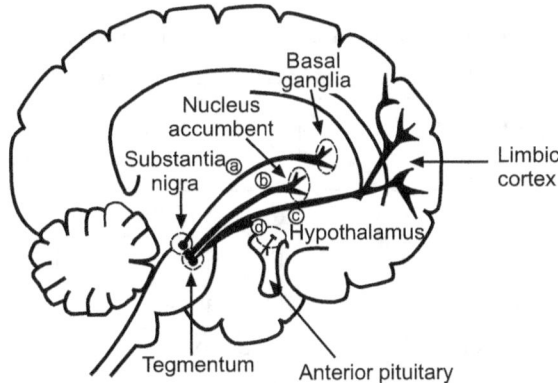

Fig. 4.1: Dopamine Pathway

a = **Nigrostriatal pathway**

b = **Mesolimbic pathway:** Increase in dopamine causes positive symptoms of schizophrenia

c = **Mesocortical pathway:** Deficit in dopamine causes negative and cognitive symptoms of schizophrenia

d = **Tuberoinfundibular pathway**

(d) Tuberoinfundibular pathway

- Increased neuronal activity of this pathway inhibits prolactin release.
- Blockade of D2 receptor increases prolactin release and causes:
  o Galactorrhea
  o Amenorrhea

Monoaminergic pathway

- Monoaminergic e.g. NA and 5-HT deficit may underline depression.

PSYCHOTROPIC DRUGS

- **Antipsychotics:** Neuroleptics, ataractic, major tranquilisers, all are use in the treatment of psychosis.
- **Antianxiety drugs:** Anxiolytic-sedatives, minor tranquilisers are used for anxiety and phobic state.
- **Antidepressants:** Used for minor as well major depressive illness, phobic state, obsessive compulsive behaviour and certain anxiety disorders.
- **Antimanic agents:** Used to control mania.

Table 4.2: Antipsychotics agents

First generation	Second generation
Chlorpromazine	Clozapine
Acetaphenazine	Risperidone
Fluphenazine	Olanzapine
Haloperidol	Quetiapine
Trifluoperazine	Ziprasidone
Triflupromazine	

First Generation Antipsychotics

- Blockade of D2 receptors in mesolimbic pathway, resulting in reduced positive symptoms of schizophrenia.
- Blockade of D2 receptors in mesocortical pathway, which is already deficient in schizophrenia, causes cognitive symptoms or worsens negative symptoms.
- Blockade of D2 receptors in nigrostriatal pathway, produces EPS such as motor abnormalities (Parkinsonism), tardive dyskinesia or hyperkinetic movement disorder.
- Blockade of D2 receptors in tuberoinfundibular pathway causes hyperprolactinemia. See the Figure 4.2.

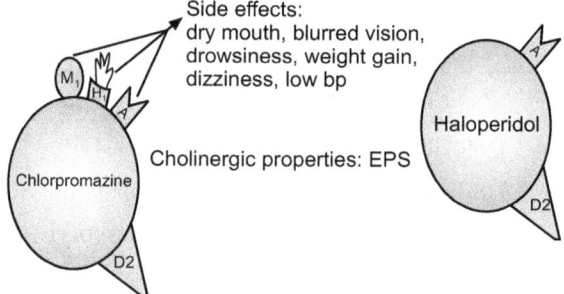

Fig. 4.2: Blockage of D2 receptor by First generation Antipsychotics

Second Generation Antipsychotics

- **In mesolimbic pathway** the action of D2 receptor blockade of antipsychotics are more robust than 5HT2A antagonism. This may help reducing positive symptoms.
- **In mesocortical pathway,** dopamine deficiency causes negative and cognitive symptoms. In mesocortical pathway, there is more 5HT2A receptors than D2 receptors. Thus 5HT antagonistic property is more profound than D2 receptor blocking property. This may help in improving negative symptoms.
- **In nigrostriatal pathway:** 5HT2A antagonists bind to 5HT2A receptors and block the release of 5HT and thus cause more DA to be released. This may reduce EPS.
- **In tuberoinfundibular pathway:** DA blocks the release of prolactin, whereas,

5HT2A causes release of prolactin. Antagonistic properties of antipsychotics cancel DA and 5HT2A action on prolactin release. (Fig. 4.3)

- The other properties of second generation antipsychotics are given in Table 4.2.

Table 4.2: Other Actions of Second Generation Antipsychotics

Clozapine	Ziprasidone	Risperidone	Quetiapine	Olanzapine
Very few EPS	Very few EPS,	EPS at high dose,	No EPS	No prolactin release
No prolactin release	No prolactin release,	Low TD,	No prolactin release	Nonsedative
Causes-agranulocytosis	No weight gain,	Less weight gain.	Weight gain	Weight gain
Weight gain	SRI and NRI, thus			Low level of TD
Seizures	act as AD and			
Sedative	anxiolytics.			

PHARMACOLOGICAL ACTION OF ANTIPSYCHOTICS

CNS: Effect differs in normal and psychotic individuals.

In Normal Individuals:

It produces indifference to the surroundings, paucity of thought, psychomotor slowing, emotional quieting, reduction in initiative and tendency to go off to sleep from which the subject is easily arousable.

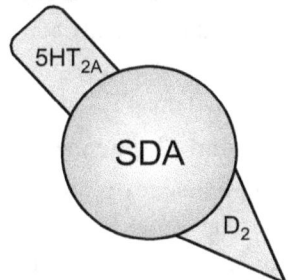

Fig. 4.3 Key: 5HT interact with 5HT2A receptors at postsynaptic level both at DA cell bodies and at axon terminals and inhibits the release of DA.

Spontaneous movements are minimized but slurring of speech, ataxia, or motor incordination does not occur. This has been referred as to neuroleptic syndrome and is quite different from sedative action of barbiturates and other similar drugs.

In Psychotics

It reduces irrational behaviour, agitation and aggressiveness and controls psychotic symptology, disturbed thought and behaviour are gradually normalised, and anxiety is relieved. Hallucination and delusion are suppressed.

Phenothiazine produces more sedation and causes greater potentiation of hypnotics, opiods etc. The sedative effect is produced immediately while antipsychotic effect takes weeks to develop.

Chlorpromazine lowers seizures' threshold and can precipitate fits in untreated epileptics. The medulary respiratory and other vital center are not affected, except at very high doses.

Neuroleptics, except thioridazine, have potent antiemetic action exerted through the CTZ. However they are ineffective in motion sickness.

Effect on ANS: Neuroleptics has varying degree of α-adrenergic blocking activity **CPZ =** Triflupromazine > Thioridazine > Fluphenazine > Haloperidol > Trifluoperazine > Clozapine > Pimozide (more potent compound has lesser α-adrenergic blocking activity).

Anticholinergic property of neuroleptic is weak and may be graded as, Thioridazine >

Chlorpromazine > Triflupromazine > Trifluperazine = haloperidol.

Phenothiazine has weak antihistaminic and antiserotonergic action as well.

Local Anesthetics: Chlorpromazine is as potent local anesthetics as procaine. However it is not used for this purpose because of its irritant action. Others have weaker membrane stabilising action.

CVS: Neuroleptic produces orthostatic hypotension by central as well as peripheral action on sympathetic tone. Higher doses of CPZ directly depress the heart and produce ECG changes. CPZ exerts some antiarrhythmic action probably due to membrane stabilising action.

Skeletal muscle: Neuroleptics have no effect on muscle fibres or neuromuscular transmission.

They reduce certain types of spasticity: the site of action being in the basal ganglia or medulla oblongata. Spinal reflexes are not affected.

Endocrine: Neuroleptics consistently increased prolactin release by blocking the inhibitory action of DA on pituitary lactotropes. This may result in galactorrhea and gynecomastica.

ACTH released in response to stress is diminished-corticosteroid levels fail to increase under such circumstances.

Decreased release of ADH may result in an increase in urine volume.

Tolerance and Dependence

Tolerance to the sedatives and hypotensive action develops within days or weeks. The antipsychotic, extrapyramidal and other actions based on DA antagonism do not display tolerance.

Physical dependence is probably absent, though some manifestation on discontinuation have been considered to be a withdrawal phenomenon. No drug seeking behaviour has been exhibited.

PHARMACOKINETICS

Oral absorption of CPZ is somewhat unpredictable and bioavailability is low. More consistent effect is produced after i.m or i.v. administration. It is highly bound to plasma as well as tissue protein-brain concentration is higher than plasma concentration. It metabolised in the liver into a number of metabolites. The effect of a single dose generally lasts for 6-8 hrs.

NOTE ON INDIVIDUAL NEUROLEPTICs

Triflupromazine: An aliphatic side chain phenothiazine somewhat more potent than CPZ. It frequently produces acute muscle dystonias in children, especially when injected as an antiemetic.

Thioridazine: Low potency phenothiazine having marked central anticholinergic action. Incidence of extrapyramidal side effect is very low. Cardiac arrhythmias and interference with male sexual function are more common. On long term use risk of eye damage.

Trifluoperazine and Fluphenazine:

These are high potency piperazine side chain phenothiazines. They have minimum autonomic actions; hypotension and sedation are not significant.

They are less likely to cause jaundice and hypersensitivity reactions. However extrapyramidal side effects are marked. They are less likely to precipitate seizure in epilepsy.

Haloperidol: It is a potent antipsychotic with pharmacological profile resembling that of piperazine substituted phenothiazines. They produce a few autonomic effects, is less epileptogenic, does not cause weight gain, jaundice is rare. It is the preferred drug for acute schizophrenia, Huntington's disease.

Trifluperidol: It is similar to but slightly more potent than haloperidol.

Domperidol: A short acting potent neuroleptic, occasionally used in anesthesia.

Penfluridol: An exceptionally long acting neuroleptic, recommended for chronic schizophrenia, affective withdrawal and social maladjustment.

Flupenthixol: It is less sedating than CPZ; indicated in schizophrenia and other psychoses, particularly in withdrawn and apathetic patients, but not in those with psychomotor agitation mania. At relatively low doses useful in depression; generally used for a short period only.

Pimozide: It is a specific DA antagonist with little α-adrenergic or cholinergic blocking activity. Because of long duration of action it is considered for maintance therapy. It prolongs the myocardial APD and carries risk of arrhythmias.

Loxapine: A dibenzoxazepine having CPZ like DA blocking and antipsychotic activity. The actions are quick and last upto 12 hrs. Sedation is less marked but neurological and cardiac toxicity is prominent in overdose.

Clozapine: An atypical and second generation antipsychotic: Pharmacologically distinct from others in that it has only weak D2 blocking action, produces a few extrapyramidal side symptoms; tardative dyskinesia is rare and prolactin level does not rise.

It suppresses positive and negative symptoms of schizophrenia.

The differing pharmacological profile may be due to relative selectivity for D4 receptors and additional 5-HT2 as well as α-adrenergic blockage. It has moderately anticholinergic, but paradoxically induce hyper salivation. Significant antihistaminic property is present.

The limitation of Clozapine is incidence of agranulocytosis and other blood dyscrasias thus there is need to weekly monitoring of leukocyte. High dose can induce seizers.

Other side effects are sedation, unstable BP, tachycardia, urinary incontinence and weight gain.

Clozapine is used only as a reserve drug in resistant schizophrenia.

Risperidone: Antipsychotic activity has been attributed to a combination of D2 + 5HT2receptor blockage. In addition it has α adrenergic blocking and antihistamic activity which contribute to efficasy as well as side effect like postural hypotension.

Risperidone is more potent D2 blocker than Clozapine; extrapyramidal side effects are less only at low doses.

Prolactin levels rise during Risperidone therapy.

Olanzapine: A new atypical antipsychotics resembles Clozapine in blocking multiple Monoaminergic (dopamine, serotonin and α - adrenergic) as well as muscarinic and antihistaminic activity.

Antipsychotic activity has been attributed to a combination of D2 + 5HT2 receptor blockage.

Both positive and negative symptoms of schizophrenia appear to be benefited. It may be combined with lithium/valproate for mania/bipolar disorder. Olanzapine is a potent antimascarinic, produces dry mouth and constipation.

Weaker D2 blockage results in few extrapyramidal side effects and little rise in prolactin levels. It is more epileptogencic than phenothiazine and causes weight gain. Agranulocytosis has not been reported with Olanzapine.

Reserpine: It is a low efficacy antipsychotic; acts by depleting brain DA, NA and 5-HT.Mental depression, suicidal tendency and other adverse effects are prominent at antipsychotic doses.

The distinct properties among antipsychotics | are given in Table 4.3.

Table 4.3: Pharmacological Distinctions among Representative Antipsychotic Drugs

Drug	Chemical Classification	Side Effects		
		Sedation	Autonomic (a)	Extrapyramidal Reaction (b)
Haloperidol	Butyrophenone	+	+	+ + +
Pimozide (c)	Diphenylbutylpiperidine	+	+	+ + +
Risperidone	Benzisoxazole	+ +	+ +	+ +
Thiothixene	Thioxanthene	+ +	+ +	+ +
Olanzapine	Thienobenzodiazepine	+	+ +	+
Clozapine	Dibenzodiazepine	+ + +	+ + +	+/-
Chlorpromazine	Phenothiazine(Aliphatic)	+ + +	+ + +	+ +
Thioridazine	Phenothiazine (Piperidine)	+ + +	+ + +	+

ADVERSE EFFECTS

CNS: Drowsiness, lethargy, mental confusion: more with low potency agents; tolerance develops; increased appetite and weight gain (not with haloperidol); aggravation of seizures in epileptics; even non epileptics may develop seizers with high doses of some antipsychotics like Clozapine.

Alpha adrenergic blockage: Postural hypotensions, palpitation, inhibition of ejaculation (especially with Thioridazine) are more common with low potency phenothiazine.

Anticholinergic: Dry mouth, blurring of vision, constipation, urinary hesitancy in elderly males (Thioridazine has the highest propensity). Some like Clozapine induce hypersalivation despite anticholinergic property, probably due to central action.

Endocrine: Amenorrhoea, infertility, gynaecomastica, galactorrhoea -due to hyperprolactinemia and low levels of gonadotropins; occurs infrequently after prolonged use.

Extrapyramidal Disturbances/Neurological Effects:

Many neurological syndromes, particularly involving the extrapyramidal motor system, occur following the use of most antipsychotic drugs. These reactions are particularly prominent with the high-potency D_2 dopamine receptor antagonists (tricyclic piperazines and butyrophenones).

Acute adverse extrapyramidal effects are less likely with aripiprazole, clozapine, quetiapine, thioridazine, and ziprasidone, or low doses of olanzapine or risperidone.

Six distinct neurological syndromes are characteristic of older neuroleptic-antipsychotic drugs. Four of these (acute dystonia, akathisia, parkinsonism, and the rare neuroleptic malignant syndrome) usually appear soon after administration of the drug. Two (tardive dyskinesias or dystonias, and rare perioral tremor) are late-appearing syndromes that evolve during prolonged treatment see the Tables 4.4 and 4.5.

Table 4.4: Characteristics of neurological syndromes

Reaction	Features
Acute dystonia	Spasm of muscles of tongue, face, neck, back; may mimic seizures; not hysteria
Akathisia	Motor restlessness; not anxiety or "agitation"
Parkinsonism	Bradykinesia, rigidity, variable tremor, mask facies, shuffling gait

Reaction	Features
Neuroleptic malignant syndrome	Catatonia, stupor, fever, unstable blood pressure, myoglobinemia; can be fatal
Perioral tremor ("rabbit syndrome")	Perioral tremor (may be a late variant of parkinsonism)
Tardive dyskinesia	Oral-facial dyskinesia; widespread choreoathetosis or dystonia

Table 4.5: Neurological Side Effects of Neuroleptic Drugs

Reaction	Features	Time of maximal risk	Proposed mechanism	Treatment
Acute dystonia	Spasm of muscles of tongue, face, neck, back; may mimic seizures; not hysteria	1 to 5 days	Unknown	Antiparkinsonian agents are diagnostic and curative*
Akathisia	Motor restlessness; not anxiety or "agitation"	5 to 60 days	Unknown	Reduce dose or change drug; antiparkinsonian agents,a benzodiazepines or propranolol b may help
Parkinsonism	Bradykinesia, rigidity, variable tremor, mask facies, shuffling gait	5 to 30 days; can recur even after a single dose	Antagonism of dopamine	Antiparkinsonian agents helpfula
Neuroleptic malignant syndrome	Catatonia, stupor, fever, unstable blood pressure, myoglobinemia; can be fatal	Weeks; can persist for days after stopping neuroleptic	Antagonism of dopamine may contribute	Stop neuroleptic immediately; dantrolene or bromocriptine c may help; antiparkinsonian agents not effective
Perioral tremor ("rabbit syndrome")	Perioral tremor (may be a late variant of parkinsonism)	After months or years of treatment	Unknown	Antiparkinsonian agents often helpa
Tardive dyskinesia	Oral-facial dyskinesia; widespread choreoathetosis or dystonia	After months or years of treatment (worse on withdrawal)	Excess function of dopamine hypothesized	Prevention crucial; treatment unsatisfactory

*Many drugs have been claimed to be helpful for acute dystonia. Among the most commonly employed treatments are diphenhydramine hydrochloride, or benztropine mesylate, followed by oral medication with the same agent for a period of days to perhaps several weeks thereafter.

a use of oral antiparkinsonian agents,

(b) Propranolol often is effective in relatively low doses. Selective β1 adrenergic receptor antagonists are less effective.

(c) Despite the response to dantrolene, there is no evidence of an abnormality of Ca^{2+} transport in skeletal muscle; with lingering neuroleptic effects, bromocriptine may be tolerated in large doses (10-40 mg per day).

Weight Gain and Metabolic Effects:

Weight gain and its associated long-term complications can occur with extended treatment with most antipsychotic and antimanic drugs.

Weight gain is especially prominent with clozapine and olanzapine; somewhat less with quetiapine; even less with fluphenazine, haloperidol, and risperidone; and is very low with aripiprazole, molindone, and ziprasidone.

Blood Dyscrasias

Mild leukocytosis, leukopenia, and eosinophilia occasionally occur with antipsychotic treatment, particularly with clozapine and less often with phenothiazines of low potency.

Bone marrow suppression, or less commonly agranulocytosis, has been associated with the use of clozapine.

Skin Reactions

Dermatological reactions including urticaria, contact dermatitis, sunburn and photosensitivity, epithelial keratopathy, opacities in cornea and in lens has been noted with antipsychotics mostly with chlorpromazine and phenothiazine.

Pigmentary retinopathy has been reported with thioridazine in excess dose.

Gastrointestinal and Hepatic Effects.

A mild jaundice, typically occurring early in therapy, may be observed in some patients receiving chlorpromazine. Pruritus is rare.

The reaction probably is a manifestation of hypersensitivity because eosinophilia and eosinophilic infiltration of the liver occur unrelated to dose.

DRUG INTERACTIONS

- Antipsychotic drugs potentiate the effect of sedatives and hypnotics, analgesics, alcohol, antihistamines.

- Chlorpromazine potentiates the sedative effects of morphine and may increase its analgesic actions.

- It potentiates the respiratory depression produced by opioid.

- Neuroleptic drugs inhibit the actions of dopaminergic agonists and levodopa and worsen the neurological symptoms of Parkinson's disease.

- Other interactions involve the cardiovascular system. Chlorpromazine, some other antipsychotic drugs block the antihypertensive effects of guanethidine, probably by blocking its uptake into sympathetic nerves.

- Low-potency phenothiazines can promote postural hypotension, possibly due to their α adrenergic blocking properties.

- Clozapine and Thioridazine potentiate the anticholinergic effect of tricyclic antidepressant and antiparkinson agents.

- The drug which induces hepatic cytochrome enzymes that enhance the metabolism of antipsychotics and many other agents e.g. carbamazepine, oxcarbazepine, phenobarbital, phenytoin.

PHARMACOLOGICAL USES

Schizophrenia: In case of Schizophrenia they produce much relief.

They control positive symptoms better than negative symptoms. However, they tend to restore cognitive, affective and motor disturbances. They are only symptomatic treatment, donot remove the cause of illness; long term treatment is required. They cause little improvement in judgment, memory and orientation. Patient with recent onset of illness respond better. Individual patient differ in their response to different antipsychotic; there is no way to predict which patient will respond better to which drug. Following table chart 4.6 may be help for drug selection.

Table 4.6: Criteria of drug selection in Psychosis

Characteristics of patient	Drug selection
Agitated, combative and violent	CPZ, Triflupromazine, Haloperidol
Withdrawn and apathetic	Trifluoperazine, Fluphenazine
Patient with mainly negative symptoms and resistant cases.	Clozapine, Olanzapine
Patient with mood elevation, hypomania	Haloperidol, Fluphenazine
If extrapyramidal side effect must be avoided.	Thioridazine, Clozapine, Olanzapine

Mania: Antipsychotics are required for rapid control. Lithium or carbamazepine may be started simultaneously or the acute phase. After 1-3 weeks when lithium has taken effect, neuroleptic may be withdrawn gradually.

Anxiety: Neuroleptics relieve anxiety but should not be used for simple anxiety because of autonomic and extrapyramidal side effects: benzodiazepines are preferable.

Antiemetics: Neuroleptics are potent antiemetic-control a wide range of drug and disease induced vomiting at doses much lower than needed in psychosis. They are effective in morning sickness but not in motion sickness probably because of dopaminergic pathway through the CTZ is not in this condition.

Other Uses:

(a) To potentiate hypnotics, analgesics and anesthetics.

(b) Intractable hiccough-may respond to parentral CPZ.

(c) Tetanus-CPZ is a secondary drug to achieve skeletal muscle relaxation.

(d) Alcoholic hallucinosis, Huntington's disease.

Questions on this Chapter

1. Write short note on antipsychotics.
2. Write the Pathophysiology of psychotic disorders.
3. Discuss first and second generation antipsychotics.
4. Write classification, pharmacological actions, adverse effects and uses of antipsychotics.

Chapter 5

ANTI-ANXIETY DRUGS

Objectives

After reading this chapter, the student will be able to:
➢ Describe the characteristics of anxiety
➢ Write the possible cause of anxiety
➢ Classify the anxiolytics
➢ Justify the use of antidepressant in treatment of anxiety

INTRODUCTION

Major therapeutic uses of anxiolytics are to relief anxiety (anxiolytics) or induce sleep (hypnotics). Hypnotic effects can be achieved with most anxiolytics drugs just by increasing the dose.

The distinction between a "pathological" and "normal" state of anxiety is hard to draw, but in spite of, or despite of, this diagnostic vagueness, anxiolytics are among the most prescribed substances worldwide.

Manifestations of anxiety
- **Verbal complaints:** The patient says he/she is anxious, nervous and edgy.
- **Somatic and autonomic effects:** The patient is restless and agitated, has tachycardia, increased sweating, weeping and often gastrointestinal disorders.
- **Social effects:** Interference with normal productive activities.

Pathology of Anxiety
- **Generalized anxiety disorder (GAD):** People suffering from GAD have general symptoms of motor tension, autonomic hyperactivity etc. for at least one month.
- **Phobic anxiety:** Simple phobias e.g. agoraphobia, fear of animals etc. Social phobias.
- **Panic disorders:** Characterized by acute attacks of fear as compared to the chronic presentation of GAD.
- **Obsessive-compulsive behaviors:** These patients show repetitive ideas (obsessions) and behaviors (compulsions).

CAUSES OF ANXIETY

1. **Medical**
   (a) Respiratory
   (b) Endocrine
   (c) Cardiovascular
   (d) Metabolic
   (e) Neurologic.

2. **Drug-Induced**
- Stimulants
  o Amphetamines, cocaine, TCAs, caffeine.
- Sympathomimetics
  o Ephedrine, epinephrine, pseudoephedrine phenylpropanolamine.

- Anticholinergics\Antihistaminergics
  - Trihexyphenidyl, benztropine, meperidine diphenhydramine, oxybutinin.
- Dopaminergics
  - Amantadine, bromocriptine, L-Dopa, carbid/levodopa.
- Miscellaneous
  - Baclofen, cycloserine, hallucinogens, indomethacin.

3. Drug Withdrawal

- Benzodiazepines (BZDs), narcotics, barbiturates, other sedatives, alcohol.

Table 5.1: Classification of Antianxiety Agents

Class	Class
Benzodiazepines	**Serotonergic agents**
Chlordiazepoxide	Buspirone
Diazepam	Trazodone
Oxazeam	**Noradrenergic agents**
Chlorazepate	Propranolol
Lorazepam	Clonidine
Prazepam	**Antihistamines**
Halazepam	Diphenhydramine
Alprazolam	Hydroxyzine
Anticonvulsant	
Gabapentin	Tiagabine
Pregabalin	Valproate
Natural Remedies	
Kava	

Benzodiazepines

The pharmacology of benzodiazepines are discussed in detail in sedatives and hypnotics. Some members of benzodiazepines have shown prolonged action; relieve anxiety at low doses without producing global CNS depression. In contrast to barbiturates, they are more selective for limbic system and have proven clinically better in both quality and quantity of improvement in anxiety and stress related symptoms. At anxiolytics doses, cardiovascular

and respiratory depression is minor. Potent benzodiazepines like Lorazepam and Alprazolam injected i.m. have adjuvant role in the management of acutely psychotic and manic patients.

Mechanism of Action

They act primarily by facilitating inhibitory GABAergic transmission, but other additional mechanisms of action have been suggested. Higher doses induce sleep and impair performance.

Pharmacokinetics determines two classes of Benzodiazepines

- Long acting forms have active metabolites with long half lives (several days).
- Example: Diazepam.
- Short acting forms without active metabolites.
- Example: Alprazolam.

Major Adverse Effects

- Sedation, impaired coordination, ataxia, physical dependence, hypersensitivity, paradoxical excitation, lightheadedness, confusional state, increased appetite, weight gain, alteration in sexual function.
- Some women fail to ovulate while on regular use of benzodiazepines.

Chlordiazepoxide

It was the first benzodiazepine to be used clinically. Its oral absorption is slow and produces a smooth long lasting effect; preferred in chronic anxiety states; often combined with other drugs in psychosomatic diseases. Its half lives 5-15 hrs. but active metabolite produces which extent the action of duration. It has poor anticonvulsant activity.

Diazepam

It is quickly absorbed and produces a brief initial phase of strong action followed by prolonged milder effect due to a two phase plasma concentration decay curve. The biological effect is longer due to active metabolite production. It is preferred in acute panic states and anxiety.

Oxazepam

It is slowly absorbed; being relatively polar, its penetration in brain is also slow. The plasma t½ is about 10 hrs. No active metabolite is produced, duration of action is shorter. Oxazepam is preferred in elderly and those with liver diseases, because its hepatic metabolism is not significant and duration of action is short.

Lorazepam

Lorazepam has slow oral absorption; being less lipid soluble than diazepam, its rate of entry in brain is slower. It has relatively shorter t½ (10-20 hrs); no active metabolite is produced. It produces sedation and amnesia when given by i.v. injection. It has been preferred for short-lived anxiety states, obsessive-compulsive neurosis and tension syndromes, as well as psychosomatic disease.

Alprazolam

Alprazolam has highly potent anxiolytic activity in addition has some mood elevating action in mild depression. It is particularly useful in anxiety associated with depression. Good response has been obtained in panic disorders with severe anxiety and autonomic symptoms. Its plasma t½ is about 12 hrs, but active metabolite is produced.

SECOND GENERATION ANXIOLYTICS

Zolpidem

Technically Zolpidem is not falls under the category of benzodiazepine. Preferentially it acts at GABA receptors and mediating hypnotic effects. Half-life of a few hours, with extended release form recently available. Less anxiolytics, cognitive and motor side-effects.

Use of Antidepressants for treatment of anxiety

Advantages: Antidepressants produces less sedation, less mental confusion and less dependence. 5-HT modulators (e.g., SSRIs) are often more effective e.g. Buspirone which is a unique antidepressant. It has $5HT_{1A}$ agonist activity. It has delayed onset of efficacy.

Buspirone

It is the most selective anxiolytic currently available in market. The anxiolytic effect of this drug takes several weeks to develop. Buspirone does not have sedative effects and does not potentiate CNS depressants and it is an alternative to benzodiazepines for generalised form of anxiety. It has a relatively high margin of safety, few side effects and does not appear to be associated with drug dependence. It has no rebound anxiety or signs of withdrawal when discontinued.

Advantages

- No sedation or impairment of performance.
- No cross-tolerance with BZDs.
- No tolerance or withdrawal.
- No abuse potential.

Disadvantages

- Nausea.
- Headache.
- Insomnia, nervousness.
- Restlessness.
- Dizziness, lightheadedness.

Mechanism of Action

Buspirone acts as a partial agonist at the $5\text{-}HT_{1A}$ receptor presynaptically inhibiting serotonin release. After chronic treatment adaptive reduction in cortical $5\text{-}HT_2$ receptors may occur. It has weak dopamine D_2 blocking activity but has no antipsychotic effect. A mild mood elevating action has been noted occasionally may be due to facilitating of central noradrenergic system.

Pharmacokinetics

It is not effective in panic disorders. Oral administration it is rapidly absorbed and undergoes extensive hepatic metabolism (hydroxylation and dealkylation) to form several active metabolites (e.g. 1-(2-pyrimidyl-piperazine, 1-PP). It is well tolerated by elderly, but may have slow clearance. The other analogs of buspirone are ipsapirone, gepirone and tandospirone.

Side effects

- Tachycardia, palpitations, nervousness, GI distress and paresthesias may occur.
- Causes a dose-dependent pupillary constriction.

α2-Adrenoreceptor Agonists

Clonidine

It is a antihypertensive agent and has been used for the treatment of panic attacks. It has been useful in suppressing anxiety during the management of withdrawal from nicotine and opioid analgesics. Withdrawal from clonidine, after protracted use, may lead to a life-threatening hypertensive crisis.

β-Adrenoreceptor Antagonists

Propranolol

It is also a hypertensive agent and used to treat some forms of anxiety, particularly when physical (autonomic) symptoms (sweating, tremor, and tachycardia) are severe. It is helpful with performance anxiety by suppressing sympathetic nervous system activity and autonomic symptoms (palpitation/tremor). Side effects with propranolol are bradycardia, hypotension, depression, nightmares, insomnia, vivid dreams and hallucinations.

Propranolol is having H_1 antihistaminic with sedative, antiemetic, antimascarinic and spasmolytic property. It is claimed to have selective anxiolytic action, but accompanying sedation is quite marked. Due to antihistaminic and sedative property, it is effective in pruritus and urticaria.

TREATMENT OF ANXIETY

Generalized Anxiety Disorder
Diazepam, lorazepam, alprazolam, buspirone.

Phobic Anxiety
(a) Simple phobia: Benzodiazépines
(b) Social phobia: Benzodiazépines.

Panic Disorders
TCAs and MAOIs, alprazolam.

Obsessive-Compulsive Behavior
Clomipramine (TCA), SSRI's.

Posttraumatic Stress Disorder
Antidepressants, Buspirone.

Questions on this Chapter

1. Discuss the pharmacology of Benzodiazepine in treatment of anxiety
2. Write the classification of anxiolytics and add note on second generation anxiolytics

Chapter 6

SEDATIVES AND HYPNOTICS

Objectives

After reading this chapter, the student will be able to:

➢ Differentiate between sedative and hypnotics

➢ Write the dose dependent effects of sedative and hypnotics

➢ Write the characteristics of different stages of normal sleep

➢ Write the treatment of benzodiazepine poisoning

INTRODUCTION

Sedatives

• Drugs that have an inhibitory effect on the CNS to the degree that they reduce-

  o Nervousness

  o Excitability

  o Irritability

  o without causing sleep

Hypnotics

• These are agents which produce calm or soothe the CNS to the point that they cause sleep.

Sedative-Hypnotics: They produce dose dependent effect which is shown in the schematic Figs. 6.11 (a) and (b)-

• At low doses, calm or soothe the CNS without inducing sleep.

• At high doses, calm or soothe the CNS to the point of causing sleep.

• By definition all sedative/hypnotics will induce sleep at high doses.

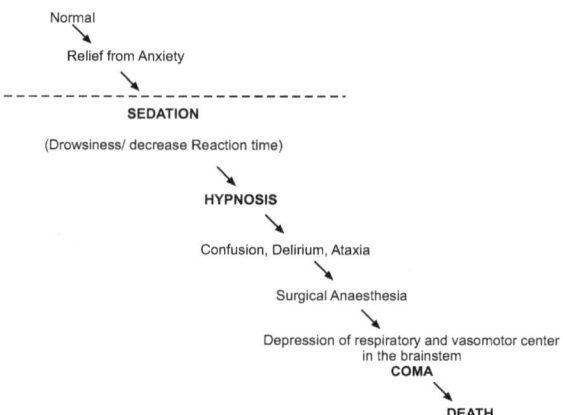

Fig. 6.1 (a): Dose dependant effects of Sedative and Hypnotics

• Normal sleep consists of distinct stages, based on three physiological measures such as electroencephalogram, electromyogram and electronystagmogram. Two distinct phases of sleep are distinguished which occur cyclically over 90 min:

(1) Non-Rapid Eye Movement (NREM): Produces 70-75% of total sleep. It consists of four stages. Most sleep occurs at stage 2.

(2) Rapid eye movement (REM). It is called as recalled dreams.

PROPERTIES OF SEDATIVE / HYPNOTICS IN SLEEP

- The latency of sleep onset is decreased (time to fall asleep).
- The duration of stage 2 NREM sleep is increased.
- The duration of REM sleep is decreased.
- The duration of slow-wave sleep (when somnambulism and nightmares occur) is decreased.
- Tolerance occurs after 1-2 weeks.
- Some sedative/hypnotics will depress the CNS to stage III of anesthesia.
- Due to their fast onset of action and short duration, barbiturates such as thiopental and methohexital are used as adjuncts in general anesthesia.

All of the anxiolytics/sedatives/hypnotics should be used only for symptomatic relief. All the drugs used alter the normal sleep cycle and should be administered only for days or weeks, never for months. These are used for short term treatment only.

Dose dependant Effects of Sedatives and Hypnotics.

Fig. 6.1 (b) shows the dose dependant effect of sedative and hypnotics. At lowest dose they are anxiolytics and at higher dose produce respiratory depression.

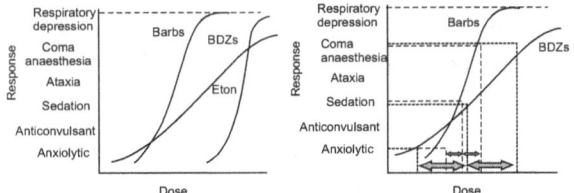

Fig. 6.1 (b): Dose dependant effect of sedative and hypnotics

MECHANISMS OF ACTIONS

(1) Enhance GABAergic transmission by
- Increasing the frequency of openings of GABAergic channels-Benzodiazepines.
- Increasing the opening time of GABAergic channels- Barbiturates.
- Increasing the receptor affinity for GABA- BDZs and BARBS.

(2) Stimulation of 5-HT$_{1A}$ receptors.

(3) Inhibit 5-HT$_{2A}$, 5-HT$_{2C}$, and 5-HT$_3$ receptors.

(I) BARBITURATES

Barbiturates first introduced in 1903 and it is standard agents for insomnia and sedation. Barbiturates are habit-forming agents. It is commonly used in insomnia and sedation due to its safety and efficacy. There are four categories of barbiturates.

- **Ultrashort Acting**

  Mephobexital, Thiamylal, Thiopental.

- **Short Acting**

  Pentobarbital, Secobarbital.

- **Intermediate Acting**

  Aprobarbital, Butabarbital.

- **Long Acting**
  - Phenobarbital.

  (a) Amobarbital, butabarbital, pentobarbital and secobarbital as sedative/hypnotics.

  (b) Thiopental and methohexital as ultrashort acting intravenous anesthetics.

  (c) Some barbiturates are potent anticonvulsants such as phenobarbital and mephobarbital as long acting anticonvulsants.

Mechanism of Actions

- Site of action :
  - Brain stem (reticular formation)
  - Cerebral cortex
- By inhibiting GABA, nerve impulses traveling in the cerebral cortex are also inhibited see Fig. 6.2.

- Barbiturates in contrast, are agonists at GABA-A receptors; (even in the absence of endogenously released GABA) thus benzodiazepines provide limited CNS depression, while barbiturates are potent CNS depressants.

Pharmacokinetics

- Barbiturates have wide range of half-lives; it ranges from 3 min to 120 hrs. They are redistributed in all body. Fast acting agents are more lipids soluble and produce the action in seconds while water soluble agents are long acting and they are slower to penetrate the CNS usually they take around (20-30 minutes). They are metabolised in liver and eliminated through kidneys. Urinalysis detects 30 hours to weeks.

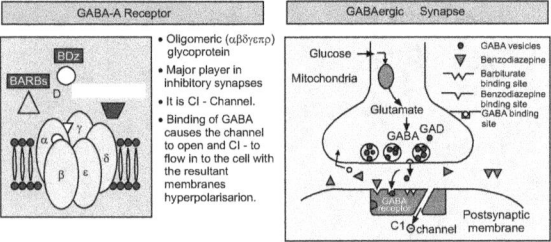

Fig. 6.2: GABAergic receptor

Pharmacological Effects

- With lower dose used in treating anxiety and at higher dose produce sedation.

- Not analgesic – no sleep/sedation with moderate pain.

- Suppressed dreaming during REM.

- Cognitive inhibition.

- Changes in thinking, judgment, motor skills, behavior for over hours or days.

(a) Effects on CNS

- Barbiturates are general CNS depressants; i.e. as one increases the dose, one can cause any degree of CNS depression, from the mildest sedation through hypnosis, anesthesia, coma and death. Ethanol potentiates the CNS depressant effects of barbiturates, as do some antihistamines and MAO inhibitors.

- Barbiturates are not analgesics. They do not block sensation until consciousness is lost. In fact they can increase sensitivity to pain.

- Barbiturates are potent respiratory depressants. Respiratory failure is the most common cause of death from overdose of barbiturates.

- Barbiturates produce euphoria

- Anesthetic doses of barbiturates attenuate cerebral edema resulting from brain surgery, head injury or cerebral ischemia. These doses may decrease infarct size and increase survival.

(b) Effects on Respiratory System

- Barbiturates reduce respiratory drive as well as the mechanisms responsible for the rhythmic character of respiration. Barbiturates can reduce the neurogenic (voluntary), hypercarbic and hypoxic drives to respiration. Protective respiratory reflexes are not inhibited until severe intoxication is present. Laryngospasm is one of the chief complications of barbiturate anesthesia.

- High dose of barbiturates results into suppression and sometimes causes death of patients.

(c) Effects on Reproductive System

- No current evidence implies that barbiturates produce any impaired fertility or teratogenicity.

(d) Effects on Liver

- Barbiturates increase the hepatic enzyme which normally metabolises most of the drugs thus concurrent use of barbiturates increases the metabolism of other drug.

(e) Psychological Effects

Barbiturates produced following psychological effects-

- Depressed behavior
- Cognitive/Motor inhibition akin to alcohol
- Low dose – reduced anxiety or emotional withdrawal, aggression or violence set/ setting determine positive or negative response.
- High doses of barbiturates produce general behavioral depression and sleep.

Physiological Dependence

- They produced wide range of effects; at low dose they produce sleep difficulties while at high dose they produce hallucinations and restlessness. They also produce disorientation and life-threatening convulsions.

Therapeutic Uses

Barbiturates are used to treat the following conditions:

- Hypnotics
- Sedatives
- Anticonvulsants
- Surgical procedures

Toxicity of Barbiturates

- Major cause of death in barbiturates toxicity is due respiratory depression: Barbiturates have a relatively low therapeutic index as a rough rule of thumb, 10 therapeutic doses taken simultaneously will be fatal outcome.

- These drugs have a high abuse potential due to their euphoric effects.
- Repeated use leads to the development of tolerance to most, but not all the effects of barbiturates i.e. tolerance does not develop to the effects of barbiturates on respiration. Therefore as tolerance develops, more drugs are needed to give the desired sedative / hypnotic/anxiolytics or euphoric effect; however the dose that kills by respiratory depression remains the same.
- Acute barbiturate withdrawal in drug abusers can cause fatal withdrawal syndrome.
- Barbiturates can cause restlessness, excitement and delirium when given in the presence of pain and may make a patient's perception of pain worse.

Drug Interactions

- Additive Effects
  - ETOH, antihistamines, benzodiazepines, narcotics, tranquilizers produce additive effects when given with barbituartes.
- Inhibited Metabolism
  - MAOIs will prolong effects of barbiturates because of inhibition of metabolising enzyme by MAOIs.
- Increased Metabolism
  - Barbiturates stimulate the metabolising enzymes thus the administration of barbiturates along with anticoagulants results into reduced anticoagulant response leading to possible clot formation.

(II) BENZODIAZEPINES

- May be divided according to primary use as hypnotics, anxiolytics and anticonvulsants.

Table 6.1: Classification of Benzodiazepines

Hypnotics	Anxiolytics	Newer Non-Benzodiazepine
Diazepam	Alprazolam	Zopiclone
Flurazepam (Long acting)	Chlordiazepoxide	Zolpidem
Nitrazepam	Buspirone	Zaleplon
Flunitrazepam	Diazepam	
Temazepam (Short acting)	Lorazepam	
Triazolam (Short acting)	Oxazepam	**Anticonvulsants**
Midazolam	Triazolam	Diazepam
Chloral hydrate	Phenobarbital	Clonazepam
Estazolam (Short acting)	Halazepam	Clobazam
Secobarbital	Prazepam	
Quazepam (Long acting)		

Benzodiazepines Pharmacology

Benzodiazepines potentiate GABAergic inhibition at all levels of the neuraxis. Benzodiazepines cause more frequent openings of the GABA-Cl channel via membrane hyperpolarisation and increased receptor affinity for GABA. Benzodiazepines act on BZ_1 (α_1 and α_2 subunit containing) and BZ_2 (α_5 subunit containing) receptors. They may cause euphoria, impaired judgement, loss of cell control and anterograde amnesic effects.

Properties of Benzodiazepines

- Benzodiazepines have a wide margin of safety if used for short periods. Prolonged use may cause dependence.
- They have little effect on respiratory or cardiovascular function as compared to BARBS and other sedative-hypnotics.
- They depress the turnover rates of norepinephrine (NE), dopamine (DA) and serotonin (5-HT) in various brain nuclei (Fig. 6.3).

Mechanism of Action

- Benzodiazepines are not general CNS depressants. A general CNS depressant can cause any degree of depression, ranging from the slightest sedation to anaesthesia, coma and death. They will not cause anaesthesia and in fact have extensively replaced the barbiturates and other sedative hypnotics because they are much less likely to cause fatal CNS depression.

- The mechanism of action of benzodiazepine is thought to be due to an allosteric effect on GABA-A receptors which facilitates or amplifies the inhibitory effect of endogenous CNS GABA. Benzodiazepines do not directly activate GABA-A receptors and require endogenous GABA to express their effects.

- Peripheral effects of benzodiazepines show few effects.

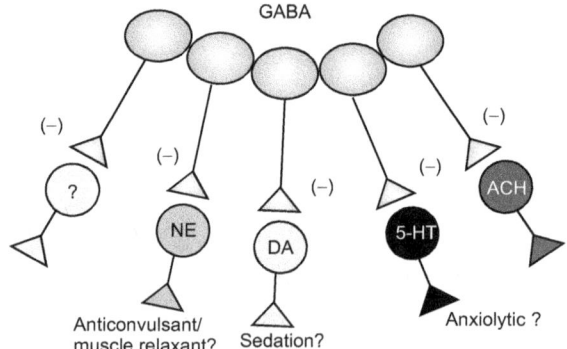

Fig. 6.3: Influence of BDZs on Bioamines level in brain nuclei

Pharmacological Actions

(a) Effects on Respiration

- Almost all benzodiazepines do not inhibit respiration in hypnotic doses in normal man (exception is midazolam), but can cause apnea when combined with other CNS depressants such as opiates and alcohol.

- In patients with obstructive sleep apnea benzodiazepines in hypnotic doses may decrease muscle tone in the upper airway and exaggerate the pathophysiological effects of apneic episodes. The presence of obstructive sleep apnea may be a contraindication to the use of any sedative hypnotic including benzodiazepines.

(b) Effects on GI System

There are a few direct effects of benzodiazepines, but sometimes used in "anxiety related" GI disorders.

(c) Effects on Liver

Benzodiazepines cause little or no induction of hepatic drug metabolising enzymes. However, the BZs are themselves metabolised extensively in the liver.

Pharmacokinetics

Drugs active at the benzodiazepine receptor are divided into four categories based on their elimination of half lives:

- A. Ultra short acting; i.e. clorazepate with t½ = 2 hours.
- B. Short acting with t½ < six hours such as triazolam.
- C. Intermediate acting with t½ of 6-24 hours such as estazolam and temazaepam.
- D. Long acting with t½ greater than 24 hours such as flurazepam, diazepam and quazepam.
- **Hepatic metabolism:** Almost all benzodiazepines undergo microsomal oxidation (N-dealkylation and aliphatic hydroxylation) and conjugation (to glucoronides).
- Rapid tissue redistribution of benzodiazepines produced long acting effects due to long half lives and elimination half lives (from 10 to > 100 hrs).

- All benzodiazepines cross the placenta and can be detected in breast milk thus there may exert depressant effects on the CNS of the lactating infant.

- Many benzodiazepines have active metabolites with half-lives greater than the parent drug. Prototype drug is diazepam, which has active metabolites (desmethyl-diazepam and oxazepam) and is long acting (t½ = 20-80 hr).

- All benzodiazepines differ in the times of onset and elimination half-lives (long half-life = > daytime sedation). The summary of benzodiazepine pharmaco-kinetics is given in Table 6.1.

Drugs metabolised to active compounds with long half lives
Diazepam, Chlordiazepoxide, Flurazepam, Prazepam, Clorazepate, Halazepam
Drugs metabolised and inactivated by metabolism
Oxazepam, lorazepam, temazepam, triazolam, midazolam

Biotransformation of Benzodiazepines

With the formation of active metabolites, the kinetics of the parent drug may not reflect the time course of the pharmacological effect. Estazolam, oxazepam and lorazepam are directly metabolised via glucoronides conjugation and they have the least residual (drowsiness) effects. All of these drugs and their metabolites are excreted in urine conjugation (Fig. 6.4).

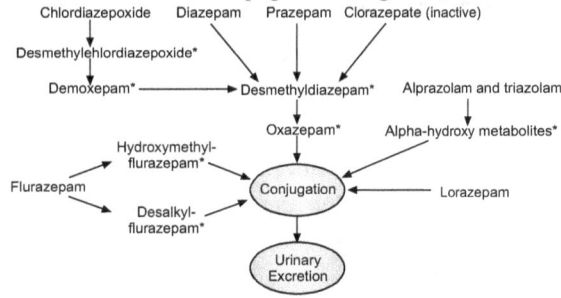

Fig. 6.4: Biotransformation of Benzodiazepines

Table 6.2: Pharmacokinetic of Benzodiazepines

Benzodiazepine	Peak Plasma Level (Hour)	Elimination Half Life (Hour)	Dosing (mg/d)	Speed of onset
Alprazolam	1-2	7-27	0.75-4	Intermediate
Chlordiazepoxide	1-4	5-30	15-100	Intermediate
Clonazepam	1-2	18-50	1.5-20	Intermediate
Diazepam	0.5-2	20-80	4-40	Very fast
Lorazepam	2-4	10-20	2-4	Intermediate
Oxazepam	2-4	5-20	30-120	Slow

Slow Elimination of Parent Drug or Active Metabolite

Flurazepam

Flurazepam produces an active metabolite which has a long half live, residual effects are likely next morning; cumulation occurs on daily ingestion peaking after 3-5 days; suitable for patients who have frequent nocturnal awaking and in whom some day time sedation is acceptable.

Relatively Slow Elimination but Marked Redistribution

Diazepam

Diazepam generates active metabolites (desmethyl-dizepam, Oxazepam). On occasional use it is free of residual effects. With regular use accumulation occurs and prolonged anxiolytic effect may be obtained. It is less likely to cause rebound insomnia on discontinuation of chronic use.

Nitrazepam

Nitrazepam produces accumulation and residual effects which can be avoided only if nitrazepam ingested occasionally. Good for patients with frequent nocturnal awaking, when some day time sedation is acceptable.

Flunitrazepam

Flunitrazepam is a potent agent and get rapidly absorbed. It has marked redistribution. The duration of action remains short only when it is used infrequently.

Relatively Rapid Elimination and Marked Redistribution

Temazepam

Absorption of temazepam is slow in case of tablet but fast when used in soft gelatin capsule. It is beneficial for people who experience difficulty falling asleep. Accumulation of temazepam can occur on daily ingestion and it does not produce active metabolite.

Ultra Rapid Elimination

Triazolam

Triazolam is very potent agent and its peak effect occurs in 1 hr. It is good for sleep induction but poor for maintaining it. Patient may wake up early in morning and feel anxious. This may be a withdrawal symptom. Rebound insomnia may occur when it is discontinued after a few night of use. It does not accumulate on repeated nightly use and so residual effects are noted in the morning if prescribed doses are not exceeded. Higher dose produce anterograde amnesia and anxiety and psychiatric disturbances are noted.

Midazolam

Midazolam has extremely rapid absorbable drug and its peak level is observed in 20 min. It can cause problem in the elderly; more liable for abuse. It is mainly used as an I.V. anaesthetic.

Indications of Benzodiazepines

Benzodiazepines are used in various conditions. They are mentioned below.

• Generalised Anxiety Disorder	• Seizure Disorders
• Panic Disorder	• Akathisia
• Insomnia	• Catatonia
• Schizophrenia	• Delirium
• Bipolar	• Balanced anesthesia
• Skeletal muscle relaxation	• Alcohol Withdrawal
• Depression	• Conscious Sedation

Adverse Effects: Benzodiazepines

- Sedation and impairment of performance in psychomotor skills such as in driving, engaging in dangerous physical activities, working using hazardous machinery. Benzodiazepines produce such adverse effects especially during initial phase of treatment.

- Benzodiazepines produced memory impairment such as anterograde amnesia (desired before surgery). There may dose-related and tolerance may not develop and it is most likely with triazolam.

- It produces disinhibition. The possible risk factors: History of aggression, impulsivity, borderline or antisocial personality.

- Benzodiazepines can be abused but chances. It can decrease when properly prescribed and supervised.

- There is drug dependence with benzodiazepines which may occur at usual doses taken beyond several weeks.

- There are withdrawal symptoms which may occur even when discontinuation is not abrupt (e.g. by 10% every 3 days). Symptoms include: tachycardia, increased blood pressure, muscle cramps, anxiety, insomnia, panic attacks, impairment of memory and concentration, perceptual disturbances, derealization, hallucinations, hyperpyrexia, seizures. The symptoms may continue for months.

- There is rebound anxiety with benzodiazepines with increased intensity.

Drug Interactions

Following are the drug interactions with benzodiazepines

- Clozapine: There issevere hypotension, respiratory or cardiac arrest and loss of consciousness.

- Cigarette smoking may decrease the sedative effects of usual benzodiazepine doses.

- Alcohol increases sedation.

- Anti-fungals may increase plasma concentration of benzodiazepines.

- Benzodiazepines reduce the effect of antiepileptic drugs.

- Combination of anxiolytics drugs should be avoided.

- Concurrent use with antihistaminic and anticholinergic drugs as well as the consumption of alcohol should be avoided.

- SSRI's and oral contraceptives decrease metabolism of benzodiazepines.

Benzodiazepine Withdrawal Symptoms

- Symptoms: Insomnia, anxiety, autonomic instability (increased heart rate and BP, tremor, diaphoresis) insomnia, muscle cramps, confusion, seizures, irritability, ataxia.

- Time frame for emergence of symptoms corresponds to half-life of the benzodiazepine. Example: Alprazolam has high risk of withdrawal- due to short half-life.

Benzodiazepine Overdose

- Benzodiazepine overdose may be intentional or secondary to accumulation of doses. The symptoms due to overdose are somnolence, impaired coordination, slurred speech, diminished reflexes, confusion, respiratory depression, hypotension.
- Treatment Options
  - Supportive and symptomatic care.
  - Gastric lavage.
  - Activated charcoal.
- I.V. hydration and maintenance of adequate airway.
- Flumazenil.
  Flumazenil is not effective against barbiturates overdose.

BENZODIAZEPINES ANTAGONIST

Flumazenil

Flumazenil is a benzodiazepine antagonist that competitively binds to benzodiazepine receptors. In benzodiazepine overdose/ poisoning Flumazenil can be used at a dose of 0.2 mg I.V. over 30 seconds, then 0.5 mg at 1 minute interval, up to 3 mg. It produces rapid response in 1-2 min, up to 10 min and duration around 1-5 hours.

It is used with caution if patient ingests tricyclic antidepressant and benzodiazepine due to risk of seizures. Continuously monitor the patients for respiratory rate and cardiac status. The side effects of flumazenil are agitation, confusion, sweating, nausea/vomiting, blurred vision, seizure. Re-sedation can occur due to short half-life, may repeat dose at 20 minutes intervals with maximum of 1 mg/dose and 3 mg/hr.

MISCELLANEOUS DRUGS

- Chloral hydrate
- Melatonin
- Meprobamate (Similar to Barbiturate)
- Zolpidem (BZ_1 selective)
- Zaleplon (BZ_1 selective)

Chloral Hydrate

Chloral hydrate is used in institutionalized patients. It displaces warfarin (anti-coagulant) from plasma proteins and it has extensive biotransformation.

Newer Non-Benzodiazepine: "Z-Hypnotics"

Zaleplon, Zolpidem, Zopiclone

These are more selective for alpha-1 subunit of benzodiazepine receptor complex. These are less likely to impact sleep stages or prevent brain from achieving deep sleep. They have lower risk of tolerance and dependence and less risk of memory impairment.

Zolpidem

Zolpidem is structurally unrelated but as effective as benzodiazepines. It produces minimal muscle relaxation and anticonvulsant action. Zolpidem is rapidly metabolised by liver enzymes into inactive metabolites. Dosage of zolpidem should be reduced in patients with hepatic dysfunction, the elderly and patients taking cimetidine. The side effects of zolpidem are dizziness, headache, and somnolence reports of sleepwalking.

Zolpidem produce pharmacological action by binds selectively to BZ_1 receptors. It facilitates GABA-mediated neuronal inhibition. The actions of zolpidem are antagonized by flumazenil.

Zopiclone

Zopiclone is indicated for maintenance insomnia, (studied for up to 6 months in clinical trial). It decreases sleep latency and improved sleep maintenance. In adults 2 mg QHS, up to 3 mg; elderly 1mg QHS, up to 2 mg. The side effects of zolpidem are metallic taste, drowsiness, dizziness, difficulty with coordination.

Zaleplon

Zaleplon is absorbed rapidly and has half life of one hour. It is a good choice if patient has difficulty falling asleep. Dosing 10 mg QHS (range 5-20 mg).

Melatonin

Melatonin is N-Acetyl-5-methoxy tryptamine, the principal hormone of the pineal gland which is secreted at night and has been found to play an important role in entraining the sleep-wakefulness cycle with the circadian rhythm. High dose of melatonin can induce sleep, but low dose donot depress CNS, but increase propensity of falling asleep. However melatonin is not dependable hypnotics; has little effect on latency and duration of sleep, especially in non-elderly insomnia.

Other Properties of Sedative/Hypnotics

- Benzodiazepines on the other hand, with their long half-lives and formation of active metabolites, may contribute to persistent postanesthetic respiratory depression.

- Most sedative/hypnotics may inhibit the development and spread of epileptiform activity in the CNS.

Questions on this Chapter

1. Write short note on Z-Hypnotics

2. Write the classification, mechanism of actions, pharmacological actions,, indications and adverse effects of Benzodiazepines

3. Discuss in benzodiazepine poisoning and their treatment

4. Write the classification, mechanism of actions, pharmacological effects and adverse effects of barbiturates.

Chapter 7

ANTIDEPRESSANT DRUGS

Objectives

After reading this chapter, the student will be able to:

➢ Describe the characteristics of depression

➢ Understand the biogenic amine theory of depression

➢ Justify the tyramine containing food should be avoided when medicated with with MAO inhibitor

➢ Understand the different mechanism associated with depression

➢ Note the advantages of SSRIs against TCA and MAO inhibitors

INTRODUCTION

Depression is an **affective disorder where a** person's mood goes far beyond the usual, normal "ups and downs." **Depression is a s**evere and long-lasting feeling of sadness that lasts much beyond the precipitating event. The major signs and symptoms of depression are low energy level, sleep disturbances, lack of appetite, limited libido, inability to perform activities of daily living, overwhelming feelings of sadness, despair, hopelessness and disorganization.

Biogenic Amine Theory of Depression

Depression results from a deficiency of norepinephrine (NE), dopamine or serotonin (5HT).Monoamine oxidase (MAO) may break them down to be recycled or restored in the neuron. Rapid fire of the neurons may lead to their depletion. The number or sensitivity of postsynaptic receptors may increase, depleting neurotransmitter levels. Following are three actions of antidepressant agents:

(i) Inhibit the effects of MAO, leading to increased NE or 5HT in the synaptic cleft.

(ii) Block reuptake by the releasing nerve, leading to increased neurotransmitter levels in the synaptic cleft.

(iii) Regulate receptor sites and breakdown of neurotransmitters, leading to an accumulation of neurotransmitters in the synaptic cleft.

CLASSIFICATION OF ANTIDEPRESSANTS

(1) Tricyclic Antidepressants (TCAs)

(A) NA + 5HT reuptake inhibitors:

Imipramine, Amitriptyline, Trimipramine, Doxepin, Dothiepin, Clomipramine.

(B) Predominantly NA reuptake inhibitors: Desipramine, Nortryptaline, Amoxapine.

(2) MAO Inhibitors (MAOIs): Moclobemide, Clorgyline.

(3) Selective Serotonin Reuptake Inhibitors (SSRIs): Fluoxetine, Fluvoxamine, Paroxetine, Sertraline, Citalopram.

(4) Atypical Antidepressants: Trazodone, Mianserin, Mirtazapine, Venlafaxine, Tianeptine, Amineptine, bupropion.

TRICYCLIC ANTIDEPRESSANTS (TCA)

Many of the antidepressant drugs are close structural relatives of postsynaptic dopamine (antipsychotic) and norepinephrine (sedative) blockers. Small structural changes are involved, if the agents can begin to gain ability to block a presynaptic event and then lose ability to affect a postsynaptic block. Chemically trycyclic compounds have 3 nucleus rings and they are extremely lipophilic in nature. It blocks reuptake of NE and serotonin, hence there is monoamine theory of depression. There is also inhibition of DA uptake, which correlates with stimulant action of tricyclic antidepressant. It takes at least two weeks for relief from the symptom of depression. All TCAs are similar. Choice depends on individual response to the drug and tolerance of adverse effects.

Adverse effects/Limitation

- Orthostatic hypotension, anticholinergic effects, sedation, cardiac toxicity, cardiac arrhythmias, seizures.

  Precautions: Overdose can cause life threatening events.

Metabolism

All the tricyclic antidepressants undergo oxidative hydroxylation followed by conjugation N-demethylation. Demethylated metabolites are less anticholinergic, less sedative more stimulatory and higher NE than 5HT uptake.

Focus on the prototype antidepressant:

Imipramine

- **Indications:** Relief of symptoms of depression; enuresis in children > 6 years of age; unlabeled consideration, control of chronic pain.

- **Actions:** Inhibits presynaptic reuptake of norepinephrine and serotonin; anticholinergic at CNS and peripheral receptors; sedating.

- **Oral route:** Onset varies; peaks within 2-4 hours.

- $T_{1/2}$: 8-16 hours, metabolised in the liver, excretion in the urine.

Amitriptyline

Amitriptyline is of the most commonly prescribed anticholinergic and sedative of the tricyclic antidepressants. Due to lack of nitrogen atom of imipramine, its metabolic inactivation mainly proceeds not at 2 – position but at 10 – position. This results into more anticholinergic and sedative action than imipramine.

Doxepin

Presence of oxygen influences oxidative metabolism as well as post and presynaptic binding affinities of doxepin. Z-isomer is more active; however drug is marketed as the mixture of isomers. The drug is an NE and 5-HT uptake blocker and has significant anticholinergic and sedative properties.

Special Characteristics of TCA

- Some amitryptyline, doxepine, trimipramine have slight H_1 antihistaminic action as well.

- **Monoamine Oxidase Inhibitors (MAOIs):** Last choice for treatment except in atypical depression.

- Tyramine containing foods can cause hypertensive crisis.

- MAO is flavin containing enzyme. It inactivates biogenic amines such as NE, dopamine, serotonin and tyramine by converting them to aldehydes, which on further oxidation or reduction produces an acid or alcohol. It is subdivided in two isozymes, MAO-A and MAO-B.

MONOAMINE OXIDASE (MAO) INHIBITOR

MAO-A

- MAO-A prefers serotonin and NE inhibition of this permits dietary tyramine to be metabolised, so selective MAO-A inhibitor-hypertension is not side effect.

- Hypertensive crisis is observed after the ingestion of food rich in tyramine such as cheese, wine and chicken liver.

- Another prominent side effect is orthostatic hypotension to lower blood pressure.

- Examples are hydrazines and hydrazides which are introduced as MAO inhibitors. They can cause hepatoxicity.

MAO – B

- It prefers dopamine selective MAO-B inhibition and is prescribed for the treatment of Parkinsonism. Most of the MAO inhibitors antidepressants are nonselective between NE and Serotonin.

- **Distribution of MAO:** Peripheral adrenergic nerve ending, intestinal mucosa and human placenta contain predominantly MAO-A. MAO-B predominates in certain areas of brain and in platelets. Liver contains both isoenzymes.

- Two hydrazine drugs isoniazide and iproniazid were used to treat tuberculosis. Later they were found to cause disproportionate elevation of mood by inhibit the degradation of biogenic amines. Its less hepatotoxic congers like phenelzine and isocarboxazide and some nonhydrazine MAO inhibitors (related to amphetamine) like tranylcypromine was used as antidepressant in the 1960s.

- The selective MAO-A inhibitors possess antidepressant property: selegiline selectively inhibit MAO-B at lower doses, but are not effective in depression.

- Selegiline is metabolized to amphetamine and at higher doses it becomes nonselective MAO inhibitor exhibiting antidepressant and excitement properties.

- The nonselective MAO inhibitors elevate the mood of depressed patient.

- **Adverse effects :** Excessive stimulation (CNS), Orthostatic hypotension, hypertensive crisis if patient eats foods containing tyramine. Drug interactions with MAO are described below.

Drug Interactions

- MAO inhibitors also inhibit a number of other enzymes as well with many food constituent and drug. In MAO inhibited patient certain tyramine containing food items such as cheese, beer, wines, pickled meat and fish, yeast extract causes hypertensive crisis. It can be treated by i.v. injection of adrenergic blocker e.g. phentolamine, prazocine or chlorpromazine.

- Reserpine, Guanethidine, tricyclic antidepressant cause excitement, rise in BP and body temperature occur when these drugs given to patient on MAO inhibitors.

- Levodopa increases the biological action of DA and NA. When Levodopa is administered to a patient on MAO inhibitors it causes excitement and hypertension.

- Its prolong the action of barbiturates, alcohol, opioids, and antihistamines.

- With pethidine MAO inhibitors show excitory action.

Focus on the MAOI Prototype

- **Phenelzine Indications:** Used in treatment of patients with depression who are unresponsive to or unable to take other antidepressive therapy.

- **Actions:** Irreversibly inhibits MAO, allowing norepinephrine, serotonin and dopamine to accumulate in the synaptic cleft.

- **Oral route:** Onset slow; duration 48–96 hours.
- **T½:** Unknown; metabolized in the liver, excreted in the urine.

Reversible Inhibitors of MAO-A

Moclobemide

It is a reversible and selective MAO-A inhibitor with short duration of action. The antidepressant action is comparable to TCAs. It lacks the anticholinergic, sedative, cognitive, psychomotor and cardiovascular adverse effect of typical TCAs and is safer in case of an overdose. It is particularly good option in elderly patients and in those with heart disease. Adverse effects are nausea, dizziness, headache, insomnia, rarely excitement and liver damage. Chances of interaction with other drugs are rare.

SELECTIVE SEROTONIN REUPTAKE INHIBITORS (SSRIS)

These are newest group of antidepressants. They specifically block the reuptake of 5HT, with little to unknown effect on NE. Do not have the many adverse effects associated with TCAs and MAOIs. They have improved tolerability, both in therapeutic use as well as in case of an overdose and is a preferred drug for prophylaxis of recurrent depression. Their relative safety and better acceptability has made them first line of treatment in depression and allowed their extensive use in anxiety, phobias, Obsessive Compulsive Disorder (OCD) and related disorders. They produce little or no sedation; do not interfere with cognitive and psychomotor function or anticholinergic side effect.

Devoid of adrenergic blocking action-postural hypotension. Weight gain is not problem. Side effect produces nervousness, restlessness, insomnia, anorexia, dyskinesia, headache and diarrhea. Incidence of epistaxis and ecchymosis reported due to impairment of platelet function. Gastric blood loss due to NSAID may be increased by SSRIs. The SSRIs inhibit drug metabolising enzymes-elevate plasma level of TCAs, haloperidol, clozapine, terfenadine, warfarin, β blocker, some BZDs and carbamazepine. Discontinuation result in parastesia, bodyache, bowel upset, agitation and sleep disturbances.

Clinical applications of SSRIs

- Depression, Obsessive Compulsive Disorders (OCDs)
- Also used in Panic attacks, Bulimia, PMDD, Posttraumatic stress disorders, Social phobias, Social anxiety disorders, Elevation of mood and increases the work capacity.

Focus on the Prototype SSRI

Fluoxetine

- It is bicyclic compound and is the longest acting agent.
- **Indications:** used in the treatment of depression, OCDs, bulimia, PMDD, panic disorders; unlabeled uses include chronic pain, alcoholism, neuropathies, obesity.
- **Actions:** Inhibits CNS neuronal reuptake of serotonin with little effect on norepinephrine and little affinity for cholinergic, histaminic, or alpha-adrenergic sites.
- **Oral route:** Onset slow; peaks in 6-8 hours, form active demethylated metabolite. T½ is around 2–4 weeks; metabolised in the liver and excreted in the urine and feces.
- **Adverse effect:** Causes more agitation and dermatological reaction than other SSRIs.

Fluvoxamine

It is a short acting SSRI with T½ a 18 hours and does not have active metabolite. It produces more nausea and discontinuation reaction has been reported.

Paroxetine

It is another short acting SSRI; T½ is 20 hours, which does not produce active metabolite. A higher incidence of gastrointestinal side effect and discontinuation reaction than with other SSRIs has been noted.

Sertraline

Drug interaction due to inhibition of CYP isoenzymes are less likely to occur with it. Plasma $T_{1/2}$ is 26 hours and it produces longer lasting active metabolite.

Citalopram

It shares with sertraline lower propensity to cause drug interaction. Its $T_{1/2}$ is 33 hours and no active metabolite is found.

Atypical Antidepressant

Trazodone

It is the first atypical antidepressant, which blocks 5-HT, α_1 adrenergic as well as $5 HT_2$ antagonistic action. It is sedative but not anticholinergic, because bradycardia (hypotension) rather than tachycardia does not interfere intra cardiac conduction-less prone to cause arrhythmia. Mild anxiolytic effect has been noted and it has benefited cases of OCD. Development of seizure does not occur. Plasma $T_{1/2}$ is 6 hrs. The major adverse effect painful penile erection resulting in impotence (α_1 adrenergic blocking potency).

Nefazodone

It is a congener of trazodone, which selectively blocks 5-HT reuptake and 5-HT_2 receptor. It is sedative but cause less postural hypotension. It has α_1 adrenergic blocking property. It is used for prophylaxis of recurrent depression.

Mianserin

Mianserin is unique in nature. It is not inhibiting either NA or 5-HT uptake; but blocks presynaptic α_2 receptor--increase release and turnover of NA in brain, which may be responsible for antidepressant effect.

Antagonistic action at 5-HT_2, 5-HT_{1c} as well as H_1 receptor. It is sedative-relieves associated anxiety and suppress panic attacks. Less prominent anticholinergic and cardiac side effects. Causes seizure in over doses. Blood dyscrasias and liver dysfunction have been reported.

Tianeptine

It increase the uptake of 5-HT and is neither sedative nor stimulant. It has shown efficacy in anxiodepressive states. Side effects are dry mouth, epigastric pain, flatulence, drowsiness, insomnia, tremor, and bodyache.

Amineptine

It enhance 5-HT uptake but has antidepressant property. It produce anticholinergic side effect including tachycardia, confusion and delirium.

Venlafaxine

It is an 5-HT and NA reuptake inhibitor (TCAs), but does not interact with cholinergic, adrenergic or histaminirgic receptor or have sedative property. Having faster of action. It does not produce usual side effect of TCAs; tend to raise rather than depress BP and is safer in overdose. Side effects are nausea, sweating, anxiety, dizziness and impotence.

Mirtazapine

It act by novel mechanism by blocking α_2 auto (on NA neurones) and hetero-(on 5-HT neurones) receptors enhancing both NA and 5-HT release. The enhancement of anti-depressive 5-HT_1 receptor action is achieved by concurrent blockage of 5-HT_2 and 5-HT_3 receptor, which have been held responsible for some adverse effects of high serotonergic tone. Severe depression is reported to be comparable to TCAs.

Bupropion

It is inhibitor of DA and NA uptake having excitation activity rather than sedative. It is metabolised into an amphetamine like compound. It is used in smoking cessation, better result has been obtained when it combined with nicotine patch. It can cause insomnia, agitation, dry mouth and nausea as side effect. Seizure occurs as a dose related side effect.

Questions on this Chapter

1. Write the classification of antidepressant and add note on Tricyclic antidepressant.

2. Discuss the applicability of MAO inhibitors in treatment of depression.

3. What is atypical antidepressant?

4. Write note on selective serotonin reuptake inhibitors.

Chapter **8**

ANTIMANIC DRUGS / MOOD STABILISING AGENTS

Objectives

After reading this chapter, the student will be able to:

➢ What are the goals of general anesthesia

➢ Write the clinical features of mania.

➢ Write the features of MDD

➢ Write the psychosocial treatment for mania

Mania is an episodic mood disorder either in severe or recurrent form which is characterised by major depression (unipolar) and bipolar disorder (manic depression). Kraepelin (1896) identified manic depression as an illness characterised by severe mood swings that are relatively independent of social and psychological forces.

Epidemiology of Mania

It is a Bipolar disorder (BPD). The prevalence is ~1% and there are no clear gender differences. The age of onset ~20 years of age and the prognosis is poorer than for major depressive disorder (MDD). The prevalence of major depressive disorder is 5-12% in males and 10-25% in females. Gender ratio is similar across cultures and the age of onset is ~25 years. MDD is common and debilitating, age of onset is shifting downward markedly.

Background of Mania

The suicide risk in manic patients is ~ 15% in which depression is one of the most co-morbid of all disorders (also co-occurs with many medical illnesses). Dysthymia and cyclothymia are risk factors for MDD and BPD. Depressive episodes have a typical duration of four months and can go untreated. Manic episodes are shorter and almost always treated. 60% of those having a depressive first episode can be expected to have subsequent episodes (risk is higher in female). Economic costs associated with mood disorders are second only to those associated with cardiovascular disease. Psychosurgery is an option for intractable MDD.

Major Depressive Episode

At least 5 of the following symptoms present for at least 2 weeks.

1. Depressed mood

2. Loss of interest or pleasure (anhedonia) characterised by

   - Significant weight loss/gain (e.g. 5% change/month).
   - Insomnia or hypersomnia nearly every day.
   - Psychomotor agitation or retardation.
   - Fatigue or loss of energy.
   - Feelings of worthlessness or excessive/inappropriate guilt.
   - Diminished ability to think or concentrate indecisiveness.
   - Recurrent thoughts of death (including suicidal thoughts/intent).

Dysthymic Disorder

Dysthymic disorder shares many of the symptoms of MDD, but symptoms are milder and remain relatively unchanged over longer periods of time (sometimes 20-30 years). There is persistently depressed mood that lasts for at least 2 years. Mean age of onset is early 20's. It is often leads to MDD (~70%) and when both are present then there is double depression. About 10% of MDD cases are preceded by dysthymia.

Manic Episode

Manic episode is characterised by euphoric or irritable mood which persist for 1 week. The symptoms in the manic episode are decreased need for sleep, pressure to keep talking, more talkative than usual, flight of ideas, feels like thoughts are racing, distractibility, increase in goal directed activity level or psychomotor agitation, involved in pleasurable activities that have high potential for harmful consequences (impaired judgment).

Bipolar Disorder

Defined as a brain disorder that causes unusual shifts in mood, energy, activity levels, and the ability to carry out day-to-day tasks. Unipolar mania may be misdiagonised as (15% of cases) bipolar disorder. 60-70% of manic episodes occur just before depressive episodes. In bipolar disorder there are mixed episodes, rapid cycling (4 episodes/year) and possibly psychotic features.

Hypomania

Hypomania is similar to mania but it is less severe and lasts at most for 4 days. There is no major impairment but clear (observable to others) change in functioning that is uncharacteristic of person when not symptomatic. There is no hospitalization, no psychotic features. When the hypomania and major depressive episode combine then it is termed as bipolar II disorder.

Cyclothymia

Dysthymic and hypomanic period's cycle over two year period (1 year in kids) with no more than 2 months of normal mood. The prevalence is around 1-4%. 1/3 to ½ BPDs are premorbid "cyclothymes" and it is equally common in men and women.

Table 8.1: Mood Disorders: Integrative Summary

Severe Depressive Episode.	MDD
Minor depressive episodes and symptoms for maximum 2 years.	Dysthymic disorder
Minor depression for maximum 2 yrs and one major depressive episode.	Double depression
At least 1 major episode.	Bipolar I
At least 1 major depression and 1 hypomanic episode.	Bipolar II
Minor depression and hypomania for maximum 2 years.	Cyclothymic disorder

Psychosocial Treatments

Behaviour Therapy: Treatment focuses on increasing person's opportunities to receive appropriate reinforcements.

Interpersonal Psychotherapy: Focuses on resolving problems in existing relationships and learning how to form new interpersonal relationships.

Cognitive-Behavioral Therapy (CBT): People get depressed because they have irrational depressogenic thoughts about self, world and future.

Patients are taught to monitor their thought processes and recognise depressive errors in thinking. Treatment involves correcting cognitive errors and substituting less depressive thoughts (e.g., my thoughts are not facts!). Behaviorally oriented homework exercises also included.

Biological Treatment:

- Lithium Carbonate
- Older Anticonvulsant: Carbamazepine, Valproate
- Newer Anticonvulsant: Lamotrigine, Gabapentin.
- Atypical antipsychotic: Olanzapine, Risperidone.
- Calcium channel blocker: Verapamil.
- Electroconvulsive Therapy.

LITHIUM CARBONATE

Lithium carbonate is small monovalent cation. It exerts prophylactic effect in bipolar manic depressive illness. Alternative drugs are carbamazepine and valproate (antiepileptic drugs).

Action and Mechanism

CNS: It is neither sedative nor euphorient, but on prolonged administration it acts as a mood stabiliser in bipolar disease.

Mechanism

Lithium carbonate affects ionic fluxes across brain cells or modifies the property of cellular membranes by replacing body sodium. There is decrease in the the release of NA and DA in the brain without affecting 5-HT release. This may correct the turnover of brain monoamines. Lithium dampens the signal transduction by inhibiting the hydrolysis of inositol-1-phosphate; as a result the supply of free inositol (for regeneration of membrane phosphatidyl-inositol), which is the source of IP3 and DAG) is reduced and affecting the hyperactive neuron (due additional supply of inositol from extracellular source) involved in manic state. See Fig. 8.1.

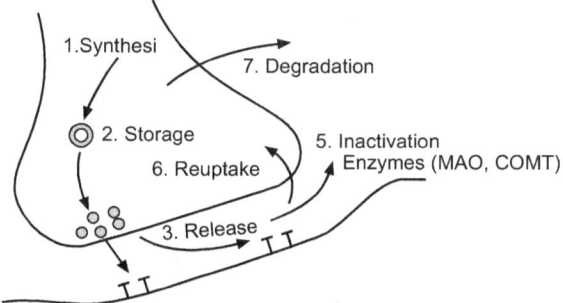

Fig. 8.1: Mechanism of Drug Action

Other Actions

- Lithium carbonate produces diabetes insipidus like state by inhibiting the action of ADH on distal tubule. There is also insulin like action on glucose metabolism.
- Lithium also increases the leukocyte count.
- Reduces thyroxine synthesis by interfering with iodination of tyrosine.

Pharmacokinetics

It is well absorbed orally and is neither protein bound nor metabolised. It first distributes in extracellular water and then gradually enters cells and slowly penetrates into the CNS. Lithium is handled by the kidney in much the same way as sodium. Lithium is secreted in breast milk. Mothers on Li treatment should not breastfeed.

Adverse Effects

Lithium carbonate produces various adverse effects they are given bellow:

- Nausea, vomiting and mild diarrhoea.
- Thirst and polyuria.
- Fine tremors and rarely seizure.
- CNS toxicity-in treatment of CNS toxicity there is no specific antidote. Osmotic diuresis and sodium bicarbonate infusion promote lithium excretion.
- Diabetic insipidus.
- Goiter.

Drug Interactions

- Diuretics (Thiazide and Furosemide) increase the plasma level of lithium by tubular reabsorption of lithium.
- There is retention of lithium by concurrent administration with tetracycline, indomethacin and ACE inhibitors.
- It reduces the pressor response of NA.
- It enhances insulin induced hypoglycemia.
- In lithium treated patient, succinylcholine and pancuronium produce prolonged paralysis.

Pharmacological Uses

- It is used in acute manic episodes.
- It is used in prophylaxis in case of bipolar disorder.
- In recurrent unipolar depression, antidepressant with lithium carbonate is often used initially and then lithium alone is continued in the maintenance phase.
- It is also used in recurrent neuropsychiatric illness and cluster headache.
- Lithium carbonate helps to recover the leukocyte count in cancer therapy induced leukopenia and agranulocytosis.
- It also used in inappropriate ADH secretion syndrome.

ALTERNATIVE TO LITHIUM

- **Carbamazepine (CBZ):** Patient who relapse on lithium therapy or those prone to rapid cycling of moods are known to fare better on combined lithium with CBZ treatment.
- **Sodium Valproate:** It may act faster than lithium. It can be useful in those not responding to lithium or CBZ or not tolerating these drugs.
- Anticonvulsant like lamotrigine, gabapentin have also been found to be effective in bipolar disorder.

  Atypical antipsychotics: olanzapine and risperidone are also used in bipolar illness. Olanzapine carries a low risk of agranulocytosis and extra-pyramidal side effect.

Questions on this Chapter

1. Discuss characteristics of mania.
2. Explain the treatment of mania.
3. Write a short note on mood stabilising agents.

Chapter 9

CNS STIMULANTS

Objectives

After reading this chapter, the student will be able to:

➢ Understand the possible effects of CNS stimulants

➢ Classify the CNS stimulants

➢ What are the different conditions associated with hyper excitation

➢ Write the molecular basis of CNS stimulation

Stimulants are substances, which tend to increase behavioral activity i.e. when administered results into elevation of mood, increase motor activity, increase alertness, decrease need for sleep, increase the brain's metabolic and neuronal activity.

MOLECULAR BASIS OF CNS STIMULATION

There is imbalance between inhibitory and excitatory processes in the brain. This hyper-excitability of neurons results from-

- Potentiation or enhancement of excitatory neurotransmission (e.g. amphetamine).

- Depression or antagonism of inhibitory transmission (e.g. Strychnine).

- Presynaptic control of neurotransmitter release (e.g. Picrotoxin).

CLASSIFICATION OF CNS STIMULANT

- **Analeptics:** It has limited range use (as respiratory stimulants).

- **Convulsant:** Strychnine, Picrotoxin, Bicuculline, Pentylenetetrazole (PTZ, Metrazol, Laptazol).

- **Methylxathines:** It has interesting stimulating properties e.g. Caffeine (cortical stimulant).

- **Central sympathomimetic agents:** amphetamine and related compounds.

- **Psychedelics:** They have a broad range of CNS effects. One effect of several of these agents is CNS stimulation.

- **Antidepressants:** It contain mainly Monoamine Oxidase (MAO) inhibitors and tricyclic agents.

ANALEPTICS (RESPIRATORY STIMULANTS)

It is a diverse chemical class of agents majority can be absorbed orally. It has a short duration of action. The primary expression of pharmacological effect is convulsions (tonic-clonic). At subconvulsant dose analeptics produce respiratory stimulation. Its pharmacological effect is terminated through hepatic metabolism. It acts through possibly common mechanism of action i.e. ability to alter movement of chloride ions across neuronal membranes.

Doxapram and Nikethamide

They act by facilitating excitatory processes rather than by depressing inhibitory. The overall effect resembles that of an amphetamine more than that of picrotoxin. It is possible to stimulate respiration with the drug without inducing generalised CNS stimulation. However, selectivity is still very low. It has very limited use in treating acute respiratory insufficiency in Chronic Obstructive Pulmonary Disease (COPD). It also has some value in correcting respiratory depression caused by O_2 therapy in COPD.

CONVULSANTS

- Strychnine
- Picrotoxin
- Bicuculline
- Pentylenetetrazole (PTZ, Metrazol, Laptazol)

Strychnine

- Strychnine is a source of accidental poisoning. It is a potent convulsant. Produces spinal convulsions. It stimulates the cerebrospinal axis. Also used to study CNS mechanism because of its relatively specific action as a glycine (motoneuron juction in spinal cord) antagonist.
- **Adverse Reactions:** Convulsion is characterised by opisthotonos, i.e. tonic extension of body and all limbs. Back is arched and only the back of the head and the heels are touching the touching the surface. All sensory stimuli produce exaggerated response and slight sensory stimulation may trigger convulsion.

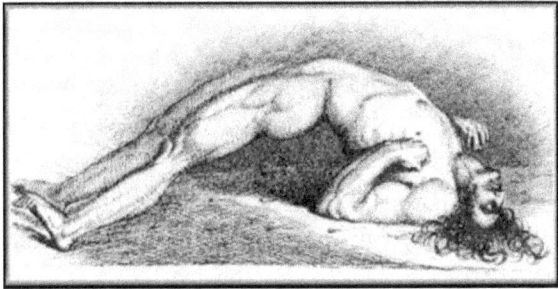

Fig. 9.1: Convulsions de to strychine poisoning

Treatment of Strychnine Poisoning

Following are the treatment options in strychnine poisoning

- Remove/reduce external sensory stimuli.
- Introduce Diazepam or Clonazepam I.V. or nitrous oxide by inhalation to depress CNS and stop convulsions which can be fatal.

Picrotoxin

- Picrotoxin is obtained from the seeds of *Anamirta cocculus*. The active ingredient is Picrotoxin. It is a potent convulsant symptoms may be vomiting, respiratory and vasomotor stimulation. Picrotoxin exerts its effects by interfering with the inhibitory effect of γ- amino butyric acid (GABA) at the level of GABA-A receptors chloride channel (It is said to jam the chloride channel).
- Pharmacologically it is used as an experimental tool for determination of certain sedative hypnotics and anticonvulsant drugs at the molecular level.

Pentylenetetrazole (PTZ)

- It is a powerful CNS stimulant that acts by depolarizing the central neurons. Low doses cause excitation and larger dose produce convulsions. The drug acts as a convulsant by interfering with chloride conductance. It binds with allosteric site on GABA-A receptors and acts as a negative modulator. Overall it has a similar effect as that of Picrotoxin.
- It is used clinically as a tool for screening latent epileptics and experimentally to screen compounds for anti-epileptic activity. In the past PTZ was used for respiratory paralysias, circulatory failure and for physical and mental improvement in old dementic patient.

Bicuculline

This synthetic convulsant has picrotoxin like action. It is a competitive GABA-A receptor (chloride channel receptor) antagonist.

PSYCHOMOTOR STIMULANTS

Drugs of Primary Importance are as follows:
Amphetamine – (Prototype compound)
Methamphetamine
Methylphenidate
    Nicotine
    Cocaine
    Fenfluramine

Characteristics of Psychomotor stimulant

- All compounds are absorbed well orally. Large portion of untransformed amphetamine is excreted unchanged.
- In the urine: Consequently, acidifying the urine with ammonium chloride hastens its clearance and thus reduces its reabsorption in the renal tubules.
- Overdose produces hyperreflexia, tremors and convulsions.
- Fatalities: Due to hyperthermia rather than cardiovascular effects.

Pharmacological Actions

- The primary effects of an oral dose are wakefulness, alertness, decrease fatigue; mood elevation, increased ability to concentrate; an increase in motor and speech activity.
- Amphetamines also diminish the awareness of fatigue; person may push exertion to the point of severe damage or even death. It stimulates the respiratory center, especially when respiration is depressed by centrally acting drugs (barbiturates and alcohol).
- Amphetamine can reverse the marked sedation and behavioral retardation resulting from reserpine-like drug. It depresses appetite by it's action on the lateral hypothalamus rather than an effect on the metabolic rate.

Mechanisms of Action

They release monoamines at synapses in the brain and spinal cord. They inhibit neuronal uptake of monoamine. They are direct agonists at DA and 5-HT receptors and antagonists at certain adrenreceptors. They may inhibit monoamine oxidase.

Therapeutic Uses for-

- Hyperkinesias: Methylphenidate.
- Narcolepsy: Amphetamine or methylphenidate.
- Obesity: Fenfluramine.

Adverse Effects

CNS: Produces Euphoria, dizziness, tremor, irritability, insomnia, convulsion (at higher doses), hyperthermia and coma.

CVS: Cardiac stimulation leads to headache, palpitations, cardiac arrhythmias, anginal pain.

Others: Weight loss, Psychotic Reaction which are often misdiagnosed as schizophrenia.

Addiction including psychic dependence, tolerance and physical dependence.

Drug Interactions

Drug interaction with tricyclic antidepressant, antihypertensive agents and with foods containing high tyramine content

NICOTINE

It is a primary active ingredient of tobacco. One of the most widely used psychoactive drugs are caffeine and alcohol. They have few or no therapeutic applications.

Pharmacological Effects

Nicotine exerts powerful effects on brain, spinal cord, peripheral nervous system, heart and various other body structures.

- Stimulation of the vomit center in the brain stem and sensory receptors in the stomach produces nausea in the early stages of smoking and tolerance develops rapidly.

- It also reduces weight gain probably by suppressing appetite.
- It stimulates the release of ADH (antidiuretic hormone) causing fluid retention.
- It reduces the activity of afferent nerve fibers from muscles causing reduction in muscle tone and partially involved with relaxation effect.
- At higher doses it can induce nervousness and tremors. At toxic overdose it produce seizures.
- Smoking associated with increased occurrence of panic attacks and panic disorders.
- In the CNS, nicotine increases psychomotor activity, cognitive functioning, sensorimotor performance, attention, memory consolidation

Nicotine can improve performance on vigilance and rapid information processing. Effects are greater for working memory rather than long term memory.

Nicotine exerts an antidepressant effect. High smoking rates among depressed individuals may be an attempt at self medication.

Nicotine exerts a potent reinforcing action. There is an indirect activation of midbrain dopamine neurons which is greatest in the early phases and diminishes over time.

Reproductive Effects

- Smoking during pregnancy increases rates spontaneous abortion, stillbirth, early postpartum death, preterm deliveries.
- Intrauterine growth retardation increasingly 40%. In an average about 2000 infant deaths per year attributed to smoking. Smoking reduces oxygen delivery to the foetus resulting in varying degree of foetal hypoxia. Foetus does not receive much oxygen. Smoking may result in irreversible intellectual and physical deficiencies.

Mechanism of Action

- Nicotine activates specific acetylcholine (ACh) receptors known as nicotinic receptors
- Nicotinic receptors are located throughout the body – Skeletal muscle, Sympathetic and parasympathetic neurons, CNS.
- ACh is released, broken down, and reabsorbed very quickly (microsecond) allowing the receptor to respond to a new molecule of Ach.
- ACh receptors work as a fast first messenger system which attached directly to ion channels and after binding result in an immediate response.
- Nicotine replaces ACh at nicotinic receptor and beats out the ACh at the binding site
- It works as an agonist and opens ion channels allowing depolarisation to occur.

Peripheral Nervous System

Activation of nicotinic receptors in the PNS resulted elevated in blood pressure and heart rate because of release of epinephrine from the adrenal glands. It increases the tone, secretions and activity of the gastrointestinal tract.

Central Nervous System

Nicotinic receptors are widely distributed and may be present at the presynaptic terminals of neurons which secrete dopamine, acetylcholine and glutamine. Activation by nicotine facilitates the release and increases the action in the brain of these neurotransmitters.

Role of Dopamine, Acetylcholine and Glutamine

- Dopamine levels are increased in the area of Ventral tegmentum, Nucleus accumbens and Forebrain. Stimulation of these areas account for the behavioral reinforcement, stimulant, antidepressant, and addictive properties of nicotine.

- Increases in acetylcholine contribute to the cognitive potentiation and memory facilitation properties of nicotine.

- Facilitation of glutaminergic neurotransmissions contribute to the improvement in memory functioning.

Tolerance

Nicotine does not appear induces a pronounced degree of biological tolerance. Smokers adjust nicotine intake to maintain 20 to 40 nanograms per milliliter of plasma. It induce physiological and psychological dependence producing habituation and rebound effects.

Withdrawal Symptoms

Withdrawal symptoms of nicotine produces intense nicotine craving, irritability, anxiety anger, difficulty in concentrating, restlessness, impatience, increased appetite, weight gain and insomnia

Pharmacokinetics

It is easily absorbed by the lungs, buccal and nasal mucosa, skin and gastrointestinal tract. Nicotine is suspended in the minute particles (tars) in smoke and orally administered blood levels of nicotine are comparable to smoking. Only about 20% of the nicotine in a cigarette is inhaled and absorbed into the bloodstream. Nicotine, which is not immediately absorbed, is rapidly metabolised by the hepatic enzyme CYP2A6. Nicotine is thoroughly distributed in the body. There are no barriers to nicotine distribution. It undergoes rapid brain penetration and cross the placental barrier. It appears in all bodily fluids. The liver metabolizes 80 to 90% of nicotine before excretion to the kidneys. The primary metabolite is cotinine and the elimination half life in chronic users is about 2 hrs.

COCAINE
(Psychomotor Stimulant)

It is local anesthetic and obtained from Coca shrub (cocaine) which is found in Peru, Colombia and Bolivia. Leaves used by natives to increase endurance and promote sense of well being.

Pharmacological Actions

The pharmacological effects of cocaine in depends upon the dosage, form in which it is administered, route of administration, frequency of administration, background of users, user expectations, history and personality of users. Pharmacologically it blockades the initiation or conduction of nerve impulses (similar with local anesthetic).

CNS:

Stimulation of CNS caused by dose and route of administration are as follows

- Euphoria and feeling of well being (not an aphrodisiac).

- Motor coordination decreases with increased dose.

- Fatigue is masked by central stimulation (borrowed energy).

- Weight loss.

- Higher doses cause depression and reparatory failure.

- Chronic administration can cause paranoia

- Dental hygiene decreases.

Cardiovascular Effects

Small doses of cocaine may slow heart rate; moderate doses increase heart rate (irregular heart beat). There is increased blood pressure (vasoconstrictor). Muscle fatigue is a direct toxic effect on heart result into conduction disturbances. It also increases body temperature, dilation of pupils and increases glucose availability.

Mechanism of Action of Cocaine

Cocaine blocks the neurotransmitter reuptake of dopamine, serotonin, norepinephrine and epinephrine (Fig. 9.2). The action of cocaine is similar to amphetamine. It increases epinephrine and increases physical energy.

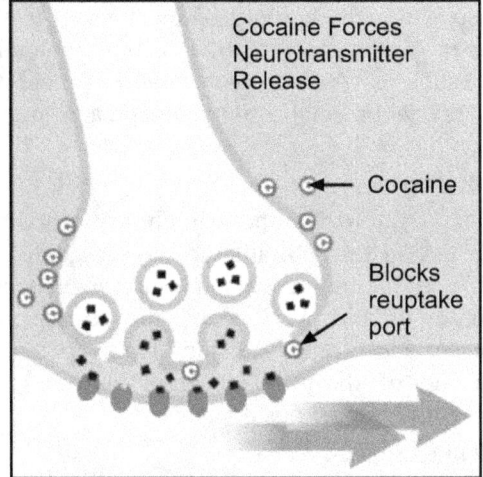

Fig. 9.2: Mechanism of action of cocaine

Dosage Forms of Cocaine

1. Cocaine Hydrochloride: It is water-soluble salt form for intranasal and intravenous use.
2. Cocaine Base Crystals: It is water-insoluble "crack" a ready to smoke base form of cocaine, which vaporizes when, heated at high temperature. Can be used intravenously.
3. Cocaine Alkaloid Paste: It is **water-insoluble** "freebase" can also be smoked like "crack."

Routes of Administration

The plasma level of cocaine at various route of administration is given in Fig. 9.3.

Oral: Duration of high is 45-90 mins. after intake and slowly diminishes.

Intranasal (snorting): There is rapid absorption and produce peek and euphoria in 15-30 min, can cause numbness, perforation of nasal septum with chronic use continual snorting limits absorption due to vasoconstriction of blood vessels.

Intravenous: Initial onset of action produce in 30-45 sec, duration of action is high 10-20 min. Initial euphoria followed by "crash" of extreme dysphoria and intense craving 40-60 min after injection. It can lead to hepatitis, AIDS, endocarditis, addiction and risk of overdose.

Smoking: By this route euphoria is more intense and the initial onset of action 8-10 sec and duration is of high 5-10 min, followed by a "crash" similar to intravenous injection, leads to chronic addiction. It can cause pulmonary disease.

Detoxification and Metabolism: It rapidly distributes to brain and is metabolised in liver.

Half-life of cocaine in plasma is only 30-90 min and with alcohol is 150 min.

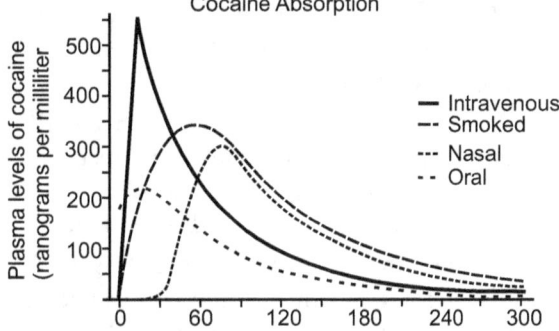

Fig. 9.3: Route of administration of cocaine

Toxicology

Overdose can occur by any route of administration. Average lethal dose is 500 mg, but is variable. Toxicological symptoms of cocaine are excitement, panic, paranoia, restlessness, chills, fever, nausea, vomiting, irregular heart rhythms, respiration and mental confusion.

There is no antidote for cocaine. Sedatives can be used to decrease CNS Stimulation.

Monitoring Use: By measuring metabolites of cocaine in urine.

Snorting and **Intravenous:** Urine sample is tested positive for metabolites for 2-4 days.

Smoking: Urine sample is tested positive for metabolites for 8-12 days.

Chronic cocaine use and withdrawal of cocaine causes dopamine depletion, rapid heartbeat, hypertension, paranoia and sleep deprivation.

Withdrawal symptoms of cocaine are decreased energy, excessive sleeping, irritable mood, depression, psychomotor retardation, nausea/vomiting. Withdrawal is almost never fatal and there is no physically dependency.

METHYLXANTINES

Caffeine

Caffeine found various beverages products but in varying amount such as in coffee the content of caffeine is 100-150 mg/cup; in tea it is 30-40 mg/cups; in cocoa it is 15-18 mg/cup.

Theophylline: It is found in tea and cocoa

Theobromine: It is present in cocoa

Mechanism of Action

They increase cyclic nucleotide concentration and blocks adenosine receptors. These are most potent at adenosine A_1 and A_{2A}. They alter intracellular calcium distribution.

Caffeine, the most widely used drug in the world, is a stimulant. Commonly found in coffee, tea, soft drinks, chocolate and a wide variety of over-the-counter medications, it is legal to buy and easily accessible. Caffeine is a physically addictive drug.

Caffeine works as an antagonistic. It blocks the adenosine receptor. Adenosine is a neuromodulator. Modulatory effect increases or decreases the rate at which neurons fire and it is works in conjunction with the G protein processes. Adenosine appears to exert sedative, depressant, and anticonvulsant actions and works to slow down the system and it is important for sleeping.

Adenosine Receptor A_1

These types of receptors inhibit excitatory neurons of dopamine, glutamate and acetylcholine secreting neurons and resulted to decrease the production of cAMP. Thus there is inhibition of the release of dopamine and glutamate and limit the release of acetylcholine. It also slows the activity of the kinase. It also reduces occurrence of the action potential. Blockade of A_1 receptors causes increased vigilance and mental activity, and creates arousal effect.

A_{2A} Receptors

It stimulates the inhibitory neurons GABA-A in turn stimulating the production of cAMP. It inhibits dopamine activity. There is increase in the activity of the kinase and increases occurrence of the action potential. Blockade of the A_{2A} receptors increases the potency of endogenous dopamine

Pharmacological Activity

Low Doses: 50-250 mg/caffeine (oral doses) increase mental alertness, decrease drowsiness, lessen fatigue.

Larger Doses: 250-600 mg/caffeine produces irritability, restlessness, tremor, insomnia, headache, palpitations and hyperesthesia GIT upset.

Large Doses: > 1000 mg overt excitement, delirium and clonic seizures.

Caffeine constricts cerebral blood vessels and decreases blood flow by about 30%. It can relieve headaches.

Cardiovascular System: Increases rate and force of the heart beat by directly stimulating myocardium (low doses). It produces tachycardia and arrhythmias at higher doses. Peripheral vasodilation deceases in blood pressure (acute administration). It produces hypotension and cardiac arrest (rapid I.V. theophyline).

Smooth Muscles: Relaxes vascular smooth muscle (Theophylline >> Caffeine).

Kidney: All xanthines are capable of producing some degree of diuresis in humans (Theophylline > Caffeine).

GIT: There is increase in the secretion of gastric acid.

Bronchi: It produces bronchial relaxation.

Miscellaneous: Xanthines shorten clotting time by increasing tissue prothrombin and factor V.

Reproductive Effects: It freely crosses the placenta to reach the foetus. Breast milk contains levels equal or higher in concentration than mothers plasma. Higher doses causes intrauterine growth retardation. Moderate consumption does not increase the risk.

Pharmacokinetics

- Caffeine is rapidly and completely absorbed into the blood stream. Significant blood levels reached in 30-45 minutes peak levels observed in about 2 hours.
- Caffeine is freely and equally distributed through total body water and can be found in almost equal concentrations throughout body and brain.
- Caffeine has 3.5 to 5 hours half life and there are extended half life for elderly, pregnant women up to ten hours.
- Decreased half life for smokers.
- Caffeine is metabolised in the liver by the CYP_{1A2} subgroup of enzymes into three metabolites.

Adverse effects: Stimulates gastric secretions in patients with ulcers. Dehydration in children due to vomiting and transient diuretic action (theophyline), allergic reaction (aminophylline), psychic dependence (caffeine) and chronic use associated with habituation and tolerance.

Quitting may cause withdrawal symptoms like headaches, drowsiness, fatigue, negative mood.

Therapeutic Uses-

- Caffeine plus ergot alkaloid (Ergotamine) used to treat migraine headaches.
- OTC preparations: Theophylline is an OTC preparation used as a prophylaxis for chronic asthma.

- Respiratory Stimulant: Bronchodilator for relief of asthmatic symptoms.

PSYCHEDELICS

These are the agents which produce an increased awareness and enhanced perception of sensory stimuli. Psychedelics are broadly grouped into (1) those have indolethylamine moiety (2) Those have phenyl ethylamine moiety.

In the first group, they have structural resemblance to 5HT while in the second group they have structural resemblance to NE and DA.

Indolethylamine Moiety

- Indolethylamine
- Dimethyltryptanine
- Bufofenine
- Psilocybin
- Psilicyn

Phenylethylamine: Pentenyltetrazole

α-Methylation increases synthetic activity which relatively are more potent than mescaline. It possesses both an indolethylamine moiety and phenethylamine.

Lysergic acid diethylamide (LSD): It is a very potent agent used to increased awareness and enhanced perception.

Antidepressants

These are mainly Monoamine Oxidase (MAO) inhibitors and tricyclic antidepressants. These are discussed in details in the chapter antidepressants.

Questions on this Chapter

1. Write the classification CNS stimulants and add note on analeptics.
2. Write the pharmacology of psychomotor stimulants.
3. Explain the therapeutic role of nicotine and cocaine as CNS stimulant.
4. What are psychedelics.
5. Write short note on methylxanthine.

Chapter 10

ANTIEPILEPTIC DRUGS

Objectives

After reading this chapter, the student will be able to:

➤ Describe the characteristics of seizures

➤ Differentiate general and partial seizures

➤ Enlist the different cellular mechanism responsible for seizures formation

➤ Write the different class of anticonvulsant

INTRODUCTION

Seizures, which result from abnormal excessive hyper-synchronous discharges of cortical neurons, affect about one in 11 people over the course of a lifetime. Many people experience an isolated unprovoked seizure that never recurs. Others suffer seizures only during the course of an acute illness that temporarily disrupts brain function. Thus, the occurrence of a seizure does not automatically lead to the diagnosis of epilepsy.

Epilepsy is a group of chronic disorders characterized by recurrent unprovoked seizures. About 1.5 million people in the United States are under treatment for epilepsy.

Antiepileptic drugs are used primarily to decrease or eliminate seizures in persons with epilepsy. They are also used to abort acute symptomatic seizures resulting from disease-induced transient brain dysfunction. The antiepileptic drugs are structurally diverse and affect disparate processes within the central nervous system (CNS).

Factors Affecting the Form of Seizure

- Location of the cells that initiate the electrical discharge.
- Neural pathways that are stimulated by the initial volley of electrical impulses.

CLASSIFICATION OF SEIZURES

- **Generalised seizures:** Begin in one area of the brain and rapidly spread throughout both hemispheres of the brain.
- **Partial seizures or focal seizures:** Involve one area of the brain and do not spread throughout the entire organ.

I. Classification of Generalised Seizures

- Tonic–clonic seizures (grand mal seizures).
- Absence seizures (petit mal seizures).
- Myoclonic seizures.
- Febrile seizures.
- Status epilepticus.

(a) **Tonic-clonic seizure:** It is major epilepsy and known as grand mal seizures. There is unconsciousness, tonic spasm of all body muscle, clonic jerking followed by prolonged sleep and depression of all CNS function. It last for 1-2 min.

(b) **Absence seizure:** It is minor epilepsy and also known as petit-mal seizure. Abrupt onset of impaired consciousness associated with staring and cessation of ongoing activities typically lasting less than 30 seconds.

(c) **Myoclonic seizure:** A brief (perhaps lasting for a second), shock like contraction of muscles which may be restricted to part of one extremity or may be generalised.

(d) **Atonic seizure:** A state of unconsciousness with relaxation of all muscles due to excessive inhibitory discharges results in fall of patient on floor.

(e) **Infantile spasm (Hypsarrhythmia):** It is seen in infants. There is intermittent muscle spasm and progressive mental deterioration. Diffuse changes in EEG are noted.

II. Classification of Partial Seizures

Simple Partial Seizures

• Occur in a single area of the brain and may involve a single muscle movement or sensory alteration.

• Diverse manifestations determined by the region of cortex activated by the seizure (e.g., if motor cortex representing left thumb, clonic jerking of left thumb results; if somatosensory cortex representing left thumb, paresthesia of left thumb results), lasting approximating 20 to 60 seconds.

• Key feature is preservation of consciousness.

Complex Partial Seizures

• It involves complex sensory changes.

• Motor changes may include involuntary urination, chewing motions, diarrhoea etc.

• Impaired consciousness lasting 30 seconds to 2 minutes, often associated with purposeless movements such as lip smacking or hand wringing.

Partial with Secondarily Generalised Tonic-Clonic Seizure

o Simple or Complex Partial Seizure evolves into a Tonic-Clonic seizures with loss of consciousness and sustained contractions (tonic) of muscles throughout the body followed by periods of muscle contraction alternating with periods of relaxation (clonic), typically lasting 1 to 2 minutes.

Table 10.1: Categorisation of Anticonvulsants by Their Proposed Mechanism

Class	Description	Drugs
Type I	Block SRF by enhancing sodium channel inactivation	Phenytoin, Carbamazepine, Oxcarbazepine, Lamotrigine, Felbamate
Type II	Multiple actions: enhance GABAergic inhibition, reduce T-calcium currents and possibly block SRF	Valproic acid, Benzodiazepines, Phenobarbital, Primidone
Type III	Block T-calcium currents only	Ethosuximide and Trimethadione
Type IV	Only enhances GABAergic inhibition	Vigabatrin
Non-categorized	Has no known effect on SRF, GABAergic inhibition or T calcium currents	Gabapentin

MODE OF ACTION OF ANTICONVULSANT

• In epilepsy, certain neurons and/or groups of neurons become hyperexcitable and begin firing bursts of action potentials that propagate in a synchronous manner to other brain structures. These may be the result of abnormalities in neuronal membrane stability or in the connections among neurons.

- It is known that the epileptic burst consists of sodium dependent action potentials and a calcium-dependent depolarizing potential. Thus it can be concluded that either reduction in inhibitory synaptic activity or enhancement of excitatory synaptic activity might be expected to trigger a seizure.

- Pharmacological studies disclosed that antagonists of the GABAA receptor or agonists of different glutamate-receptor subtypes (NMDA, AMPA or kainic acid) trigger seizures.

Cellular Mechanisms of Seizure Generation

➢ **Excitation (Figure 10.1 and 10.2)**

▪ Ionic-inward Na+, Ca++ currents.

▪ Neurotransmitter: Glutamate, Aspartate.

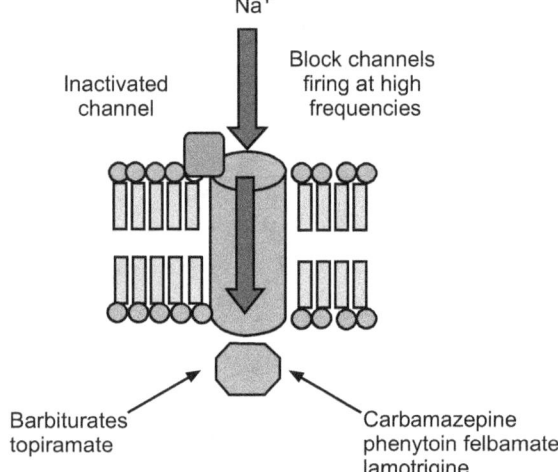

Fig. 10.1: Inward sodium channel

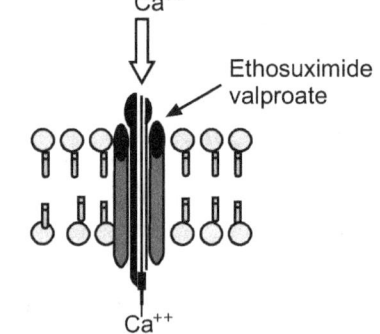

Reduction in the flow of Ca^{++} through T- type Ca^{++} channels in thalamus

Fig. 10.2: Inward Calcium channel

➢ **Inhibition**

▪ Ionic-inward Cl; outward K^+ currents.

▪ Neurotransmitter: GABA.

The inhibition of GABAergic transmission mediated through chloride channel refers Fig. 10.3.

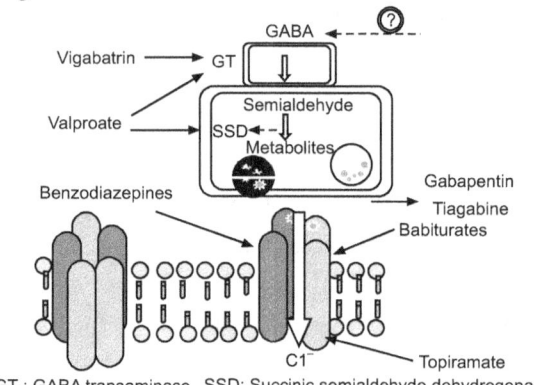

GT : GABA transaminase SSD: Succinic semialdehyde dehydrogenase

Fig. 10.3: Inhibitory GABAergic neurotransmission through chloride channel.

PHENYTOIN

Phenytoin (diphenylhydantoin) is effective against all types of partial and tonic-clonic seizures but not absence seizures. Phenytoin was first synthesised in 1908 by Biltz, but its anticonvulsant activity was not discovered until 1938. In contrast to the earlier accidental discovery of the antiseizure properties of bromide and phenobarbital, phenytoin was the product of a search among nonsedative structural relatives of phenobarbital for agents capable of suppressing electroshock convulsion. Since this agent is not a sedative in ordinary doses, it was established that antiseizure drugs need not induce drowsiness and encouraged the search for drugs with selective antiseizure action.

Pharmacological Effects

Central Nervous System: Phenytoin shows antiseizure activity without producing CNS depression. At higher dose than anticonvulsant they produce excitory sign. The most prominent action of phenytoin is to modify the pattern of maximal electroshock seizures while it does not inhibit clonic seizures evoked by pentylenetetrazol.

Mechanism of Action

Phenytoin inhibit the firing action potential of spinal cord neurons which are mediated by voltage gated sodium channel. The inhibitory activity of phenytoin are produced at therapeutic concentration which are present in CSF. At concentrations five to tenfold higher, multiple effects of phenytoin are evident, including reduction of spontaneous activity by reducing calcium influx depolarization and enhancement of responses to GABA; these effects may underlie some of the unwanted toxicity associated with high levels of phenytoin.

Adverse Effects

- Adverse effects are observed at therapeutic concentration of phenytoin. There are results of gum hypertropy, hirsutism, acne, hypersensitivity reaction, megaloblastic anemia, osteomalacia, hyperglycemia and foetal abnormality.

- At high plasma concentration it produces ataxia, vertigo, drowsiness, behaviour alteration, mental confusion, hallucination, epigastric pain, nausea and vomiting.

- when injected intravenously it produces local vascular injury, fall in BP and cardiac arrhythmias.

Drug Interactions

- Phenobarbitone competitively inhibits phenytoin metabolism and drug like chloramphenicol, isoniazide; cimetidine, dicumarol and warfarin inhibit the phenytoin metabolism and can precipitate its toxicity.

- Carbamazepine and phenytoin increase each other's metabolism.

- Phenytoin induces microsomal enzymes and increases degradation of steroids, digoxin, doxycyclin, theophylin.

- Valproate displaces protein bound phenytoin and decreases its metabolism; plasma level of unbound phenytoin increases.

- Sucralfate binds phenytoin in gastrointestinal tract and decreases its absorption.

Therapeutic uses

- It is used in generalised tonic-clonic seizures, simple and complex partial seizures while it is ineffective in absence seizures.

- It also used in Status epilepticus, Trigeminal neuralgia, Cardiac arrhythmias.

PHENOBARBITONE

Phenobarbital was the first effective antiseizure agent. It has relatively low toxicity and it is inexpensive. Most barbiturates have antiseizure properties. However, only some of these agents, such as phenobarbital, exert maximal antiseizure action at doses below those required for hypnosis. It inhibits tonic hindlimb extension in the maximal electroshock model; clonic seizures evoked by pentylenetetrazol and kindled seizures.

Mechanism of Action

At therapeutic concentration phenobarbitone increased the GABA-A receptor-mediated current by increasing the duration of bursts of GABA-A receptor-mediated currents without changing the frequency of bursts. At higher concentration phenobarbitone inhibits repetitive firing. Hypnosis produces due to some antagonistic effects on calcium channel.

Pharmacokinetic Properties

A complete oral absorption peak level occurs in plasma after several hours of administration. Plasma protein binding found to be 40% to 60% and around 25% of the dose is eliminated by kidney in unchanged form and remaining metabolised in liver.

Adverse Effects

- At initial therapy sedation is produced and at chronic tolerance develops. At excessive doses nystagmus and ataxia.

- There is also reported irritability and hyperactivity in children, and agitation and confusion in the elderly to phenobarbitone.

- There is also observed hypoprothrombinemia with hemorrhage in the new borns of mothers who have received phenobarbitone during pregnancy.

- Megaloblastic anemia and osteomalacia reported at chronic phenobarbital therapy.

Drug Interactions

- Valproic acid increases the plasma concentration of phenobarbitone.

- Phenobarbitone increases the metabolism of co-administered drug e.g. oral contraceptives.

Therapeutic Uses

- It is used in generalised tonic-clonic and partial seizures.

PRIMIDONE

It is a deoxybarbiturate, converted by liver to phenobarbitone and phenylethyl-malonamide so its mechanism of action is similar to phenobarbitone. Activity of primidone is mainly due to its metabolite because the plasma t½ of primidone is less than of its metabolites. Antiepileptic efficacy and side effect are similar to phenobarbitone. Additionally it is known to produce anemia, leukopenia and psychotic reaction. It is successfully used in generalised tonic-clonic seizures and partial seizures. It is adjuvant to phenytoin and carbamazepine.

CARBAMAZEPINE

It is chemically related to imipramine and was initially use as an antiseizure agent in 1974. It has been employed since the 1960s for the treatment of trigeminal neuralgia. It is now considered to be a primary drug for the treatment of partial and tonic-clonic seizures. It is therapeutically useful in manic-depressive patients. Carbamazepine produces antidiuretic effects by enhancing ADH action.

Mechanism of Action

Mechanism of carbamazepine is similar to phenytoin. It inhibits the repetitive firing of action potential of spinal cord which is mediated by voltage gated sodium channel. The metabolite of carbamazepine also contributes to action of carbamazepine by inhibiting the repetitive firing.

Pharmacokinetic Properties

Carbamazepine is absorbed slowly and peak concentrations in plasma usually are observed 4 to 8 hours after administration. It is distributed in all tissue. The plasma protein binding is found to be 75%. It is metabolised hepatically by cytochrome enzyme to active metabolite 10, 11-epoxide which is further metabolised to inactive compounds, which are excreted in the urine principally as glucuronides. Carbamazepine is also inactivated by conjugation and hydroxylation.

Drug Interactions

- Carbamazepine is enzyme inducer thus drugs which are hepatically metabolised can be more rapidly degraded thus the efficacy is reduced when coadministered with it. e.g. the efficacy of oral contraceptives reduced when concurrently administered with carbamazepine.

- Metabolism of carbamazepine is induced by phenobarbitone, phenytoin and valproate and vice versa.

- Erythromycin, fluoxetine, isoniazide inhibits the metabolism of carbamazepine.

Adverse Effects

- At higher doses carbamazepine produce hyperirritability, convulsions, and respiratory depression. Chronic therapy to carbamazepine produces drowsiness, vertigo, ataxia, diplopia and blurred vision. There is increase in the frequency of seizures at overdose of carbamazepine.

- Other adverse effects include nausea, vomiting, serious hematological toxicity (aplastic anemia, agranulocytosis), and hypersensitivity reactions (dermatitis, eosinophilia, lymphadenopathy, splenomegaly).

- They are also found to elevate the hepatic transaminase with carbamazepine. There is also incidence of minor foetal malformation with carbamazepine therapy.

Therapeutic uses

- Use in generalised tonic-clonic and both simple and complex partial seizures.

- Use in Trigeminal and glossopharyngeal neuralgias.

- Use in Bipolar affective disorders (mania).

OXCARBAZEPINE

Oxcarbazepine is prodrug of carbamazepine which is immediately converted to active metabolite; a 10-mono-hydroxy derivative, which is inactivated by glucuronide conjugation and eliminated by renal excretion. Its mechanism of action is similar to that of carbamazepine. Similar to carbamazepine it induces the hepatic microsomal enzyme which reduces the anticoagulant effect of warfarin and also reduces plasma levels of oral contraceptives.

ETHOSUXIMIDE

Ethosuximide is a primary agent for the treatment of absence seizures. The most prominent characteristic of ethosuximide at nontoxic doses is it protects against clonic motor seizures induced by pentylenetetrazol but does not inhibit tonic hindlimb extension of electroshock seizures or kindled seizures.

Mechanism of Action

It reduces the threshold of calcium current in thalamic neurons without modifying the sodium voltage dependence. Ethosuximide does not inhibit repetitive firing of action potential or enhance GABA responses at clinically relevant concentrations.

Pharmacokinetic Properties

It is absorbed orally and peak plasma concentration observed within 3 hours after a single oral dose. It is distributed all over the body and its concentration in the CSF is similar to that in plasma. It metabolises by hepatically by microsomal enzyme and excreted unchanged in urine.

Toxicity

- Gastrointestinal like nausea, vomiting and anorexia; and CNS effects including drowsiness, lethargy, euphoria, dizziness, headache and hiccough. Parkinson like symptoms and photophobia also has been reported.

- Restlessness, agitation, anxiety, aggressiveness, inability to concentrate, and other behavioural effects observed in psychiatric patients.

- Urticaria and other skin reactions, including Stevens-Johnson syndrome, as well as systemic lupus erythematosus, eosinophilia, leukopenia, thrombocytopenia, pancytopenia, and aplastic anemia also have been reported.

Therapeutic Uses

- Effective in absence seizures but not in tonic-clonic seizures.

VALPROIC ACID

Pharmacologically valproic acid is similar to phenytoin and carbamazepine. At nontoxic doses it inhibits tonic hindlimb extension in maximal electroshock seizures and kindled seizures. And at subtoxic doses it inhibits the clonic motor seizures induced by pentylenetetrazol.

Mechanism of Action

Similar to phenytoin and carbamazepine it inhibits repetitive firing of action potential induced by depolarisation of cortical or spinal cord neurons which are mediated through voltage gated sodium channel. It also reduces the threshold of calcium current at slightly higher concentration. Due to presence of these actions it may be effective against partial and tonic-clonic seizures and absence seizures respectively. Valproate also augments the release of inhibitory transmitter GABA probably by increasing its synthesis.

Pharmacokinetic properties

There is rapid oral absorption of valproic acid and peak plasma concentration is attained in 1 to 4 hours. It is 90% bound to plasma protein and distributed all over the body, apparent volume of distribution for valproate is about 0.2 L/kg. The concentration of valproate in CSF is equal to blood. Valproate metabolises hepatically and less than 5% is excreted unchanged in urine. The half-life of valproate is approximately 15 hours.

Adverse Effects

- Gastrointestinal symptoms, include anorexia, nausea and vomiting.
- The CNS related effects observed are sedation, ataxia and tremors.
- At chronic valproate therapy there are skin rashes, alopecia and stimulation of appetite and weight gain observed.
- In liver there is elevation of hepatic transaminase which results into hepatitis.
- There are also microvesicular steatosis without evidence of inflammation or hypersensitivity reaction.
- Acute pancreatitis and hyperammonemia also have been frequently associated with the use of valproic acid.
- Valproic acid can also produce teratogenic effects such as neural tube defects.

Drug Interactions

- Inhibit the metabolism of phenytoin, phenobarbital, lamotrigine and lorazepam

Therapeutic Uses

- Effective in the treatment of absence, myoclonic, partial and tonic-clonic seizures.

BENZODIAZEPINES

Benzodiazepines are primarily used as anxiolytic and sedative. At higher doses it is used as antiseizure. Diazepam and lorazepam are used in the management of status epilepticus. In animal experimental model clonazepam has reported to antagonizes the effects of pentylenetetrazol (PTZ) induced seizures while it do not produced any effects on seizures induced in maximal electroshock model.

Mechanism of Action

Benzodiazepines at non-sedating doses enhance the GABA-mediated synaptic inhibition. It increases the frequency of opening at GABA- activated chloride channel. At higher concentrations it decreases the firing of action potential of neurons which is similar to the effects of phenytoin, carbamazepine and valproate.

Pharmacokinetic properties

It is absorbed well orally and maximal plasma concentration is obtained within 1 to 4 hours. Due to high lipid solubility it is bound 99% to plasma protein. It is metabolised hepatically into N-desmethyl-diazepam. Both diazepam and N-desmethyl-diazepam are slowly hydroxylated to other active metabolites, such as Oxazepam. The half-life of diazepam in plasma is between 1 and 2 days, while that of N-desmethyl-diazepam is about 60 hours.

Clonazepam is metabolised principally by reduction of the nitro group to produce inactive 7-amino derivatives. The half-life of clonazepam in plasma is about 1 day. Lorazepam is metabolised chiefly by conjugation with glucuronic acid; its half-life in plasma is about 14 hours.

Adverse Effects

- Clonazepam produce drowsiness and lethargy. Muscular incordination and ataxia are less frequent.
- Other side effect includes hypotonia, dysarthria, dizziness, behavioural disturbances, aggression, hyperactivity, irritability and difficulty in concentration.
- Both anorexia and hyperphagia have been reported.
- Increased salivary and bronchial secretions may cause difficulties in children.
- Cardiovascular and respiratory depression may occur after the intravenous administration of diazepam, clonazepam or lorazepam, particularly if other antiseizure agents or central depressants have been administered previously.

Therapeutic Uses

- Clonazepam used in absence seizures and myoclonic seizures.
- Diazepam is used in treatment of status epilepticus because of its short duration of action, lorazepam is more frequently is used.

GABAPENTIN

Gabapentin is centrally active GABA agonist. Due to its high lipid solubility it easily crosses the blood brain barrier.

Mechanisms of Action

Gabapentin inhibits clonic and tonic hindlimb seizures by pentylenetetrazol and electroshock respectively. Gabapentin may act on GABA receptor and promote non vesicular release of neurotransmitter through a poorly understood mechanism. Gabapentin also binds with an amino acid sequence of the L type of voltage-sensitive Ca^{2+} channel while it does not affect the current of other type of calcium channels.

Pharmacokinetics

- It is absorbed orally and is not bound to plasma protein and is excreted unchanged in urine. Its half life is found to be 4 to 6 hours.

Therapeutic Uses

- Effective for partial seizures.

Adverse effect

- It is well tolerated; the most common adverse effects are dizziness, ataxia and fatigue.

LAMOTRIGINE

Lamotrigine is used in seizures induced by maximal electroshock also in partial and generalized seizures but not in clonic seizures which is induced by pentylenetetrazol.

Mechanism of action

It blocks the repeated firing of action potential of spinal cord mediated by voltage gated sodium channel similar to those of phenytoin and carbamazepine. This may well explain lamotrigine's actions on partial and secondarily generalised seizures.

Pharmacokinetics properties

It is absorbed completely at orally and metabolised primarily by glucuronidation. The plasma half-life of a single dose is 15 to 30 hours which is affected when coadministered with phenytoin, carbamazepine, or Phenobarbital. It reduces the half-life and plasma concentrations of lamotrigine while with valproate there is increase in plasma concentration of lamotrigine

Adverse effects

- When lamotrigine is used with other antiseizure drug it produces dizziness, ataxia, blurred or double vision, nausea, vomiting, and rash.

- It is also reported to produce Stevens-Johnson syndrome and disseminated intravascular coagulation with lamotrigine.

Therapeutic Use

- It is used in partial and secondarily generalised tonic-clonic seizures.

LEVETIRACETAM

It is new antiseizure agent for partial and secondarily generalised tonic-clonic seizures examined in the kindling model, while is ineffective against maximum electroshock- and pentylenetetrazol-induced seizures. The mechanism by which levetiracetam exerts these antiseizure effects is unknown.

Pharmacokinetics properties

Orally it is rapidly and completely absorbed and is not bound to plasma proteins. 95% of the drug and its inactive metabolite are excreted in the urine. As compared to other antiseizure there are no any interaction of leviracetam with other antiseizure drugs, oral contraceptives or anticoagulant because it neither induces nor substrate for cytochrome enzyme or glucuronidation for metabolism.

Therapeutic Use

- It is used for partial or generalised epilepsy.

Adverse Effects

- The drug is well tolerated. The most frequently reported adverse effects are somnolence, asthenia and dizziness.

TIAGABINE

In addition to other drug it is also approved for treating partial seizures. Tiagabine inhibits the GABA transporter and thereby reduces GABA uptake into neurons and glia. Tiagabine increases the duration of inhibitory synaptic currents in neuron of hippocampus. It prolongs the effect of GABA at inhibitory synapses through reducing its reuptake. Tiagabine inhibits maximum electroshock seizures and generalised tonic-clonic seizures in the kindling model, results suggestive of clinical efficacy against partial and tonic-clonic seizures.

Adverse effects: The common adverse effects are dizziness, somnolence, and tremor. Patients with a history of spike-and-wave discharges have been reported to have exacerbations of their EEG abnormalities.

TOPIRAMATE

Topiramate is a sulfamate-substituted monosaccharide. It reduces voltage-gated Na^+ currents similar to phenytoin. In addition, topiramate activates a hyperpolarizing K^+ current, enhances postsynaptic GABAA-receptor currents and also inhibit activation of the AMPA-kainate-subtype(s) of glutamate receptor. Topiramate is also a weak carbonic anhydrase inhibitor. Topiramate inhibits maximal electroshock and pentylenetetrazol-induced seizures as well as partial and secondarily generalized tonic-clonic seizures in the kindling model.

Pharmacokinetics properties

It is rapidly absorbed orally and binds to plasma protein, metabolised hepatically and excreted mainly unchanged in the urine. Its half-life is about 1 day.

Adverse Effects

- The most common adverse effects are somnolence, fatigue, weight loss and nervousness.

- It can precipitate renal calculi, which is most likely due to inhibition of carbonic anhydrase.

- There is also reported to produce cognitive impairment and change in the taste of carbonated beverages.

Drug interactions

- Concurrent administration with oral contraceptive reduces its plasma concentration suggesting the need for higher doses of oral contraceptives when coadministered with topiramate.

Therapeutic Use

- It is used in partial and primary generalised epilepsy.
- Effective as therapy for refractory partial epilepsy and refractory generalised tonic-clonic seizures.

FELBAMATE

Felbamate is found to be effective in both the maximal electroshock and pentylenetetrazol seizure models. Mechanically it inhibits NMDA-associated responses and potentiates GABA-mediated responses. Due to this dual action, it may contribute in partial and secondarily generalised seizures.

ZONISAMIDE

Zonisamide is a sulfonamide derivative and inhibits the T-type Ca^{2+} currents. In addition it also inhibits repetitive firing of spinal cord neurons mediated by voltage gated sodium channel similar to actions of phenytoin and carbamazepine. Zonisamide inhibits tonic hindlimb extension evoked by maximal electroshock and inhibits both partial and secondarily generalised seizures in the kindling model while it does not inhibit minimal clonic seizures induced by pentylenetetrazol, suggesting that the drug will not be effective clinically against myoclonic seizures.

Pharmacokinetics properties

It is completely absorbed orally and has a long half-life (about 63 hours), and is about 40% bound to plasma protein. Approximately 85% of an oral dose is excreted in the urine.

Therapeutic Uses

- It is used in refractory partial seizures.

Adverse Effects

- The most common adverse effects are somnolence, ataxia, anorexia, nervousness and fatigue.
- It is also found that 1% of individuals develop renal calculi due to inhibitory activity on carbonic anhydrase.

ACETAZOLAMIDE

- It is carbonic anhydrase inhibitor proven effective in absence seizures. Adverse effects are minimal when it is used in moderate dosage for limited periods.

USES OF ANTI-EPILEPTICS IN SPECIAL GROUPS

In Pregnancy

- There is increased risk of birth defects due to use of antiepileptic drugs during pregnancy. The risk observed is higher in first trimester with use of valproate and carbamazepine. Therefore, antiepileptic drugs should not be used in women of childbearing potential unless clearly indicated clinically for the treatment of epilepsy.
- Some antiepileptics may precipitate megaloblastic anemia by interfering with folic acid metabolism. Thus, supplemented with folic acid when women of childbearing potential receive antiepileptics.
- There are hemorrhagic complications like maternal and neonatal hemorrhage due to use of antiepileptics in pregnancy because of vitamin K depletion. Treatment of the mother with vitamin K during the last 4 weeks of pregnancy, and of the newborn at birth, appears to reduce hemorrhagic complications to antiepileptics.

In Breast-feeding

- Most of the antiepileptic drugs are excreted in breast milk. Ethosuximide reaches relatively high concentrations in breast milk and frequently attains therapeutic concentrations in the infant's blood.

In Children

- Most of the antiepileptic drugs have been used extensively in children. There are few pharmacokinetic and safety data pertinent to neonates and young infants; phenobarbital has been used most extensively in this group, but other primary antiepileptic drugs are commonly used.

In Elderly

- There is little information available regarding drug pharmacokinetics, safety and efficacy in elderly. The elderly are more sensitive to dose-related adverse effects.

The clearance of drug like phenytoin, gabapentin decreases in elderly and is probably due to decline in proportion to the age-related decline in renal function thus there is need to reduce the doses of drug in elderly. Starting dosages should generally be lower in the elderly and regular clinical follow-up should be scheduled to survey for both desired and undesired drug effects.

Seizure Type	Drugs of Choice	Alternative
Partial-onset seizures		
Simple and complex Partial seizures	Carbamazepine or phenytoin	**Monotherapy:** Oxcarbazepine, phenobarbital, primidone, topiramate
	or valproate or lamotrigine	**Adjunctive therapy:** Gabapentin, levetiracetam, topiramate, tiagabine, Zonisamide
Secondarily generalized seizures	Carbamazepine or phenytoin	**Monotherapy:** Oxcarbazepine, phenobarbital, primidone, topiramate
	or valproate or lamotrigine	**Adjunctive therapy:** Gabapentin, levetiracetam, tiagabine, zonisamide
Generalized-onset seizures		
Tonic-clonic	Valproate	Carbamazepine, phenytoin, phenobarbital, primidone, felbamate, topiramate (adjunctive), lamotrigine (adjunctive)
Absence	Ethosuximide or valproate	Clonazepam, lamotrigine (adjunctive)
Myoclonic	Valproate	Clonazepam, Zonisamide
Tonic	Valproate	Felbamate, clonazepam, topiramate (adjunctive), lamotrigine (adjunctive)
Atonic	Valproate	Felbamate, clonazepam, ethosuximide, topiramate (adjunctive), lamotrigine (adjunctive)

Questions on this Chapter

1. Discuss in detail the different types of seizures.

2. Explain in detail the cellular mechanisms of seizures formation.

3. Write the classification of anticonvulsant and add note on phenytoin.

4. Explain the pharmacology of GABAergic inhibitors in treatment of seizures.

5. Discuss the pharmacology of sodium channel inactivators in treatment of seizures.

6. Write the treatment of seizures in special groups.

Chapter 11

PHARMACOTHERAPY OF PARKINSON'S DISEASE

Objectives

After reading this chapter, the student will be able to:

➢ Identify the cardinal features of Parkinson's disease
➢ Understand the possible cause of Parkinson's disease
➢ Understand the role of L-Aromatic Amino Acid Decarboxylase (AADC) in the dopaminergic nerve terminals
➢ Understand the catecholamine synthetic pathway
➢ Understand the use of Carbidopa along with levodopa

INTRODUCTION

- Parkinson's disease (PD) is often referred to as a chronic neurodegenerative disorder involving primarily the dopaminergic nigrostriatal input to the basal ganglia.

- PD is a disorder that affects numerous and diverse sub-populations of neurons throughout the brain and may actually progress in a caudal-to-rostral fashion from the inferior brainstem to the cerebral hemispheres.

- This is a critical point when considering the approaches that we take towards symptomatic therapies for PD, and in understanding the lack of responsiveness of many motor and non-motor features of PD to modern dopaminergic treatments.

Causes of Parkinson's Disease

- Viral infection
- Blows to the head
- Brain infection
- Atherosclerosis
- Exposure to certain drugs
- Environmental factors

Clinical Features of PD

There are various features of PD; the primary features are tremor, rigidity and bradykinesia while others are anteroflexed posture, postural instability, freezing/festinating gait, poor balance and frequent falls on floor. There are also problem of walking, drooling and speech is affected, mask like expression. If PD is untreated, the symptoms progress over several years to end stage disease in which the patient is rigid, unable to move, unable to breathe properly.

PD usually progresses gradually as a "triad" of tremor, rigidity and bradykinesia, although many other motor and non-motor symptoms/signs are common. The "cardinal" motor features are:

- **Tremor:** Usually a unilateral resting tremor of the hands/arms or feet/legs, or a jaw tremor. Head tremor is very atypical.

- **Rigidity:** Usually appendicular >> axial, unilateral at onset, and "cog-wheeling" in quality (the resistance to passive movement appears to start and stop through the full range of motion of the joint). The abnormal tone may be noticed by patients as "stiffness" or "dragging" of a limb, and by observers as diminished arm swing with gait.

- **Bradykinesia:** Slowness and reduced amplitude of movement. This is noticed as slow gait, reduced blink frequency, blunted facial expressions etc.

- **Postural instability, freezing, gait imbalance:** These are usually late manifestations of the disease, but are very disabling and poorly responsive to medication.

- Although tremor, rigidity and bradykinesia are often responsive to dopamine replacement therapy, patients usually become less responsive to medication as the disease progresses.

- In addition, later disease stages are typically complicated by motor fluctuations (with treatment responsive "on" and unresponsive "off" phases) and dyskinesias (hyperkinetic, "fidgety," choreiform movements) that require more "creative" management strategies.

- Other motor features, such as postural instability, freezing, and gait imbalance, are typically not responsive to modern medical therapy.

- Many non-motor features of PD are also very disabling: depression, anxiety, daytime fatigue, disrupted sleep architecture, visual disturbances, gastrointestinal problems, autonomic disturbances, and cognitive decline, to name a few.

- Most non-motor manifestations do not respond to the treatments used for motor problems.

Dopamine receptors

- Dopamine receptors exist in 2 families, denoted D_1-like (D_1 and D_5 receptors) and D_2-like (D_2, D_3, and D_4 receptors), with the D_2 receptor itself appearing to be the most important for PD therapy.

- The D_1-like receptor family activates adenylate cyclase via Gs (stimulation of G protein) to increase cAMP, the D_2-like family inhibits adenylate cyclase via Gi (inhibition of G protein) to decrease cAMP.

Dopamine Receptors: D_1

D_1 receptors are found primarily on dendrites of neurons in the striatum and subthalamic nucleus. Role of D_1 receptors in PD therapy not as clear as that of D_2 receptors. Activation of D_1 receptors increases cAMP. D_1 activation appears to stimulate direct pathway putaminal GABA/dynorphin neurons that project to the GPi.

Dopamine Receptors: D2

D_2 receptors are found primarily on dendrites of neurons in the striatum, substantia nigra pars compacta, ventral tegmental area and STN. D_2 receptors play the major role in PD therapy. Activation of D_2 receptor family members (D_{2-5}) decreases cAMP. D_2 activation appears to inhibit indirect pathway putaminal GABA/enkephalin neurons that project to the GPe.

CLASSIFICATION

The main hallmark of Parkinson's is deficiency of dopamine in brain. Thus Levodopa is used to correct the state of dopamine deficiency because the dopamine its does not able to cross the blood brain barrier. Recently a number of levodopa potentiators and dopamine agonist have been developed as adjuvants (Fig. 11.1).

(I) Drug Affecting Brain Dopaminergic System.

- **Dopamine Precursor:** Levodopa

- **Peripheral Decarboxylase Inhibitors:** Carbidopa, Benserazide.

- **Dopaminergic Agonist:** Bromocriptine, Pergolide, Piribedil, Ropinirole, Pramipexole.

- **MAO-B Inhibitor:** Selegeline

- **COMT Inhibitor:** Entacapone, Tolacapone.

- **Dopamine Facilitator:** Amantadine

(II) Drug Affecting Brain Cholinergic System

- Central anticholinergic: Trihexyphenidyl, Procyclidine, Biperiden.

- Antihistaminic: Orphenadrine, Promethazine.

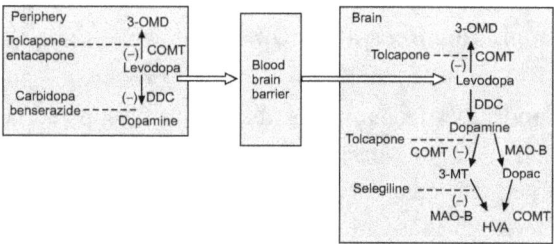

Fig. 11.1: Site of action of Antiparkinsonism

Levodopa

- This is the most effective agent for PD regarding symptomatic control of tremor, rigidity and bradykinesia, and was the first major advance in PD therapy. It is not helpful for postural instability, freezing and balance problems that complicate the later stages of disease progression.

- Dopamine (DA), the "major deficient neurotransmitter" in PD, does not cross the blood-brain barrier (BBB) and cannot therefore be directly supplemented in patients.

- Its orally bioavailable precursor, levodopa, does cross the BBB, where it can be converted to DA via L-Aromatic Amino Acid Decarboxylase (AADC) in the dopaminergic nerve terminals of the striatum.

- However, AADC is found so abundantly in the periphery (gut) that up to 99% of an oral dose of levodopa will be decarboxylated prior to having a chance to cross the BBB, leaving only ~1% available for use in the brain. Thus, historically, large doses of levodopa need to be administered to be symptomatically effective, producing not only anti-PD relief but also significant nausea, vomiting and other peripheral dopaminergic side effects.

Pharmacokinetics

- Levodopa has an onset of clinical action of ~30 minutes and a half-life of ~50 minutes.

- It is absorbed in the small bowel by active amino acid transport, thus, reduced gastric emptying time, low gastric pH and high protein meals will reduce its absorption speed and efficiency.

- A large number of dopamine metabolites are known; most are excreted in the urine. The various metabolites are given in Fig. 11.2.

Adverse Effects

At Initial therapy

- The potential side effects of levodopa are similar to the DA agonists, and occur in a dose-dependent fashion: nausea, vomiting, fatigue/somnolence, hypotension, orthostasis, vivid dreams, psychosis, hallucinations, confusion, hypersexuality and cramps.

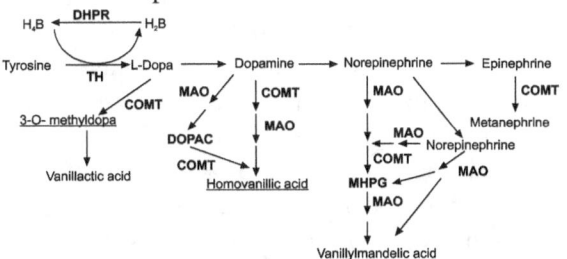

Fig. 11.2: Catecholamine metabolic pathway

Catecholamine metabolic pathways: TH = tyrosine hydroxylase (the major rate-limiting enzyme), L-DOPA = L-dihydroxy-phenyla-lanine, COMT = catechol-O-methyl transferase, MAO = monamine oxidase, DOPAC = dihydro-xyphenylacetic acid, B4H = tetrahydrobiopterin

- As with the other dopaminergic drugs, the risk of side effects and their severity can be diminished by starting at a low dose and slowly titrating up of levodopa.

- Peripheral decarboxylation of levodopa and release of dopamine into the circulation may activate vascular dopamine receptors and produce orthostatic hypotension. The actions of dopamine at α and β adrenergic receptors may induce cardiac arrhythmias, especially in patients with pre-existing conduction disturbances.

- A common and troubling adverse effect is the induction of hallucinations and confusion; these effects are particularly common in the elderly and in those with pre-existing cognitive dysfunction and often limit the ability to treat parkinsonian symptoms adequately.

At prolonged therapy

- Levodopa has a theoretical risk of "activating" melanoma, so should probably

not be used in such patients, and withdrawal of this and the other dopaminergic drugs should occur over a period of at least 7 days to decrease the risk of precipitating a neuroleptic malignant-like syndrome (potentially life-threatening hyper-stimulation syndrome of dysautonomia, hyperpyrexia and rigidity).

- Despite its effectiveness against PD, most patients taking levodopa will develop motor fluctuations and/or dyskinesias at some point in their life as a function of total time on the medication and total dose. There is evidence that delaying the use of levodopa may delay the onset of motor fluctuations and dyskinesias.

Drug Interactions

- Administration of levodopa with nonspecific inhibitors of MAO, such as phenelzine and tranylcypromine, markedly increase the actions of levodopa and may precipitate life-threatening hypertensive crisis and hyperpyrexia; nonspecific MAO inhibitors always should be discontinued at least 14 days before administration of levodopa

- Pyridoxine: abolishes therapeutic effect by enhancing peripheral decarboxylation of levodopa, less is available to cross BBB.

- Antihypertensive agents and levodopa attenuated posture hypotension.

- Atropine and other anticholinergic drugs have additive antiparkinsonism effect with low doses of levodopa.

- Phenothiazines, butyrophenones, metoclo-pramide reverse therapeutic effect by blocking DA receptors.

- Reserpine abolishes levodopa action by preventing entry of DA into synaptic vesicle.

Carbidopa

- The second major advance in PD therapy came with the discovery of carbidopa, an inhibitor of AADC that does not itself cross the BBB.

- The effect of combining carbidopa with levodopa is that peripheral conversion to DA is significantly diminished, but central conversion is not affected. Thus, levodopa can be effectively concentrated within the brain, decreasing the total oral dosage needed for symptomatic relief by at least 70%, and diminishing the potential for nausea, vomiting, and severe hypotension caused by high levels of peripheral DA.

- The addition of carbidopa increases the half-life of levodopa to ~90 minutes, and significantly extends the symptomatic drug action, but does not affect the time to onset of clinical effect.

- The development of extended-release versions of carbidopa-levodopa further extend the length of time of drug action, but at the expense of prolonged time to onset of action (~90 minutes) and reduced oral absorption fidelity (~70% of regular Sinemet a combination of carbidopa-levodopa).

DOPAMINE AGONISTS

- Dopamine agonists are useful for PD-related tremor, rigidity and bradykinesia. They may play a "protective" role against the development of motor complications and dyskinesias in later stages of PD (due to sustained, non-pulsatile activation of DA receptors), and may have "neuroprotective" properties against disease progression via non-dopaminergic mechanisms. For these reasons, many physicians use DA agonists as their first-line therapy in PD.

- The DA agonists are divided into ergotamine and non-ergotamine groups, with the latter being most heavily used by physicians today due to the lower incidence of side effects.

Catecholamine Synthesis

Tyrosine hydroxylase is the rate-limiting enzyme in catecholamine synthesis. The synthetic pathway given in Fig. 11.3.

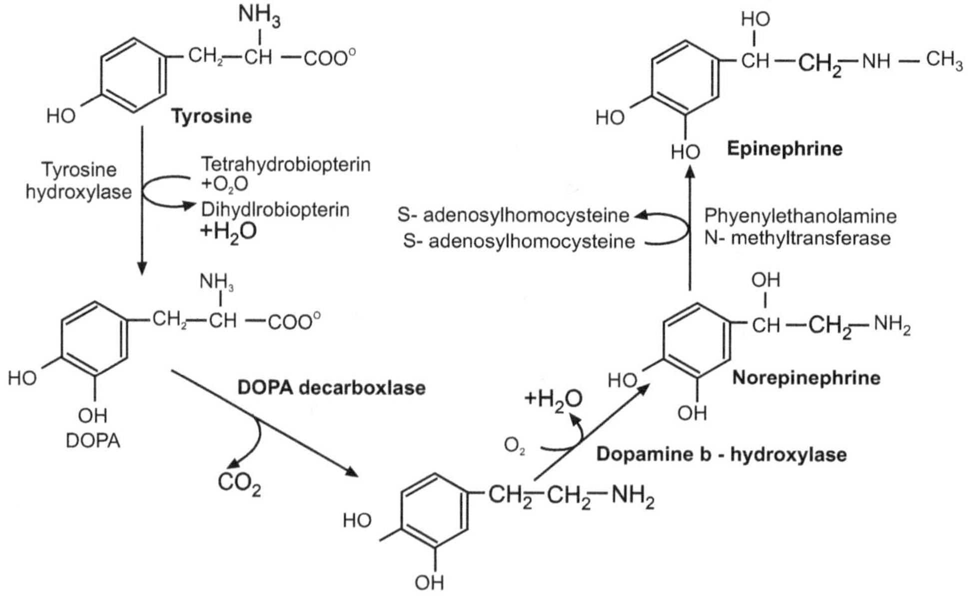

Fig. 11.3: Biosynthesis of catecholamine

Limitations

- Compared with levodopa, these agents are generally less effective for symptomatic therapy against the cardinal motor features of PD, less likely to produce dyskinesias themselves, and more likely to cause "dopaminergic" side effects such as neuropsychiatric disturbances (confusion and hallucinations), sedation, dizziness, dyspnea (trouble breathing), leg edema (diuretic insensitive), hypotension (sometimes acute), and orthostasis (position-dependent hypotension).

- A particularly notable potential problem is the so-called "sleep attack," a sudden overwhelming sleepiness that occurs without warning or without a sufficient prodrome to allow for appropriate protective measures to be taken.

Pergolide and Bromocriptine

These are DA "ergot" agonists with broad dopaminergic and non-dopaminergic agonist properties, acting on $D_3 > D_2 >> D_{1, 4, 5}$ dopamine receptors as well as on $5\text{-}HT_{1/2}$ serotonergic receptors and alpha 1/2 adrenergic receptors. These agents have hepatic metabolism and, in addition to the dopaminergic side effects listed above, they exhibit ergot-specific effects such as Raynaud's phenomenon, serous fibrosis, pericarditis, pericardial effusion, cardiac valvulopathy and rhinitis/cough.

Pramipexole and Ropinirole

These are DA "non-ergot" agonists with more specific activity on $D_3 > D_{2, 4}$ not D_1 or D_5 receptors. 5-HT and alpha adrenergic activity is essentially absent. These agents have long half-lives of up to 8 hours, high oral bioavailability, and steady state plasma levels are reached within 2 days (4-5 half-lives). Approximately 90% of a pramipexole dose is eventually excreted unchanged by the kidneys, whereas ropinirole exhibits hepatic metabolism like the other DA agonists. In addition to their potential dopaminergic side effect profiles, pramipexole and ropinirole may cause uncontrolled impulsive behaviours such as hypersexuality. On the brighter side, these agonists may be used as potent anti-depressant agents as fluoxetine/Prozac. They appear to "delay" the onset of motor fluctuations and dyskinesias in PD patients (compared to levodopa) and may have neuroprotective properties.

Apomorphine

- It is a dopaminergic agonist and has high affinity for D_4 receptors; moderate affinity for D_2, D_3, D_5, and low affinity for D_1 receptors. There is also some affinity toward adrenergic receptors.

- Apomorphine is highly emetogenic and it requires antiemetic therapy prior and post treatment of apomorphine.

- The side effects of apomorphine include QT prolongation, abuse reaction, pain at site of injection, at frequent dosing cause hallucinations, dyskinesia and abnormal behaviour. Because of these potential adverse effects, use of apomorphine is appropriate only when other measures, such as oral dopamine agonists or COMT inhibitors, have failed to control the "off" episodes.

MONO AMINO OXIDASE (MAO)

There are two isoenzymes of monoamine oxidase MAO-A and MAO-B. The MAO-B is predominant in the stratum and responsible for most of the oxidative metabolism of dopamine in the brain. Inhibition of MAO-B enzyme results in inhibition of dopamine metabolism. Examples of this enzyme inhibitor are given as follows.

MAO-B Inhibitors

Selegiline

Selegiline inhibits the MAO-B enzyme thus no enzyme available in striatum for metabolism of dopamine, resulting in increased in the availability and prolonging in activity of dopamine in striatum. MAO-B inhibitors selectively inhibit the "B" form of the enzyme thus reducing in the MAO-A related "cheese effect" (potentially life-threating "hyper-activation" autonomic state with hypertension, hyperpyrexia, and seizures). The reactions are associated with the consumption of foods containing tyramine or combined therapy with some anti-depressant and catecholaminergic agents. Thus, the judicious combination of these agents with levodopa and DA agonists is generally safe, although typically not very clinically effective in practice.

CATECHOL-O-METHYL TRANSFERASE (COMT) INHIBITORS

- These agents also reduce dopamine catabolism, increasing its striatal availability, and effectively prolong the half-life of levodopa to "smooth out" its clinical effect.

- "On" time ("no" symptoms) is generally increased, "off" time (PD symptoms) decreased, and side effects are generally dopaminergic (levodopa doses may therefore need to be lowered).

- The main agent available for use in clinical practice is entacapone, and its "sister" agent tolcapone having similar mechanism of action is a reversible inhibitor of peripheral COMT.

- Tolcapone has a relatively long duration of action, allowing for administration two to three times a day, and appears to act by both central and peripheral inhibition of COMT.

- The duration of action of entacapone is short, around 2 hours, so it usually is administered simultaneously with each dose of levodopa/carbidopa.

- The action of entacapone is attributable principally to peripheral inhibition of COMT.

- The common adverse effects of these agents are similar to those observed in patients treated with levodopa/carbidopa alone and include nausea, orthostatic hypotension, vivid dreams, confusion, and hallucinations.

- An important adverse effect associated with tolcapone is hepatotoxicity.

DOPAMINE FACILITATOR

Amantadine

- It is an antiviral agent used in treatment of Influenza A and also has Antiparkinsonism activity. Pharmacologically amantadine alters the dopamine release in brain. This mechanism is thought to be involved in Antiparkinsonism effect of amantadine. Additionally it has anticholinergic property.

- The most significant action of amantadine may be its ability to block NMDA glutamate receptors which correlates to its antidyskinetic property.

- It is used in treatment of mild Parkinsonism disease.

- Amantadine usually is administered in a dose of 100 mg twice a day and is well tolerated.

- Adverse effects like dizziness, lethargy, anticholinergic effects, and sleep disturbance, as well as nausea and vomiting, have been observed occasionally with Amantadine.

MUSCARINIC RECEPTOR ANTAGONISTS

Several muscarinic antagonists used in the treatment of PD, including trihexyphenidyl, benztropine mesylate and diphenhydramine hydrochloride. Diphenhydramine also is a histamine H_1 antagonist. All have modest antiparkinsonian activity that is useful in the treatment of early PD or as an adjunct to dopamimetic therapy. The adverse effects of these agents due to their anticholinergic properties. Mostly they show sedation and mental confusion, constipation, urinary retention and blurred vision.

Questions on this Chapter

1. Give the classification of Antiparkinsonism agents and add note on Carbidopa.

2. Discuss the pharmacology of Levodopa.

3. Discuss the role of MAO inhibitors in PD.

Chapter 12

PHARMACOTHERAPY OF ALZHEIMER'S DISEASE

Objectives

After reading this chapter, the student will be able to:

➤ Understand the causes for Alzheimer's Disease.

➤ Understand the clinical manifestation of Alzheimer's disease

➤ Learn about the neurotransmitters involved in process of memory

➤ Justify the use of cholinesterase inhibitors in symptomatic treatment of Alzheimer's disease.

Alzheimer's is a neurodegenerative disease of the brain that causes problems with memory, thinking and behaviour. It is not a normal part of aging. Alzheimer's gets worse over time. Although symptoms can vary widely, the first problem many people notice is forgetfulness that is severe enough to affect their ability to function at home or at work, or to enjoy lifelong hobbies. The disease may cause a person to become confused, lost in familiar places, misplace things or have trouble with language.

PATHOPHYSIOLOGY OF AD

• AD is characterised by the formation of senile plaques, which are spherical accumulations of the β-amyloid protein accompanied by degenerating neuronal processes which is the main feature of AD.

• There is marked impairment of memory and reasoning ability.

• There are neuronal losses of many neurotransmitter substances. The selective deficiency of acetylcholine in AD, as well as the observation that central cholinergic antagonists such as atropine can induce a confusional state bears some resemblance to the dementia of AD.

• It is important to note that the deficit in AD is far more complex, involving multiple neurotransmitter systems, including serotonin, glutamate, and neuropeptides, and that in AD there is destruction of not only cholinergic neurons but also the cortical and hippocampal targets that receive cholinergic input.

CAUSES AND RISK FACTORS

Alzheimer's disease involves the failure of nerve cells, why this happens is still not known. However, they have identified certain risk factors that increase the likelihood of developing Alzheimer's.

Age

The greatest known risk factor for Alzheimer's is increasing age. Most individuals with the illness are 65 and older. The likelihood of developing

Alzheimer's approximately doubles every five years after age 65. After age 85, the risk reaches nearly 50 percent.

Family History and Genetics

Another risk factor is family history. Research has shown that those who have a parent, brother or sister with Alzheimer's are two to three times more likely to develop the disease. The risk increases if more than one family member has the illness.

Scientists have so far identified one gene that increases the risk of Alzheimer's but does not guarantee an individual will develop the disorder. Research has also revealed certain rare genes that virtually guarantee an individual will develop Alzheimer's. The genes that directly cause the disease have been found in only a few hundred extended families worldwide and account for less than 5 percent of cases. Experts believe the vast majority of cases are caused by a complex combination of genetic and non-genetic influences.

Aluminium

During the 1960s and 1970s, aluminum emerged as a possible suspect in causing Alzheimer's disease. This suspicion led to concerns about everyday exposure to aluminum through sources such as cooking pots, foil, beverage cans, antacids and antiperspirants. Since then, studies have failed to confirm any role for aluminum in causing Alzheimer's. Almost all scientists today focus on other areas of research, and few experts believe that everyday sources of aluminum pose any threat.

Other Risk Factors

Age, family history and genetics are all risk factors we can't change. Now, research is beginning to reveal clues about other risk factors that we may be able to influence. There appears to be a strong link between serious head injury and future risk of Alzheimer's. It's important to protect your head by buckling your seat belt, wearing your helmet when participating in sports and "fall-proofing" your home.

One promising line of research suggests that strategies for overall healthy aging may help keep the brain healthy and may even offer some protection against Alzheimer's. These measures include eating a healthy diet; staying socially active; avoiding tobacco and excess alcohol; and exercising both body and mind.

Some of the strongest evidence links brain health to heart health. The risk of developing Alzheimer's or vascular dementia appears to be increased by many conditions that damage the heart and blood vessels. These include heart disease; diabetes; stroke and high blood pressure; or high cholesterol. Work with your doctor to monitor your heart health and treat any problems that arise.

Studies of donated brain tissue provide additional evidence for the heart-head connection. These studies suggest that plaques and tangles are more likely to cause Alzheimer symptoms if strokes or damage to the brain's blood vessels are also present.

SIGNS AND SYMPTOMS OF ALZHEIMER'S DISEASE

It may be hard to know the difference between a typical age-related change and the first sign of Alzheimer's disease. Ask yourself: Is this something new? For example, if the person was never good at balancing a checkbook, struggling with this task is probably not a warning sign. But if their ability to balance a checkbook has changed a lot, it is something to share with a doctor. Some people may recognize changes in themselves before anyone else notices. Other times, friends and family will be the first to observe changes in the person's memory, behaviour or abilities. To help, the Alzheimer's Association has created this list of warning signs for Alzheimer's disease. Every individual may experience one or more of these in different degrees. If you notice any of them, please see a doctor.

1. Memory loss that disrupt daily life

One of the most common signs of Alzheimer's, especially in the early stages, is forgetting recently learned information. Others include forgetting important dates or events; asking for the same information over and over; relying on memory aides (e.g., reminder notes or electronic devices) or family members for things they used to handle on their own.

2. Challenges in planning or solving problems

Some people may experience changes in their ability to develop and follow a plan or work with numbers. They may have trouble following a familiar recipe or keeping track of monthly bills. They may have difficulty concentrating and take much longer to do things than they did before.

3. Difficulty completing familiar tasks at home, at work or at leisure

People with Alzheimer's disease often find it hard to complete daily tasks. Sometimes, people may have trouble driving to a familiar location, managing a budget at work or remembering the rules of a favourite game.

4. Confusion with time or place

People with Alzheimer's can lose track of dates, seasons and the passage of time. They may have trouble understanding something if it is not happening immediately. Sometimes they may forget where they are or how they got there.

5. Trouble understanding visual images and spatial relationships

For some people, having vision problems is a sign of Alzheimer's. They may have difficulty reading, judging distance and determining colour or contrast. In terms of perception, they may pass a mirror and think someone else is in the room. They may not realise they are the person in the mirror.

6. New problems with words in speaking or writing

People with Alzheimer's may have trouble following or joining a conversation. They may stop in the middle of a conversation and have no idea how to continue or they may repeat themselves. They may struggle with vocabulary, have problems finding the right word or call things by the wrong name (e.g., calling a watch a "hand-clock").

7. Misplacing things and losing the ability to retrace steps

A person with Alzheimer's disease may put things in unusual places. They may lose things and be unable to go back over their steps to find them again. Sometimes, they may accuse others of stealing. This may occur more frequently over time.

8. Decreased or poor judgment

People with Alzheimer's may experience changes in judgment or decision-making. For example, they may use poor judgment when dealing with money, giving large amounts to telemarketers. They may pay less attention to grooming or keeping themselves clean.

9. Withdrawal from work or social activities

A person with Alzheimer's may start to remove themselves from hobbies, social activities, work projects or sports. They may have trouble keeping up with a favourite sports team or remembering how to complete a favorite hobby. They may also avoid being social because of the changes they have experienced.

10. Changes in mood and personality

The mood and personality of people with Alzheimer's can change. They can become confused, suspicious, depressed, fearful or anxious. They may be easily upset at home, at work, with friends or in places where they are out of their comfort zone.

TREATMENT OF ALZHEIMER'S DISEASE

At present, there is no cure for the treatment available for Alzheimer's disease, while the symptomatic therapy can manage the disease and provide the better quality of life. In addition to symptomatic therapy, physical exercise and social activity are important to maintain overall good health. Modification of the living environment of the affected person can help to maintain comfort and dignity.

A. Non-Pharmacological Approaches

The major approach for the people with Alzheimer's is to compensate for cognitive capacity that decline in patient by providing friendly environment, helping hand, activities, communication and programme. There are the following treatment domains that can compensate the cognitive dysfunction in Alzheimer's.

Physical Environment Treatment Plan: Physical environment promotes safety and reduces fear regarding cognition. The physical environmental strategy proven effectively in improving resident behaviour and improving levels of brain functioning. It is a natural mapping process in which it is helpful in providing the knowledge necessary for correct use of things by the user. It promotes feelings of security and mastery, decreased level of frustration.

Accepting Nature: The most important cornerstone of non-pharmacological treatment is to understand and to help the patient of Alzheimer's. There is need for strong communication between the people with limited words of recognition. There is always helping hand to the patients of Alzheimer's as well as to support and provide the justification for everything to reduce the fear.

Motivation: This involves

- Maintaining positive emotion as well as assisting with activities of daily living of Alzheimer's patients.

- Providing a helping hand and motivating the patients that he or she can do things for themselves.
- Use specific skill and strategy to ensure that the person with Alzheimer's is participating in his/her own care activities.

Therapeutic activities and programming: People with dementia experience more psychiatric symptoms such as anxiety, depression, delusion and hallucinations. Thus plan such therapeutic activities and programme that can change the negative emotions quickly and promote the feelings of success. The caregivers plan success oriented activities that focus on patient's cognitive strengths and avoid skills that expose their weakness.

Self-control Behaviours: This type of treatment therapy focuses on the behaviors of patients rather than their emotions. There are a number of factors that can trigger negative thoughts in the patient, thus such factors have to be first identified and eliminated so there may reduction in unpleasant behavior. There are various techniques that are reported to reduce the behavioral disturbances in a patient of Alzheimer's. Thus the behavior of patient has to be analysed for their negative feelings and thoughts and such intervention planned that can manipulate the triggering factors.

Communication modalities: There are multiple communication strategies that can be used such as use of familiar music, touching sensation, smell of certain food and use of non-verbal perception in Alzheimer's. There is impairment of receptive and expressive language abilities in Alzheimer's. Thus the communication with such patient is not done with words. Communication should be done with look, tone and hug that reflect the feelings of safety and personal care.

B. Pharmacological Approaches

It is important to remember that there is no medicine available for complete treatment of Alzheimer's. There are several prescription drugs currently approved by U.S. Food and Drug Administration (FDA) for symptomatic relief in Alzheimer's. Symptomatic treatment of Alzheimer's may help the patients with comfort, dignity and independence for longer period of time. Such treatment can also assist and encourage the caregivers.

The main approach toward treatment of AD is to improve the cholinergic transmission in the brain. Recently several clinical trials shown that the anticholinesterase increases the level of acetyl choline in brain by preventing its breakdown through cholinesterase enzyme.

Some studies on Physostigmine indicate that there is temporary improvement in memory following physostigmine in patients with AD. There is limited use of physostigmine in Alzheimer's because of its short half-life and tendency to produce symptoms of systemic cholinergic excess at therapeutic doses.

Other anticholinesterases are tacrine, donepezil, rivastigmine and galantamine: Reports of all these agents' show that they improve the memory performance of Alzheimer's. There are reported side effects of tacrine such as abdominal cramps, anorexia, nausea, vomiting, and diarrhea at therapeutic dose level. As there is also reported literature of elevations of serum transaminases due to these side effects, tacrine is not used widely. Instead of tacrine, donepezil, rivastigmine and galantamine show similar improvement in memory. Comparatively there are less frequent and less severe side effects than those observed with tacrine; they include nausea, diarrhea, vomiting, and insomnia.

Treatment for Mild to Moderate Alzheimer's

Drugs like cholinesterase inhibitors may delay or prevent behaviour symptoms especially cognitive related. The drugs includes rivastigmine, donepezil, galantamine, tacrine. Anticholinestrase agents are also used in the treatment of Alzheimer's. These drugs prevent the breakdown of acetylcholine (neuro-transmitter involved in memory and thinking). In Alzheimer's there is less amount of acetylcholine in brain therefore the problem of cognitive decline. Cholinesterase inhibitors prevent the hydrolysis of acetylcholine and thereby increase the level and improve the cognitive performance.

Drug name	Category	Actions
Memantine	N-methyl D-aspartate (NMDA) antagonist	Blocks the toxic effects associated with excess glutamate and regulates glutamate activation
Galantamine	Cholinesterase inhibitor	Prevents the hydrolysis of acetylcholine and stimulates nicotinic receptors to release more acetylcholine in the brain
Rivastigmine	Cholinesterase inhibitor	Prevents the breakdown of acetylcholine and butyrylcholine (a brain chemical similar to acetylcholine) in the brain
Donepezil	Cholinesterase inhibitor	Prevents the breakdown of acetylcholine in the brain

Treatment for Moderate to Severe Alzheimer's

Memantine, an N-methyl D-aspartate (NMDA) antagonist, is prescribed for use in case of moderate to severe Alzheimer's disease. They produce delay in progression of some symptoms of Alzheimer's. Mechanically, memantine acts by regulating glutamate level which is an important brain neurotransmitter. When there is excess amount of glutamate, it results in brain cell death. NMDA antagonist work differently as compared to cholinesterase inhibitors. The drug allows maintaining and performing certain daily functions e.g. ability to use of bathroom independently for little longer than without medicine.

Therapeutic targets for disease modification in Alzheimer's

There are more than 200 pharmaceutical agents under clinical trial for treatment of Alzheimer's disease. These agents are categorised into anti-amyloid agents and other pathophysiological targeted drugs. Anti-amyloid drugs are designs to block or inhibit the overproduction or aggregation β-amyloid protein. They are also designed to favour the clearance of β-amyloid protein from the brain. Other category of drugs are categorised according to their mechanism of action like neurotransmitter and cell signaling agents, neuroprotective agents, Tau based therapies, glial cell modulators. There are also undergoing stem cell research and gene therapy for treatment of Alzheimer's disease.

There is role of immune response in Alzheimer's disease. Immune response removes the excess soluble β-amyloid form from circulation and thereby prevents the formation of β-amyloid plaque. Anti- β-amyloid immunotherapeutic agents are designed to stimulate the soluble β-amyloid derivative immunogens to minimize the risk of secondary inflammatory responses or vasogenic oedema. These vaccines increase the immune response to raised antibodies against β-amyloid monomers and oligomers.

Questions on this Chapter

1. Discuss etiopathogenesis of Alzheimer's disease.

2. Write the signs and clinical manifestations of Alzheimer's disease

3. Discuss the various treatment approaches for Alzheimer's disease.

Chapter 13

OPIOID ANALGESICS AND ANTAGONISTS

Objectives

After reading this chapter, the student will be able to:
➢ Understand the mechanism of pain
➢ Differentiate the different types of pain
➢ Understand opioids receptors
➢ Enlist the endogenous opioids
➢ Enlist the applications of opioid analgesic
➢ Write the function of long acting opiate antagonists

INTRODUCTION TO PAIN

- Pain is an unpleasant sensory and emotional experience associated with actual or potential tissue damage.

- Pain may be classified along temporal lines with acute pain arising as a warning of disease or threat to the body. This is generally associated with identifiable injury, surgery/trauma, or illness, and typically resolves within three months. Chronic pain arises from extension of acute discomfort beyond the time expected for typical resolution or healing. Often lacking clear pathology, this pain extends beyond 6 months and may last for years.

- The origins of pain may be distinguished as either "nociceptive" or "neuropathic".

- Nociceptive pain, or "somatic" pain, involves activation of the peripheral receptors of an intact nervous system, often as a result of tissue damage.

- Neuropathic pain arises from aberrant somatic sensory processing in either the peripheral or central nervous system.

PAIN PATHWAYS

- The neurobiology of acute pain involves initial stimulation of the receptor.

- The terminal processes of peripheral nerve fibers, which may involve either encapsulated or free nerve endings, transduce energy into electrical impulse.

- Local tissue damage resulting in release of algesic substances (prostaglandins, histamine, serotonin, bradykinin, substance P) which cause noxious stimuli (pain) which transduce by nociceptors and transmitted by A-delta and C nerve fibers to the neuraxis.

- The trigeminal nerve carries painful impulses from the head and face with synapses in the spinal trigeminal nucleus (trigeminal nucleus caudalis).

- Subsequent signals carried in the spinothalamic tract and the trigeminothalamic tract will synapse in the sensory thalamus and then somatosensory cortex. These pathways are largely involved with the primary transmission of pain, and associated connections with limbic system will provide the emotional elements to the experience of pain.

Pain produces segmental reflex responses which increases the skeletal muscle tone and spasm. It is also associated with increase in oxygen consumption and lactic acid production.

Pain also stimulate sympathetic neurons result in tachycardia, increased SV cardiac work, and myocardial oxygen consumption, lower muscle tone in GI and urinary tracts.

Pain types

Nociceptive pain
➢ It stimulates nociceptive receptor.
➢ It has intact neural pathways.
➢ It is usually opioids sensitive.

Neuropathic pain
➢ It damages the neural structures.
➢ It is usually opioids resistant.

ANALGESICS

- Analgesics are broadly divided into two main categories, the Opioids and nonopiods.
- Acetaminophen, acetylsalicylic acid, nonsteroidal anti-inflammatory drugs, and the atypical opioid tramadol are included among the nonopioids.
- Acute migraine management with selective 5-HT1 agonists (triptans) will be used to illustrate non-analgesic interruption of pain generation and transmission.

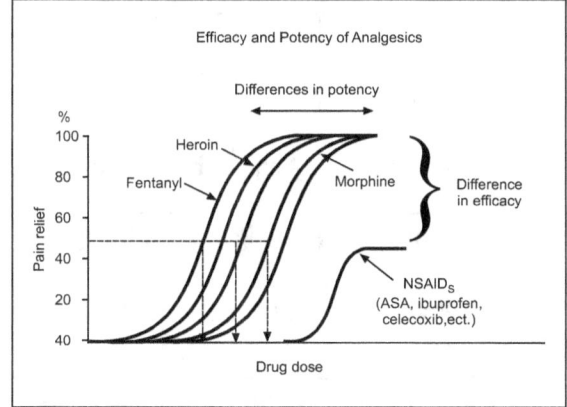

Fig. 13.1: Efficacy and Potency of Analgesics

Opioids Analgesics

History

- "Opium" is a Greek word meaning "juice," or the exudate from the poppy Papaver somniferum.

- "opiate" is a drug extracted from the exudate of the poppy
- "opioid" is a natural or synthetic drug that binds to opioid receptors producing agonist effects.
- Used for thousands of years to produce:
  - Euphoria
  - Analgesia
  - Sedation
  - Relief from diarrhoea
  - Cough suppression
- An opioid is defined as any natural or synthetic compound with morphine-like properties.
- Morphine was isolated from opium in the early 1800's and since then has been the most effective treatment for severe pain
- Morphine, codeine, and papaverine are clinically useful components derived directly from the poppy.
- The opioids agents are generally subdivided by their activity at opioid receptors (agonist, antagonist or mixed) and by their binding at specific receptors (mu, kappa or delta).

All opioids are "Narcotics"—they are covered by the 1970 Comprehensive Drug Abuse Prevention and Control Act.

Classified by Schedule:
   I.   Heroin;
   II. Oxycodone
   III. Hydrocodone
   IV. Codeine- Propoxyphene

Three Opioids Receptors (see Table 13.1)
  ❖ **Mu**
  ❖ **Kappa**
  ❖ **Delta**

Delta Receptor:
- It is unclear what delta receptor is responsible for. Delta agonists show poor analgesia and little addictive potential. May regulate mu receptor activity.

Mu (μ)-Receptor:
There are two types of μ receptors.
- **Mu-1**
  - Located outside the spinal cord.
  - Responsible for central interpretation of pain.

- **Mu-2**
  - Located throughout CNS.
  - Responsible for respiratory depression, spinal analgesia, physical dependence, and euphoria.

Kappa Receptor
- It produces only modest analgesia.
- Produces little or no respiratory depression.
- It produces little or no dependence.
- Produces dysphoric effects.

Table 13.1: Principle of Opioids receptor

	mu (μ)	kappa (κ)	delta (δ)
Localisation	.... cerebral cortex		
	.... hippocampus		
	.... midbrain .... amygdale		
	.... periphery		
Functions	analgesia euphoria constipation respiratory depression physical dependence	analgesia micturition	analgesia emotion/reward seizures
Typical Ligands	morphone fentanyl β-endorphin naloxone	pentazocine dynorphins	enkephalins

Mu Receptor Activation

Table 13.2 shows the different effects mediated through activation of mu-1 and mu-2 receptor.

Table 13.2: Responses of Mu-1 and Mu-2 receptor activation

Response	Mu-1	Mu-2
Analgesia	+	+
Respiratory Depression	-	+
Euphoria	-	+
Dysphoria	-	+
Decrease GI motility	-	+
Physical Dependence	-	+

TERMINOLOGY

- **Pure Agonist:** has affinity for binding plus efficacy
- **Pure Antagonist:** has affinity for binding but no efficacy; blocks action of endogenous and exogenous ligands
- **Mixed Agonist-Antagonist:** produces an agonist effect at one receptor and an antagonist effect at another
- **Partial Agonist:** has affinity for binding but low efficacy

Table 3.3: Mu and Kappa Receptors

Drugs	Mu	Kappa
Pure Agonists	Agonist	Agonist
Agonist-Antagonist	Antagonist	Agonist
Pure Antagonists	Antagonist	Antagonist

ENDOGENOUS OPIOIDS (OPIOIDS RECEPTOR)

- Three distinct families of endogenous opioids have been identified.
- These involve peptides classified as **enkephalins, endorphins, and dynorphins**. Each family is derived from a distinct precursor polypeptide and possesses a characteristic anatomical distribution.

➢ Endorphins - pro-opiomelanocortin (POMC)

➢ Enkephalins - proenkephalin

➢ Dynorphins – prodynorphin

➢ Endormorphins - pro-opiomelanocortin (POMC)

- The precursors are designated as proenkephalin, proopiomelanocortin, and prodynorphin. These precursor molecules, and other peptides derived from their conversion, are not confined to the central nervous system and may be found in the adrenal gland, pancreas, and enteric nervous system.

Enkephalin

- Enkephalins, agonists at the delta opioids receptor, are derived from the precursor proenkephalin.

- The enkephalins enjoy a wide distribution in the central nervous system and in the sympathetic nervous system.

- Enkephalin-containing neurons project from the entorhinal cortex to the molecular layer of the dentate gyrus in hippocampus, while additional descending long axons from the pons and medulla also contain enkephalin peptides.

Dynorphins

- Dynorphins are agonists at the kappa opioid receptor and derivatives of prodynorphin.

- Fibers containing dynorphins follow distributions similar to those of the enkephalins, with important projections extending from the dentate gyrus to the CA3 pyramidal cells.

- It is suspected that connections between presumptive dopaminergic neurons and neurons containing enkephalins and endorphins may be potentially responsible for endogenous reward properties of opioids.

Endorphins

- Endorphins, derived from proopiomelanocortin, are agonists at the mu opioid receptor and are contained in neurons originating from the medial hypothalamus, diencephalons, and pons.

- It is the endorphins that are most prominently active in pain-modulatory pathways.

MECHANISM OF OPIOIDS AT CELLULAR LEVEL

- The membrane mechanisms of opioids agents are variable, but often involve inhibition of N-type calcium channel conduction presynaptically and enhancement of potassium conduction postsynaptically.

- These effects, combined with inhibition of adenylate cyclase, result in inhibition of neuronal activity via presynaptic blockade of neurotransmitter release or postsynaptic hyperpolarization. Neuronal stimulation, when it occurs, appears to arise through depression of inhibitory interneurons.

- Opioid-induced analgesia may arise from action at several sites within the peripheral and central nervous systems. Although opioids do not appear to alter the response threshold of afferent nociceptive nerve terminals, they may decrease conduction of impulses along primary afferent fibers.

- Opioids binding sites have been documented at substantia gelatinosa in the dorsal horn of the spinal cord (laminae I and II), and direct inhibition of pain impulse conduction appears to occur at this level.

- Opioids also appear to activate descending pain modulatory pathways arising from the periventricular and periaqueductal grey matter regions. Neurons from these regions project to medullary nuclei (Raphe nuclei), which subsequently project fibers through distinct pathways in the spinal cord.

- Alteration of limbic and emotional responses to pain also may occur through activation of opioids pathways

Primary Effect of Opioids Receptor Activation

- Reduction or inhibition of neurotransmission, due largely to opioids-induced presynaptic inhibition of neurotransmitter release.

- Involves changes in transmembrane ion conductance.

  - Increase potassium conductance (hyperpolarization)

  - Inactivation of calcium channels

Table 13.4: Effects of Opioids Analgesics

✓ Analgesia	✓ Bradycardia
✓ Cough suppression	✓ Respiratory depression
✓ Sedation	✓ Nausea/vomiting
✓ Vasodilatation	✓ Muscle hypertonia
✓ Constipation	✓ Biliary spasm
✓ Urinary retention	✓ Histamine release
✓ Euphoria	✓ Tolerance

MECHANISM OF ACTION OF OPIOIDS

- Activation of peripheral nociceptive fibers causes release of substance P and other pain-signaling neurotransmitters from nerve terminals in the dorsal horn of the spinal cord
- Release of pain-signaling neurotransmitters is regulated by endogenous endorphins or by exogenous opioids agonists by acting presynaptically to inhibit substance P release, causing analgesia

Numerous opioids are available for clinical analgesic purposes.

- **Pure Opioid Agonists**: opium, morphine sulfate, codeine, meperidine, oxycodone, fentanyl, methadone, hydromorphone (one of the most potent oral agents), sufentanil (1000 times more potent than morphine and 10 times more potent than fentanyl), pentazocine, propoxyphene
- **Partial Agonists or Mixed Agonist/Antagonists:** buprenorphine, nalbuphine. These drugs are less addictive.
- **Agonist at other types of opioids receptors (kappa and delta receptors):** butorphanol, pentazocine, propoxyphene. They are less addictive.

Most of these agents are lipophilic with rapid absorption and wide distribution. Metabolism is largely hepatic. Onset, duration of action, potency, and route of administration are the bases for agent selection.

The most common antitussive opioid in clinical use is codeine, while the synthetic opioids diphenoxylate and loperamide are examples are agents used for the treatment of diarrhea. Dextromethorphan is the d-isomer of a codeine analog and is also used in cough suppression.

Morphine and most other are clinically used opioids agonists

Table 13.5: Classification of Opioids Analgesics

Natural opium alkaloids	Semisynthetic opiates	Synthetically manufactured
Morphine Codeine	Diacetylmorphine (Heroin) Pholcodiene	Meperidine Diphenoxylate Loperamide Fentanyl Sufentanil Remifentanil Methadone Propoxyphene Tramadol

NATURAL OPIUM ALKALOIDS

Morphine and Releated Drugs

It is the principal alkaloid in opium and still widely used, therefore described as prototype.

Pharmacological effect of Morphine and related drugs:

(A) CNS

- Morphine-and related drugs produce some CNS effect. It has both **depressant and stimulant** effect in the CNS.
- Morphine-and related drugs produce **depressant effects** which are as follows
  - Analgesia
  - Drowsiness
  - Changes in mood
  - Respiratory depression
  - Cough depression
  - Temperature regulation
  - Vasomotor depressant
- The **stimulant effects** are as follows:
  - Stimulation of CTZ
  - Stimulation of vagal center
  - Stimulation of certain cortical areas and hippocampus cells.

Depressant effect of Morphine

Analgesia:

- Morphine-and related drugs produces analgesia without loss of consciousness.

- When therapeutic doses of morphine are given to patients with pain, pain get less intense the patient experiences less discomfort while some drowsiness commonly occurs.
- When morphine in the same dose is given to a normal, pain-free individual the person experiences unpleasant effect, such as nausea and vomiting.
- Analgesic effects of opioids arise from their ability to directly inhibit the ascending transmission of nociceptive information from the spinal cord dorsal horn.
- Simultaneous administration of morphine at spinal and supraspinal sites results in synergy in analgesic response, with a tenfold reduction in the total dose of morphine necessary to produce equivalent analgesia at either site alone.
- Opioids can also produce analgesia when administered peripherally.
- Opioid receptors are present on peripheral nerves and will respond to peripherally applied opioids and locally released endogenous opioid compounds when up-regulated during inflammatory pain states.

Drowsiness
- Morphine and similar drugs produce drowsiness and it is occur without disturbance of motor coordination.
- Higher dose progressively cause sleep and coma.
- It has no anticonvulsant action while fits may occur.

Effect on Mood
- Opioids produce euphoria, tranquility, and other alterations of mood.
- However, there is separate neurological mechanism involved in mood alterations which are distinct from those involved in physical dependence and analgesia.
- The effect are mostly like due to dopaminergic pathways, particularly involving the nucleus accumbens. Whereas nalorphine like drug inhibit DA pathway and produce aversion.

Respiratory depression
- Morphine-like opioids depress respiration by a direct effect on the brainstem respiratory centers.

- The respiratory depression is dose dependant.
- Therapeutic doses of morphine in humans depress all phases of respiratory activity.
- Opioids also produce transient respiratory depression in the neonate because of transplacental passage of opioids.

Cough suppression
- Morphine and related opioids also depress the cough reflex by a direct effect on a cough center in the medulla.
- Suppression of cough by such agents appears to involve receptors in the medulla that are less sensitive to naloxone than those responsible for analgesia.

Regulation of temperature
- Opioids alter the equilibrium point of the hypothalamus thus body temperature falls slightly. However, chronic high dosage may increase body temperature.

Vasomotor center
- When the dose of morphine exceeds it result into depression of vasomotor center and it contribute to fall in blood pressure.

Stimulant effect of Morphine
Miosis:
- Morphine and most μ and κ agonists cause constriction of the pupil by an excitatory action on the parasympathetic nerve.

Nausea and Emetic Effects
- Opioids and related drug cause a direct stimulation of the chemoreceptor trigger zone (CTZ) for emesis in the area postrema of the medulla.

Convulsions
- At higher doses morphine and related opioids produce convulsions.
- Morphine-like drugs produce excitatory effects probably result from inhibition of the release of GABA by interneurons especially hippocampal pyramidal cells.
- Selective δ agonists produce similar effects.
- However, with most opioids, convulsions occur only at doses far in excess of those required to produce profound analgesia, and seizures are not seen when potent μ agonists are used to produce anesthesia.

- Naloxone is more potent in antagonizing convulsions produced by some opioids (e.g., morphine, methadone, and propoxyphene) than those produced by others (e.g., meperidine).

Vagal center:

- It produces bradycardia by stimulating vagal center.

(B) Neuroendocrine Effects

- Morphine inhibits the release of gonadotropin-releasing hormone and corticotropin-releasing hormone. Thus it results into decreasing concentrations of luteinizing hormone, follicle-stimulating hormone, ACTH, and β-endorphin.

- The administration of μ agonists increases the concentration of prolactin in plasma probably by reducing the dopaminergic inhibition of its secretion.

- Although some opioids enhance the secretion of growth hormone.

- Morphine can release ADH and reduce urine volume.

- Although κ-receptor agonists inhibit the release of antidiuretic hormone and cause diuresis, the administration of μ-opioid receptor agonists tends to produce antidiuretic effects in humans.

(C) CVS:

- Therapeutic doses of morphine like opioids produce peripheral vasodilation, reduced peripheral resistance by increasing the release of histamine, and an inhibition of baroreceptor reflexes.

- However, vasodilation is partially blocked by H_1 antagonists, but it is effectively reversed by naloxone.

- Morphine may exert its well-known therapeutic effect in the treatment of angina pectoris and acute myocardial infarction by decreasing preload, inotropy, and chronotropy.

- Morphine has been shown to produce cardioprotective effects.

- Very large doses of morphine can be used to produce anesthesia; however, decreased peripheral resistance and blood pressure are troublesome.

- Fentanyl and sufentanil, which are potent and selective μ agonists, are less likely to cause hemodynamic instability during surgery in part because they do not cause the release of histamine.

- Morphine-like opioids should be used with caution in patients who have a decreased blood volume because these agents can aggravate hypovolemic shock. The concurrent use of certain phenothiazines may increase the risk of morphine-induced hypotension. However, opioid-induced respiratory depression and CO_2 retention can result in cerebral vasodilation and an increase in cerebrospinal fluid pressure; the pressure increase does not occur when PCO_2 is maintained at normal levels by artificial ventilation.

(D) Skin:

- The skin of the face, neck, and upper thorax frequently becomes flushed because of dilation of cutaneous blood vessel by morphine.

- The dilation may be due to release of histamine and may be responsible for the sweating and some of the pruritus.

- Histamine release probably accounts for the urticaria commonly seen at the site of injection.
  Pruritus is a common and potentially disabling complication of opioid use.

(E) GIT: The usual gastrointestinal effects of morphine primarily are mediated by μ and δ opioid receptors in the bowel and produce constipation at less than analgesic doses and may account for troublesome gastrointestinal side effects. Although some tolerance develops to the effects of opioids on gastrointestinal motility, patients who take opioids chronically remain constipated. Following are the factors who contribute in producing constipation.

- Activation of opioid receptors on parietal cells enhances secretion, while increased secretion of somatostatin from the pancreas and reduced release of acetylcholine. Relatively low doses of morphine increase the esophageal reflux by decreasing gastric motility, thereby prolonging gastric emptying time.

- Morphine diminishes biliary, pancreatic, and intestinal secretions and delays digestion of food in the small intestine.

- In the presence of intestinal hypersecretion that may be associated with diarrhea, morphine-like drugs inhibit the transfer of fluid and electrolytes into the lumen by naloxone-sensitive actions on the intestinal mucosa and within the CNS.

- Opioids act on the submucosal plexus and decreases in the basal secretion by the release of norepinephrine and stimulation of α_2 adrenergic receptors on enterocytes.

- There are also inhibition of the stimulatory effects of acetylcholine, prostaglandin E_2, and vasoactive intestinal peptide.

- Opoids either diminishe or abolishe the propulsive peristaltic waves in the colon and resulting in delay in the passage of bowel contents causes desiccation of the feces.

- The tone of the anal sphincter is augmented greatly, and reflex relaxation in response to rectal distension is reduced.

(F) Smooth muscle
Biliary Tract

- Morphine constricts the sphincter of Oddi resulting in spasm. Fluid pressure also may increase in the gallbladder and produce symptoms that may vary from epigastric distress to typical biliary colic.

- Spasm of the sphincter of Oddi probably is responsible for elevations of plasma amylase and lipase. Atropine only partially prevents morphine-induced biliary spasm, but opioid antagonist and nitroglycerin prevent or relieve it.

Ureter and Urinary Bladder

- Morphine may increase the tone and amplitude of the contractions of the ureter.

- Morphine increases the tone of the external sphincter and the volume of the bladder; catheterization sometimes is required after therapeutic doses of morphine.

Uterus

- Slightly prolongs labour.

(G) ANS

- Cause mild hyperglycemia due to central sympathetic stimulation.

- Opoids also have some weak anticholinesterase action.

(H) Immune system

- Opioids modulate immune function by direct effects on the cells of the immune system and indirectly via centrally mediated neuronal mechanisms.

- The acute central immunomodulatory effects of opioids may be mediated by activation of the sympathetic nervous system, whereas the chronic effects of opioids may involve modulation of the hypothalamic-pituitary-adrenal (HPA) axis.

Opioid antagonist

Opioid antagonist is described as a receptor antagonist which work differently and opposite of an opioid agonist. Opioid antagonist binds to opioid receptor more strongly with higher affinity than that of the agonists that results in blocking of opioid response. There are different opioid antagonists but most commonly used in opioid addiction treatment are Nalaxone and Naltrexone. These are called competitive antagonists and they prevent the normal response that are produced by opioids. Thus the user will not feel the effects of heroin, morphine, and other opiates after use of opioid antagonist. Released of endorphins is also blocked when such antagonist used.

Some of the opioid antagonists are considered as selective antagonists and they work on specific type of opioid receptor. They block opioid receptor i.e. mu opioid receptor, delta opioid receptor, and kappa opioid receptor. There are also other types of opioid receptors available but most widely used receptors are the above three. These receptors are most widely used in the treatment of opioid dependence and treatment.

The receptors most affected by opioid agonists include:

- The mu opioid receptors, when activated by an opioid agonist, results in the most common opioid effects such as analgesia, euphoria, sedation, respiratory depression, constipation, reduced blood pressure, and impaired thinking and balance. In the prefrontal cortex of the brain, it contributes to the person's decisions and addictive behaviours after adaptations.

- Delta opioid receptors cause seizures at high doses of an opioid agonist.

- Kappa opioid receptors alter the perceptions or pain, mood, consciousness, and motor control.

Opioid antagonists block these receptors and thereby reverses the above physiological responses which are produce by opiates.

Examples of Opiate Antagonists

There are various types of opioid antagonist existing but the most common ones are given below-

- Naloxone
- Naltrexone
- Narcan
- Narcon
- Narcotan
- Vivitrex
- Zynol

Long-Acting Opiate Antagonist

Naltrexone is the most commonly used long-acting opioid antagonists which can stay in the system for about 96 hours after its initial dose and has a half-life of between 4 and 10 hours.

It is the most suitable drug for the treatment of opiate addiction because of its long acting effect on user and requires fewer doses. Due to its long duration of action, there is no need for frequent visits to the doctor as well as it reduce the risk of a dose being missed.

Naltrexone

The use of naltrexone is common in the treatment of opiate addiction such as heroin or morphine. The patient stays away from opiates use due to lack of pleasurable experience when used.

Some people respond well with Naltrexone as a treatment for opiate dependence while others have to take the drug every day and this is very difficult process and the risk of missing a dose is too high. Naltrexone has long acting drug and there is reduce the risk of dose missing which is major advantage with this drug for its use in drug addiction treatment.

Naloxone

Naloxone is considered an opioid inverse agonist and is used in the treatment of opiate overdose rather than the treatment of opiate addiction.

In case of opioid overdosing, naloxone can stop the effects of opiates. It enables the user to breathe properly. Naloxone is most widely used in the emergency treatment of opioid overdose and thereby reduces the rate of fatality.

Naloxone is most widely used as morphine antagonist. When morphine is administered, it quickly enter the body and binds to the opioid receptor. In case of overdose of morphine, naloxone may be administered. When the naloxone is given in the event of an overdose, there is competition with morphine for the binding site at the same receptor. As naloxone has more affinity than morphine for binding to opioid receptor it results in reversal of the morphine effects.

Summary

- The central nervous system effects of the opioid agents are the most clinically important and include analgesia, sedation and cough suppression.

- The analgesia is relatively selective, with sparing of other sensory modalities and maintenance of consciousness.

- Direct suppression of the cough reflex at the cough center in the medulla is another clinically important benefit from the use of opioids.

- Although constipation is often considered a significant adverse event in the clinical use of opioids, this effect may prove to be clinically advantageous in the treatment of diarrhoea.

- Additional central nervous system properties include pupillary miosis, direct stimulation of the chemoreceptor trigger zone resulting in nausea/vomiting, and euphoria.

- Respiratory depression via direct effect on brain stem's, respiratory centers is discernable at low doses, and such respiratory depression remains the major source of death from opioid overdose.

- Adaptation syndromes noted with extended use of opioids include tolerance, physical dependence and addiction.

The overall effects of opioids appear to be immunosuppressive, and increased susceptibility to infection and this action may be due to effects on neutrophils is through a nitric oxide-dependent inhibition of NF-κB activation. Others have proposed that the induction and activation of MAP kinase also may play a role.

Questions on this Chapter

1. Write a short note on opioids receptor.
2. What are the endogenous opioids.
3. Classify opioids analgesic and add a note on effects.
4. Discuss in detail the mechanism of opioids.
5. Write in detail the pharmacological actions of morphine and its toxicity.
6. Write short note on opoid antagonist.

Chapter 14

NON-STEROIDAL ANTI-INFLAMMATORY AGENTS

Objectives

After reading this chapter, the student will be able to:

➢ Understand the synthesis of Prostaglandins and Leukotrienes

➢ Understand the pathological and physiological role of prostaglandins

➢ Understand the function of Thromboxanes and leukotrienes

➢ Enlist the various inhibitory effects of NSAIDs

➢ Understand the future prospective of COX-2 inhibitors

INTRODUCTION

Non-steroidal anti-inflammatory agents (NSAIDs) are a chemically diverse class of drugs (>70 NSAIDs are in use) that have anti-inflammatory, analgesic, and antipyretic properties. Among the most frequently prescribed drugs worldwide 70 million people/day prescribed NSAIDs and some 230 million people/day take OTC NSAIDs. Most of these agents are nonselective blockers of the hydrophobic channel of cyclooxygenase 1 and 2, but there are newer selective cyclooxygenase 2 (Cox-2) inhibitors that are commercially available. Since they do not belong to steroid group and they do not possess adverse reactions associated with steroids.

PROSTAGLANDINS

Prostaglandins are a group of lipid like compounds that exhibit a wide range of pharmacologic activities. They appear to be hormones that regulate cell function under normal and pathological conditions.

Properties of PGs (see Table 14.1 and Figure 11.1)

Arachidonic acid metabolism

Eicosanoids like prostaglandins and leukotrienes are derived from arachidonic acid. Arachidonic acid is a 20-carbon essential fatty acid and is a component of membrane phospholipids. During cellular damage or infection, enzyme phospholipase A_2 interact with membrane phospholipids releasing arachidonic acid from them. Acid so released then forms or synthesize required eicosanoids. This released of arachidonic acid from membrane phospholipids is stimulated by variety of stimuli such as physical, chemical, hormonal and neurochemical.

Physiological and pathological role of Prostaglandins (summaries in Table 14.1)

(a) **Pain:** Prostaglandins help in mediate painful stimuli; they don't directly produce pain but increase the sensitivity of pain receptors towards other pain-producing substances (like bradykinin). PGI2 and PGE2 sensitize nerve endings to bradykinin, histamine and substance P.

(b) **Inflammation:** Increased prostaglandin synthesis is usually detected at the site of local inflammation. Certain type of prostaglandins causes increase in blood flow, capillary permeability and increasing the effect of histamine and bradykinin. Other types of prostaglandins increase vascular permeability. PGI2, PGD2 and PGE2 are vasodilators resulting into edema and erythema formation which results into inflammation. Beside this prostaglandin PGI2 provides protection to gastric mucosa while PGE2 helps in maintaining renal blood flow.

(c) **Fever:** Prostaglandins (PGE2) seems to be pyretogenic (substance elevating body temperature during fever) Prostaglandins appear to alter the thermoregulatory system.

(d) **Platelets:** PGI2 and PGD2 inhibit platelet aggregation while TXA2 stimulates platelet aggregation.

(e) **Uterus:** PGD2 bring contractions in uterine walls.

(f) **Dysmenorrhea:** Some studies have shown close association between excessive amounts of prostaglandins in the endometrium of the uterus and those suffering from painful cramps during menstruation.

(g) **Thrombus Formation:** Blood clot formation (deep vein thrombosis) is associated with a prostaglandin called thromboxanes or TXA2, which causes platelet aggregation resulting in clot formation.

(h) **Other Pathologies:** Prostaglandins have been associated with cardiovascular disorders, hypertension, respiratory dysfunction (asthma), neurologic disorders (multiple sclerosis, allergic encephalo-myelitis, endocrine dysfunction (Bartter's syndrome, diabetes mellitus) and other diseases.

(i) Beside above mention roles PGE2 helps in keeping ductus arteriosus open during birth.

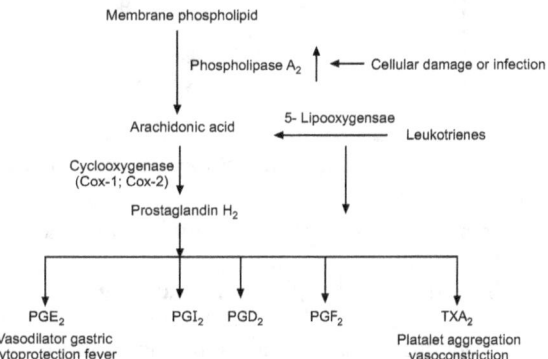

Fig. 14.1: Site and properties of PGs

Table 14.1: Role of Prostaglandin

Pathologic	Physiologic
Fever	Temperature control
Asthma	Bronchial tone increases(dilation by PGE2)
Ulcers	
Diarrhea	Cytoprotection
Dysmenorrhea	Intestinal mobility increase
Produce Inflammation	Myometrial tone
Increases the bone erosion	Semen viability
Enhanced pain inducing effects of bradykinin	Enhance vessel permeability
	Produce vasodilation (PGE2, PGD2)

Functions of Thromboxanes

- Cause platelets to aggregate.
- Causes vasoconstriction.
- Causes smooth mm contraction.
- Enhances function of inflammatory cells.

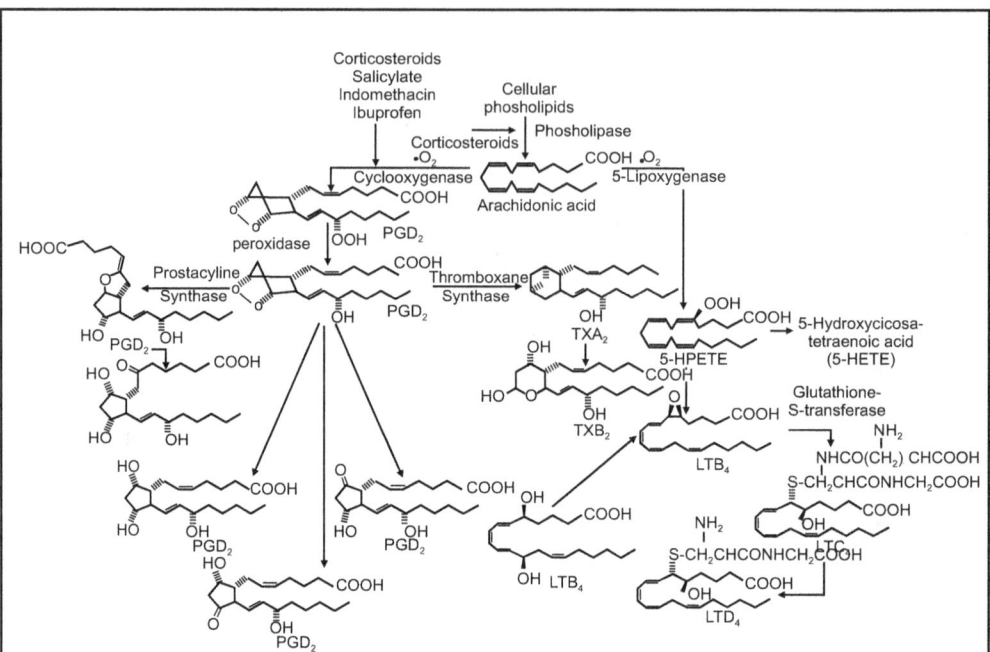

Fig. 14.2: Biosynthetic pathway of prostaglandin and leukotrienes

Functions of Leukotrienes
- Increases vessel permeability and leakiness.
- Stimulates platelet aggregation.
- Stimulates neutrophils pavementing.
- Act as powerful chemotactic signals for: monocytes, macrophages and neutrophils.

CYCLOOXYGENASE ENZYME (COX)

There are 3 COX enzymes: (see Fig. 14.3)
- COX-1 → "constitutively" expressed in most tissues; supports platelets and helps to maintain stomach lining.
- COX-2 → "inducible"; undetectable in most tissues; triggers pain and inflammation.
- COX-3 recently identified.
- The anti-inflammatory effects of NSAIDs are carried out by COX-2 inhibition.
- The GI adverse effects are caused by COX-1 inhibition.

COX-2 Specific Inhibitors
- Inhibition of COX-2 is thought to mediate the anti-pyretic, analgesic and anti-inflammatory actions of NSAIDs.
- Simultaneous inhibition of COX-1 results in unwanted side effects (gastrointestinal ulcerations).
- Research has recently been focused on the development of NSAIDs with greater selectivity for COX-2 over COX-1.

- Inhibition of COX2 removes the protective constraints on thrombogenesis, hypertension, and artherogenesis.
- Side effects include risk of heart attack and stroke.

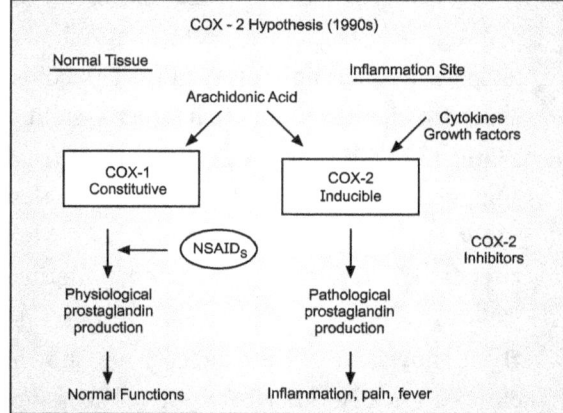

Fig. 14.3: Cyclooxygenase Enzyme

Non-Steroidal Anti-inflammatory Agents

Properties of NSAIDs
- All NSAIDs have common therapeutic indications.
- Shows almost common adverse effects.

- Though NSAIDs have common therapeutic indications and adverse effects but they differ greatly in their pharmacokinetics and potency.
- They belong to different chemical families.
- They all have common mechanism of action i.e. cyclooxygenase inhibition.
- NSAIDs shows different selectivities for COX I and II enzyme.

Pharmacokinetics of NSAIDs

They are absorbed completely i.e. NSAIDs show 100% absorbance. NSAIDs produce negligible first-pass hepatic metabolism. They are tightly bound to albumin and metabolized predominantly in liver by cytochrome P450 system. After complete metabolism NSAIDs are eliminated from body by excretion through kidney.

Effects of NSAIDS

NSAIDs exhibits inhibitory effects, it inhibits

- Cyclooxygenase enzymes
- Lipoxygenase enzymes
- Superoxide generation
- Lysosomal enzyme release
- Neutrophil activity
- Lymphocyte function
- Cytokine release
- Cartilage metabolism

Common Pharmacological Effects

- Analgesic (CNS and peripheral effect) may involve non-PG related effects.
- Antipyretic (mediated through CNS) effect.
- Anti-inflammatory (except acetaminophen) mainly due to PG inhibition.
- Some NSAIDs shown to have inhibited activation, aggregation, adhesion of neutrophils and release of lysosomal enzymes.
- Some are Uricosuric.

Mechanism of Non-Steroidal Anti-Inflammatory Agents

The anti-inflammatory properties

Substances such as prostaglandins, histamine, thromboxane and leukotrienes are mediators of inflammation. The anti-inflammatory properties of the NSAIDs ensure that the release of the prostaglandins, histamines, thromboxanes and leukotrienes is inhibited in the area of tissue injury.

Prostaglandins are chemicals produced by the body that promote inflammation, pain, and fever. NSAIDs are thought to act by inhibiting prostaglandin synthesis. NSAIDs achieve by inhibiting the action of the enzyme cyclooxygenase (COX), which is responsible for synthesis of prostaglandins.

Physiological Effects of NSAIDs

(1) Analgesic properties

Whereas the opioids are the drugs of choice for the treatment of moderate-to-severe pain, the NSAIDs are most frequently used for mild-to-moderate pain. Prostaglandins by themselves do not cause pain but lower the threshold of the C fiber nociceptors. As a result, lower concentrations of bradykinin and histamine are required to activate the nociceptor. Activation of nociceptor results into pain and inflammation. NSAIDs produce analgesia by reducing capillary permeability, stabilizing the mast cell and by inhibit prostaglandin production. Beside this it also inhibits bradykinin from stimulating pain receptors.

(2) Anti-pyretic properties

The hypothalamus regulates the set point at which body temperature is maintained. This point is elevated during fever, and NSAIDs promote its return to normal. The concentration of cytokines such as IL-1B, IL-6, interferons α and β and TNF-α are frequently increased during inflammation which stimulate the synthesis of PGE_2 near the hypothalamic area. This synthesis of prostaglandin alters the temperature regulation by hypothalamus.

(3) Anti-Thrombolytic Action of Aspirin

- A single dose of aspirin approximately doubles the mean bleeding time of normal persons for a period of 4-7 days.

- These medications have varying capabilities to prolong the clotting time. They all inhibit one of the clotting factors as well as inhibit platelet aggregation (Figure 11.4).

- Since platelets only have COX-1, the COX-2 specific drugs are not anti-thrombolytic.

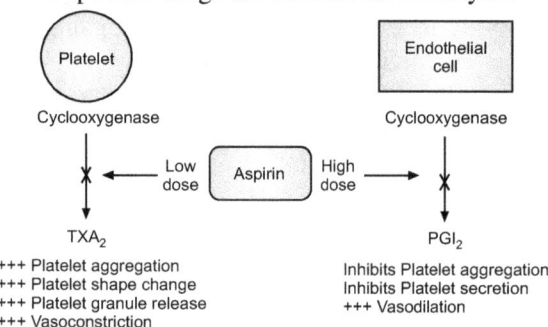

Fig. 14.4: Pharmacology of Aspirin

(4) NSAIDs a anti-coagulants i.e. they prevent blood coagulation.

(5) Anti-cancer property

A number of studies in both animals and in humans have shown an up-regulation of COX-2 in colonic cancers. A large body of epidemiological evidence points to an inverse association between aspirin use and colorectal cancer risk. The mechanism, the dose and duration required for maximal efficacy still are not completely clear.

(6) Prevention or relief of symptoms of Alzheimer's disease: In Alzheimer's disease there is inflammatory changes occurs in β-amygloid plaque. Use of NSAIDs prevents or relief such types of changes.

(7) Gastrointestinal ulceration

It is estimated that 2-4% of chronic NSAID users develop upper gastrointestinal tract bleeding; as many as 20,000 deaths occur annually due to this. PGI2 and PGE2 serve as cytoprotective agents in the gastric mucosa by inhibiting acid secretion, enhancement of mucosal blood flow, stimulation o bicarbonate and mucus secretion. Thus inhibition of this prostaglandins by NSAIDs adversely affect gastrointestinal tract.

(8) Renal function

NSAIDs have little effect on renal perfusion in individuals with normal cardiac output. In individuals with a reduced cardiac output, the local vasodilating effect of prostaglandins is critical to counter the vasoconstrictive compensatory mechanisms mediated by norepinephrine and angiotensin II.

(9) Inhibition of uterine motility

Prostaglandin such as PGD_2 is responsible for bringing contractions in uterine walls. Consumption of NSAIDs results into prolongation of gestation period.

(10) Hypersensitivity Reaction

NSAIDs produce hypersensitivity reactions. It is manifested by symptoms that range from vasomotor rhinitis with profuse watery secretions, angioedema, generalized urticaria, bronchial asthma to laryngeal edema, bronchoconstriction, flushing, hypotension and shock.

(11) Use of NSAIDs for sports injuries

- NSAIDs are mainstay in the treatment of many types of mild-to-moderate pain.

- They are effective in treating pain and inflammation arising from acute and chronic musculoskeletal disorders.

- Treat fever or prevent excessive blood clotting.

- Could hamper the inflammation/healing process.

Common Adverse Effects of NSAIDs

- Platelet Dysfunction.

- Prolonged bleeding time

- Gastritis and peptic ulceration with bleeding (inhibition of PG + other effects).
- Acute Renal Failure in susceptible individuals.
- Sodium ion, water retention and edema.
- Analgesic nephropathy.
- NSAIDs may also cause central nervous system toxicity: resulting into headache, confusion, dizziness, mood alteration, depression and aseptic meningitis.
- Prolongation of gestation and inhibition of labor.
- Hypersensitivity: it is not immunologic but due to prostaglandins inhibition.

Table 14.2: Classification of NSAIDs

(A) Nonselective COX inhibitors

Acetic acid	Propionic acid	Anthranilic acid derivatives	Salicylate
Diclofenac Etodolac Indomethacine Sulindac Tolmetin	Fenoprofen Flurbifrofen Ibuprofen Ketoprofen Naproxen Oxaprozin Ketorolac	Mefenamic acid Meclofenamate Meclofenamic acid **Oxicam derivatives:** Peroxicam, Tenoxicam, Lornoxicam	Asprin Diflunisal

(B) Selective COX-2 inhibitors

Celocoxib
Rofecoxib
Valdecoxib
Parecoxib
Lumiracoxib
Etoricoxib

(C) Preferential COX-2 inhibitors

Nimesulide
Meloxicam
Nabumetone (Naphthylakanone-acetic acid derivative)

(D) Analgesic, Antipyretics and poor anti-inflammatory agents

Paraaminophenol derivative	Pyrazone derivatives	Benzoxazocine derivatives
Acetaminophen (paracetamol)	Metamizole Propiphenazole Phenylbutazone Oxyphenbutazone	Nefopam

SALICYLIC ACID

Aspirin

Aspirin is acetylsalicylic acid. In body it is rapidly converted into salicylic acid which is responsible for its activity.

Mechanism of Action of Acetyl salicylic acid (ASA)

Inhibits the activity of enzyme COX (cyclooxygenase or prostaglandin synthase) and therefore inhibits prostaglandin synthesis.

Pharmacokinetics

It is rapidly absorbed from gastrointestinal tract through passive diffusion and distributed throughout most body tissues and 80-90% is bound to plasma proteins, mainly albumin. It displaces several other drugs from plasma protein resulting in higher effective plasma concentrations. It get rapidly hydrolyzed in blood and liver to salicylic acid (half-life is approximately 15 minutes). A constant amount (not percentage) of the drug is metabolized per hour i.e. show Zero order kinetics. Inactivation occurs mainly in the hepatic endoplasmic reticulum and mitochondria and is mainly through the formation of conjugates that are excreted in the urine.

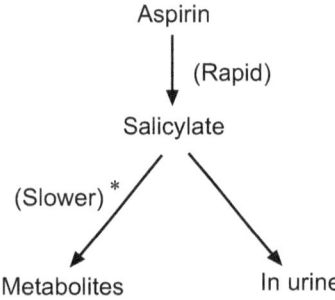

Dosage

- Analgesic/antipyretic dose for adults is 325-650 mg every 4 hrs which results in a plasma concentration of approximately 60 mg/ml. The half-life is 2-3 hours.

- Anti-inflammatory dose is usually 4-6 g daily which results in a plasma concentration of 150-300 mg/ml. The half-life is usually 12 hours.

- Fatal dose is 10-30 g resulting in plasma concentrations exceeding 450 mg/ml. The half-life can be as long as 15-30 hours.

Pharmacologic effects of Acetyl salicylic acid

Aspirin shows dose dependant effects which have been shown schematically in Fig. 14.5.

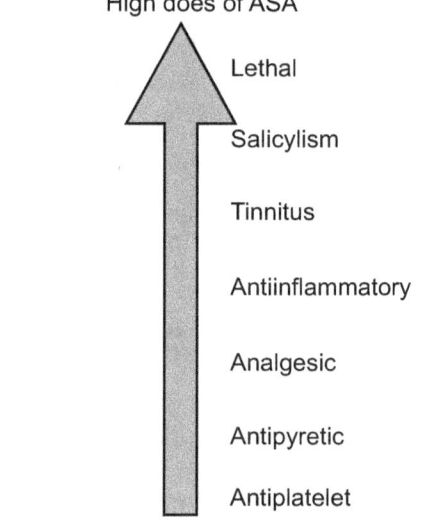

Fig. 14.5: doses dependant effect of Aspirin

- **Analgesic:** The analgesic action mediated by reducing the synthesis of prostaglandins.

- **Antipyretic:** Acetyl salicylic acids reduce prostaglandin synthesis in the hypothalamus and induce peripheral vasodilation and sweating.

- **Anti-inflammatory:** Prostaglandins can induce swelling

- **Respiration.** Salicylates increase oxygen consumption and CO_2 production (especially in skeletal muscle) at full therapeutic doses.

- **Antiplatelets:** Acetyl salicylic acid irreversibly binds to platelet (4-7 days lifetime; clotting back to normal after 36 hrs).

- **Effect of Acetyl salicylic acid on platelet aggregation mediators**
  Throboxane and prostaglandin both having opposite effects on platelet; throboxane increases the platelet aggregation results into clotting of blood and PGI2 cause bleeding by inhibiting platelet aggregation. Asprin at low dose it decreases the platelet

aggregation by inhibiting the throboxane secretion while at high doses it increases the platelets aggregation and results into clotting of blood (Fig. 14.6).

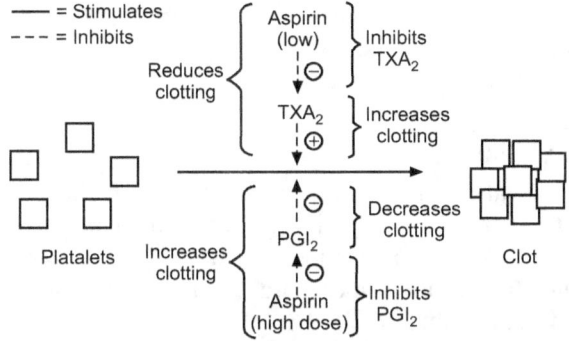

Fig. 14.6: Effect of Asprin on blood clotting

- **Gastrointestinal Effects.** The ingestion of salicylates may result in epigastric distress, nausea and vomiting. Salicylates may also cause gastric ulceration, exacerbation of peptic ulcer symptoms (heartburn, dyspepsia), gastrointestinal hemorrhage and erosive gastritis.

- **Cardiovascular Effects.**

  Low doses of aspirin (<100 mg daily) are used widely for cardioprotective effects. At high therapeutic doses (>3 g daily), as might be given for acute rheumatic fever, salt and water retention can lead to an increase in circulating plasma volume and decreased hematocrit (*via* a dilutional effect). Due to direct effect on vascular smooth muscle there is tendency for the peripheral vessels to dilate. As results cardiac output and work are increased.

- **Uricosuric Effects.**

  It shows dose dependant uricosuric effects. Low doses (1 or 2 g per day) may decrease urate excretion and elevate plasma urate concentrations; intermediate doses (2 or 3 g per day) usually do not alter urate excretion; large doses (more than 5 g per day) induce uricosuria and lower plasma urate levels.

- **Hepatic Effects.**

  Salicylates can cause hepatic injury, usually in patients treated with high doses of salicylates that result in plasma concentrations of more than 150 mg/ml. There is an increase in serum levels of hepatic transaminases, but some patients note right upper quadrant abdominal discomfort and tenderness. However, the use of salicylates is contraindicated in patients with chronic liver disease.

- **Metabolic Effects**

  The metabolic effect may occur with usual doses of salicylate used in the treatment of rheumatoid arthritis which can result in the inhibition of a number of ATP-dependent reactions by uncoupling of oxidative phosphorylation results in increase in O_2 uptake and CO_2 production.

  Large doses of salicylates may cause hyperglycemia and glycosuria and deplete liver and muscle glycogen.

  Toxic doses of Acetyl salicylic acid may decrease aerobic metabolism and increase the production of strong organic acids.

- **Endocrine Effects**

  There are competitive displacement of thyroxine and triiodothyronine from transthyretin and the thyroxine-binding globulin in plasma by salicylates. This results into decreases thyroidal uptake and clearance of iodine, but increases O_2 consumption and the rate of disappearance of thyroxine and triiodothyronine from the circulation.

- **Local Irritant Effects.**

  Salicylic acid is irritating to skin and mucosa and destroys epithelial cells. After treatment with salicylic acid, tissue cells swell, soften, and desquamate.

NSAIDs and Pregnancy

NSAIDs generally used in pregnancy because of following effects of prostaglandins on pregnancy which ultimately cause to labor pain and preterm delivery (gestation).

(i) Excessive amounts of prostaglandins in the endometrium of the uterus and those suffering from painful cramps during menstruation results into contraction leading to dysmenorrhea.

(ii) Before parturition, there is induction of COX-2, prostaglandin E_2 and $F_{2\alpha}$ in the myometrium during labor.

(iii) Opening of the ductus arteriosus, particularly in fetuses older than 32 weeks' gestation.

(iv) Pregnancy induce hypertension which is believed to be due to imbalance between TXA-2 and PGI2.

Thus, NSAIDs may prevents all these effects of prostaglandins but it is risky because it may lead to low birth weight babies, delayed or prolonged labour, haemmorhage, closing of ductus arteriosus thus impairing fetal circulation. Some NSAIDs, particularly Indomethacin, have been used off-label to terminate preterm labor. There is a relative contraindication to the use of all NSAIDs, and their use must be weighed against potential fetal risk.

Table 14.3: Usual dose of Aspirin and their effects

Usual dose	Effect
80-160 mg	Antiplatelets
325-1000 mg	Analgesic, antipyretic
325 mg-6 grams	Anti-inflammatory, tinnitus
6-10 grams	Respiratory alkalosis
10-20 grams	Fever, dehydration, acidosis
> 20 grams	Shock, coma

Adverse Reactions of Acetyl salicylic acid

(i) Gastrointestinal effects (vomiting, gastric bleeding, nausea etc.): Direct irritation or from prostaglandin synthesis inhibition (prostaglandins are responsible for inhibiting gastric acid secretion and stimulation of cytoprotective mucus). Salicylates can exacerbate preexisting ulcers, gastritis or hiatal hernia.

(ii) Irreversibly interferes with clotting mechanisms by reducing platelet adhesiveness (stickiness).

(iii) Reye's syndrome: chickenpox or influenza.

(iv) Allergies are rare, but asthmatics more likely to have allergies.

(v) NSAIDs may show cross-hypersensitivity to other NSAIDs.

Special Problems Associated With Salicylate in Children

Reyes Syndrome is associated with a virally induced fever with the concomitant use of aspirin. Reyes Syndrome shows symptoms such as cerebral edema, encephalopathy and disorientation and confusion.

Aspirin Toxicity

(A) Salicylism

Salicylism is mild intoxication with aspirin. It is commonly experienced when the daily dose exceeds 4 g. symptoms arising due low mentioned are some characteristics (symptoms) of Salicylism.

❖ Headache, timmitus, dizziness, hearing impairment and dim vision

❖ Confusion and drowziness

❖ Sweating and hyperventilation

❖ Nausea, vomiting

❖ Marked acid-base disturbances

❖ Hyperpyrexia

❖ Dehydration

❖ Cardiovascular and respiratory collapse, coma convulsions and death

(B) Changes in acid-base balance

Altered acid-base balance is one of the outcomes of aspirin toxicity. There is increased O_2 consumption and CO2 production as a result of the uncoupling of oxidative phosphorylation. The increased CO_2 stimulates respiration for balancing the overproduction of CO_2 and maintaining the level of plasma CO_2. Salicylates directly stimulate the respiratory center in the medulla resulting in hyperventilation.

$$\xrightarrow{\hspace{2cm}}$$
$$\downarrow CO_2 + H_2O \rightleftharpoons H_2CO_3 \rightleftharpoons H^+ HCO_3^-$$
(Respiratory alkalosis)

It is compensated by renal excretion of bicarbonate. After toxic doses or prolonged exposure, salicylates have a depressant effect on the medulla.

$$\xleftarrow{\hspace{2cm}}$$
$$\downarrow CO_2 + H_2O \rightleftharpoons H_2CO_3 \rightleftharpoons H^+ HCO_3^-$$
(Respiratory and metabolic acidosis)

Aspirin Toxicity: Treatment

Several methods are used to treat aspirin toxicity. Below mention are some such measures:

- Since, the drug is rapidly absorbed in gastrointestinal tract, the formost measure in reducing aspirin toxicity is to reduce its absorption. This is achieved by using active activated chaecoal, emetics and gastric lavage.

- Enhance excretion –Excretion of drug is enhanced either by alkalinize urine, forced dieresis and haemodialysis.

- Supportive measures - fluids, decrease temperature, bicarbonate, electrolytes, glucose etc.

Drug Interactions

- Low dose of Aspirin and concomitant use of other NSAIDS. This combination therapy increases gastrointestinal adverse events over either class of NSAID alone.

- Aspirin increases the plasma concentration of warfarin, sulphonylureas, phenytoin and methotrexate by displacing it from binding site.

- Aspirin also displace the binding of thyroxine.

- It antagonizes the action of Probencid because of inhibition of tubular secretion of uric acid.

- It also reduces the effects of Spironolactone by competitively inhibiting active transport in proximal tubule.

Contraindications

Aspirin should not be used as a therapy in individual with following conditions:

- In peptic ulcer and bleeding
- Liver diseases cause hepatic necrosis.
- In diabetes
- In pregnant women
- Should be avoiding in breast feeding mother.

Aspirin - Therapeutic Uses

(i) Used as good antipyretic and analgesic agent.

(ii) Anti-inflammatory: rheumatic fever, rheumatoid arthritis, other rheumatological diseases. High dose needed (5-8 g/day)

(iii) Prophylaxis of diseases due to platelet aggregation.

(iv) An effective in treatment regimen for pre-eclampsia and hypertension of pregnancy due to excess TXA2.

Diflunisal

(i) Diflunisal is a difluorophenyl derivative of salicylic acid and it is not converted to salicylic acid *in-vivo*.

(ii) Diflunisal is more potent anti-inflammatory agent than aspirin and appears to be a competitive inhibitor of cyclooxygenase.

(iii) It is devoid of antipyretic effects because of poor penetration into the central nervous system.

(iv) It has also more potent analgesic activity than aspirin and has been used primarily as an analgesic in the treatment of osteoarthritis and musculoskeletal strains or sprains. The usual initial dose is 500 to 1000 mg, followed by 250 to 500 mg every 8 to 12 hours.

(v) Diflunisal does not produce auditory side effects and appears to cause fewer and less intense gastrointestinal and antiplatelet effects than aspirin.

PROPIONIC ACID DERIVATIVES

- Ibuprofen
- Fenoprofen
- Ketoprofen
- Naproxen
- Oxaprozin
- Flurbiprofen
- Ketorolac

General Characteristics Feutures

- These are similar to aspirin in effectiveness but differ in potency, duration of action and have fewer gastrointestinal effects.

- All are nonselective cyclooxygenase inhibitors with the effects and side effects common to other NSAIDs.

- They have lower analgesic, antipyretic and anti-inflammatory efficasy compare to asprin.
- They are used in the symptomatic treatment of rheumatoid arthritis, osteoarthritis, ankylosing spondylitis, acute gouty arthritis. They are also used as analgesics, for acute tendinitis and bursitis and for primary dysmenorrhea.
- Naproxen is most potent inhibitor of prostaglandin synthesis and also has prominent inhibitory effects on leukocyte function.
- They inhibit the platelet aggregation thus prolonging the bleeding time.
- All propionic acid derivatives NSAIDs are capable of entering the brain and crossing the placenta.
- Ibuprofen is the drug of choice for treatment of dental pain when NSAIDs are indicated.

Drug interactions

All propionic acid derivatives interfere with the action of antihypertensive and diuretic agents, increase the risk of bleeding with warfarin and increase the risk of bone marrow suppression with methotrexate. Ibuprofen one of the propionic acid derivatives interfere with the antiplatelets effects of aspirin; similar interaction has been observed between aspirin and naproxen.

Ibuprofen

Ibuprofen is rapidly absorbed by orally; food decreases the rate but not the extent of absorption. The half-life is roughly 2 hours. 400 mg of Ibuprofen is usually more effective than many other pain relievers. Ibuprofen is thought to be better tolerated than aspirin and indomethacin and has been used in patients with a history of gastrointestinal intolerance to other NSAIDs. While other adverse effects are similar to Aspirin.

Naproxen

Naproxen is absorbed fully when administered orally. Food delays the rate but not the extent of absorption. Peak concentrations in plasma occur within 2 to 4 hours and are somewhat more rapid after the administration of naproxen sodium. It is potent inhibitors of leukocyte migration.

Ketoprofen

In addition to COX inhibition, it stabilizes lysosomal membranes and antagonizes the actions of bradykinin. Ketoprofen cause fluid retention and increased plasma concentrations of creatinine.

Fenoprofen

Oral doses of Fenoprofen are readily but incompletely (85%) absorbed. Remaining other properties are similar to Ibuprofen.

Flurbifrofen

Flurbiprofen is more effective than ibuprofen but gastric effects are more.

Oxaprozin

Its pharmacokinetic properties differ considerably. Peak plasma levels are not achieved until 3 to 6 hours after an oral dose, while its half-life of 40 to 60 hours allows for once-daily administration. Remaining properties are similar to other propionic acid derivatives.

Naproxen

Naproxen is longer acting agent. It is more efficacious and better tolerated in anti-inflammatory doses.

Ketorolac

Ketorolac is a propionic acid derivative and has potent analgesic but only a moderately effective anti-inflammatory activity. Ketorolac has a rapid onset of action, extensive protein binding and a short duration of action. Oral bioavailability is about 80%. It is used as an alternative treatment option for moderate pain after opioid therapy. Unlike opioids, tolerance, withdrawal and respiratory depression do not occur. Ketorolac is used widely in postoperative patients, but it should not be used for routine obstetric analgesia. Side effects at usual oral doses include somnolence, dizziness, headache, gastrointestinal pain, dyspepsia, nausea and pain at the site of injection.

ANTHRANILIC ACID DERIVATIVES/FENAMATE

- Mefenamic acid
- Meclofenamic acid
- Flufenamic acid

They include Mefenamic, Meclofenamic, and Flufenamic acids and all are derivatives of N-phenylanthranilic acid. They have no more advantages over aspirin and frequently causing gastrointestinal effects. They have been used in the short-term treatment of pain in soft-tissue injuries, dysmenorrheal, in rheumatoid and osteoarthritis.

Mefenamic acid has central and peripheral actions while Meclofenamic acid antagonizes directly certain effects of prostaglandins. These drugs are absorbed rapidly and have short durations of action. They develops common gastrointestinal side effects at therapeutic doses. Diarrhea, which may be severe and associated with steatorrhea and inflammation of the bowel, has been reported in many cases. Autoimmune hemolytic anemia is a potentially serious but rare side effect of anthranilic acid derivatives.

ACETIC ACID DERIVATIVES

- Diclofenac
- Tolmetin
- Indomethacin
- Sulindac

DICLOFENAC

Diclofenac is a phenylacetic acid derivative and as an anti-inflammatory agent. Lumiracoxib is an analog of Diclofenac which is selective inhibitor of COX-2. Diclofenac has analgesic, antipyretic and anti-inflammatory activities. Potency of diclofenac is greater than indomethacin, naproxen or several other NSAIDs against COX-2. There is a cardiovascular hazard at chronic therapy with diclofenac. It has rapid absorption, extensive protein binding and a short half-life while its duration of therapeutic effect is considerably longer because of accumulation in synovial fluid after oral administration. It is used in symptomatic treatment of rheumatoid arthritis, osteoarthritis, ankylosing spondylitis, musculoskeletal pain, postoperative pain and dysmenorrhea.

Adverse effects

- It produces gastrointestinal side effects.
- Modest elevation of hepatic transaminases in plasma. Therefore, transaminases should be measured during the first 8 weeks of therapy with diclofenac, and the drug should be discontinued if abnormal signs or symptoms develop.
- It also produces central nervous system effects, rashes, allergic reactions, fluid retention, edema and rarely impairment of renal function.

TOLMETIN

Tolmetin is aryl (pyrole) acetic acid derivative and exerts an anti-inflammatory, analgesic and antipyretic agent. It is equivalent in efficacy to moderate doses of aspirin.

Pharmacokinetics:

Tolmetin demonstrates rapid and complete absorption, extensive plasma protein binding and a short half-life. Accumulation of the drug in synovial fluid begins within 2 hours and persists for up to 8 hours after a single oral dose.

Uses:

It is use in treatment of osteoarthritis, rheumatoid arthritis, juvenile rheumatoid arthritis and ankylosing spondylitis.

Adverse effects:

Gastrointestinal side effects are the most common and gastric ulceration has been observed. Neurological side effects are similar to those seen with indomethacin and aspirin.

Recommended dose 200 to 600 mg three times a day.

INDOMETHACIN

Indomethacin is an indole acetic acid derivative with prominent anti-inflammatory and analgesic-antipyretic properties similar to those of the salicylates. It is more potent inhibitor of the cyclooxygenase than aspirin. Indomethacin has distinct analgesic properties and may involve central and peripheral actions. Indomethacin also inhibits the motility of polymorphonuclear leukocytes and depresses the biosynthesis of mucopolysaccharides.

Pharmacokinetics

Oral indomethacin has excellent bioavailability. Peak concentrations occur 1 to 2 hours after dosing. Indomethacin is 90% bound to plasma proteins and tissues. Concentration in synovial fluid is equal to that in plasma within 5 hours of administration.

Adverse effects

Gastrointestinal, Hepatic and Pancreas: It produces dose related adverse effects e.g. gastrointestinal including diarrhea, ulcerative lesions of the bowel, peptic ulcer, acute pancreatitis and rarely causes hepatitis.

Central Nervous System: Adverse effects on central nervous system include frontal headache, dizziness, vertigo, light-headedness and mental confusion. Seizures have been reported, as have severe depression, psychosis, hallucinations and suicide.

Blood: Hematopoietic reactions include neutropenia, thrombocytopenia and rarely aplastic anemia. Impairment in platelet function has also been reported.

Uses

- Indomethacin is more potent than aspirin in relieving joint pain, swelling and tenderness, increasing grip strength and decreasing the duration of morning stiffness. Also used in treatment of ankylosing spondylitis and osteoarthritis and acute gout although it is not uricosuric.

Drug Interactions

- Indomethacin does not directly modify the effect of warfarin, but platelet inhibition and gastric irritation increase the risk of bleeding.
- Indomethacin antagonizes the natriuretic and antihypertensive effects of furosemide and thiazide diuretics.

SULINDAC

Sulindac is indole acetic acid derivative and closely related to indomethacin. Its analgesic and anti-inflammatory effects are comparable to those achieved with aspirin. While the adverse effects are similar to indomethacin but the intensity is much lower. It is present as prodrugs which generate active anti-inflammatory sulfide metabolite. The sulfide metabolite is potent more than 500 times than sulindac as an inhibitor of cyclooxygenase.

There is a lower incidence of gastrointestinal toxicity with sulindac compared with indomethacin. In contrast to other NSAIDs, it do not alter renal prostaglandin levels and therefore might avoid the association with hypertension in susceptible individuals.

Pharmacokinetics

About 90% of the sulindac is absorbed after oral administration and peak concentrations attained within 1 to 2 hours, while its metabolite takes about 8 hours at oral administration. The half-life of sulindac itself is about 7 hours, but the active sulfide has a half-life as long as 18 hours.

Uses

Sulindac is used mainly for the treatment of rheumatoid arthritis, osteoarthritis, ankylosing spondylitis and acute gout. The usual dose is 150 to 200 mg twice a day in adult. It also used to prevent colon cancer in patients with familial adenomatous polyposis.

OXICAM DERIVATIVES

- Piroxicam
- Tenoxicam
- Lornoxicam
- Others

PIROXICAM

Piroxicam is a long acting NSAID and is highly effective as an anti-inflammatory. It inhibits cyclooxygenase as well as proteoglycanase and collagenase in cartilage. Beside this, it also inhibits activation of neutrophils and decreases the production of IgM rheumatoid factor.

Pharmacokinetics

Piroxicam is absorbed completely after oral administration and its peak concentrations in plasma occur within 2 to 4 hours. It is extensively (99%) bound to plasma proteins. There is a variable half-life in plasma which is roughly 50 hours. Steady state concentration in plasma and synovial fluid attained after 10 days of administration.

Uses

Used in treatment of rheumatoid arthritis and osteoarthritis. Piroxicam is less suited for treatment in acute analgesia but is used extensively treatment of acute gout.

Other Oxicam derivative under investigation which have been designed to reduce gastrointestinal irritation.

The efficacy and toxicity of these drugs are similar to those of piroxicam.

These include several prodrug of Piroxicam

- Ampiroxicam
- Droxicam
- Pivoxicam
- Lornoxicam
- Cinnoxicam
- Sudoxicam

Lornoxicam is unique among the enolic acid derivatives in that it has a rapid onset of action and a relatively short half-life (3 to 5 hours).

PREFERENTIAL COX-2 INHIBITORS

- Meloxicam
- Nabumetone
- Nimesulide

MELOXICAM

Meloxicam is a newer congener of Piroxicam which has both COX-1 and COX-2 selectivity. But preferentially inhibits COX -2 enzyme for its activity. It is mostly use in osteoarthritis (dose-7.5 to15 mg) and rheumatoid arthritis (15mg). It has significantly less gastric injury as compared to piroxicam. At the therapeutic dose level there is decrease in platelet production.

NABUMETONE

Nabumetone is a prodrug; which is absorbed rapidly and is converted in the liver to one or more active metabolites, principally 6-methoxy-2-naphthylacetic acid (6-MNA), a potent inhibitor of COX-2 than COX-1. This metabolite, inactivated by *O*-demethylation in

the liver, is then conjugated before excretion, and is eliminated with a half-life of about 24 hours. It possesses analgesic, antipyretic and anti-inflammatory properties. It is used in treatment of rheumatoid arthritis and osteoarthritis and soft tissue injury. The typically dose is 1000 mg once daily.

Side effects

It produces lower abdominal pain and diarrhea, while the gastrointestinal ulceration appears to be lower than with other NSAIDs. Other side effects include rash, headache, dizziness, heartburn, tinnitus, and pruritus.

NIMESULIDE

Nimesulide is a sulfonanilide compound preferentially acts on COX-2 than COX-1. It also inhibits neutrophil activation, decreases cytokine production, decreases degradative enzyme production and activation of glucocorticoid receptors.

Nimesulide is anti-inflammatory, analgesic and antipyretic. It shows fewer incidences of gastrointestinal adverse effects. There is a risk of cardiovascular and cerebrovascular events with Nimesulide due to these reason, it has been withdrawal from US market.

SELECTIVE COX-2 INHIBITORS

- Celecoxib
- Rofecoxib
- Valdecoxib
- Parecoxib
- Lumiracoxib
- Etoricoxib

CELOCOXIB

Celocoxib is a selective COX-2 inhibitor and exerts anti-inflammatory, analgesic and antipyretic effects. It has low ulcerogenic potential. It do not affecting to COX-1 activity in gastrointestinal mucosa at maximal dose also. Celocoxib is used in treatment of rheumatoid arthritis and comparatively is more effective than naproxen and diclofenac.

There is risk of thrombosis, hypertension and accelerated artherogenesis so it should be avoided in patients prone to cardiovascular or cerebrovascular disease. For treatment of osteoarthritis the recommended dose is 200mg/day as a single dose or as two 100-mg doses while in rheumatoid arthritis, the recommended dose is 100 to 200 mg twice per day.

Pharmacokinetics

It is slowly absorbed and around 98% bound to plasma protein metabolized predominantly by CYP2C9. Its peak plasma levels occur at 2 to 4 hours post dose. The elimination half-life is approximately 11 hours.

ROFECOXIB

There is an incidence of serious thromboembolic events in individual receiving 25 mg of Rofecoxib. It has superiority over NSAIDs in terms of gastrointestinal outcomes. It is used in treatment of osteoarthritis, rheumatoid arthritis, and dysmenorrhea, dental, musculoskeletal and postoperative pain.

It do not produce any effects on TXA2 production by platelets. It has mild gastrointestinal complaint over other NSAIDs. It also produces headache and dizziness. Rofecoxib is also known to rise in blood pressure due to edema formation in pedal.

Rofecoxib is contraindicated in individual with severe hepatic and renal disease; it should also be avoided in patients who are receiving rifampicin, warfarin and methotrexate.

VALDECOXIB

Valdecoxib has been recently introduced in market and has COX-2 selectivity which has similar tolerability and efficasy as rofecoxib. It elevates the risk of heart attack and stroke and so should be avoided in patients prone to these conditions. There are reports of skin reactions (Stevens-Johnson syndrome, and erythema multiforme) with valdecoxib.

Pharmacokinetics

Valdecoxib is absorbed rapidly (1 to 2 hours) and undergoes extensive hepatic metabolism. The half-life is approximately 7 to 8 hours. Concomitant administration of valdecoxib and fluconazole or ketoconazole results to increase plasma levels of valdecoxib by inhibiting the metabolism of valdecoxib.

PARECOXIB

Parecoxib is a prodrug of valdecoxib which is absorbed rapidly (approximately 15 minutes) and converted (15 to 52 minutes) by deoxymethylation to valdecoxib. It is the only coxib available by injection and has been use when patients are unable to take oral medication. Remaining properties are similar to valdecoxib.

LUMIRACOXIB

Lumiracoxib is unique among the coxib in being a weak acid. Its acidic nature allows it to penetrate well into areas of inflammation. It is rapidly and well absorbed, with peak plasma concentrations occurs in 1 to 3 hours. Potency of lumiracoxib is similar to naproxen with much greater COX-2 selectivity. It is used in treatment of osteoarthritis, rheumatoid arthritis and dysmenorrhea. There is little or no evidence of gastric injury at high therapeutic doses.

ETORICOXIB

Etoricoxib is incompletely (83%) absorbed and has a long half-life of approximately 20 to 26 hours. There is a moderate hepatic impairment with etoricoxib. Once-daily medicine used for symptomatic relief in the treatment of osteoarthritis, rheumatoid arthritis, and acute gouty arthritis.

Caution to use COX-2 inhibitor due to following limitations

- Inhibition of COX2 removes the protective constraints on thrombogenesis, hypertension and artherogenesis.
- Side effects include risk of heart attack and stroke.
- Indications not seen due to shortness of trial studies before approval.

Future prospective of COX-2 Inhibitors

- There is predominant role of COX-2 in neocortex and hippocampus.
- Studies for role of COX-2 inhibitors in Alzheimer's are in progress.
- Cox-2 inhibition results into regression of neoplastic polyps and prevention of their development.
- Role in Cancer prevention is in progress.

DRUG HAVING POOR ANTI-INFLAMMATORY ACTIVITY

ACETOAMINOPHEN: (Paracetamol)

Paracetamol has analgesic and antipyretic activity. It exhibits less effect on peripheral COX and shows few drug-drug interactions. It has poor or no anti-inflammatory activity. While it produce analgesic effects. The major side effect of paracetamol is liver toxicity at higher dose. It may also inhibit COX selectively in central nervous system. It is only a weak inhibitor of peripheral COX due to presence of peroxide which is generated at site of inflammation. It also inhibits effects of substance P in central nervous system.

Paracetamol inhibits effects of glutamate in nervous system while there is no effect on cardiovascular system. It does not affect platelet function or clotting function and not also uricosuric.

It is valuable in patient with peptic ulcer, aspirin hypersensitivity and in children with a febrile illness in whom aspirin is contraindicated.

Mechanisms of Action

There is central effect (COX) at level of spinal cord (little effect on peripheral COX-1 or COX-2). This spinal antinociceptive effect is amplified by acetaminophen in the brain. The brain effect is mediated by an opioid mechanism expressed at the level of spinal cord. In contrast to aspirin it does not stimulate respiration, cellular metabolism and neither affects acid base balance.

Pharmacokinetics

Rapidly absorbed from gastrointestinal tract and reaches a peak plasma level in 30 to 60 minutes. It gets metabolized in liver mainly through glucuronic acid conjugation and half life is approximately 2 hours. A small percentage undergoes cytochrome P450 mediated N-hydroxylation forming a highly reactive intermediate. Paracetamol is associated with hepatoxicity which is a major side effect when taken in large doses (10 to 15 g) while it is neutralized with the sulphydryl reducing agent such as N-acetylcysteine which is discuss below.

Adverse effects

It is generally well tolerated at therapeutic dose level while occasionally produce nausea and rashes. It is also reported to produce leucopenia but is rare. It is also reported to cause nephropathy which in turn leads to loss of urine concentrating ability resulting into kidney shrinks.

PARACETAMOL POISONING

Paracetamol poisoning generally occurring in patient who has low hepatic glucuronide conjugating ability which is generally observed in infants and children. It also occurs at high dose more than 150 mg/kg at which there is saturation of enzyme responsible for metabolism.

Generally paracetamol metabolized by glucuronide and sulphate conjugation. Administration in toxic doses results into saturation of glucuronide capacity to metabolism and depletion of glutathione (GSH) enzyme. As a result, toxic metabolite N-acetyl-p-benzoquinoneimine (NABQI) of paracetamol starts accumulating in hepatocytes leading to hepatotoxicity.

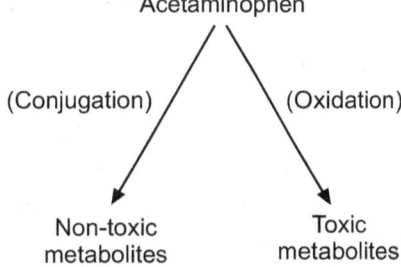

Role of glutathione:

It detoxify the minor metabolite of paracetamol which is toxic, The toxic metabolite rapidly eliminated by conjugation with GSH and then further metabolized to a mercapturic acid and excreted into the urine.

Effects of toxic metabolites NAPQI:

The highly reactive NAPQI metabolite binds covalently to cell macromolecules of liver leading to dysfunction of enzymatic systems (hepatocellular levels of GSH become depleted).

Thus, hepatocytes become susceptible to oxidative stress and apoptosis.

Manifestation of paracetamol poisoning:

- Early manifestations are nausea, vomiting, abdominal pain and liver tenderness.
- Plasma transaminases become elevated approximately 12 to 36 hours after ingestion.
- Hepatic damage is manifest within 2 to 4 days of ingestion of toxic doses, with right subcostal pain, tender hepatomegaly, jaundice and coagulopathy.
- Renal impairment may occur. Liver enzyme abnormalities typically peak within 72 to 96 hours after ingestion.

Treatment of poisoning:

- Activated charcoal should be given within 4 hours of ingestion which decreases acetaminophen (paracetamol) absorption by 50% to 90% and is the preferred method of gastric decontamination. Gastric lavage generally is not recommended.
- N-Acetylcysteine (NAC) is use for preventing the hepatic injury. NAC therapy should be used in acetaminophen poisoning which detoxifying NAPQI by serving as a GSH substitute.
- NAC may also provide against extrahepatic injury by its antioxidant and anti-inflammatory properties.
- While the adverse reaction to NAC include rash, urticaria, nausea, vomiting, diarrhea and rare anaphylactoid reactions.
- Hypoglycemia can result from liver failure therefore plasma glucose should be monitored closely; besides this, other supportive measure, as needed should be taken.

PYRAZOLONE DERIVATIVES

Previously antipyrine and amidopyrine were available for its antipyretic and analgesic activity, but there were incidences of agranulocytosis thus they were withdrawn from market. While other drug viz. oxyphenbutazone which shows bone marrow depression and other toxicity, due to this it is rarely prescribed for its antipyretic and analgesic activity. Available drugs in category of pyrazolone derivative which are using are metamizole and propiphenazole.

Metamizole and Propiphenazole

- Potent analgesic and antipyretic but shows poor anti-inflammatory action.
- Donot produce uricosuric action.
- Produce gastric irritation and pain at site of injection.
- Reported to show agranulocytosis with metamizole but not with propiphenazole, while the other risks are lower than asprin.

Phenylbutazone and oxyphenbutazone

- These are COX inhibitors and have a potent anti-inflammatory activity while poor analgesic and antipyretic activity.
- It produces uricosuric action.
- It is more toxic than asprin and shows variety of reactions including CNS, hypersensitivity as well as bone marrow depression.

BENZOXAZOCINE DERIVATIVES

Nefopam

- It is non-opioid drug but the efficacy is approaching to morphine.
- It is used in reliving musculoskeletal pain which is not responding to other non-opioid drug.
- It produces sympathomimetic and anticholinergic side effects.

Summary

- Prostaglandins are chemicals produced by the body that promote inflammation, pain, and fever
- NSAIDs acts by inhibiting prostaglandin synthesis. This is done by inhibiting the action of the enzyme cyclooxygenase (COX).
- Simultaneous inhibition of COX-1 results in unwanted side effects (gastrointestinal ulcerations).
- COX-2 is an inducible enzyme that is synthesized only during inflammation.

- Aspirin - Inhibits COX1 and COX2
- COX-1 inhibitors: Decrease pain and increase gastric distress.
- COX-2 specific inhibitors: decrease gastric distress, increase heart problems.
- Aspirin: Inhibits clotting of blood for a prolonged period (7-14 days) and beneficial in preventing blood clots, heart attacks and strokes.
- Selective COX-2 inhibitors: specifically designed to avoid the gastrointestinal side effects associated with COX-1 inhibition.
- NSAIDs interact with anti-hypertensive drugs, phenytoin, anti-coagulants and methotrexate.
- Acetaminophen and aspirin are equally efficacious (blocks same degree of pain) and potent (require the same dose for effect) as analgesics and antipyretics.
- Acetaminophen does not possess any significant anti-inflammatory effect probably due to the degree of prostaglandin synthesis inhibition at different sites.
- Acetaminophen (paracetamol) does not produce any effect on cardiovascular or respiratory systems, no gastric bleeding, does not affect platelet adhesiveness and is remarkably free of drug interactions.
- Toxic metabolite of acetaminophen on accumulation may cause hepatic necrosis.
- Alcohol stimulates oxidizing enzymes that metabolize acetaminophen.

- Combination generally used in patient NSAID +Acetaminophen which has greater analgesic effect than either alone and avoids adverse effects of opioids.

Agent	Duration	COX
Ibuprofen	4-6 hours	1, 2
Naproxen	12 hours	1, 2
Indomethacin	4-8 hours	1, 2
Ketorolac	3-6 hours	1, 2
Piroxicam	48-72 hours	1, 2
Celecoxib	12-24 hours	2

Questions on this Chapter

1. Write a detail on COX enzyme and its inhibitors.
2. Write the physiological effects of NSAIDs
3. Write the classification of NSAIDs and add note on Aspirin toxicity.
4. Write the mechanism, pharmacological action and adverse effects of Aspirin.
5. Write short note on Propionic acid derivatives.
6. Write the pharmacology of Indomethacin.
7. Write short note on Paracetamol poisoning.

Chapter 15

PHARMACOTHERAPY OF RHEUMATOID ARTHRITIS

Objectives

After reading this chapter, the student will be able to:

➢ Write the pathogenesis of rheumatoid arthritis

➢ What are the disease modifying therapy

➢ Write the importance of immunosuppressant in rheumatoid arthritis

➢ Write the different surgical procedure available for rheumatoid arthritis

INTRODUCTION

Rheumatoid arthritis is autoimmune disease. Antigen stimulates the initial autoimmune response and the genetic mechanisms promote its development. Antigen-antibody complex activate the complement and elicit the release of various mediators, causing inflammation. The detailed pathogenesis of rheumatoid arthritis is largely unknown; it appears to be an autoimmune disease driven primarily by activated T cells. These activated cells give rise to T cell-derived cytokines, such as IL-1 and TNF-α. Activation of B cells and the humoral responses are also evident, although most of the antibodies generated are IgG of unknown specificity. This antibody generation is believed to be elicited by polyclonal activation of B cells rather than from a response to a specific antigen.

Many cytokines, including IL-1 and TNF-α, have been found in the rheumatoid synovium. Glucocorticoids interfere with the synthesis and actions of cytokines, such as IL-1 or TNF-α. The actions of these cytokines are accompanied by the release of prostaglandins and thromboxane A_2 (TXA$_2$). COX inhibitors appear to block only their pyrogenic effects. In addition, many actions of the prostaglandins are inhibitory to immune responses, including suppression of the function of helper T cells and B cells and inhibition of the production of IL-1.

Thus, it has been suggested that COX-independent effects may contribute to the efficacy of NSAIDs in this disease.

An impact of adhesive interactions, salicylate and certain NSAIDs can directly inhibit the activation and function of neutrophils, by blockade of integrin-mediated neutrophil responses. The treatment of rheumatoid arthritis is aimed at reducing this inflammation by inhibiting the cytokine production or its action also is aimed at to suppress the immune response by inhibiting the activation of B cells, thereby decreasing the pain and attempting to slow the joint destruction. In the management of arthritic condition the therapy is chosen on the basis of patient condition and severity.

TREATMENT METHODS

Treatment of rheumatoid arthritis involves following methods:

- Oral Drugs
- Disease modifying therapy
- Intra-articular Drugs
- Physical Treatment
- Surgery
- External Analgesics
- Nutritional Supplements

ORAL THERAPY

Non-Steroidal Anti-inflammatory Agents (NSAIDs)

NSAIDs reduce the arthritic condition by eliminating inflammations but this therapy doesn't eliminate signs and symptoms of arthritis. They have no major effect on the underlying disease process. Some NSAIDs such as Ibuprofen and Naproxen are considered safest for long term treatment of rheumatoid arthritis. In many cases they can control the symptoms while the disease process remits spontaneously. Nonprescription drugs (over the counter products) promoted as "arthritis pain relievers" should be viewed with some skepticism. The FDA expert panel has advised that nonprescription drugs should not be labeled for this purpose. Aspirin can be given to patient up to 4000mg daily without prescription but there need prescription and should be taken under close medical supervision if it more than 5300 mg.

Side Effects

Large amounts of drugs may cause stomach irritation, gastrointestinal bleeding (severe or mild), ringing in the ears and temporary hearing loss. To control such side effects, physicians may reduce the dosage

DISEASE-MODIFYING ANTIRHEUMATIC DRUG [DMARD]

When a patient does not respond adequately or if doctor believes that it's advisable to attempt to prevent permanent damage to the joints, disease-modifying antirheumatic drugs are used these includes as bellow.

- Gold salts
- Penicillamine
- Hydroxychloroquine (an anti-malarial drug)
- Immunosuppressant: Methotrexate, Azathioprine, Cyclosporin. (A chemo-therapeutic agent also used against cancer).
- Sulfasalazine (a drug used for treating inflammatory bowel disease).
- Corticosteroid

Gold

Gold is considered as one of the most effective agents for arresting the rheumatoid process and for preventing involvement of additional pain. It reduces chemotaxis, phagocytosis, macrophage and lysosomal activity, monocytes differentiation and inhibits cell mediated immunity, but the exact mechanism of action is unknown. It also lowers the rheumatoid factor level. By affecting on synovial membrane and collagen it prevents the joint destruction and promotes the healing of bone.

The major limitation to gold therapy is that it's get heavily bound to plasma and tissue protein, especially in kidneys; thus stays in body for years resulting into high toxicity. It produces vasodilation, postural hypotension, dermatitis and rashes, albunuria, hepatitis, peripheral neuritis, encephalopathy, eosinophilia and bone marrow depression. Due to these unavoidable side effects, Aurafin is now being used as an effective alternative to gold. It contains gold but in less erconcentration. Due to less gold concentration it produces less toxic reactions.

D-Penicilamine

It is a copper chelating agent with gold like activity in rheumatoid arthritis. It is less efficacious than gold and it does not heal the erosionated bone. Toxicity of Penicilamine is similar to same.

Chloroquine and Hydrochloroquine

They are less effective and less toxic than gold. Both are found to reduce the monocytes interleukin and B lymphocyte. For treatment of rheumatoid arthritis long term therapy by these agent is necessary. Prolonged consumption results into accumulation of these drugs into tissues and produce toxicity like retinal damage and corneal opacity. While this type of toxicity is less common with hydrochloroquine.

Sulfasalazine

Sulfasalazine is a mixture of sulphapyridine and 5-amino salicylic acid which has anti-inflammatory activity and primarily used in ulcerative colitis. It inhibits the generation of superoxide radicals and cytokine elaboration by suppressing inflammatory cells.

Immunosuppressants

Methotrexate

Methotrexate has prominent immuno-suppressant and anti-inflammatory activity. It shows beneficial effects in rheumatoid arthritis because of inhibition of cytokine production, chemotaxis and cell mediated immune reaction. Onset of symptoms relief is rapid and thus it preferred for initial treatment in rheumatoid arthritis.

Azathioprine

It is a potent suppressant of cell mediated immunity. It acts by affecting selectively the differentiation and function of T cell and natural killer cell.

Cyclosporine

Cyclosporine is T cell specific immunosuppressant used in rheumatoid arthritis.

Corticosteroid

Corticosteroid has potent immunosuppressant and anti-inflammatory properties. It is used for treating rheumatoid arthritis in combination with other drugs. For long term therapy it is given in low dose in combination with NSAIDs and in case of severe cases it is given in high dose.

INTRA-ARTICULAR

This treatment method is used when only one or two joints are involved. In this case steroid drug is injected into affected joints. This provides considerable relief but should only be done sparingly, because repeated injections can cause cartilage degeneration, damaging the joint.

PHYSICAL TREATMENT

Rest is most important during acute flare-ups (i.e. acute pain and inflammation). But under moderate conditions exercise is the best physical treatment. Besides preventing and relieving pain it also helps in maintaining joint flexibility and muscle strength. While doing exercise care should be taken to avoid activities that are strenuous, involves high impact or require sudden twisting and turning. Walking, bicycling, swimming are advised. In addition to these exercise hot or cold packs, whirlpool baths, ultrasound diathermy or paraffin baths are also of great help in relieving pain.

SURGERY

It is generally best to operate as the need arises rather than wait until the patient has many severely damaged joints.

Types of Operations

- Arthrodesis: Fusion of a diseased joint to relieve pain.
- Joint Replacement: Synthetic materials can be used or rebuild afflicted joints.
- Arthroplasty: Reconstruction of a diseased joint using patient's own tissue
- Osteotomy: Separation or cutting of a joint that has become fused or has shifted to an abnormal position.
- Autologous Chondrocyte Transplantation (ACT): a small amount of cartilage from a healthy joint is cultivated in a lab and is implanted into a damaged joint.

EXTERNAL ANALGESICS

These products are promoted for the relief of aches and pains due to arthritis. Some products of this type have been part of folk medicine for thousands of years. Liniments, rubs, poultices, plasters, and balms mildly stimulate nerve endings in the skin providing warmth and coolness. If the external analgesic combines with rubbing motion then it may loosen tight muscles and it will more benefit to relive the pain from arthritis.

NUTRITIONAL SUPPLEMENTS

Green-lipped mussel was one of the best nutrition source in case of rheumatoid arthritis. It harvested in New Zealand and made into supplement capsules. FDA has now banned green-lipped mussels; however there are still similar products out there. Superoxide dismutase (SOD) is an enzyme involved in the body's defense against free radicals.

SOD claims to reduce inflammation in arthritis. Capsules of omega-3 fatty acids, commonly referred to as fish oils, are believed to be also natural curative agents for arthritis. Agents like glucosamine and chondrotin sulfate may control the pain of osteoarthritis but the quality of the supporting evidence is not high.

GUIDELINES FOR PEOPLE WITH ARTHRITIS

- Be aware that there is no specific cure for most forms of arthritis.

- Avoid spas or clinics that encourage self-diagnosis by mail or allege therapeutic value of such treatments as mineral salts and baths.

- Understand that just because a product is marketed does not ensure that the claims for it are justified.

- Contact a local Arthritis Foundation for help.

- Individuals wishing to use an unproven approach should discuss this with their physician to minimize their chances of deceiving themselves or selecting a dangerous method.

Questions on this Chapter

1. Write the classification of Antirheumatic agents and add note on immuno-suppressant in rheumatic arthritis.

2. Write the disease modifying therapy for rheumatoid arthritis.

3. Discuss the different treatment methods for rheumatoid arthritis.

Chapter 16

PHARMACOTHERAPY OF GOUT

Objectives

After reading this chapter, the student will be able to:
➢ Explain the hyperuricemic state of gout
➢ Differentiate between acute and chronic gout
➢ Understand the mechanism of colchicine
➢ Write the mechanism of uricosuric agent

Gout and Hyperuricemia

Gout is a hyperuricemic state (> 6 mg/dl) that is effectively diagnosed through the detection of monosodium urate crystals in the synovial fluid of the involved joint. Condition causing hyperuricemia include excessive synthesis of uric acid and excessive synthesis of purines which are precursors of uric acid. Uric acid has low water solubility, especially at low pH. When the blood level of uric acid is high, it get precipitated and deposited in joints, kidney and subcutaneous tissue. If remains untreated it may precipitate an acute attack of gout.

Acute gout manifested as a severe inflammation in a joints due to precipitation of urate crystals in the joint space. The joints become red, swollen and extremely painful which required immediate treatment.

Chronic gout: If the manifestation of acute gout is not treated immediately pain and stiffness persist in a joint and gout become chronic. Other features of chronic gout are hyperuricemia, chalk like urate stone under the skin and in kidney. It may also cause progressive disability and permanent deformities.

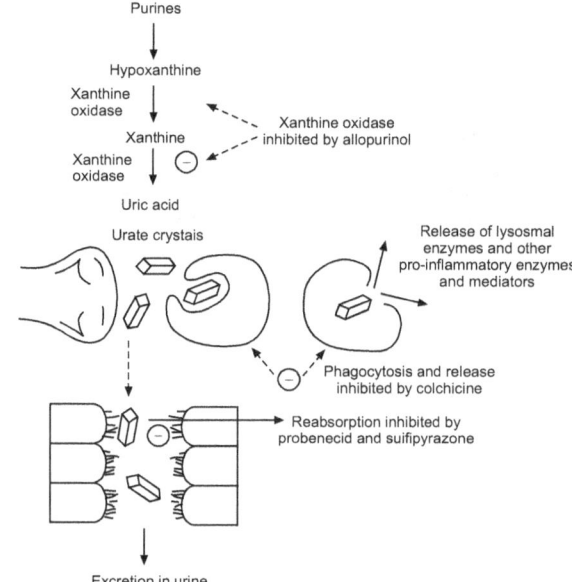

Fig. 16.1: Hyperuricemic state of Gout and targeted site

The hyperuricemic state may be corrected either by inhibiting the synthesis of uric acid by allopurinol or by enhancing the elimination of uric acid by uricosuric agents (Figure 16.1).

TREATMENT OF ACUTE AND CHRONIC GOUT

(A) TREATMENT OF ACUTE GOUT
NSAIDs

Several NSAIDs are reported to be used in the treatment of acute gout at high doses for   3-

4 days; e.g. etoricoxib, indomethacin, naproxen, sulindac, and celocoxib. Aspirin is not indicated in the treatment of gout because at low doses it inhibits urate excretion and at high doses it shows uricosuric action along with the risk of renal calculi. When aspirin is given in combination with uricosuric agents then it inhibits the action of uricosuric agents.

CORTICOSTEROIDS

Corticosteroids suppress the symptoms of gout rapidly within hours of therapy. Intra-articular glucocorticoids are useful if only a few joints are involved and septic arthritis has been ruled out. Systemic steroids are rarely indicated. They are very effective and produce rapid response (e.g colchicines) and they are reserved as treatment regimen in cases which do not respondito colchicine or cannot tolerate NSAIDs, e.g. Prednisolone.

COLCHICINE

It is an anticancer agent having antimitotic effects which arrests cell division in G-1 phase by interfering with microtubule and spindle formation. This effect of colchicine is similar to vinca alkaloids. Colchicine also alters neutrophil motility. Colchicine decreases the secretion of chemotactic factors by activated neutrophils. It inhibits the release of histamine-containing granules from mast cells, the secretion of insulin from pancreatic β cells, and the movement of melanin granules in melanophores.

Colchicine is also reported to decrease body temperature, increase the sensitivity to central depressants, depress the respiratory center, enhance the response to sympathomimetic agents, constrict blood vessels, and induces hypertension by central vasomotor stimulation. It enhances gastrointestinal activity by neurogenic stimulation but depresses it by a direct effect and alters neuromuscular function.

Pharmacokinetic

It is rapidly absorbed orally and peak plasma concentrations occur 0.5 to 2 hours after dosing. It is 50% bound to plasma protein and metabolised by deacetylation in the liver. The plasma half-life of colchicine is approximately 9 hours.

Adverse effects

- Oral administration produces adverse effects such as nausea, vomiting, diarrhea, and abdominal pain as the gastrointestinal tract is particularly susceptible to colchicine toxicity; it reported to show
- Acute intoxication causes hemorrhagic gastropathy and ascending paralysis of the central nervous system.
- It has narrow margin of safety by intravenous administration because this route shows serious systemic toxicity in addition to gastrointestinal severity.
- Colchicine toxicity is associated with bone marrow suppression.
- Chronic use of colchicine may lead to agranulocytosis, thrombocytopenia and disseminated intravascular coagulation, nephropathy and azoospermia in cases of severe poisoning.
- Proteinuria, hematuria and acute tubular necrosis have been reported in severely intoxicated patients.

Supportive measures

- Fluid repletion. Activated charcoal may decrease total colchicine exposure.
- Hemodialysis.
- Colchicine antibodies and the use of granulocyte colony-stimulating factor to treat the leucopenia.

Uses

- Colchicine is used as a preventive measure in case of recurrent gout. It also relieves acute attacks of gout.
- It reduces pain, swelling, and redness within 12 hours of its intake. Symptoms completely vanish within 48 to 72 hours.
- Colchicine should only be repeated after a week. If administered early, it may results into cumulative toxicity.
- Use of colchicine is contraindicated in patient with cardiac, renal, hepatic, or gastrointestinal diseases.

(B) TREATMENT OF CHRONIC GOUT

URICOSURIC AGENT

Uricosuric agents increase the rate of excretion of uric acid from body by inhibiting the reabsorption of urate; they act by affecting specific transporter. They compete for urate with transporters involved in urate transport thereby inhibiting its reabsorption by anion exchange system. Following are the examples of uricosuric agents.

PROBENECID

Probenecid is an endogenous compound which increases the excretion of uric acid by inhibiting its reabsorption.

Pharmacokinetics

Oral bioavailability of probenecid is excellent; it is absorbed completely and peak concentrations in plasma are reached in 2 to 4 hours. The plasma protein binding is found to be 95%. The half-life of the drug in plasma is dose-dependent and varies from less than 5 hours to more than 8 hours.

Adverse effects

- Probenecid has been reported to show mild gastrointestinal irritation.
- Hypersensitivity reactions usually are mild.
- Substantial over dosage with probenecid results in central nervous system stimulation, convulsions and death from respiratory failure.

Interactions

- Salicylate interferes with the activity of probenecid. When administered concurrently, the uricosuric action of probenecid decreases.
- Probenecid inhibits the tubular secretion of a number of drugs, such as methotrexate and Clofibrate. Certain NSAIDs such as naproxen, ketoprofen, and indomethacin, some diagnostic agents e.g. indocyanine green and bromosulphthalein (BSP) and rifampicin shows higher plasma concentrations when administered concurrently with probenecid.

Uses

- It is used for the treatment of gout in which the starting dose is 250 mg twice daily, and it is increased over 1 to 2 weeks to 500 to 1000 mg twice daily.
- Probencide is generally not used alone in gouty patients with overproduction of uric acid because it precipitates an attack of gout so probenecid is concomitantly administered either with colchicine or NSAIDs.

SULFINPYRAZONE

Sulfinpyrazone is related to Phenylbutazone which lacks anti-inflammatory and analgesic activity but has potent uricosuric effects. Sulfinpyrazone potently inhibits the renal tubular reabsorption of uric acid but at small doses it decreases the excretion of urate.

Pharmacokinetics

Sulfinpyrazone is well absorbed orally and is 99%bound to plasma protein and displaces other anionic drugs that have their highest affinity for the same binding site. Its plasma half-life is about 3 hours. The uricosuric effect of a single dose of sulphinpyrazone lasts for 10 hours. Excretion takes place by active secretion at proximal tubule.

Adverse effects

Sulfinpyrazone produces mild gastro-intestinal irritation and hypersensitivity reactions. Depression of hematopoiesis has also been demonstrated, periodic blood cell counts are therefore advised during prolonged therapy.

Drug Interactions

- It induces hypoglycemia by inhibiting the metabolism of the sulfonylurea.
- The hepatic metabolism of warfarin also is impaired.
- The uricosuric action of sulfinpyrazone is additive when it is given concurrently with probenecid, but when it is given with salicylate, it antagonises the uricosuric effects of sulphinpyrazone.

Uses

As similar with probenecid, concomitant colchicine is indicated early in the course to avoid precipitating an attack of gout in hyperuricemic patient. Therapy starts with a dose of 100-200 mg twice daily and it is gradually increased according to the response; maximal daily dose may reach upto 800 mg.

URIC ACID SYNTHESIS INHIBITOR

ALLOPURINOL

Allopurinol is an analog of hypoxanthine. Previously it was synthesised as a purine antimetabolite for cancer chemotherapy. However, it had no anticancer activity but found to inhibit an enzyme xanthine oxidase which is responsible for uric acid synthesis. Allopurinol is a short acting competitively inhibitor of xanthine oxidase at low concentrations and is a noncompetitive inhibitor at high concentrations.

Its metabolite oxypurine is long acting and a noncompetitive inhibitor of xanthine oxidase.

In the absence of allopurinol, the dominant urinary purine is uric acid. During allopurinol treatment, the urinary purines include hypoxanthine, xanthine and uric acid. The concentration of uric acid in plasma is reduced and purine excretion increased. Allopurinol facilitates the dissolution of urate crystals and prevents the development or progression of chronic gouty arthritis by lowering the uric acid concentration in plasma.

Pharmacokinetics

Orally administered allopurinol is absorbed rapidly. Its peak level is attain within 60 min. of its administration. It is not bound to plasma protein and metabolised to alloxantine (oxypurine). Oxypurinol is excreted by glomerular filtration and is counterbalanced by some tubular reabsorption. The plasma half-life of allopurinol is approximately 1 to 2 hours and of oxypurinol approximately 18 to 30 hours.

Drug Interactions

- Allopurinol shows complex interaction with probenecid; it increases the half-life of probenecid and enhances its uricosuric effect, while probenecid shortens the half-life of alloxantine by increasing the clearance, thus there need to increase the dose of allopurinol when given along with probenecid.

- Allopurinol potentiates the effect of mercaptopurine and its derivative azathioprine by inhibiting the enzymatic degradation thus it is essential to reduce the dose of mercaptopurine and its derivative when it is given along with allopurinol

- Allopurinol also potentiates the effect of warfarin and theophylline by inhibiting their metabolism.

- It has also been reported to show some skin reaction when administered with penicillin.

Adverse effects

- The most common adverse effects are hypersensitivity reactions; rarely toxic epidermal necrolysis or Stevens-Johnson syndrome may also occurs.

- Fever, malaise and myalgias occur more frequently in those with renal impairment.

- Transient leukopenia or leukocytosis and eosinophilia are rare reactions.

Contraindications

Allopurinol is contraindicated in patients showing hypersensitivity reactions to the medication. It is also contraindicated in nursing mothers and children, except those with malignancy or certain inborn errors of purine metabolism (e.g., Lesch-Nyhan syndrome).

Uses

- It is indicated in chronic gout.

- It is also used in secondary hyperuricemia due to cancer chemotherapy or other drugs which can be controlled by allopurinol.

- In the management of gout, it is recommended to use allopurinol therapy with colchicine and to avoid starting allopurinol during an acute attack of gouty arthritis.

- For chronic treatment an initial daily dose of 100 mg which is increased by 100-mg increments at weekly intervals. Those with more severe gout may require 400 to 600 mg/day.

- Allopurinol also used in Kala-azar as it inhibits *Leishmania* by altering its purine metabolism.

RASBURICASE

Rasburicase is a recombinant enzyme produced by a genetically modified *Saccharomyces cerevisiae* strain that causes oxidation of uric acid into the soluble and inactive metabolite allantoin. It is capable of lowering urate levels more effectively than allopurinol. Rasburicase is indicated to use in cancer therapy for management of elevated plasma uric acid levels.

Adverse effects

- Haemolysis in G6PD-deficient patients, methemoglobinemia, acute renal failure and anaphylaxis.

Other adverse reactions include vomiting, fever, nausea, headache, abdominal pain, constipation and diarrhea.

Questions on this Chapter

1. Write a note on uricosuric agents.
2. Elaborate on the treatment of acute gout.
3. Discuss the pharmacology of colchicine.
4. What is the treatment for chronic gout.?
5. Write a short note on uric acid synthesis inhibitors.

Chapter 17

DRUGS USED IN BRONCHIAL ASTHMA AND COPD

Objectives

After reading this chapter, the student will be able to:
- Understand the clinical picture of Asthma and COPD
- Understand the various management approaches for asthma
- Differentiate between asthmatic reliever and controller
- Understand the schematic representation for pathogenesis of asthma
- Explain the role of leukotrienes in asthma

INTRODUCTION

Asthma and COPD are common disorders (affecting 10 and 30 million Americans, respectively) and show several similarities in their clinical features. The clinical hallmarks of asthma are recurrent, episodic bouts of coughing, shortness of breath, chest tightness and wheezing. In mild asthma, symptoms occur only occasionally but in more severe forms of asthma, frequent attacks of wheezing, dyspnea occur, especially at night. Asthma is characterised physiologically by increased responsiveness of the trachea and bronchi to various stimuli and by widespread narrowing of the airways. Its chronic pathological features are contraction of the smooth muscles of the airways, leading to reversible airflow obstruction, mucosal thickening from edema and cellular infiltration along with airway inflammation and persistent airway hyperreactivity (AHR), and airway remodeling (Figure 17.1).

Obstruction increases resistance to air flow and decreases flow rates. Impaired expiration causes hyperinflation of alveoli distal to obstruction and thus increasing the work of breathing. If remained untreated, it can lead to airway damage that is irreversible.

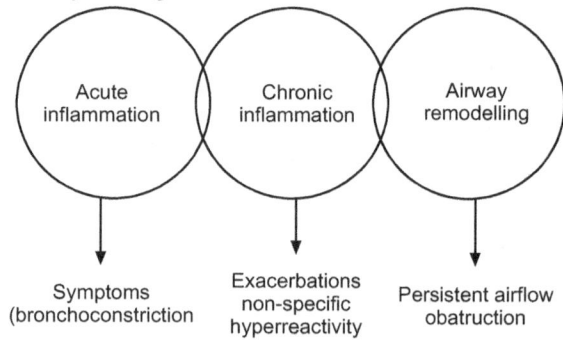

Fig. 17.1: Pathological features of Asthma

THE FUNDAMENTAL PATHOGENESIS OF ASTHMA

The fundamental pathogenesis of asthma involves several processes which are shown in schematic Fig. 17.2. Chronic inflammation of the bronchial mucosa is prominent, with infiltration of activated T-lymphocytes and eosinophils. This results in subepithelial fibrosis and the release of chemical mediators that can damage the epithelial lining of the airway. Many of these mediators are released following activation and degranulation of mast cells in the bronchial tree.

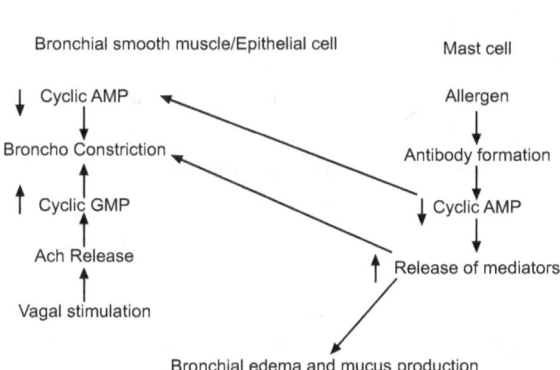

Fig. 17.2: Pathogenesis process of Asthma

Some of these mediators act as chemotactic agents for other inflammatory cells. They also produce mucosal edema, which narrows the airway and stimulates smooth muscle contraction, leading to bronchoconstriction. Excessive production of mucus can cause further airway obstruction by plugging the bronchiolar lumen (Fig. 17.3).

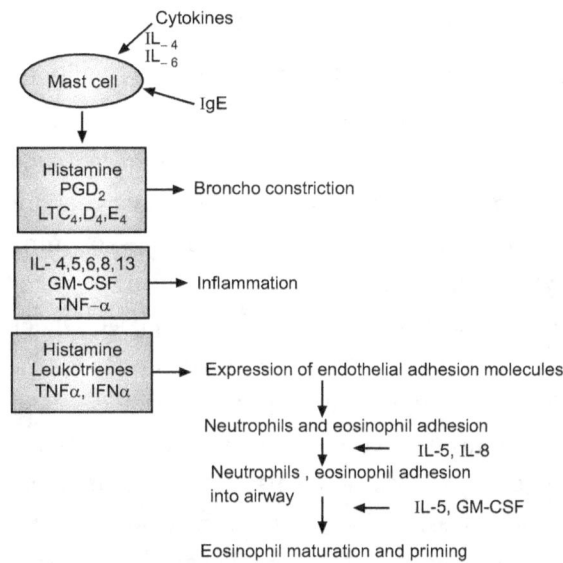

Fig. 17.3: Activation of mast cells results in secretion of several mediators that contribute to the pathogenesis of asthma. These mediators produce bronchoconstriction and initiate both the acute inflammatory response and attract cells responsible for maintaining chronic inflammation. IL, interleukin; GM-CSF, granulocyte and macrophage colony-stimulating factor; PG, prostaglandin; TNF, tissue necrosis factor; IFN interferon

Factors Influencing Asthma Development and Expression

There are number of factors responsible for the development of asthma. Host factors such as a genetic predisposition is responsible for the induction of atopy and airway hyper-responsiveness. Asthma may be due to gender and obesity. Some environmental factors like indoor allergens, outdoor allergens, occupational sensitisers, tobacco smoke, air pollution, respiratory infections and improper diet lead to development of asthma. Some factors e.g. allergens, respiratory infections, exercise, hyperventilation, weather changes, sulphur dioxide, food, additives and drugs like beta blockers also exacerbate the asthmatic condition.

Clinical manifestations

During remission, the individual is asymptomatic and pulmonary function tests are normal. Later on with the passage of time symptoms like frequently occurring cough, dyspnea and wheezing exhalation appear. Under mild conditions, attacks are usually of one to two hours duration, but in the chronic state, symptoms may be severe and continue for days or even weeks. All this is an outcome of bronchospasm. If bronchospasm is not reversed by usual measures, the individual is considered to have severe bronchospasm or status asthmaticus. If the condition persists for longer duration then it can be life threatening.

General Goals of Asthma Therapy

- First and foremost goal of asthma therapy is prevention of chronic symptoms and asthma exacerbations during the day and night.

- Due to asthma, patient's day to day activities, otherwise normal of human beings are very badly affected. So the major priority should be to maintain normal activities levels in the affected individuals.

- In asthma, due to damage to bronchial smooth muscle and epithelial cells of the airway, normal functioning is compromised to a greater extent.

- During therapy, care should be taken that patients face no or minimal side effects from medications. Thus another important goal of therapy is to do all possible efforts to bring lung functioning back to normal or at least near normal.

Approach for treatment

- Prevention of antigen: antibody reaction by avoiding contact with allergen and irritant.

- Suppression of inflammation and bronchial hyperreaction by corticosteroids.

- Prevention of release of mediators from mast cell by stabilising mast cells. The drugs commonly used for this purpose are sodium cromoglycolate, necorandil and ketotifen.

- Antagonism of release of mediators by antagonizing LT release and by using antihistamines.

- Blocking of constrictor neurotransmitter by using anticholinergic drugs in order to avoid bronchoconstriction.

- Mimicking the dilator neurotransmitters by using sympathomimetic agents (B_2 agonist).

- Use of bronchodilators like methylxanthine in order to counteract bronchoconstrictions.

Management

- Triggers like allergens and irritants should be avoided.

- In case of an acute attack, the patient should be treated with corticosteroids and inhaled beta-agonists.

- In chronic disease conditions, management is based on severity of asthma and includes regular use of inhaled anti-inflammatory medications – corticosteroids, chromolyn sodium or leukotriene inhibitors. Beside these inhaled bronchodilators are also used.

- Immunotherapy is another important means of disease management in patients; it includes allergy shots etc.

GENERAL PHARMACOLOGIC APPROACH TO THE TREATMENT OF ASTHMA

- The available agents for treating asthma can be divided into two general categories:

  1. Drugs that inhibit smooth muscle contraction, i.e., the so-called "quick relief medications" or bronchodilators (beta-adrenergic agonists, methyl-xanthines, and anticholinergic). These

are commonly referred to an "asthmatic relievers"

2. Agents that prevent and/or reverse inflammation, i.e., the "long-term control medications" (glucocorticoids, leukotriene inhibitors and receptor antagonists, and mast cell-stabilising agents, or cromones). Such agents are known as "asthmatic controllers".

"Asthmatic Relievers"

Asthmatic relievers include short-acting Bronchodilators such as-

(a) β2-adrenergic agents

(b) Anti-cholinergic (Parasympatholytic) agents

"Asthmatic Controllers"

Asthmatic controllers include agents such as-

(a) Corticosteroids

(b) Long-Acting bronchodilators

    (i) β2-adrenergic agents

    (ii) Methylxanthines

(c) Cromolyn sodium

(d) Leukotriene inhibitors

(e) Anti-IgE monoclonal antibodies

TREATMENT OF ASTHMA

1. Aerosol Delivery of Drugs

Topical application of drugs to the lungs can be accomplished by use of aerosols. This approach should in theory produce high local concentrations in the lungs with a low systemic delivery, thus reducing chances of systemic side effects. The critical delivery determinant of any particulate matter to the lungs is the size of the particle. Particles >10 μm are deposited primarily in the mouth and or pharynx; particles <0.5 μm are inhaled to the alveoli and exhaled without being deposited in the lungs. The most effective particles have a diameter of 1-5 μm.

Other important factors for deposition are rate of breathing and breath-holding after inhalation. Even under ideal circumstances only a small fraction of the aerosolized drug (~2-10%) is deposited in the lungs. A large volume spacer attached to metered-dose inhalers can improve markedly the ratio of inhaled to swallowed drug.

"Asthmatic Relievers"

Bronchodilators

The bronchial tree is one of the organs that receive dual sympathetic and parasympathetic innervation. The predominant adrenoceptor in the bronchial tree are β2, causes relaxation. As mentioned below, a subtype of muscarinic cholinergic receptor, M3 mediates smooth muscle contraction in the lungs. Bronchodilators are a group of agents that causes rapid relaxation of bronchial smooth muscle. Three classes of bronchodilators are in current use: β-adrenergic agonists, theophylline and anticholinergics drugs.

β-adrenergic agonists

β-agonists produce bronchodilation by directly stimulating β_2-receptors in airway smooth muscle. Activation of β_2 receptors results in activation of adenyl cyclase via a stimulatory guanine-nucleotide binding protein [G protein (Gs)] and increases intracellular cyclic 3'5'-adenosine monophosphate (cAMP). This activates protein kinase A, which then phosphorylates several target proteins within the cell leading to relaxation of bronchial smooth muscle (Fig. 17.4).

β_2 agonists have other beneficial effects including inhibition of mast cell mediator release, prevention of microvascular leakage and airway edema and enhanced mucociliary clearance. The inhibitory effects on mast cell mediator release and microvascular leakage suggests that β_2 agonists may also modify acute inflammation. β_2 agonists, however, have no effect on chronic inflammation.

β_2 agonists were developed through substitutions in the catecholamine structure of norepinephrine (NE). NE differs from epinephrine in the terminal amine group, and modification at this site confers beta receptor selectivity; further substitutions have resulted in β_2 selectivity. The selectivity of β_2 agonists is obviously dose dependent. Inhalation of the drug aids selectivity since it delivers small doses to the airways and minimises systemic exposure. As shown in table below, β agonists are generally divided into short (4-6 h) and long (>12 h) acting agents.

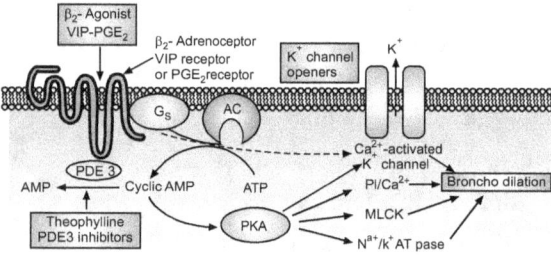

Fig. 17.4: Molecular mechanism of bronchodilators

Activation of $\beta2$ adrenoreceptors, vasoactive intestinal peptide (VIP) and prostaglandin E2 (PGE2) receptors results in activation of adenylyl cyclase (AC) via a stimulatory G-protein (Gs) and an increase in cAMP concentration. This activates protein kinase A (PKA), which phosphorylates several targeted proteins resulting in opening of calcium-activated potassium channels (Kca), decreased phosphoinositides (PI) hydrolysis, increased Na+/K+ ATPase and decreased myosin light chain kinases (MLCK) activity, which finally lead to relaxation of airway smooth muscle.

Adrenergic Bronchodilators

Table 17.1: Classification of Adrenergic Bronchodilators

Short-Acting Agents	Long acting
Catecholamines	Salmeterol
• Epinephrine	Formoterol
• Isoproterenol	
• Isoetharine	
Resorcinol agents	
• Metaproterenol	
• Saligenin agents	
• Albuterol	
Pirbuterol	
Bitolterol	

Short-acting β_2 adrenergic receptor agonists, such as albuterol, are the preferred treatment for rapid symptomatic relief of dyspnea associated with asthmatic bronchoconstriction. With topical delivery there are relatively few side effects with these agents at therapeutic doses. At higher doses, these agents may lead to increased heart rate, cardiac arrhythmias, and central nervous system effects which are associated with β adrenergic receptor activation. Beside these side effects, such as muscle cramps and metabolic disturbances also limits oral administration.

Modes of action

Adrenergic bronchodilators act in the following ways-

• Relax airway smooth muscle

• Enhance mucociliary clearance

• Decrease vascular permeability

• May modulate mediator release from mast cells and basophils.

Role in therapy

Adrenergic bronchodilators are medication of choice for the treatment of acute exacerbations of asthma and useful in the pretreatment of exercise-induced bronchospasm (EIB). Beside these are also used to control episodic bronchoconstriction. But increased used or even daily use of these agents is a warning of deterioration of asthma and indicates the need to institute or to intensify regular anti-inflammatory therapy.

Side Effects Seen with Beta Agonists

Some side effects associated with β-agonists are tremor, palpitations and tachycardia, headache, insomnia, rise in blood pressure, nervousness, dizziness and nausea.

Adrenergic Bronchodilators – Long-Acting Agents

An agent included under long acting adrenergic bronchodilators includes-

(i) Sustained-released albuterol

(ii) Salmeterol

(iii) Formoterol

Modes of administration

These drugs administered either by aerosol delivery mechanism or orally as a tablet and capsule.

Mechanisms of action

Mechanism of action is the same as that of short-acting beta-2 agonists. The only difference being that their effects persist for at least 12 hours i.e. they are long acting agents than short acting beta-2 agonist.

Role in therapy

Long-acting inhaled beta-2 agonists should be the choice of treatment when standard introductory doses of inhaled glucocorticoids fail to achieve control of asthma before raising the dose of inhaled glucocorticoids. Because long-term treatment with these agents does not appear to influence the persistent inflammatory changes in asthma, this therapy should be combined with inhaled glucocorticoids (Fluticosone propionate – salmeterol and bedesonide-formoterol inhalers).

Side effects

Inhaled beta-2 agonists' cause fewer systemic adverse effects (e.g., cardiovascular stimulation, skeletal muscle tremors and hypokalemia) than oral therapy particularly if the oral regimen includes theophylline.

ANTICHOLINERGIC (PARASYMPATHOLYTIC) BRONCHODILATORS

Anticholinergics bronchodilators are grouped into two categories viz. (i). Tertiary ammonium compounds: which include agents such as Atropine sulphate and Scopolamine; (ii). Quaternary ammonium compounds: including agents such as Ipratopium and Tritropium.

Tertiary Ammonium Compounds	Quaternary Ammonium Compounds
Atropine sulfate	Ipratropium
Scopalamine	Tiotropium

Mode of administration: Anticholinergic bronchodilators are administered through inhalation.

Mechanisms of action

Anticholinergics bronchodilators block the release of acetylcholine from cholinergic nerves in the airways thus reducing intrinsic vagal cholinergic tone to the airways. It also blocks reflex bronchoconstriction caused by inhaled irritants. They do not diminish the early and late allergic reactions and have no effect on airway inflammation. Anticholinergics bronchodilators are less potent bronchodilators than inhaled beta-2 agonists and in general, have a slower onset of action (30-60 min to maximum action).

Human airways are innervated by a supply of efferent, cholinergic parasympathetic autonomic nerves. Motor nerves derived from the vagus form ganglia within and around the walls of the airways. This vagally derived innervations extends along the length of the bronchial tree, but predominates in the large and medium-sized airways. Postganglionic fibers derived from the vagal ganglia supply the smooth muscle and submucosal glands of the airways as well as the vascular structures. Release of acetylcholine (ACh) at these sites results in stimulation of muscarinic receptors and subsequent airway smooth muscle contraction and release of secretions from the submucosal airway glands.

Three pharmacologically distinct subtypes of muscarinic receptors exist within the airways: M1, M2 and M3 receptors.

- M1 receptors are present on peribronchial ganglion cells where the preganglionic nerves transmit to the postganglionic nerves.

- M2 receptors are present on the postganglionic nerves; they are activated by the release of acetylcholine and promote its reuptake into the nerve terminal.

- M3 receptors are present on smooth muscle. Muscarinic receptor activation of these M3 receptors leads to a decrease in intracellular cAMP levels, resulting in contraction of airway smooth muscle and bronchoconstriction.

Atropine is the prototype anticholinergic bronchodilator. Ipratropium is a quaternary amine, which is poorly absorbed across biologic membranes. Atropine and ipratropium antagonise the actions of acetylcholine at parasympathetic, postganglionic, effector cell junctions by competing with acetylcholine for M3 receptor sites. This antagonism of acetylcholine results in airway smooth muscle relaxation and bronchodilation. Ipratropium is given exclusively by inhalation from a metered-dose inhaler or a nebulizer. Inhaled ipratropium has a slow onset (about 30 minutes) and a relatively long duration of action (about 6 hours).

Recently, **tiotropium**, a structural analog of ipratropium, has been approved for treatment of COPD. Like ipratropium, tiotropium has high affinity for all muscarinic receptor subtypes but it dissociates from the receptors much more slowly than ipratropium, especially M3 receptors. This permits once a day dosing. It is formulated for use with an oral inhalator.

Role in therapy

- Additive effect when nebulized together with a rapid-acting beta-2 agonist for exacerbations of asthma.

- It is recognised that Ipratropium can be used as an alternative bronchodilator for patients who experience adverse effects such as tachycardia, arrhythmias and tremors from beta-2 agonists.

Side effects

Dryness of the mouth and bitter taste are some effects of anticholinergics bronchodilators therapy.

ASTHMATIC CONTROLLERS

Below mentioned are some asthmatic controllers

"Asthmatic Controllers"
(i) Corticosteroids
(ii) Long-Acting bronchodilators • β2-adrenergic agents • Methylxanthines
(iii) Cromolyn sodium/Nedrocromil
(iv) Leukotrienes inhibitors
(v) Anti-IgE monoclonal antibodies

Corticosteroids

- Beclomethasone dipropionate
- Budesonide
- Flunisolide
- Fluticasone
- Tramcinolone acetonide

Physiological effects of Glucocorticoids

- Regulation of carbohydrate, protein and lipid metabolism.

- Maintenance of fluid and electrolyte balance.

- Preservation of normal functioning of the cardiovascular system, immune system, kidney, skeletal muscle, endocrine system and nervous system.

- Preservation of organismal homeostasis.

The impact of glucocorticoids on homeostasis is illustrated by the potent anti-inflammatory and immunosuppressive actions of these hormones. However, glucocorticoids, generates many adverse side effects. Since physiological glucocorticoids (i.e. cortisol) bind with reasonably high affinity to the mineralocorticoid receptor, so alterations in fluid and electrolyte handling (mediated physiologically by the mineralocorticoid receptor) and ensuing hypertension are important side effects of glucocorticoids therapy.

Pharmacology of Glucocorticoids for the Treatment of Asthma

Chemical modification of cortisol can dramatically influence its half-life and efficacy. For example, prednisolone has enhanced glucocorticoid activity with reduced mineralocorticoid activity. Prednisolone is also metabolised much more slowly than cortisol.

The fluorinated glucocorticoids dexamethasone and betamethasone have very long half-lives, are potent glucocorticoids and have no detectable mineralocorticoid action.

Cortisone must be enzymatically reduced by 11β-hydroxysteroid reductase (typically in liver) in order to be active. (Table 17.1)

Glucocorticoids Withdrawal

Since glucocorticoids suppress their own synthesis through a feedback mechanism that operates at the pituitary (i.e. reduced ACTH synthesis) and the brain (reduced CRH synthesis). Thus rapid cessation of glucocorticoid therapy may leads to acute adrenal insufficiency, which can be debilitating.

Fig. 17.5: Hypothalamic-Pituitary-Adrenal (HPA) Axis: Regulation of Cortisol Synthesis and Secretion

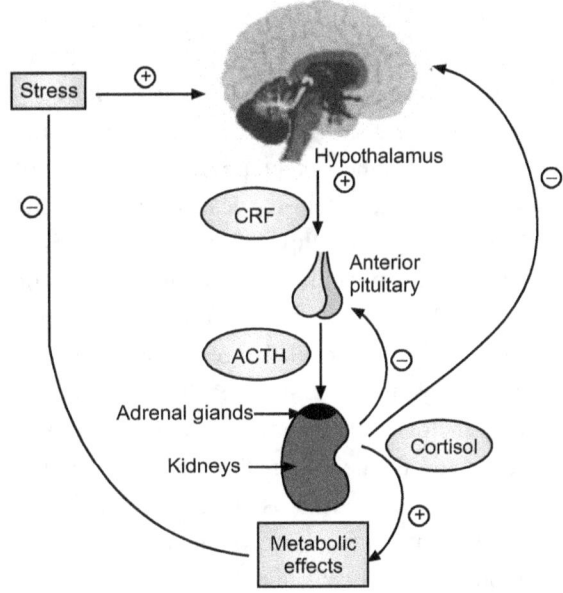

Fig. 17.5: The above diagram shows the regulation of cortical synthesis and secretion by the feedback mechanism in which stress produced leads to increase in the synthesis and secretion of cortisol and when excess amount is secreted, it reduce the stress and decrease the synthesis and secretion of cortisol.

Table 17.2: Relative Potencies of representative Corticosteroids

Compound	Anti-inflammatory potency	Na+-retaining Potency	Duration of action*
Cortisol	1	1	S
Cortisone	0.8	0.8	S
Prednisone	4	0.8	I
Prednisolone	4	0.8	I
Triamcinolone	5	0	I
Betamethasone	25	0	L
Dexamethasone	25	0	L

*S, short (*i.e.*, 8–12 hour biological half-life); I, intermediate (*i.e.*, 12–36 hour biological half-life); L, long (*i.e.*, 36–72 hour biological half-life).

Delivery of Glucocorticoids

Systemic glucocorticoids are not routinely used for asthma treatment as they can produce side effects. But still they are used for acute asthma exacerbations and chronic severe asthma. However, the development of **aerosol delivery systems** for glucocorticoids has led to dramatic increase in the therapeutic index of glucocorticoid treatment for less severe, chronic asthma. Thus, this allows for the generalised anti-inflammatory actions of this hormone to be exploited. Various glucocorticoid formulations are available for aerosol delivery that differs in their affinity for the glucocorticoid receptor. Various factors influence the choice and dose of the drug used including the severity of the disease and the devises used for drug delivery. However, maximal improvement of lung function may not occur until several weeks after treatment.

Inhaled glucocorticoids are used prophylactically to control asthma rather than acutely to reverse asthma symptoms. As with all prophylactic therapies, compliance is a significant concern. Several systemic effects of inhaled steroids have been described and include dermal thinning and skin capillary fragility. Inhaled steroids may have local side effects due to the deposition of inhaled steroid in the oropharynx. The most common problems are hoarseness and dysphonia. Oropharyngeal candidiasis occurs in 5% of patients. Even with proper use of aerosol devices, typically 10% of inhaled glucocorticoids are deposited in lung with the remainder swallowed and absorbed in the gut. Thus, even inhaled glucocorticoids have the potential to exert systemic effects.

Glucocorticoids: Side Effects

- **Skin:** They produce atrophy, striae rubre distensae, delayed wound healing, steroid acne, perioral dermatitis, erythema, patechia and hyperchosis.

- **Skeleton and muscle:** They produce muscle atropy/myopathy, osteoporosis, bone necrosis.

- **Eye:** In case of eye glaucoma and cataracts are some side effects of glucocorticoids therapy.

Central Nervous System: Glucocorticoids may affect central nervous system by producing disturbances in mood, behaviour, memory and cognition, steroid dependence, cerebral atropy.

Systemic Glucocorticoids produce following types of side effects

- **Electrolyte, metabolism and endocrine system:** Causes Cushing's syndrome, diabeties mellitus, adrenal atrophy, growth retardation, hypogonadism, delayed puberty, increased sodium retention and potassium excretion.

- **Cardiovascular system:** They may affect functioning of cardiovascular system thus producing hypertension, dyslipedemia, thrombosis and vasculitis.

- **Immune system:** Glucocorticoids serve as immunosuppressants hereby increasing the risk of infection e.g. candidiasis and reactivation of latent viruses e.g.cytomegaloviruses in asthmatic patients on glucocorticoid medication.

- **Gastrointestinal tract:** It produces distress in gastrointestinal tract thus producing peptic ulcer, gastrointestinal bleeding and pancreatitis.

Inhaled Glucocorticoids produce the following types of side effects

- Local adverse effects include oropharyngeal candidiasis, dysphonia and occasional coughing from upper airway irritation.

- Since inhaled glucocorticoids show some systemic absorption so the risks of systemic adverse effects will depend on the dose and potency of the glucocorticoids as well as its bioavailability, absorption in the gut, metabolism by the liver and the half-life of its systemically absorbed fraction.

XANTHENES AGENTS

Naturally Occurring Agents	Synthetic Derivatives
Caffeine (Coffee and kola beans; tea leaves) Theophylline (Tea leaves) Theobromine (Cocoa seeds or beans)	Dyphylline Proxyphylline Enprophylline

Methylxanthines

Mode of administration: Methylxanthines are administered orally or parenterally.

Mechanisms of action

The bronchodilator effect may be related to phosphodiesterase inhibition (>10 mg/L); while anti-inflammatory effect is due to an unknown mechanism and may occur at lower concentrations (5-10 mg/L). The latter mechanism may involve the inhibition of cell surface receptors for adenosine, which modulate adenyl cyclase activity i.e. contraction of isolated smooth muscle and to provoke histamine release from mast cells. Most studies have showed little or no effect of methyxanthine on airway hyperresponsiveness.

Role in therapy

Sustained release of theophylline is effective in controlling asthma symptoms and improving lung function. Many salts of theophylline have been marketed, the most common being aminophylline, which is the ethylenediamine salt.

Theophylline has been in clinical use since the 1930s. It is a weak, non-selective inhibitor of phosphodiesterase (PDE). PDE inhibition results in an increase in cAMP and cGMP. Another hypothesis regarding mechanism of action is adenosine receptor inhibition, which may prevent the release of mediators from mast cells. Monitoring theophylline level is advised when high dose therapy (i.e.> 10mg/kg body weight) is used or when patient develops adverse effects on the usual dosage.

Concurrent administration of phenobarbitol or phenytoin increases activity of cytochrome P-450 (CYP), which results in increased metabolic breakdown. Reduced clearance is also seen with certain drugs, which interfere with the CYP system, such as cimetidine, erythromycin, ciprofloxacin, allopurinol, zileuton, and zafirlukast. Viral infections and vaccinations may also reduce clearance.

Unwanted side effects may be seen at higher plasma concentrations, although they may occur in some patients even at low concentrations. The most common side effects are anorexia, nausea and vomiting, headache, abdominal discomfort, and restlessness.

Side effects (serum concentrations > 15 µg/mL)

Unwanted side effects are observed at high serum concentration i.e. >15 µg/mL. The usual side effects of the gastrointestinal tract include nausea and vomiting. In the central nervous system the side effect could be a seizure. Some cardiovascular side effects include tachycardia and arrhythmias. Stimulation of respiratory center is one of the important side effects exhibited in the pulmonary system.

Monitoring theophylline levels is advised when high-dose therapy (>10 mg/kg body weight) is used or when a patient develops an adverse effect on the usual dosage.

CROMOLYN AND NEDROCROMIL SODIUM

The drugs cromolyn sodium and nedocromil sodium are commonly grouped together as chromones (also called cromoglycates). The specific action of chromones is to block or attenuate the effects of immunologic and non-immunologic stimuli in both asthmatics and normal individuals. For example, they preventboth early and late asthmatic responses to inhaled allergens such as pollen, and they reduce airway reactivity resulting from exposure to a range of inhaled irritants such as sulphur dioxide and cold air. Their precise mechanism of action is not known. The current hypotheses proposed to explain the effects of these drugs include-

- Cromones enhance phosphorylation of a cell membrane protein that is responsible for the termination of mediator release from mast cells (stabilisation of the mast cell membrane).
- Chromones suppresses firing of sensory C-fiber nerve endings.
- Chromones have variable inhibitory actions on other inflammatory cells that may participate in allergic inflammation including macrophages and eosinophils.
- Chromones inhibit the synthesis of IgE antibody by B-lymphocytes.
- Chromones may act on specific chloride channels in mast cells and sensory neurons.
- Cromones are widely used in pediatrics, but have suffered from limited efficacy in adult populations. These agents are extremely safe, and side effects are very rare. These two chromones are available for inhalation by either metered dose inhaler or nebulizer solution.

Role in therapy

- May be used as a controller in mild, persistent asthma. When administered prophylactically, these medications inhibit early and late-phase allergen-induced airflow limitation and acute after exposure to exercise, cold dry air and sulphur dioxide.
- At present, inconclusive data is available on the effectiveness of these drugs on reducing airway hyper responsiveness. A 4-6 week therapeutic trial may be required to determine the efficacy for individual patients.

Side effects

At low serum concentration, it shows minimal side effects such as coughing, throat irritation, wheezing, chest tightness and mouth dryness.

Pharmacokinetics

For asthma, cromolyn is given by inhalation using either solutions (delivered by aerosol spray or nebulizer) or, in some countries, powdered drug is mixed with lactose and delivered by a special turboinhaler. Once absorbed, the drug is excreted unchanged in the urine and bile in about equal proportions.

Peak concentrations in plasma occur within 15 minutes of inhalation, and excretion begins after some delay such that the biological half-life ranges from 45 to 100 minutes.

LEUKOTRIENES MODIFIERS

The generation of cysteinyl leukotrienes (CysLT) e.g. LTC4, LTD4 and LTE4 from arachadonic acid requires the action of the 5-lipoxygenase enzyme (5-LOX). This is regulated by different factors such as various stimuli, cell types, genetics of the host and cytokine stimulation. Expression, distribution and activation of specific receptors regulate the actions of CysLTs. CysLTs induce bronchospasm by local effects on smooth muscle, mucus, and edema. Their modulation of the immune response, collagen deposition, and recruitment and activation of inflammatory cells increase chronic airway obstruction and bronchial hyper-responsiveness. Several leukotriene-modifying drugs have been developed for clinical use including leukotriene receptor antagonists such as zafirlukast and montelukast and a 5'-lipoxygenase enzyme inhibitor i.e. zileuton.

Leukotrienes Synthesis Pathway

Synthesis of leukotriene takes place through arachidonic acid. Below figure 15.6 shows the pathway involved in synthesis of Leukotriene.

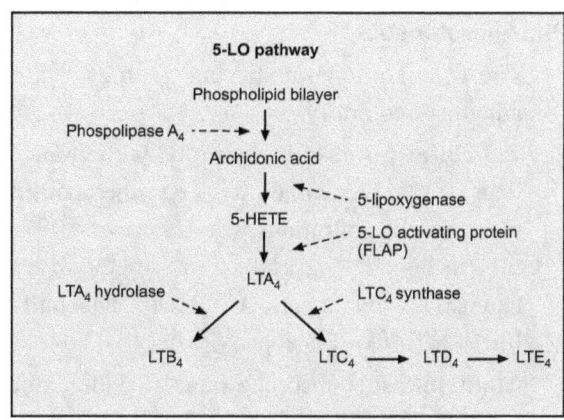

Fig. 17.6: Synthesis of leukotrienes

Role of Leukotrienes in the Pathogenesis of Asthma

The role of leukotrienes in pathogenesis has been shown in below figure 15.7. It involves various inflammatory reactions which are produced by systemic leukotrienes as a result of their action on target cell.

Mode of administration: Leukotriene modifiers are generally administered by oral route.

Mechanism of action

Receptor antagonists block the CysLT1 receptors on airway smooth muscle and thus inhibit the effects of cysteinyl leukotrienes that are released from mast cells and eosinophils. 5-lipoxygenase inhibitors on the contrary blocks the synthesis of leukotrienes.

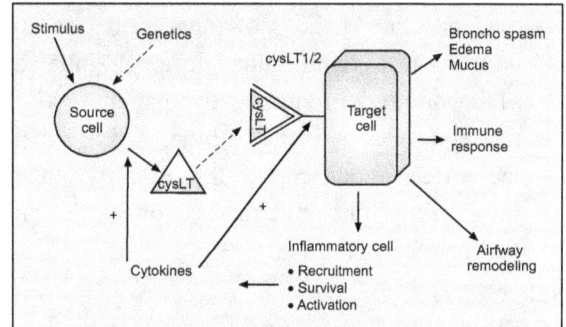

Fig. 17.7: Role of Leukotrienes in pathogenesis of Asthma

Pharmacokinetics

- The leukotriene-modifying drugs are administered orally.

- **Zafirlukast** is absorbed rapidly, with greater than 90% bioavailability. At therapeutic plasma concentrations, it is over 99% protein-bound. Zafirlukast is metabolised extensively by hepatic CYP2C9. The half-life of zafirlukast is approximately 10 hours.

- **Montelukast** is absorbed rapidly, with about 60% to 70% bioavailability. At therapeutic concentrations, it is highly protein-bound (99%). It is metabolized extensively by CYP3A4 and CYP2C9. The half-life of montelukast is between 3 and 6 hours.

- **Zileuton** is absorbed rapidly on oral administration and is metabolised extensively by CYPs and by UDP-glucuronosyltransferases. The parent molecule is responsible for its therapeutic action. Zileuton is a short-acting drug with a half-life of approximately 2.5 hours and also is highly protein-bound (93%).

Role in therapy

- These agents have a small and variable bronchodilator effect, reduce symptoms, improve lung function and reduce asthma exacerbations.

- Effect of these drugs is less than that of low-doses of inhaled glucocorticoids. There is evidence that the use of these drugs as an add-on may reduce the dose of inhaled glucocorticoids required by patients with moderate to severe asthma. Note that leukotriene modifiers are less effective than long-acting inhaled beta-2 agonists as an add-on therapy.

Side effects

These drugs are usually well tolerated, and a few if any class-related effects have been recognised.

- Zileuton has been associated with liver toxicity and monitoring liver test is recommended.

- There are several reports of Churg-Strauss syndrome associated with the leukotriene modifier therapy (typically associated with a reduction of systemic glucocorticoids).

ANTI-IgE THERAPY

Agents directed at diminishing the production of IgE through effects on interleukin 4 or on IgE itself have been discuss below (Figure 15.8).

- Soluble recombinant IL-4 receptor that can be delivered by aerosol.

- Recombinant human monoclonal antibody that forms complexes with free IgE (rhuMAb or omalizumab blocks the interaction of IgE with mast cells and basophils. All these anti-IgE agents attenuates the early-phase and late phase airway obstruction response to allergen and suppressed the accumulation of eosinophils in the airways.

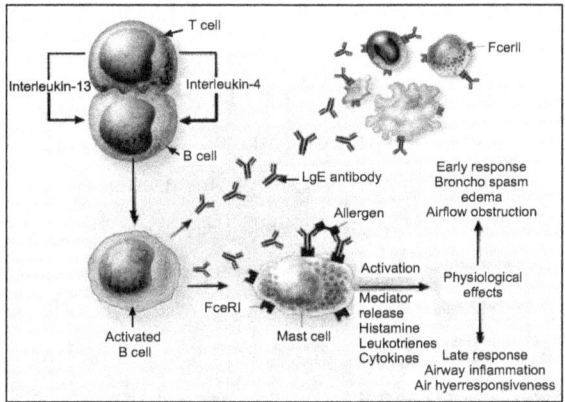

Fig. 17.8: Role of IgE in Pathogenesis of Asthma.

Omalizumab is a recombinant humanised monoclonal antibody against IgE that is being used for asthma treatment. When bound to Omalizumab, IgE is unable to bind to IgE receptors (FceRI) on mast cells and thereby blocks the inflammatory process at an early step. Omalizumab also reduces the amount of FceRI on the surfaces of basophils, further enhancing its anti-inflammatory actions.

Pharmacokinetics

Omalizumab is given by a single subcutaneous injection at every 2 to 4 weeks. It's bioavailability is about 60% and peak plasma concentration is attained after 7 to 8 days. The serum elimination half-life is 26 days. The elimination of omalizumab-IgE complexes occurs in the liver reticuloendothelial system. Some intact omalizumab is also excreted in the bile.

Toxicity

The most frequent adverse effect of omalizumab therapy is injection-site reactions such as redness, stinging, bruising and indurations.

Anaphylaxis has also been reported in 0.1% of treated patients.

CHRONIC OPHTHALMIC PULMONARY DISEASE (COPD)

COPD is characterised by airflow limitation caused by chronic bronchitis or emphysema often associated with long term tobacco smoking. This is usually a slowly progressive and largely irreversible process, which consists of increased resistance to airflow, loss of elastic recoil, decreased expiratory flow rate and overinflation of the lung.

The degree of broncodilatory response at the time of testing, however, does not predict the degree of clinical benefits to the patient and thus bronchodilators are given irrespective of the acute response obtained in the pulmonary function laboratory. COPD exhibits some following characteristics features-

(i) Pathological changes that cause reduced expiratory air flow.

(ii) Does not show major reversibility in response to pharmacological agents.

(iii) Associated with abnormal inflammatory response of the lungs to noxious particles or gases.

(iv) Primary cause is cigarette smoking. Both active and passive smoking have been implicated. Other risks are occupational exposures and air pollution.

USE OF ASTHMA DRUGS IN COPD

Emphysema can be prevented or its progression can be slowed down if the patient stops smoking. Pharmacological interventions can help patients to stop smoking. Nicotine gum, nicotine transdermal patches and the antidepressant agent bupropion are moderately useful when combined with other interventions such as support groups and physician encouragement. Clonidine may be helpful in reducing the craving for cigarettes. The pharmacological treatment of established emphysema resembles that of asthma largely because the inflammatory/bronchospastic component of a patient's disease is the aspect amenable to therapy. For patients with emphysema who have a significant degree of active inflammation with bronchospasm and excessive mucus production, symptomatic use of inhaled ipratropium or a β_2 adrenergic agonist may be helpful.

Ipratropium or tiotropium usually produces almost the same modest degree of bronchodilation in patients with COPD as do maximal doses of β-2 adrenergic agonists. As in asthmatic patients, continuous use of bronchodilators is controversial, with some studies suggesting that it is associated with an unfavourable course of COPD. A subgroup of patients may respond favorably to short courses of oral glucocorticoids. However, except for the treatment of acute bronchospastic episodes, glucocorticoids have given mixed results in the treatment of COPD. In some patients, theophylline may be effective; in others who have a profound response to β2 adrenergic agonists, theophylline fails to produce additional bronchodilation beyond that achieved by maximal doses of the inhaled β-adrenergic agonist. In a minority of patients, emphysema results from a genetic deficiency of the plasma proteinase inhibitor α 1-antiproteinase (also called α1-antitrypsin). Lack of these plasma proteinase inhibitors causes destruction of lung tissue due to unopposed action of neutrophil elastase and other proteinases. Purified α 1-*antiproteinase* from human plasma is available for intravenous replacement.

USE OF ASTHMA DRUGS IN RHINITIS

Seasonal allergic rhinitis (hay fever) is caused by deposition of allergens on the nasal mucosa, resulting in an immediate hypersensitivity reaction. This reaction usually is not accompanied by asthma because the allergenic particles are too large to be inhaled into the lower airways (*e.g.,* pollens).

Treatment for allergic rhinitis is similar to that for asthma. Topical glucocorticoids, including beclomethasone, mometasone, budesonide, flunisolide, fluticasone and triamcinolone can be highly effective with minimal side effects, particularly if treatment is instituted immediately prior to the allergy season. Topical glucocorticoids can be administered twice daily (beclomethasone and flunisolide) or even once daily (budesonide, mometasone, fluticasone, and triamcinolone).

Cromolyn usually requires dosing three to six times daily for full effect. Rare instances of local candidiasis have been reported with glucocorticoids and probably can be avoided by rinsing the mouth after use. Unlike in asthma, antihistamines afford considerable, though incomplete, symptomatic relief in allergic rhinitis.

Nasal decongestants rely on β adrenergic agonists (*e.g.,* pseudoephedrine and phenyl-ephrine) as vasoconstrictors. Anti-cholinergic agents such as ipratropium bromide are effective in inhibiting parasympathetic reflex-evoked secretions from serous glands lining the nasal mucosa.

Future pharmacological directions for Asthma and COPD

1. **Vasoactive intestinal peptide analogs.** Vasoactive intestinal peptide (VIP) is a potent relaxant of constricted human airways *in vitro* but it is degraded in the airway epithelium and ineffective in asthmatic patients. A more stable cyclic analogue of VIP (Ro-25-1553) has a more prolonged effect in-vitro and in-vivo and is effective in asthmatic patients by inhalation.

2. **Prostaglandin E2.** PGE agonists that are selective for lung receptors subtypes are being considered for exploration as bronchodilators/anti-inflammatory drugs.

3. **Atrial natriuretic peptides (ANP).** Intravenous infusion of ANP produces a significant bronchodilating effects and provides protection against bronchoconstriction induced by inhaled broncoconstrictors such as methacholine. ANP, however, is a peptide and subjected to rapid enzymatic degradation. A related peptide, urodilatin, is less susceptible to degradation and has a longer duration of action. It is as potent as salbutamol when given i.v.

4. **Phosphodiesterase 4 (PDE4) inhibitors.** Based on the actions of theophylline, there has been interest in developing PDE4 inhibitors. In animal models of asthma, PDE4 inhibitors reduce eosinophil infiltration and airway hyperresponsiveness responses to allergens. THE PDE4 inhibitor

cilomilast has been clinically tested for COPD but the drug causes emesis, a common side effect with this class (this could be due to inhibition of PDE4D). There is hope that selective inhibitors of PDE4B might have more therapeutic potential.

5. **Pharmacogenomics.** It is suggests that the 16th amino acid position of the β_2 adrenergic receptor is associated with significant pharmacogenomic effect, namely down regulation of the receptor and responsiveness of patients using β-agonists.

Key Points

- Short-acting beta2-agonists: Therapy of choice for relief of acute symptoms and prevention of EIB.

- Anticholinergics: May provide some additive benefit to inhaled beta2-agonists in severe exacerbations. May be an alternative for patients who do not tolerate inhaled beta2-agonists.

- Systemic corticosteroids: Used for moderate-to-severe exacerbations to speed and prevent recurrence of exacerbations.

- Corticosteroids: Most potent and effective anti-inflammatory medication currently available

- Cromolyn sodium and nedrocromil: Mild-to-moderate anti-inflammatory medication.

- Leukotriene inhibitors: May be considered an alternative therapy to low dose inhaled corticosteroids or cromolyn sodium or nedrocromil for patients >12 years of age with mild persistent asthma.

- Long-acting beta2-agonists: These drugs are typically used concurrently with anti-inflammatory medications for long-term control of symptoms, especially nocturnal symptoms.

- Methylxanthines: Sustained release theophylline is a mild-to-moderate bronchodilator used principally as an adjuvant to inhaled corticosteroids for prevention of nocturnal asthma symptoms.

Questions on this Chapter

1. Discuss the pathogenesis and management approaches for the Asthma.
2. Classify anti-asthmatic agents and add a note on beta agonists.
3. Discuss the role of corticosteroid in Asthma.
4. Discuss the involvement of cholinoceptor in asthma and add brief on its therapeutic target.
5. Discuss the pharmacotherapy of COPD.

Chapter 18

NASAL DECONGESTANTS, EXPECTORANTS, AND ANTITUSSIVE AGENTS

Objectives

After reading this chapter, the student will be able to:

➢ Describe the term congestion and decongestion

➢ Describe expectorant and mucolytics

➢ Justify the use of antihistamines as nasal decongestants

➢ Enlist the various cough suppressants

DECONGESTANTS

Congestion in the nose, sinuses and chest is due to swollen, expanded or dilated blood vessels in the membranes of the nose and air passages. These membranes have an abundant supply of blood vessels with a great capacity for expansion (swelling and congestion). Histamine stimulates these blood vessels to expand as described previously.

Nasal Decongestant

Antihistamines:

Diphenhydramine, Tripelennamine, Promethazine, Cyclizine, Loratidine and Desloratadine

α-Adrenergic Agents:

Pseudoephedrine and Phenylephrine

Decongestants, on the other hand, causes constriction or tightening of the blood vessels in those membranes. As a result of much of the blood is forced out of the membranes so that they shrink, and the air passages open up again. Decongestants are chemically related to adrenalin, the natural decongestant, which is a sympathomimetic. Side effect of decongestants is a jittery or nervous feeling. They can cause difficulty in going to sleep, and they ccan elevate blood pressure and pulse rate. Should not be used by a patient who has an irregular heart rhythm (pulse), high blood pressure, heart disease or glaucoma.

Some patients taking decongestants experience difficulty with urination. Furthermore, decongestants are often used as ingredients in diet pills. Typical decongestants are phenylephrine and pseudoephedrine both are α-adrenergic agents Histamine is an important body chemical that is responsible for the congestion, sneezing and runny nose that a patient suffers with an allergic attack or an infection.

Antihistamine decongestant drugs block the action of histamine, therefore reducing the allergy symptoms.

Antihistamines should be taken before allergic symptoms get well established. The most annoying side effect that antihistamines produce is drowsiness. Though desirable at bedtime, it is a nuisance to many people who need to use antihistamines in the daytime. These drugs are not recommended for daytime use for people who may be driving automobiles or operating equipment that could be dangerous. Newer non-sedating antihistamines, available by prescription only, do not have this effect. The first few doses may result in excessive sleepiness but subsequent doses are usually less troublesome.

Many H_1 antihistamines have been conventionally added to antitussive/expectorant formulation. They afford relief in cough due to their sedative and anticholinergic actions, but lack selectivity for cough center. But they do not exert expectorant action and may even reduce secretions by anticholinergic action. They have been specially promoted for cough in respiratory allergic states. Commonly used antihistamines are Chlorpheniramine, Diphenhydramine and Promethazine.

EXPECTORANTS

Expectorant

Guaifenesin, Guaiacol

Sodium Potassium citrate and Ammonium salt

Mucolytics:

Bromohexine, Ambroxol, Acetylcysteine and Carbocysteine

Guaifenesin

Expectorants are drugs that loosen and clear mucus and phlegm from the respiratory tract. Guaifenesin, an expectorant is an important ingredient in many cough medicines.

Expectorants come in several forms, including capsules, tablets, and liquids. A lingering cough could be a sign of a serious medical condition. Coughs that last more than seven days or are associated with fever, rash, sore throat, or lasting headache should be brought to medical attention and the patient should consult a physician as soon as possible. Expectorants increase bronchial secretion or reduce its viscosity, facilitating its removal by coughing, they loosen the cough which becomes less tiring and more productive.

Guaifenesin is not meant to be used for coughs associated with asthma, emphysema, chronic bronchitis or smoking. It should also not be used for coughs that are producing a large amount of mucus.

Some studies have suggested that guaifenesin causes birth defects. Women who are pregnant or plan to become pregnant should check with their physicians before using any products that contain guaifenesin. Side effects may include vomiting, diarrhea, stomach upset, headache and skin rash.

Sodium and potassium citrate: They increase bronchial secretion by salt action.

Potassium Iodide: It is secreted by bronchial glands and in this process irritates them thus increasing the volume of secretion. It is dangerous in patients sensitive to iodine and interferes in iodide function test. Prolonged use can induce goiter and hypothyroidism.

Guaiacol: It is obtained from wood creosote or is synthetically prepared. Guaiacol and its derivative guaiphenesin are believed to directly increase bronchial secretion and mucosal ciliary action.

Ammonium Salts: These are gastric irritants reflexly enhance bronchial secretion and sweating. Expectorant doses are subemetics but often nauseating because of unpleasant taste.

MUCOLYTICS

Bromhexine: A derivative of alkaloid vasicine obtained from *Adhatoda vasica*. It is a potent mucolytic and mucokinetic. It is capable of inducing thin copious bronchial secretion. Bromohexine depolymerises mucopolysacchride directly by liberating lysosomal enzyme-network of fibers in tenacious sputum is broken. It is particularly useful in case where mucus plugs are present. Side effect includes rhinorrhea and lacrymation, gastric irritation and hypersensitivity.

Ambroxol: It is a metabolite of bromohexine with similar mucolytic action, uses and side effects.

Acetylcysteine: It opens disulfide bonds of mucoproteins which are present in sputum, thus making it less viscid. Unlike other mucolytics, it has to be administered directly to the respiratory tract.

Carbocisteine: It liquefies viscid sputum in the same way as acetylcysteine but is administered orally. Some patients of chronic bronchitis have been shown to benefit from corbocisteine.

ANTITUSSIVES
(COUGH SUPPRESSANTS)

Antitussive
Opioids
Codeine, Pholcodeine, Ethylmorphine and Morphine
Non-Opioids
Noscapine, Dextromethorphan, Oxeladin and Chlophedianol
Methyl xanthine
Theobromine

A cough medicine is a drug used to treat coughing and related conditions. Dry coughs are treated with cough suppressants (antitussives) that suppress the body's urge to cough, while productive coughs (coughs that produce phlegm) are treated with expectorants that loosen mucus from the respiratory tract. Cough suppressants may act centrally (on the brain, and specifically the vagus nerve) or locally (on the respiratory tract) to suppress the cough reflex. Centrally acting suppressants include Dextromethorphan (DM), Noscapine, Ethyl morphine, and Codeine.

Recent studies have found that theobromine, a compound found in cocoa, is more effective as a cough suppressant than prescription codeine. This molecule suppresses the "itch" signal from the nerve in the back of the throat that causes the cough reflex. It is possible to get an effective dose from dark chocolate, which contains more cocoa than milk chocolate.

They act on the central nervous system thus raising the threshold of cough center or act peripherally in the respiratory tract to reduce tussal impulses or both these actions. Antitussive drugs aim to control rather than eliminating cough. Antitussives should only be used for dry unproductive cough or if cough is unduly tiring, disturbing sleep or is hazardous.

OPIOIDS

Codeine: Codeine is an alkaloid obtained from opium. Qualitatively it is similar to but less potent than morphine. It has higher selectivity for cough center and is treated as a standard antitussive. It suppresses the cough for about 6 hours. The antitussive action of codeine is blocked by nalaxone indicating that it is exerted through opioid receptor in brain. The chief drawback of codeine therapy is excessive constipation. At higher doses respiratory depression and drowsiness can occur. Like morphine it is contraindicated in asthma.

Pholcodeine: Similar in efficacy as an antitussive like codeine but is longer acting. It suppresses the cough for about 12 hours or even more.

Ethylmorphine: Drug ethylmorphine is similar to codeine in all aspects.

Morphine: It is antitussive in subanalgesic doses.

NONOPIOIDS

Noscapine: It depresses the cough but does not have narcotic, analgesic or dependence inducing properties. It is nearly equipotent antitussive as codeine and is especially useful in treating spasmodic cough. Headache and nausea occur occasionally as side effects. Use of noscapine is contraindicated in asthma patients. In such individual it may release histamine and produce bronchoconstriction which in turn may lead to asthmatic attack.

Dextromethorphan: It is synthetic with selective antitussive action (raise the threshold of cough center). It is effective as codeine and does not depress mucociliary function of airway mucosa and is practically devoid of constipating and addicting action. Its antitussive action is not blocked by Naloxone: not exerted through opioids receptor.

Oxeladin: A synthetic centrally acting antitussive, devoid of opiod side effects.

Chlophedianol: It is similar to oxeladin and has a slow onset and longer duration of antitussive action.

Methyl Xanthine (Theobromine): Methyxanthine is also used as an antitussive agent. For detail pharmacology refer anti-asthmatic chapter.

Questions on this Chapter

1. Write a short note on expectorant and mucolytics.
2. Write a short note on antitussive agents.
3. What are nasal decongestants, explain in detail.

Chapter 19

PHARMACOTHERAPY OF PEPTIC ULCER

Objectives

After reading this chapter, the student will be able to
- Understand the mechanism involved in gastric secretion
- Have a basic knowledge about peptic ulcer
- Differentiate between gastric and duodenal ulcer
- The different defense mechanisms available against gastric acid
- Understand the role of cytoprotective factors
- Understand Zollinger-Ellison Syndrome

INTRODUCTION

Peptic ulcer occurs in that part of gastrointestinal tract (GIT) which is exposed to gastric acid and pepsin i.e. stomach and duodenum. It results due to imbalance between aggressive (acid, pepsin, and *H. Pylori*) and the defensive (gastric mucus and bicarbonate secretion, prostaglandin, nitric oxide, innate resistant of the mucosal cells) factors. In gastric ulcer, acid secretion is generally low or normal while in duodenal ulcer, acid secretion is high in about half of the patients but normal in rest of patients. Production of acid, whether normal or high, does contributes to ulceration as an aggressive factor; its reduction is the main approach of the ulcer treatment. An understanding regarding the control of gastric acid secretion will helps in elucidating the target of antisecretory drug action.

PHYSIOLOGY OF GASTRIC SECRETION

Three main factors are believed to be involved in gastric acid secretion i.e. neuronal (acetylcholine), endocrine (gastrin) and paracrine (histamine). Gastric acid secretion is a complex, continuous process in which multiple central and peripheral factors contribute to a common endpoint i.e. to the secretion of H^+ by parietal cells. Neuronal (acetylcholine), paracrine (histamine) and endocrine (gastrin) factors all regulate acid secretion. Their specific receptors (M_3, H_2, and CCK_2 receptors, respectively) are on the basolateral membrane of the parietal cells in the body and fundus of the stomach. The H_2 receptor is a GPCR (G Protein Couple Receptor) that activates the G_s-adenylyl-cyclase-cyclic AMP-PKA pathway. Acetyl-choline and gastrin signal through GPCRs that couple to the G_q-Phospholipase-C-Inositol Triphosphate (IP_3)-Ca^{2+} pathway in parietal cells. In parietal cells, the cyclic AMP and the Ca^{2+}-dependent pathways activate H^+, K^+-ATPase (the proton pump), which exchanges hydrogen and potassium ions across the parietal cell membrane and secretes the acid. The summary of acid secretion is given in pathway in Fig. 19.1.

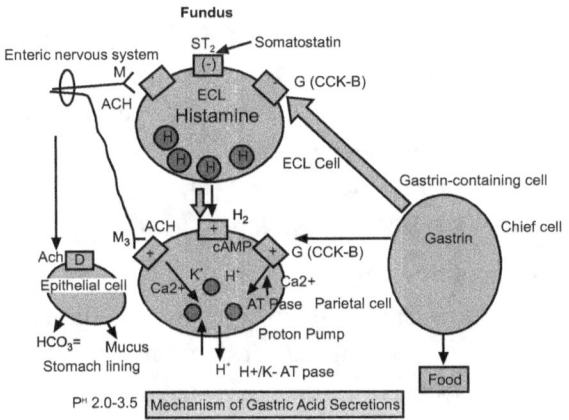

Fig. 19.1: Acid secretion pathways

- Gastrin → ECL cell → Histamine → Parietal cell → ↑ cAMP → H^+/K^+ ATPase (Proton Pump) → Acid secretion
- Gastrin → Parietal cell → ↑ Ca^{2+} → H^+/K^+ ATPase (Proton Pump) → Acid Secretion
- ACh → ECL cell (M?) → Histamine → parietal cell → ↑ cAMP → H+/K+ ATPase (proton pump) → acid secretion
- ACh → parietal cell (M3) → ↑ Ca^{2+} → H^+/K^+ ATPase (Proton Pump) → Acid Secretion
- PGE_2/PGI_2 → Parietal Cell (EP_3) → ↓ cAMP → H_+/K_+ ATPase (Proton Pump) →Acid Secretion Inhibition

GASTRIC DEFENSES AGAINST ACID

High concentrations of H^+ in the gastric lumen require defense mechanisms to protect the esophagus and the stomach. The primary defense mechanism in esophagus is the lower esophageal sphincter, which prevents the reflux of acidic gastric contents into the esophagus. The stomach protects itself from acid damage by a number of mechanisms. One key defense is the secretion of a mucus layer that protects gastric epithelial cells. Mucus production is stimulated by prostaglandins E_2 and I_2, which also directly inhibits gastric acid secretion by parietal cells. A second important part of the normal mucosal defense is the secretion of bicarbonate ions by superficial gastric epithelial cells. Bicarbonate ions neutralise the acid in the region of the mucosal cells, thereby raising pH and preventing acid-mediated damage. The Fig. 19.2 shows the site of action of drugs which are used for treating gastroesophegeal reflex diseases (GERD).

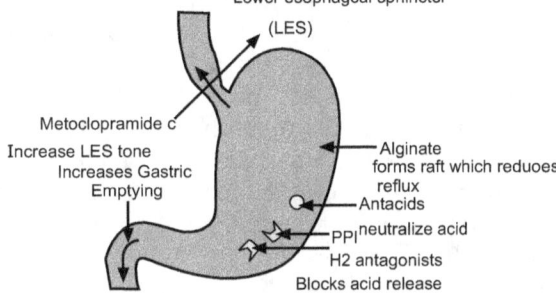

Fig. 19.2: The sites of actions of drugs used to treat gastroesophegeal reflux disease (GERB) Classification

Drugs used for treating peptic ulcers can be classified as follows.

Drugs Class	Examples
Agents that Neutralise Acids (Antacids)	$NaHCO_3$, $Al(OH)_3$, $Mg(OH)_2$
Agents decreasing Gastric Acid Secretion (a) H_2 Receptor Blockers (b) Proton Pump Inhibitors (c) M_1 selective Muscarinic Antagonist	Cimetidine, Ranitidine, Famotidine,Omeprazole Pirenzipine
Agents Enhancing Mucosal Defense Mechanism (Cytoprotective Factors)	Sucralfate, Misoprostol, Bismuth subsalicylate
Eradication of *Helicobacter pylori* Infection (anti-microbial agents)	Triple Combination Therapy: (i) Bismuth + (ii) Metronidazole + (iii) Tetracycline (or) + (iv) Amoxicilin or Clarithromycin

Drugs which decrease the gastric acid secretion and anti-ulcerogenic agents.

Below mention are some characteristics features of these drugs.

PROTON PUMP INHIBITORS

Omeprazole

Esomeprazole

Lansoprazole

Rabeprazole

Lansoprazole

All the proton pump inhibitors chemically differ in their substitution but pharmacologically they are same.

Proton pump inhibitors are present in prodrugs forms which require activation in an acid environment. As soon as they reach the systemic circulation, the prodrug diffuses into the parietal cells of the stomach and accumulates in canaliculi for activation. The activated form of proton pump inhibitor binds covalently with sulfhydryl groups of cysteines in the H^+, K^+-ATPase (the proton pump) and blocks the acid secretion.

The acidic pH in the parietal cell acid canaliculi is the only condition required for drug activation and since food stimulates acid production, these drugs ideally should be given about 30 minutes before meals. Concurrent administration of drug along with food may reduce the rate of absorption of proton pump inhibitors. After absorption it is highly bound to plasma protein and is metabolised hepatically by hepatic cytochrome enzymes. Hepatic disease reduces the clearance of esomeprazole and lansoprazole. Thus, in patients with severe hepatic disease, dose reduction is recommended for esomeprazole and lansoprazole.

Adverse Effects

The most common side effects are nausea, abdominal pain, constipation, flatulence and diarrhoea.

Drug Interactions

- The proton pump inhibitors are extensively metabolised by cytochrome enzymes thus it interferes in clearance of other drugs which are metabolised by the same route e.g. warfarin, diazepam, cyclosporine, phenytoin, theophylline etc.

- Chronic treatment with omeprazole decreases the absorption of vitamin B_{12}.

Therapeutic Uses

Proton pump inhibitors are principally used to promote healing of gastric and duodenal ulcers associated with *H. pylori* infections and to treat gastroesophageal reflux disease (GERD). They are also used or treating pathological hypersecretory conditions like Zollinger-Ellinson Syndrome (ZES).

H₂-RECEPTOR ANTAGONISTS

Cimetidine

Ranitidine

Famotidine

Nizatidine

- H_2 receptor blocker inhibits acid production by inhibiting the binding of histamine to H_2 receptors on the basolateral membrane of parietal cells.

- They suppress 24-hour gastric acid secretion by about 70% but the potency is somewhat less than proton pump inhibitors.

- The H_2-receptor antagonist predominantly inhibits basal acid secretion, which accounts for their efficacy in suppressing nocturnal acid secretion. The other properties of H_2 receptor antagonists are mentioned in Table 16.1.

Adverse Effects

- H_2 receptor blockers are well tolerated in low doses; the incidence of adverse effects found to be less than 3%.

- Side effects usually are minor and include diarrhoea, headache, drowsiness, fatigue, muscular pain and constipation.

- Less common side effects includes those affecting the CNS (confusion, delirium, hallucinations, slurred speech and headaches), which occur primarily with intravenous administration of the drugs or in elderly subjects.

- Long-term use of cimetidine at high doses decreases testosterone binding to the androgen receptor and inhibits a CYP that hydroxylates estradiol.

- They are also reported with various blood dyscrasias, including thrombocytopenia.

Drug Interactions

- Cimetidine inhibits CYPs (e.g., CYP1A2, CYP2C9, and CYP2D6), and thereby can increase the levels of a variety of drugs that are substrates for these enzymes.

- Ranitidine also interacts with hepatic CYPs but interferes only minimally with hepatic metabolism of other drugs.

- Slight increases in blood-alcohol concentration may result from concomitant use of H_2-receptor antagonists.

Therapeutic Uses

- These drugs are used to promote healing of gastric and duodenal ulcers, to treat uncomplicated GERD and to prevent the occurrence of stress ulcers.

AGENTS THAT ENHANCE MUCOSAL DEFENSE

Prostaglandin Analogs: Misoprostol

Mechanism

Prostaglandin E_2 (PGE_2) and prostacyclin (PGI_2) are synthesised by the gastric mucosa and binds to the EP_3 receptor on parietal cells and stimulate the G_i pathway, thereby decreasing intracellular cyclic AMP and gastric acid secretion. PGE_2 also can prevent gastric injury by cytoprotective effects by stimulation of mucin and bicarbonate secretion and increased mucosal blood flow.

Table 19.1: H_2 Receptor Antagonists Used in Peptic Ulcer Disease

Drug	Bioavailability	Elimination	Half life	Comments
Cemetidine	60-70	Renal	1-3	Inhibits P-450 enzymes
Ranitidine	50	Renal/Liver	2-3	No effect on P-450 enzymes
Famotidine	40-50	Renal/biliary	3-4	No effect on P-450 enzymes
Nizatidine	95	Renal	1.5	No effect on P-450 enzymes

Pharmacokinetics

- It show rapid oral absorption and is metabolised extensively by de-esterification producing active metabolite misoprostol acid. The peak plasma concentration reaches at 60 to 90 minutes and lasts for up to 3 hours. Food and antacids decreases the rate of misoprostol absorption, resulting in delayed and decreased peak plasma concentrations of the active metabolite.

- The free acid is excreted mainly in the urine, with an elimination half-life of about 20 to 40 minutes.

Adverse Effects

- Diarrhoea, with or without abdominal pain and cramps.

- It causes exacerbations of inflammatory bowel disease.

Therapeutic Uses

Misoprostol is used to prevent NSAID-induced mucosal injury.

SUCRALFATE (ULCER PROTECTIVE)

Mucosal erosion and ulceration produced due to presence of acid and pepsin-mediated hydrolysis of mucosal proteins can be prevented by ulcer protective agent sucralfate.

Mechanism

- Sucralfate undergoes cross linking in acidic environment to form viscous sticky polymer that adhere to epithelial cells and ulcers thus preventing the damage to mucosal barrier by inhibiting hydrolysis of mucosal proteins by pepsin

- Sucralfate may have additional cytoprotective effects, including stimulation of local production of prostaglandins and epidermal growth factor.

- Sucralfate also binds with bile salts, thus, some clinicians use sucralfate to treat individuals with the syndromes of biliary esophagitis or gastritis.

Therapeutic Uses

- Sucralfate is used for prophylaxis of stress ulcers.

- It is also used in several other conditions associated with mucosal inflammation/ulceration that may not respond to other acid suppressant.

- On administered by rectal enema, sucralfate has also been used for treating radiation proctitis and solitary rectal ulcers.

Adverse Effects

The most common side effect of sucralfate is constipation.

Drug Interactions

Sucralfate forms a viscous layer in the stomach that may inhibit absorption of other drugs, including phenytoin, digoxin, cimetidine, ketoconazole, and fluoroquinolone antibiotics. Sucralfate therefore should be taken at least after 2 hours of the administration of other drugs.

ANTACIDS

Sodium bicarbonate, $CaCO_3$, $Mg(OH)_2$, $Al(OH)_3$, Magaldrate and Simethicone

Effectiveness and choice of antacid depends upon various factors including palatability. The effectiveness of antacid preparations is expressed as milliequivalents of acid-neutralizing capacity. Sodium bicarbonate, $CaCO_3$, $Mg(OH)_2$ and $Al(OH)_3$, Magaldrate and Simethicone are some common examples of antacide. Below mentioned are some characteristics features of these antacids.

- **Sodium bicarbonate** effectively neutralises acid; it is highly water-soluble and is rapidly absorbed from the stomach. It is contraindicated in cardiac or renal failure because of sodium loads may pose a risk for patients.

- Depending on particle size and crystal structure, $CaCO_3$ rapidly and effectively neutralizes gastric H^+, but the release of CO_2 from bicarbonate- and carbonate-containing antacids can cause belching, nausea, abdominal distention, and flatulence. Calcium also may induce rebound acid secretion, necessitating more frequent administration.

- Combinations of Mg^{2+} (rapidly reacting) and Al^{3+} (slowly reacting) hydroxides provide a relatively balanced and sustained neutralising capacity.

- **Magaldrate** is a hydroxymagnesium aluminate complex which is converted rapidly into $Mg(OH)_2$ and $Al(OH)_3$ in gastric acid. Although fixed combinations of magnesium and aluminium theoretically counteract the adverse effects of each other on the bowel (Al^{3+} can relax gastric smooth muscle, producing delayed gastric emptying and constipation).

- **Simethicone** is a surfactant that may decrease foaming and esophageal reflux, hence is included in many antacid preparations.

In general, antacids should be given in suspension form because of greater neutralising capacity than powder or tablet dosage forms. Antacids are cleared from the empty stomach in about 30 minutes. However, in the presence of food there is elevation of gastric pH to about 5 and this condition prolongs the neutralising effects of antacids and it will remain for about 2 to 3 hours.

OTHER ACID SUPPRESSANTS AND CYTOPROTECTANTS

Irenzepine and telenzepine both are M_1 muscarinic receptor antagonists used to reduce basal acid production by 40% to 50%. They suppress neural stimulation of acid production *via* actions on M_1 receptors of intramural ganglia. They also produce undesirable anticholinergic side effects and also increase the risk of blood disorders.

Rebamipide

Rebamipide exerts a cytoprotective effect by increasing prostaglandin generation in gastric mucosa and by scavenging reactive oxygen species.

Ecabet

Ecabet is a cytoprotective agent which appears to increase the formation of PGE_2 and PGI_2 and thus is used for ulcer therapy.

Carbenoloxone

Carbenoloxone is a derivative of glycyrrhizic acid found in licorice root. Its exact mechanism of action is not clear, but it may alter the composition and quantity of mucin.

Bismuth compounds

- It is cytoprotective agent and effective as cimetidine for treatment of peptic ulcers. It is frequently prescribed in combination with antibiotics to eradicate *H. pylori* and prevents ulcer recurrence.

- Bismuth compounds bind to the base of ulcers and promote the production of mucin and bicarbonate which have significant antibacterial effects.

PROKINETICS

Prokinetics are the agents that promote upper gastrointestinal motility and enhance coordinated contraction of the antrum and duodenum. It also increases gastric emptying and relief of gastric stasis. The other action of prokinetics is to decrease reflux oesophagitis/heartburn and decreasing regurgitation of gastric contents and emesis by increasing release or action of ACh for prokinesis. Fig 19.3 shows the receptors and drugs acting on particular site for prokinesis.

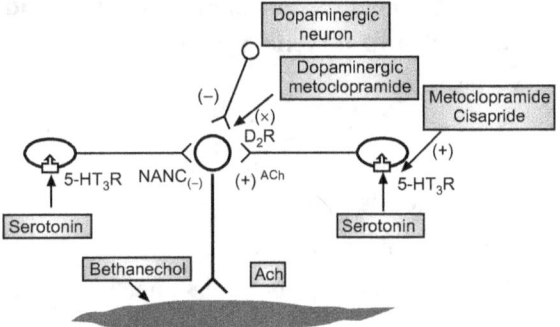

Fig. 19.3: Action of Prokinetics agents

Prokinetic Agents

Below mentioned are some prokinetic agents:

Category	Prototype	Mechanism of action
Muscarinic agonist	Bethanachol	GI motility
Anticholinestrase	Neostigmine	GI motility, inhibit ACh degradation
Dopamine D_2 blockers	Metaclopramide Domperidome	Blocks inhibitory D_2 receptor
5-HT_4 agonists	Cisapride, Metaclopramide Tegaserod, Prucalopride	Activates excitatory 5-HT_4 receptors
Motilin Agonist – Peptide hormone – GI M cells	Erythromycin	Activate neural and smooth muscle motilin receptor

Note: All the prokinetic drugs enhance cholinomimetic effect by modulating cholinergic neurons.

Disadvantages (Bethanachol and Neostigmine)

- Produce non-specific muscarinic effect
- Increases salivation
- Diarrhea, gastric and pancreatic secretion.

Advantages

- Dopamine D_2 Blockers: Metoclopramide, Domperidone
- 5-HT_4 agonists: Cisapride, metoclopramide
- Motilin agonist: Erythromycin

Brief comparative Pharmacology and Indications of Prokinetic Agents

Metaclopramide

1. Besides being $5HT_4$ receptor agonist metoclopramide is also a selective D_2 dopamine antagonist (anti-emetic).
2. It crosses the blood brain barrier.
3. It exhibits hyperprolactinemia and extrapyramidal side effects. Besides this, it also shows anti-emetic effect.

Domperidone

1. Domperidone is D_2 selective antagonist.
2. It does not cross blood brain barrier.
3. CNS related symptoms are least and causes hyperprolactinemia (dopamine inhibits prolactin release).

Cisapride

Cisapride is a serotonergic receptor agonist. It activates 5-HT_4 receptor and increases the release of cAMP. It does not exhibit D_2 receptor activity, CNS related side effects, hyperprolactinemia and also does not have anti-emetic effect. It causes upper gastrointestinal motility and promotes colonic hypermotility and relieves constipation. The major side affects of cisapride is ventricular arrhythmia by torsades de pointes because blocking of K^+ channels in the heart. It also blocks K^+ channels in gastrointestinal tract.

Erythromycin

1. Erythromycin is macrolide antibiotic and acts as a motilin agonist.
2. It increases gastric emptying and duodenal contraction and useful in diabetic gastric paresis.

Newer therapies

- CCK_1 receptor antagonist – Loxiglumide: Effective in suppressing transient lower esophageal relaxations (tLESRs) in gastroesophageal reflux disease.
- GABA agonists – Baclofen.

THERAPEUTIC STRATEGY FOR SPECIFIC ACID PEPTIC DISORDERS

GASTROESOPHEGEAL REFLUX DISEASE

- Most of the symptoms of gastroesophegeal reflux disease (GERD) reflect injurious effects of the refluxed acid-peptic content on the esophageal epithelium, providing the rationale for suppression of gastric acid. The goals of GERD therapy are complete resolution of symptoms and healing of esophagitis.
- GERD is a chronic disorder that requires long-term therapy. "step-down" approaches maintain symptomatic remission by either decreasing the dose of the proton pump inhibitor or switching to an H_2-receptor antagonist.
- Proton pump inhibitors heal the esophagitis **by** approximately 80% and 90% after 4 weeks and 8 weeks of therapy respectively while the corresponding healing rates with H_2-receptor antagonists are 50% and 75% with the same duration of therapy.
- Although some patients with mild GERD symptoms may be managed by nocturnal doses of **H_2-receptor antagonists**, twice-daily dosing usually is required.

Severe Symptoms of GERD

In patients with severe symptoms or extraintestinal manifestations of GERD, twice-daily dosing with a proton pump inhibitor may be required. However sometimes, patients with continuing symptoms on twice-daily proton pump inhibitors are often treated by adding an H_2-receptor antagonist at night as this can further suppress acid production.

Therapy for Extra intestinal Manifestations of GERD

Proton pump inhibitors have been used in higher doses and for longer periods of time than those used for patients with more classic symptoms of GERD.

GERD and Pregnancy

Mild cases of GERD during pregnancy should be treated with antacids or sucralfate as the first-line drugs. If symptoms persist, H_2-receptor antagonists can be used, with ranitidine. While the proton pumps inhibitors are reserved for women with intractable symptoms or complicated reflux disease. In this situation, lansoprazole is considered the preferred choice among the proton pump inhibitors.

PEPTIC ULCER DISEASE

Peptic ulcer occurs due to imbalance between mucosal defense factors (bicarbonate, mucin, prostaglandin, nitric oxide, and other peptides and growth factors) and injurious factors (acid and pepsin). The patient with duodenal ulcers produces more acid than do control subjects, particularly at night (basal secretion). Although patients with gastric ulcers have normal or even diminished acid production. *H. pylori* and nonsteroidal antiinflammatory drugs (NSAIDs) are the causative factors for ulcer. Up to 60% of peptic ulcers are associated with *H. pylori infection* of the stomach which leads to impaired production of somatostatin by D cells, increased acid production and reduced duodenal bicarbonate production. Proton pump inhibitors are more preferable because they relieve symptoms of duodenal ulcers and promote healing more rapidly than H_2-receptor antagonists.

HELICOBACTER PYLORI INFECTION

Helicobacter pylori infection has been associated with gastritis and the subsequent development of gastric and duodenal ulcers, gastric adenocarcinoma, and gastric B-cell lymphoma. Single-antibiotic regimens are ineffective in eradicating *H. pylori* infection which leads to microbial resistance.

Questions on this Chapter

1. Discuss the mechanism of acid secretion and add a note on proton pump inhibitors.

2. Write in detail about the pharmacology of H_2 receptor antagonist.

3. Discuss the therapeutic strategies for various acid peptic disorders.

4. Write short note on antacids and cytoprotective agents.

Chapter 20

PHARMACOLOGY OF EMETICS AND ANTI-EMETICS

Objectives

After reading this chapter, the student will be able to:

➢ Describe the process of emesis

➢ Mention the key receptors involved in the process of emesis

➢ Enlist the drugs associated with emesis

➢ Write the indications for antiemetic

EMESIS

Emesis or vomiting is a reflex coordinated by emetic center in medulla. There is nonruminant, forceful ejection of contents of stomach and proximal duodenum into mouth. In case of poisoning, toxic substances can be removed by vomiting by reflex action from stomach and intestine. Horses, rabbits and rodents do not normally vomit because of absence of vomiting center. The main vomiting center the Chemoreceptor Trigger Zone (CTZ) and Nucleus Tractus Solitaries (NTS) receive the afferent impulses arising in gastrointestinal tract, throat and other viscera. Toxins and drugs can enter CSF and stimulate receptors in CTZ. The Fig. 20.1 represents the different area of emesis in brain.

The CTZ and NTS are covered by a variety of receptors e.g. histamine, dopamine, serotonin, cholinergic, opioids which send the impulse to the vomiting center; thus these sites could be the target for antiemetic action.

Important receptors in CTZ

• Serotonin (5-HT$_3$)

• Dopamine (D$_2$) – particularly in dogs

• Opioid

• Histamine (not demonstrated in cats)

• Muscarinic

IMPORTANT RECEPTORS IN EMETIC CENTER

• Alpha-2-adrenergic – particularly in cats

• Serotonin (5-HT$_{1A}$)

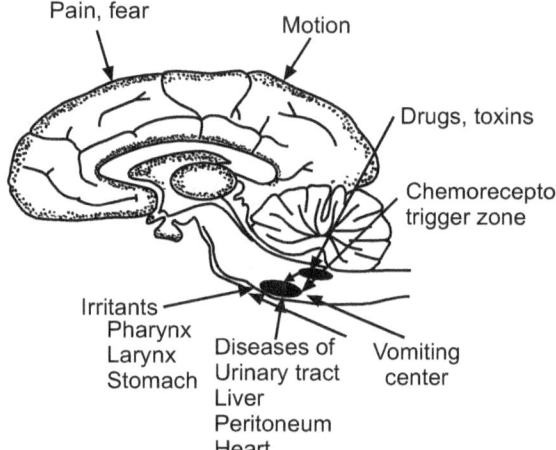

Fig. 20.1: Different Emetic centers in brain

The major emetic stimuli, pathways and structures mediating the emetic reflex and nausea are as follows.

The flow chart given in Fig. 20.2 shows the stimuli and the pathway of emetics. Strong stimulus e.g. endogenous or exogenous toxins or drugs, visual and emotional factors, stimulus to labyrinth, mechanical stimulus, pain, stimulus to cardiovascular system etc. cause activation of CTZ center resulting in vomiting. The endogenous or exogenous toxins or drugs enters into cerebrospinal fluid and activates CTZ center to produce vomiting. Motion sickness occurs in traveling because of CTZ activation due to attack of stimulus on labyrinth to nerve VIII and then to cerebellum which ultimately reaches to CTZ activation and leads to vomiting. The mechanical stimuli activate the CTZ center. In which CTZ receives the signal from gut or pharynx through sympathetic nerve or vagus nerve. Pain activates sympathetic system resulting in secretion of saliva or gastric fluid which cause retching and vomiting.

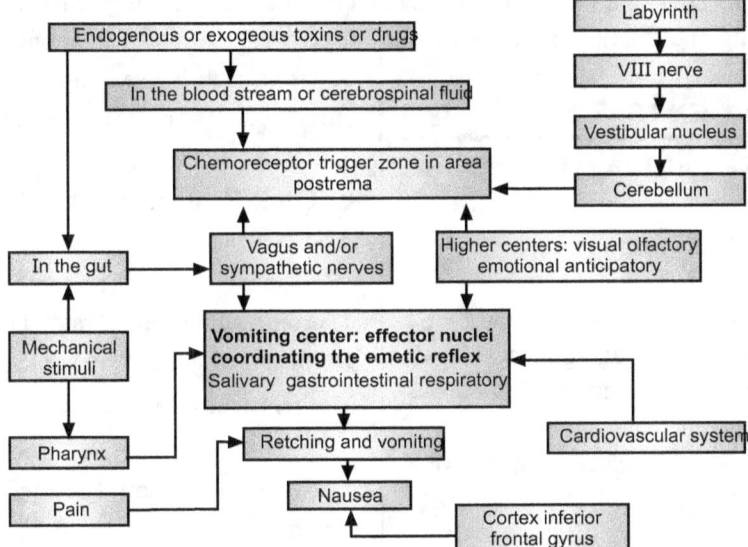

Fig. 20.2: Pathway of Emesis

EMETIC AGENTS

Emetic agents are the drugs that induce vomiting. Usually these agents remove about 40-60% stomach contents. It is contraindicated to use in those who have ingested caustic substances, don't have a normal swallowing reflex, are not totally conscious, are having seizures, in shock or dyspneic. Emetic agent cannot produce vomiting in horses, rabbits, rodents because of absence of taste buds.

Apomorphine

It is a semisynthetic derivative of morphine. It stimulates D_2 receptors in CTZ center. At higher doses it produces protracted vomiting, excitement/sedation. An overdose of apomorphine results into cardiac and respiratory depression which can be reversed with use of naloxone; a morphine antagonist.

Xylazine

It is a tranquilizer but at lower doses can be used as an emetic by acting as alpha2-adrenergic agonist. It is contraindicated in hypertension, peptic ulcer and pregnancy.

3% Hydrogen Peroxide

3% Hydrogen peroxide can also be used to produce emesis. It may cause esophagitis and gastritis.

Table Salt Solution

Salt solution produces the emesis by activating sympathetic system which causes vomiting. At higher concentration it can cause salt toxicosis characterised by neurological signs, including seizures.

Activated Charcoal

Activated charcoal is commonly used in case of poisoning. It administered orally to adsorb toxins or drugs to prevent or reduce their systemic absorption. It is not very effective in adsorbing alcohols, caustic alkalies, nitrates, mineral acids or petroleum distillates. The usual side effects of activated charcoal are emesis at rapid administration, constipation or diarrhoea; black faeces, staining and floating of dry powder in GIT.

ANTIEMETIC AGENTS

PHENOTHIAZINE DERIVATIVES (NEUROLEPTIC)

Prochlorperazine, Chlorpromazine, Haloperidol

These agents have antiemetic property by acting on dopamine receptor antagonist at CTZ; mild histamine receptor antagonist.High doses block α_2- receptors at emetic center.

These agents also produce tranquilising effect. They are contraindicated in animals with seizure.

ANTICHOLINERGIC AGENTS

Hyoscine, Dicyclomine

Anticholinergics are more effective for motion sickness in travelling. They act as a antiemetic probably by blocking nerve conduction impulses across the cholinergic link in the pathway leading from the vestibular apparatus in the vomiting center. They produce sedation and other anticholinergics side effect, thus suitable for short brisk journey.

H₁ RECEPTOR ANTAGONISTS

These are antihistaminic agents mainly used in prevention of motion sickness and lesser in case of morning sickness. They prevent the emesis by blocking input from vestibular apparatus to CTZ. Their antiemetic effects are based on anticholinergics, antihistaminic and sedative properties. Commonly used anti-histaminic are promethazine, diphenhydramine, promethazine, cyclazine, cinnarizine etc. Beside their antiemetic effects they produce side effects such as sedation and dryness of mouth .

5-HT₃ RECEPTOR ANTAGONISTS

Serotonin receptor are present on inhibitory myenteric interneurones and in CTZ/NTS center. The agents which block the serotonin receptor can prevent emesis formation. The commonly used 5-HT₃ receptor antagonist for antiemetics is ondasetron. It is used commonly to prevent/treat emesis due to cancer chemotherapy and it is well tolerated.

PROKINETIC (MOTILITY-PROMOTING) AGENTS

These are the agents which promote gastrointestinal transit rate. The commonly used prokinetic as antiemetic are as follows:

Metoclopramide

Metoclopramide is used to increase the gastrointestinal motility, now it is widely used antiemetic. The antiemetic effect of metoclopramide is mainly due to dopamine receptor blocking activity; additionally it has 5-HT₃ receptor blocking activity at vagal afferents.

It is used to block the apomorphine induced vomiting. The gastrokinetic effects of metoclopramide contribute to its antiemetic effects. Prokinetic effect in stomach and proximal small intestine is due to increase in Ach release from enteric neurons, increased force of contractions and promotes gastric emptying. It is contraindicated in presence of gastrointestinal obstruction. It is generally well tolerated. Sedation, dizziness, diarrhoea and muscle dystonia are the major side effects of metoclopramide.

P/Neurokinin-1 Receptor Antagonist Prototype: Aprepitant

- **Indications:** It is used in prevention of acute and delayed nausea and vomiting associated with emetogenic cancer chemotherapy.
- **Actions:** Selectively blocks human substance P/neurokinin 1 (NK1) receptors in the CNS, preventing nausea and vomiting caused by highly emetogenic chemotherapeutic agents
- **Oral route:** Onset rapid, plasma peak level obtained in 4 hours of administration.
- T½: 9–13 hrs.; metabolised in the liver and excreted in urine and faeces

Contraindications to Use of Substance P/Neurokinin 1 Receptor Antagonists

This drug is contraindicated in patients with history of allergy to antiemetic, impaired renal or hepatic function, pregnancy or lactation, coma or semiconscious state, CNS depression, hypotension or hypertension, active peptic ulcer and in CNS injury.

Indications for Antiemetics

- **Phenothiazine**

It is used in prevention and controlling of nausea and vomiting, including that associated with anesthesia; severe vomiting; intractable hiccoughs.

- **Anticholinergics**

Anticholinergics are used in nausea and vomiting associated with motion sickness or vestibular (inner ear) problems.

- **5-HT$_3$ receptor blockers/substance P/neurokinin 1 receptor antagonists**

Used in nausea and vomiting with emetogenic chemotherapy.

Implementation for the Patient Receiving Antiemetics

- Assess patient carefully for potential drug-drug interactions.
- Provide comfort and safety measures.
- Provide support and encouragement.

Questions on this Chapter

1. Discuss the pharmacology of emetic agents.
2. Discuss the pathogenesis of emesis.
3. Discuss in details the pharmacology of antiemetic.
4. Which are the different receptors involved in the process of emesis? Write the therapeutic target for antiemetic actions.

Chapter 21

PHARMACOTHERAPY OF CONSTIPATION

Objectives

After reading this chapter, the student will be able to:

➢ Enlist the characteristics features of laxatives

➢ Write the mechanism by which laxative acts

➢ Write the mechanism by which anthraquinone produce the action

➢ Write the mechanism by which bisocodyl produce the action

➢ Understand the action of castor oil

➢ Enlist the limitations of stimulant purgatives

INTRODUCTION

Constipation is a disorder of gastrointestinal tract characterised by infrequent stooling and difficult to pass the stools. It results into abdominal bloating or discomfort. Normally stool contains 70-85% of water and the frequency is ≥ 3/week. In order to treat constipation, laxatives are frequently employed before surgical, radiological, and endoscopic procedures where an empty colon is desirable. The terms laxatives, cathartics, purgatives, aperients, and evacuants often are used interchangeably. There is a distinction, however, between laxation (the evacuation of formed fecal material from the rectum) and catharsis (the evacuation of unformed, usually watery fecal material from the entire colon). Most of the commonly used agents promote laxation, but some are actually cathartics that act as laxatives at low doses.

The common and general causes of constipation are dietary (fibre), drugs, hormonal disturbances, neurogenic disorders, systemic illnesses, irritable bowel syndrome, colonic motility and disorder of defecation or evacuation. Some secondary causes of constipation are hypothyroidism, diabetes and use of medications like opiates and anticholinergics.

For treating constipation it is necessary to re-educate patient and maintain normal frequency of stool. Change the diet by increasing the fiber and consumption of more fluid. The medication use in treatment of constipation is laxative.

LAXATIVE AGENTS

Laxative agents exhibit the following characteristics features:

• Increases bulk of intestinal contents, stretching mucosa thus stimulating peristalsis.

- Increases fluid volume of intestinal contents.
- It may cause flatulence, cramping and diarrhoea.
- Speeds up or improves movement of intestinal contents when movement becomes slow or sluggish (constipation)
- Increases the tone of the GI tract and stimulates motility throughout the system.

Mechanism of Action of Laxatives

Laxatives generally act in one of the following ways:

1. Enhancing retention of intraluminal fluid by hydrophilic or osmotic mechanisms.
2. Decreasing net absorption of fluid by effects on small and large bowel fluid and electrolyte transport.
3. Altering motility by either inhibiting segmenting (non-propulsive) contractions or stimulating propulsive contractions. Based on their actions, laxatives have been classified into different groups.

CLASSIFICATION OF LAXATIVES

Laxative can be classified into following three classes:

1. Luminally Active Agents

Luminally active agents are of the following types:

(a) Hydrophilic colloids; bulk-forming agents (bran, psyllium etc.)

(b) Osmotic agents (non-absorbable inorganic salts or sugars)

(c) Stool-wetting agents (surfactants) and emollients (docusate, mineral oil)

2. Non-specific Stimulants or Irritants

These laxatives have their effect on fluid secretion and motility. Diphenylmethanes (bisacodyl), anthraquinones (senna and cascara) and castor oil are common example of non-specific stimulants or irritants.

3. Prokinetic Agents (Acting Primarily on Motility)

$5\text{-}HT_4$ receptor agonists and opioid receptor antagonists are some common Prokinetic agents. These agents act primarily on GI motility.

However, recent studies indicate considerable overlap among these traditional categories. A variety of laxatives, both osmotic agents and stimulants, increase the activity of nitric oxide (NO) synthase and the biosynthesis of platelet-activating factor in the gut. Platelet-activating factor is a phospholipid proinflammatory mediator that stimulates colonic secretion and GI motility. Nitric oxide also may stimulate intestinal secretion and inhibit segmenting contractions in the colon, thereby promoting laxation. Agents that reduces the expression of NO synthase or its activity can prevent the laxative effects of castor oil, cascara, and bisacodyl (but not senna), as well as magnesium sulfate.

BULK FORMING AGENTS

Increased intake of bulk forming agent is most appropriate method for prevention and treatment of constipation. While it has some drawbacks that the onset of action shows to take 3-4 days thus there is need to administer for prolong period of time to show full effects of bulk forming agents. Its relief pattern is poor. Taste of bulk forming agents is lousy and present in powder form which is inconvenient for patient to consume. It is more suitable for mild constipation. Fiber such as cellulose derivatives, psyllium seeds (Metamucil), bran are used as antidiarrhoeal agents by absorbing water from intestinal contents and used as laxatives by increasing bulk of intestinal contents, stretching mucosa and thereby stimulating peristalsis. The bulk forming agents must be given with lot of water because there may further dry out intestinal contents and cause constipation.

DIETARY FIBRE: BRAN

Bran consists of unabsorbable cell wall and other constituent of vegetable food-cellulose, pectin, glycoprotein and other polysaccharides. Bran consisting of 40% dietary fibre absorbs water from intestine, swells and increases water content of feces thus softening it and facilitates colonic transit. It supports the bacterial growth in colon which contributes to the faecal mass. Certain dietary fibre such as gums, lignins, pectins etc. bind bile acids and promote their excretion in faeces. It also enhances the degradation of cholesterol in liver and lowers the plasma LDL cholesterol.

Applications

- It increases the bulk of intestinal contents, stretching mucosa, thereby stimulating peristalsis.
- Must be given with lot of water or may further dry out intestinal contents and cause constipation.

Drawbacks

Bran has the following drawbacks:

- It is unpalatable.
- Require to ingest large quantity.
- Full effect requires daily administration for at least 3-4 days.
- It does not soften faeces already present in colon or rectum.
- It should not be used in patient with gut ulceration, adhesion, stenosis and when faecal impaction is possible.

PSYLLIUM AND ISPAGHULA

- Both contain natural colloidal mucilage which forms a gelatinous mass by absorbing water.
- They act in 1-3 days

- They should not be swallowed dry (may cause esophageal impaction)

METHYLCELLULOSE AND CORBOXYMETHYLCELLULOSE

These are semi synthetic, colloidal, hydrophilic derivatives of cellulose. Generous amount of water must be taken with all bulk forming agent. The choice of different bulking agent is a matter of personal preference.

STOOL SOFTENER

DOCUSATES

{Dicotyl Sodium Sulfosuccinate (DOSS)}

- It is an anionic detergent. It softens the stool by net water accumulation in the lumen by an action on the intestinal mucosa.
- It emulsifies the colonic contents and increases penetration of water into faeces.
- It can disrupt the mucosal barrier and enhance absorption of many non-absorbable drugs e.g. liquid paraffin, should avoid the combination with it.
- It is a mild laxative.
- Cramps and abdominal pain can occur. It is bitter; liquid preparation may cause nausea. Hepatotoxicity is feared on prolonged use.

LIQUID PARAFFIN

- It is viscous liquid; mixture of petroleum hydrocarbon.
- It is pharmacologically inert.
- Taken for 2-3 days, it softens stools and is said to lubricate hard scybali by coating them.

Disadvantage

- Unpleasant to swallow because of oily consistency.
- May produce foreign body granulomas in the intestinal submucosa, mesenteric lymph nodes, liver and spleen.

- During swallowing it may trickle into lungs cause lipid pneumonia.

- Carries away fat soluble vitamin with it into the stool; deficiency may occur on chronic use.

- Leakage of the oil past anal sphincter may cause embarrassment.

- May interfere with healing in the anorectal region.

Due to above reason it should be used occasionally.

OSMOTIC PURGATIVE

Osmotic purgatives are not absorbed in the intestine; they retain water osmotically and increase the peristaltic activity. Other mechanisms contributing to their effects are production of inflammatory mediators. Magnesium containing salts releases the cholecystokinin which accumulates intraluminal fluid and electrolyte and increases the intestinal motility by purgative action. All inorganic salts used as osmotic purgative have similar action and differs only in dose, palatability and risk of systemic toxicity. Magnesium sulfate, magnesium hydroxide, magnesium citrate, sodium phosphate, sodium sulphate and sodium potassium tartarate are common inorganic salts used as osmotic purgative. It is found that every additional miliequivalent of Mg^{2+} increases the faecal weight by about 7 gm. The usual dose of magnesium salts contains 40 to 120 mEq of Mg^{2+} and produces 300 to 600 ml of stool within 6 hours.

Limitations

It is bitter in taste and may induce nausea. Bitter taste can be masked with citrus juices. However, they must be used with caution and should be avoided in patients with renal insufficiency, cardiac disease, or preexisting electrolyte abnormalities and in patients on diuretic therapy.

NON-DIGESTIBLE SUGARS AND ALCOHOLS

Lactulose (synthetic disaccharide of galactose), fructose, sorbitol and mannitol are common examples of non-digestible sugars and alcohols with laxative action. Lactulose and fructose resists intestinal disaccharidase activity while sorbitol and mannitol is hydrolysed to fatty acid in the colon which stimulates GI motility osmotically.

Limitations

- At lower doses they cause abdominal discomfort, distention and flatulence however these subside after continued administration.

- Use of sorbitol and mannitol may result into trapping of ammonia accompanied by hydrolysis into fatty acid as they drop the luminal pH.

POLYETHYLENE GLYCOL (PEG)-ELECTROLYTE SOLUTIONS

It is highly osmotic in nature and due to this property it is retained in the lumen. It is used for cleaning of colon which is very necessary for radiological, surgical and endoscopic procedures. PEG contains an isotonic mixture of sodium sulfate, sodium bicarbonate, sodium chloride and potassium chloride which avoids net transfer of ions across the intestinal wall.

STIMULANT PURGATIVES

Stimulant purgative are powerful purgative. Some of the stimulant increases the motility by acting on myenteric plexuses. The more important mechanism of action is accumulation of water and electrolyte in the lumen by altering absorptive and secretory activity of the mucosal cell. They inhibit Na-K ATPase at the basolateral membrane of villous cell which results in reduced transport of sodium and accompanying water into the interstitium.

Secretion is enhanced by activation of cyclic AMP in crypt cells and by increased PG synthesis. The commonly used stimulant purgatives are diphenylmethane derivatives, anthraquinones and some fixed oil.

Limitations

- Larger doses produces excess purgation, fluid and electrolyte imbalance. Hypokalemia can occur on regular use.
- Long term use can produce colonic atony.
- Stimulates ulcer production.
- It produces subacute or chronic intestinal obstruction.

(I) DIPHENYLMETHANE
(Bisacodyl and Phenolphthalein)

The commonly used diphenylmethanes derivatives are phenolphthalein and bisacodyl. Phenolphthalein is an indicator and used as purgative. As an indicator it produces pink urine if urine is alkaline. It is partly absorbed and reexcreted in bile: enterohepatic circulation is more important for action of phenolphthalein. Bisacodyl is activated in intestine by deacetylation. Their primary site of action is colon. Bisacodyl act by irritating the rectal mucosa this cause reflex increase in motility. Due to irritating nature of Bisacodyl it may cause inflammation and mucosal damage. Eacuation occurs after 30 minutes of its administration.

Limitations

- Produces fluid evacuation and cramps in some individuals.
- Morphological alteration in the colonic mucosa has been observed. Mucosa become leakier.
- Allergic reactions producing skin rashes, fixed drug eruption and Steven-Johnson syndrome have been reported.

- Phenolphthalein has been found to produce tumor in mice.
- Bisacodyl produces inflammation and mucosal damage.

(II) ANTHRAQUINONES
(Senna and Cascara)

Anthraquinone purgatives are commonly known as emodins and require 6-7 hours for producing action. They are not active as such, the unabsorbed glycoside (small intestine) passes into colon where bacteria liberates the active anthrol form, which either acts locally or is absorbed into circulation-excreted in bile to act on small intestine. If taken at bed time evacuation generally occurs in the morning. Cramp and excessive purging occur in some cases. The active principle is believed to act on the myenteric plexus to increase peristalsis and decrease segmentation. They also inhibit salt and water absorption in the colon. Senna anthraquinone has been found to stimulate PGE2 production in rat intestine leading to increase the peristaltic activity. The activity of senna is block by Indomethacin thereby reduces the purgative action of senna. Skin rashes and fixed drug eruption are seen occasionally with use of anthraquinones purgatives. Regular use for 4-12 months causes colonic atony and mucosal pigmentation (melanosis).

(III) FIXED OIL (Castor oil)

Castor oil is obtained from *Ricinus communis*: it is used on skin as emollient. It mainly contains triglycerides of ricinoelic acid which is a polar long chain fatty acid. This is hydrolysed in the ileum by lipase to recinoelic acid and glycerol. Recinolic acid is believed to irritate the mucosa and stimulate intestinal contractions. Its primary action involves decreased intestinal absorption of water and electrolytes and enhanced secretion by a detergent like action on the mucosa. Structural damage to the villous tips has also been observed with fixed oil. Purgative action occurs within 2-3 hours of intake.

Limitation

Unpalatability, frequent cramping, possibility of dehydration and on regular use produces intestinal mucosal damage.

PROKINETIC AND OTHER AGENTS FOR CONSTIPATION

Prokinetics regulates the gastrointestinal motility by enhancing gastrointestinal transit by acting on specific receptor in gastrointestinal tract.

The prokinetic agent commonly used in constipation is cisapride but it does not produce consistent effect.

Another prokinetic agent is misoprostol a synthetic prostaglandin analog which is used for protection against gastric ulcer resulting from NSAIDs. Prostaglandins can stimulate colonic contractions, particularly in the descending colon and cause diarrhoea. Other agents which are used in improving frequency and stool consistency by unknown mechanism are colchicine, a microtubule formation inhibitor which is used for gout.

ENEMAS AND SUPPOSITORIES

The major constituent of enema and suppository is glycerin which is a trihydroxy alcohol that is absorbed orally, but acts as a hygroscopic agent and lubricant when given rectally. It stimulates the water retention and produces peristalsis and bowel movement in less than an hour. Local discomfort, burning, or hyperemia and bleeding limits the use of rectal glycerin. Suppositories containing sodium stearate cause local irritation.

Questions on this Chapter

1. Write the classification of laxative and add note on stool softener.

2. Discuss in details the pharmacology of stimulant purgatives.

3. Write a note on osmotic purgative.

4. Discuss the pharmacology of Luminally active agents.

Chapter 22

PHARMACOTHERAPY OF DIARRHOEA

Objectives

After reading this chapter, the student will be able to:

➢ Learn the composition and importance of ORS

➢ Understand the possible causes of a diarrhoea

➢ Understand the functions of antidiarrhoeal agents

➢ Write the mechanism of secretory and osmotic diarrhoea

➢ Write the mechanism of bismuth subsalicylate in treatment of diarrohea

Diarrhoea is a condition of frequent passage of poorly formed stool. There is passage of excess water in feaces. In diarrhoea the excessive fluid weight is around 200g/day.

MECHANISM

There is an increase in the osmotic load in the intestine because of excessive secretion as well as absorption of water and electrolyte. There is also salt absorption in ileum and colon. All these changes result in an increase in the osmotic load which leads to altered motility and rapid transit rate. There is also exudation of protein and fluid.

DIARRHOEA CAUSES

Diarrhoea may be acute or chronic. All acute enteric infections produce secretory diarrhoea. Many bacterial toxins e.g. cholera toxin, exotoxin producing strains of *E. coli, Staphylococcus aureus and Salmonella typhi* activate adenyl cyclase which enhances secretion of fluid and electrolyte.

Viral and parasitic infections also increase the water and electrolyte secretion resulting into diarrhoea.

Many disease conditions like irritable and inflammatory bowel syndrome cause chronic diarrhoea. Some medicines may also induce diarrhoea such as frequent use of laxatives and antacids; antibiotic therapy such as clindamycin, cefuroxime, augmentin; antihypertensives viz. reserpine, guanethedine, methyldopa; some cholinergics bethanechol and metoclopramide; and prostaglandin analogue.

MANAGEMENT OF DIARRHEA

There are several ways to manage diarrhoea while the very first approach is use of rehydration fluid and electrolyte balance. The use of antimicrobial therapy may mask clinical picture of diarrhoea, delay clearance of organism and increase risk of systemic invasion because of inhibition of intestinal microbial flora.

CLASSIFICATION AND FUNCTIONS OF ANTIDIARRHOEAL DRUGS

- These agents act to increase transit time in the intestine to allow greater absorption of fluid.
- They soothe irritation to the intestinal wall.
- They block gastrointestinal muscle activity to decrease peristaltic movement.
- They affect CNS activity to cause gastrointestinal spasm and stop movement.
- They may cause constipation.

Table 22.1: Classification of Antidiarrhoeal agents

Class	Drugs
Oral rehydration therapy	ORS
Bulk forming and hydroscopic agents	Carboxyl methyl cellulose, calcium polycarbophil
Bile acid sequestering agent	Cholestyramine, Bismuth subsalicylate
Antimotility and antisecretory agents	Opioids – Diphenoxylate, Dipfenoxin, Loperamide
Alpha 2 adrenergic agents	Clonidine
Hormones	Somatostatin
Plant alkaloids	Berberine

ORAL REHYDRATION THERAPY

Oral rehydration therapy is a mixture of glucose and electrolytes that can prevent dehydration. It is present in mixed formula using glucose electrolyte or rice-based physiological solution. In severe cases, dehydration and electrolyte imbalances are the principal risk, particularly in infants; children and elderly thus oral rehydration therapy is of great importance in such cases. These therapies provide nutrient-linked cotransport of water and electrolytes in most cases of acute diarrhoea. Sodium and chloride absorption is linked to glucose uptake by the enterocyte; this is followed by movement of water in the same direction. These rehydration therapies provide symptomatic relief in acute diarrhoea.

BULK-FORMING AND HYDROSCOPIC AGENTS

Common examples of bulk forming and hydroscopic agent are carboxymethyl cellulose and calcium polycarbophil which absorbs the water and increases stool bulk. These are used in mild chronic diarrhoeas; in patients suffering with irritable bowel syndrome. Mechanically, they work as gels to modify stool texture and viscosity and to produce a perception of decreased stool fluidity. They also bind to bacterial toxin and bile acid .

BILE ACID SEQUESTRANTS

Cholestyramine

Cholestyramine is used in bile salt-induced diarrhoea, antibiotic associated diarrhoea and mild colitis. It interrupts the normal enterohepatic circulation of bile salts and reaches colon where they stimulate the water and electrolyte secretion. It is also used in clearing of pathogen from bowel thus used in colitis. It is also useful in relief of pruritus associated with biliary obstruction and biliary cirrhosis. In such conditions, excessive bile acids are thought to be deposited in the skin which cause irritation.

Bismuth Subsalicylate

- It is used in a mixture of magnesium aluminium silicate clay. Due to the low pH of the stomach, the bismuth subsalicylate reacts with hydrochloric acid to form bismuth oxychloride and salicylic acid.

- It is thought that bismuth exhibits antisecretory, anti-inflammatory and antimicrobial effects. Nausea and abdominal cramps are also relieved by bismuth.

- It is used in prevention and treatment of traveler's diarrhoea, gastroenteritis. It is also used in treatment of *H. pylori* infection.

- The adverse effects produce by bismuth are dark stools and black staining of the tongue.

ANTIMOTILITY AND ANTISECRETORY AGENTS

Opioids

Opioids used in treatment of diarrhoea acts by several different mechanisms. Principally, it is mediated through either μ- or δ-opioid receptors on enteric nerves, epithelial cells, and muscle. Diphenoxylate, difenoxin and loperamide are some commonly used opioids.

Principally, they act via peripheral μ -opioid receptors. Please refer chapter opioid analgesic for mechanism of action of opioid in details.

Loperamide

- Loperamide is an orally active antidiarrhoeal agent which is more potent than morphine and act by increasing intestinal transit time and anal sphincter tone. Additionally, it has antisecretory activity against cholera, *E. coli* toxin by acting on G-protein receptor.

- It is used in all form of diarrhoea. An overdose may produce CNS depression and paralysis.

Diphenoxylate and Difenoxin

- These are piperidine derivative and structurally related to meperidine. They are more potent than morphine for treatment of diarrhoea.

- They are potentially abused and cause CNS depression. High doses produce anticholinergic effects. Excessive use may cause constipation and toxic megacolon may also develop.

Other Opium-Containing Compounds

Enkephalins are neurotransmitters which inhibit intestinal secretion without affecting motility.

ALPHA-2 ADRENERGIC RECEPTOR AGONISTS

Clonidine

- It acts on enteric neuron and enterocytes. It stimulates absorption and inhibits the secretion of fluid and electrolytes thereby increasing the intestinal transit time.

- They are effective in treating chronic diarrhoea in diabetic patients. It is also used in patients with diarrhoea caused by opiate withdrawal.

- Side effects such as hypotension, depression and perceived fatigue have been observed.

HORMONE

Somatostatin

- Somatostatin is a hormone secreted from pancreas and gastrointestinal tract. It is highly effective in treating severe secretory diarrhoea such as chemotherapy-induced diarrhoea, diarrhoea associated with human immunodeficiency virus (HIV), and diabetes-associated diarrhoea by inhibiting secretion of hormone including serotonin and various other GI peptides e.g., gastrin, vasoactive intestinal polypeptide, insulin, secretin etc.

- Side effects such as transient nausea, bloating and pain at the site of injection are common. Long-term therapy can lead to formation of gallstone and hypo- or hyperglycemia.

OTHER AGENTS USED IN DIARRHOEA

- **Calcium channel blocker reduces** intestinal motility and promotes intestinal electrolyte and water absorption; its significant side effect is constipation.

  Berberine is a plant alkaloid which is commonly used in bacterial diarrhoea and cholera. It exhibits antimicrobial activity as well as inhibits smooth muscle contraction and secretion. It also delays the intestinal transit by antagonising the effect of acetylcholine and blocking the entry of Ca^{2+} into cells.

Questions on this Chapter

1. Discuss in detail pharmacology of Antidiarrhoeal agents.

2. Write short note on bile acid sequestering agents.

3. Write the classification of antidiarrhoeal and add note on antimotility and antisecretory agents.

QUESTION BANK OF PUNE UNIVERSITY
B. PHARM PHARMACOLOGY EXAMINATION

October 2010

1. Define pain and add a note on Pathophysiology of pain. **[2008 pattern - 8 M]**
2. Discuss the etiology of chronic peptic ulcers. **[2008 pattern - 3 M]**
3. Discuss the etiology of chronic obstructive airway disease. **[2008 pattern - 3 M]**
4. Write a note on Alzheimer's. **[2008 pattern - 5 M]**
5. Write a note on Parkinson's disease. **[2008 pattern - 5 M]**
6. Discuss the pharmacotherapy of Parkinson's disease. **[2004 pattern - 10 M]**
7. Discuss the mechanism of action and adverse reactions of the following drugs:
   [2004 pattern - 15 M]

    (a) Diazepam, (b) Morphine, (c) Lithium carbonate
8. Discuss various stages of anesthesia. Add a note on pre and post-anesthetic medications.
   [2004 pattern - 15 M]
9. Write a note on any three : **[2004 pattern - 15 M]**
    (a) Selective serotonin reuptake inhibitors.
    (b) COX-2 inhibitors.
    (c) Classification of seizure and drug employed in its management.
    (d) Local anesthetics.

***

April 2011

1. Classify bronchodilator drugs. Give rational approaches of pharmacotherapy of asthma.
   [2004 pattern - 15 M]
2. Write the pharmacological account on barbiturates. **[2004 pattern - 10 M]**
3. Classify NSAIDs. Explain the pharmacology of Aspirin. **[2004 pattern - 15 M]**
4. Explain the pharmacotherapy of rheumatoid arthritis. **[2004 pattern - 7.5 M]**
5. Write the pharmacological account on antianxiety agents. **[2004 pattern - 7.5 M]**
6. Write a note on Pharmacotherapy of Alcoholism. **[2004 pattern - 5 M]**
7. Write a note on Tricyclic antidepressants. **[2004 pattern - 5 M]**
8. Write a note on Opoid dependence D) Halothane. **[2004 pattern - 5 M]**
9. Classify Opioid analgesics. **[2008 pattern - 3 M]**
10. Classify the drugs used in the treatment of Parkinsonism. **[2008 pattern - 3 M]**
11. What is pre-anaesthetic medication? Explain in brief. **[2008 pattern - 3 M]**
12. What are the advantages of benzodiazepines over barbiturates. **[2008 pattern - 3 M]**
13. Short note on Morphine poisoning. **[2008 pattern - 5 M]**
14. Short note on Treatment of Alzheimer's disease. **[2008 pattern - 5 M]**
15. Short note on Tricyclic antidepressants. **[2008 pattern - 5 M]**

16. Short note on Status epilepticus.   [2008 pattern - 5 M]
17. Explain in detail the pharmacotherapy of peptic ulcer.   [2008 pattern - 10 M]
18. Explain the mechanism of action of local anesthetics.   [2008 pattern - 3 M]
19. Classify anti-emetics.   [2008 pattern - 3 M]
20. Classify laxatives.   [2008 pattern - 3 M]
21. Classify anti-asthmatics.   [2008 pattern - 3 M]
22. Write short note on Emetics.   [2008 pattern - 5 M]
23. Write short note on Pharmacotherapy of cough.   [2008 pattern - 5 M]

***

October 2011

1. Explain the mechanism of action, the pharmacological actions adverse effects and therapeutic uses
    of Diazepam.   [2008 pattern - 10 M]
2. What is the mechanism of action of NSAID's.   [2008 pattern - 3 M]
3. What are the signs, symptoms and treatment of barbiturate poisoning. [2008 pattern - 3 M]
4. What are SSRI? Explain in brief.   [2008 pattern - 3 M]
5. Write short note on Pre anesthetic medication.   [2008 pattern - 5 M]
6. Write short note on MAO inhibitors.   [2008 pattern - 5 M]
7. Write short note on Opioid antagonists.   [2008 pattern - 5 M]
8. Explain the drug therapy in diarrhea.   [2008 pattern - 10 M]
9. Classify local anesthetics.   [2008 pattern - 3 M]
10. Classify laxatives.   [2008 pattern - 3 M]
11. Classify drugs used in the treatment of Gout.   [2008 pattern - 3 M]
12. What are Proton pump inhibitors? Explain in brief.   [2008 pattern - 3 M]
13. Write short note on Expectorants.   [2008 pattern - 5 M]
14. Write short note on Bronchodilators.   [2008 pattern - 5 M]
15. Write short note on Antiemetics.   [2008 pattern - 5 M]
16. Write a note on Pharmacotherapy of cough.   [2004 pattern - 5 M]
17. Explain the stages of general anesthesia. Add note on pharmacology of Halothane.
                                                                          [2004 pattern - 10 M]
18. Discuss the socio-economical implications of depression and explain pharmacology of tricyclic
    antidepressants.   [2004 pattern - 15 M]
19. Give the pharmacological account of barbiturates.   [2004 pattern - 15 M]
20. Pharmacotherapy of Alzheimer's disease.   [2004 pattern - 5 M]
21. Antimaniac drugs.   [2004 pattern - 5 M]
22. Physiology of sleep.   [2004 pattern - 5 M]
23. Pharmacotherapy of alcoholism.   [2004 pattern - 5 M]
24. Write short notes on Laxative.   [2004 pattern - 5 M]

***

April 2012

1. What is the mechanism of action, the pharmacological actions, adverse effects and therapeutic uses of Phenytoin. **[2008 pattern - 10 M]**
2. Classify neuromuscular blockers. **[2008 pattern - 3 M]**
3. Explain the mechanism of action of benzodiazepines. **[2008 pattern - 3 M]**
4. Write the Stages of general anesthesia. **[2008 pattern - 5 M]**
5. Write a note on Levodopa. **[2008 pattern - 5 M]**
6. Write a note on Chronic alcoholism. **[2008 pattern - 5 M]**
7. Explain the pharmacotherapy of gout. **[2008 pattern - 10 M]**
8. Explain the role of beta 2 agonists in treatment of asthma. **[2008 pattern - 3 M]**
9. Classify drugs used in the treatment of peptic ulcer. **[2008 pattern - 3 M]**
10. Write the Pharmacotherapy of Cough. **[2008 pattern - 5 M]**
11. Write short note on Local anesthetics. **[2008 pattern - 5 M]**

***

October 2012

1. Classify sedative Hypnotics. Write a note on Pharmacology of Benzodiazepines. **[2008 Pattern - 10 M]**
2. Metabolism of Alcohol. **[2008 Pattern - 3 M]**
3. Classify NSAIDs. **[2008 Pattern - 3 M]**
4. Explain the properties of an Ideal Anaesthetic. **[2008 Pattern - 3 M]**
5. Neuropharmacology of epilepsy. **[2008 Pattern - 3 M]**
6. Advantages of Benzodiazepines over Barbiturates. **[2008 Pattern - 3 M]**
7. Write short note on treatment of Parkinson's disease. **[2008 Pattern - 5 M]**
8. Write note on Opoid dependence. **[2008 Pattern - 5 M]**
9. Classify bronchodilator drugs. Give rational approaches of pharmacotherapy of asthma. **[2008 Pattern - 10 M]**
10. Classify anti asthamatics. **[2008 Pattern - 3 M]**
11. Explain the mechanism of action of local anesthetics. **[2008 Pattern - 3 M]**
12. Classify anti-ulcer agents. **[2008 Pattern - 3 M]**
13. Classify Anti-tussives. **[2008 Pattern - 3 M]**
14. Pharmacotherapy of gout. **[2008 Pattern - 5 M]**
15. Pharmacotherapy of cough. **[2008 Pattern - 5 M]**

***

April 2013

1. Classify General Anesthetics. **[2008 Pattern - 3 M]**
2. Explain preanaesthetic medication in brief. **[2008 Pattern - 3 M]**
3. ADME of Alcohol. **[2008 Pattern - 3 M]**
4. Classify opioid analgesics. **[2008 Pattern - 3 M]**
5. Mode of action of Benzodiazepines. **[2008 Pattern - 3 M]**
6. Pharmacotherapy of alcoholism. **[2008 Pattern - 5 M]**
7. Morphine poisoning. **[2008 Pattern - 5 M]**
8. Classify antitussive agents. Explain the pharmacotherapy of cough. **[2008 Pattern - 10 M]**

9. What are SERM ? Explain in brief.   [2008 Pattern - 3 M]
10. Classify anti-emetics.   [2008 Pattern - 3 M]
11. Pharmacotherapy of Rheumatoid Arthritis.   [2008 Pattern - 5 M]
12. Local anesthetics.   [2008 Pattern - 5 M]

***

October 2014

1. Classify antidepressant drugs. Discuss mechanism of action, pharmacological actions, therapeutic uses and adverse drug reactions of Fluoxetine.   [2008 Pattern - 10 M]
2. Explain why levodopa is combined with Carbidopa.   [2008 Pattern - 3 M]
3. What do you mean by redistribution of barbiturates.   [2008 Pattern - 3 M]
4. Explain the various mechanisms by which general anesthetics acts. [2008 Pattern - 3 M]
5. Classify NSAIDs.   [2008 Pattern - 3 M]
6. Write on barbiturate poisoning.   [2008 Pattern - 5 M]
7. Write on Nootropics.   [2008 Pattern - 5 M]
8. Classify drug for peptic ulcers. Discuss the pharmacotherapy of H. *Pylori*. [2008 Pattern - 5 M]
9. Classify expectorant and antitussive.   [2008 Pattern - 3 M]
10. Classify drugs for constipation.   [2008 Pattern - 3 M]
11. Explain the mechanism of action of salbutamol.   [2008 Pattern - 3 M]
12. Write on rheumatoid arthritis.   [2008 Pattern - 5 M]
13. Write on Antiemetics.   [2008 Pattern - 5 M]
14. Write on local anesthetics.   [2008 Pattern - 5 M]

***

April 2015

1. Classify antiepileptic drugs. Discuss mechanism of action, pharmacological actions, therapeutic uses and adverse drug reaction of phenytoin.   [2008 pattern - 10 M]
2. Write therapeutic uses and adverse effects of imipramine.   [2008 pattern - 3 M]
3. What do you mean by redistribution of barbiturates.   [2008 pattern - 3 M]
4. Write the therapeutic uses and adverse effects of morphine.   [2008 pattern - 3 M]
5. Explain why levodopa is combined with Carbidopa.   [2008 pattern - 3 M]
6. Explain the mechanism of action of barbiturates.   [2008 pattern - 3 M]
7. Classify antipsychotics.   [2008 pattern - 3 M]
8. Write on Nootropics.   [2008 pattern - 5 M]
9. Explain drug therapy in Peptic ulcer.   [2008 pattern - 10 M]
10. Classify antidiarrhoeal agents.   [2008 pattern - 3 M]
11. Classify anesthetics as per their clinical uses.   [2008 pattern - 3 M]
12. Write the drugs used in treatment of rheumatoid arthritis.   [2008 pattern - 3 M]
13. Classify antiemetic drugs.   [2008 pattern - 3 M]
14. Drug therapy of Asthma.   [2008 pattern - 3 M]

***

www.ingramcontent.com/pod-product-compliance
Lightning Source LLC
Chambersburg PA
CBHW080822020726
47501CB00009B/2377

* 9 7 8 9 3 5 1 6 4 1 1 0 0 *